'With *Unforgiven*, Barrie has delivered yet another dark, propulsive thriller which her fans are sure to devour. While not an easy read due to the difficult subject matter, *Unforgiven* is compelling, gritty and fast-paced — all things a great thriller should be.'

—Better Reading

'A gritty, twisty journey of suspense. Recommended.'

—*Canberra Weekly*

'If you like a read that keeps you on the edge of your seat, this addictive, suspenseful novel is for you.'

—*Woman's Day*

'Aussie thriller writer Sarah Barrie dives into dark and complex … drama and suspense aplenty in the gritty tale set on the Central Coast.'

—*Sunday Telegraph*

'Sarah Barrie is a fabulous author who brings thriller and mystery together in stories that are page turners and I cannot recommend this one enough.'

—*Chiller Thriller reviews*

Sarah Barrie is the author of nine novels including her bestselling print debut *Secrets of Whitewater Creek*, the Hunters Ridge and Calico Mountain trilogies, and a new crime series starring Constable Lexi Winter. In a past life, while gaining degrees in arts, science and education, Sarah worked as a teacher, a vet nurse, a horse trainer and a magazine editor, before deciding she wanted to write novels. About the only thing that has remained constant is her love of all things crime.

Her favourite place in the world is the family property, where she writes her stories overlooking mountains crisscrossed with farmland, bordered by the beauty of the Australian bush, and where, at the end of the day, she can spend time with family, friends, a good Irish whiskey and a copy of her next favourite book.

Also by Sarah Barrie

UNFORGIVEN

SARAH
BARRIE

First Published 2021
Second Australian Paperback Edition 2023
ISBN 9781038906618

UNFORGIVEN
© 2021 by Sarah Barrie
Australian Copyright 2021
New Zealand Copyright 2021

Except for use in any review, the reproduction or utilisation of this work in whole or in part in any form by any electronic, mechanical or other means, now known or hereafter invented, including xerography, photocopying and recording, or in any information storage or retrieval system, is forbidden without the permission of the publisher.

This book is sold subject to the condition that it shall not, by way of trade or otherwise, be lent, resold, hired out or otherwise circulated without the prior consent of the publisher in any form of binding or cover other than that in which it is published and without a similar condition including this condition being imposed on the subsequent purchaser.

All rights reserved including the right of reproduction in whole or in part in any form.

This is a work of fiction. Names, characters, places, and incidents are either the product of the author's imagination or are used fictitiously, and any resemblance to actual persons, living or dead, business establishments, events, or locales is entirely coincidental.

Published by
HQ Fiction
An imprint of Harlequin Enterprises (Australia) Pty Limited (ABN 47 001 180 918),
a subsidiary of HarperCollins Publishers Australia Pty Limited (ABN 36 009 913 517)
Level 19, 201 Elizabeth St
SYDNEY NSW 2000
AUSTRALIA

® and TM (apart from those relating to FSC®) are trademarks of Harlequin Enterprises (Australia) Pty Limited or its corporate affiliates. Trademarks indicated with ® are registered in Australia, New Zealand and in other countries.

A catalogue record for this book is available from the National Library of Australia
www.librariesaustralia.nla.gov.au

Printed and bound in Australia by McPherson's Printing Group

*To all the perfectly imperfect parents who love their kids and try their best.
And to all the kids who should have had those parents but didn't.*

The Spider and the Fly

'Will you walk into my parlour?' said a spider to a fly;
"Tis the prettiest little parlour that ever you did spy.
The way into my parlour is up a winding stair,
And I have many pretty things to shew when
you are there.'
'Oh no, no!' said the little fly, 'to ask me is in vain,
For who goes up your winding stair can ne'er come
down again.'

Mary Howitt (1829)

My townhouse is a small eighties box at the end of a row of identical boxes in the dankest corner of suburban Ourimbah. Its backyard is a steep slope of unstable mountainside thick with scrub, stunted gumtrees and insects that hum like distant traffic for most of the year. Though the sun never penetrates the damp three-by-five-metre paved courtyard, the skeleton of an arbour leans heavily over the small space, held up by the privet-lined wooden fence of an annoying neighbour and the twisting, clinging ropes of wisteria and Madeira vine that slowly devour it. Lantana encroaches from two sides, adding colour to the otherwise endless green void. The courtyard is cold, dark and never dries out. Moss and mould are at home here. And so am I.

Inside, the heavy drill curtains are drawn, to dissuade another annoying neighbour from popping in and because the driveway gets sun. The faint glow of it sneaking around the edges of the curtains is already too much to tolerate.

I have to stop drinking. This is not an epiphany, more a daily mantra when I wake sometime between eleven and one. It means I miss breakfast, often lunch. Dinner might be JD or scrounged with whatever change I have in my pocket; a street kebab, a hotdog. My body is constantly on that verge between thin and too skinny, my skin is pale against the black hair I occasionally hack off without too much skill. The fact that my sister calls the effect 'fragile' makes me laugh. There's nothing fragile about who I am. What I am is *deliberate*. But, God, I have to stop drinking.

I drop my head back against the smooth vinyl lounge and close eyes that feel too heavy in their sockets, like they want to sink right back down into unconsciousness with me. A churning nausea crawls up from my stomach and touches base with the back of my throat, tags a headache that migrates up my jaw before settling in my temples, forming a tight band across my forehead. I drag my head up, and my eyes open long enough to take another careful sip of the hot black coffee I'd poured into yesterday's mug on my way from the kitchen to the lounge. I hope for the best.

I give in to the need to close my eyes again. If the world can stay silent, dark and still, there may be a slight chance of riding this out without full toilet-bowl-hell-hangover breaking loose.

On the edge of oblivion, images drift through the fog of my mind and hold, refusing to let go. Last night. The very dreamy Jonathan Davies of the chiselled features, stunning baby blues and long, dark lashes. A tall, muscular power-house, precision toned and sculpted to be appreciated. So commanding, so sure of himself. The images form into a memory and I groan in resignation.

Shit. I have to get up. His body is still in the boot.

CHAPTER ONE

Friday, March 5

Hurry up!

I catch a glimpse of the hotel's archaic clock radio as I bounce up and down on Henry Elliot's erection. 8:43pm. I take pride in my work, and I like to make sure my clients get their money's worth. But tonight there's somewhere else I need to be and Henry's distracted, taking longer than usual.

The hotel walls are a dull beige—scuffed and scarred from furniture being carelessly bumped against them. A darker rectangular patch shows the place a cheap painting used to hang. I've spent a fair bit of time staring at that painting over the years and I kind of miss its cringy, colourful landscape. I wonder what happened to it. By the door, a roundish indentation suggests someone's attempted to put their fist through the gyprock. Maybe the painting was a victim of whatever drunk did that little bit of angry redecorating.

The walls are thin and I can hear someone snoring up a storm in the room next door. The shattering rumble is competing with the noise from the crowd downstairs and the blaring of an impatient driver's horn on the road outside. I tune it all out and stretch up, lifting my arms over my head and squeezing my shoulder blades together. The move might look like a posture of wild abandon but in reality I'm just trying to stop anything from cramping. My eyes catch the movement of a daddy-long-legs as it picks its way along the corner of the ceiling and my mind wanders again. I remember hearing that they're highly toxic, but their fangs are too small to penetrate human skin. Probably a fallacy.

Okay, my patience is running thin. I'm considering a change of position, maybe adding some more serious sound effects, but then with pure gratitude I hear the quick catch of his breath. His hands grip my hips and convulse and—there it is—the breathy snort that trills into something like a happy horse whinny.

I relax and wait it out, give him a moment to pant and mop at his brow as though he's been doing all the work rather than starfishing underneath me, then slide off his ample belly with a smile I know he thinks means I enjoyed the hell out of it. In reality it's the two-fifty in cash and the JD waiting for me in the pub downstairs that puts this smile on my face. I take another glance at the clock and grimace. There won't be much time. I'll have to drink fast.

'That's some stamina you've got there,' Henry puffs, his eyes warm in his damp face.

'All part of the service,' I reply. I hope I can get off the bed without my legs giving way.

The hotel window is open a crack and the early March air is cool with the predicted southerly change. My skin prickles. I move off the bed and self-consciously reach for the lingerie I'd tossed on the floor. I can fuck a client six ways to Sunday without batting an eyelid but somehow picking up the pieces afterwards is always awkward. I have this way of switching off when I'm working that flicks back to life in the aftermath. I suppose the cleaning-up process highlights the emptiness of the experience; in a relationship, this'd be the part where you snuggle into your partner feeling all warm and fuzzy. I think. I wouldn't really know. But what I do know is you wouldn't be getting showered and dressed while the other participant reaches for a wad of cash in his wallet.

I don't often question what I do, so it annoys me that whatever conscience I own has decided to start gnawing at me now. What I do makes a few lonely men happy and keeps a roof over my head. Both of these are good things. Important things.

I shake off my thoughts and visit the tiny bathroom, give myself a quick moment to enjoy the shower spray. When I come out Henry's still sprawled naked on the bed.

'Lexi, honey, it's my birthday on Tuesday. Think you can fit in a couple of hours for a little get-together? I'm going to call in and see Mum, then the girls from the bank and a few of my friends were thinking beers at the pub. Just casual, shouldn't run late. Should leave us some alone time after.'

For the sake of appearances I pretend to ponder that. But of course I can. I only see three long-term clients these days, leftovers from when I had no choice but to take on anyone for whatever they offered just to stay alive. It gives me enough to get by, and that's fine. I can't be bothered dealing with strangers or the rough, kinky or downright warped requests anymore.

'Sure. Is that what you've been dreaming about tonight?'

'Dreaming about? It's always you,' he says with a wink. But I know he's lying.

'Come on, you got something going on the side here, Henry?'

I sometimes wonder why he hasn't found a Mrs Right. He's on a slippery slope towards fifty and there's no denying he's let himself go, but he has a pleasant enough face, is well versed in basic manners and hygiene and has a gorgeous waterfront home and million-dollar inheritance from a great aunt secured in the bank he manages.

I sit on the edge of the bed. 'Someone to buy you a birthday cake? Celebrate with you? Stay the night?'

'I'd be happy for you to do all those things.'

I pull a face and Henry chuckles. 'Marry me and I'll give you everything you've ever wanted.'

'It's a tempting offer. But I'm not the domestic type.'

He shifts up to lean on his elbow. His face goes endearingly red. 'Actually, there might be someone.'

'Oh?'

'A new investment manager. She was helping me with my portfolio last week and we just kind of clicked. I don't want to think too much of it yet. She's quite a bit younger and I would have said out of my league but I don't think I was misinterpreting the signals.'

Oh you poor, sweet, blind man, I think as warning bells clang, but I punch him playfully on the arm. 'Good for you! But make sure you have fun and protect that big heart of yours.' *And big bank balance.* Maybe I'm just cynical.

'Oh … I don't know,' he groans, dropping back down on the mattress. He stares at the roof for several seconds before his gaze shifts back to me. 'You really think I should ask her out?'

Now I'm playing counsellor and I've got no one to blame but myself—I started it. 'Sure. If she can't make it, I'll be available. Let me know.'

'She'll be there. She's on staff and they're all coming. But maybe if she sees me with you …'

My left eyebrow lifts in amusement. 'Are you trying to make her jealous, Henry?'

'Not exactly, it's just that with someone like you on my arm she might see me as more … appealing.'

I lean over and kiss him. 'If she doesn't already know how amazing you are, she doesn't deserve you. Text me a time.' Before I can surprise myself even more with all this *niceness* I take the money he's tossed on the pillow, blow him another kiss and walk out.

The narrow hallway is dimly lit and the lingering stench of stale alcohol, vomit and cheap air freshener follows me down the stairs. All three odours seem to be permanent fixtures of the place. I push through a heavy glass door to the noise and general chaos of the busy lounge and head straight for the bar. Tom, the skinny Canadian bartender, is wiping down the counter with an overused checkered cloth. He greets me with his usual all-over stare of appreciation and a jerk of his head.

'Usual?'

'Thanks. Make it a double.' I slide onto a bar stool and dump my bag by my feet. The bar is still damp under my elbows as I lean on it but I leave them there.

His big, friendly grin flashes as he grabs the bottle. 'That *is* the usual.'

'So make it a double double.'

He doesn't bother to measure the shots, just pours me a glass two-thirds full. Tom's always generous with quantities.

'Rough night at the office?' he asks, sliding the glass across the bar before glancing at the door to upstairs.

I shake my head and toss back half the contents of my drink, feel it burn down my throat. 'I'm in a hurry. Need to be somewhere.'

'Want any food to go?'

'Nah, but thanks.'

'Hey, before you gulp that down and rush off,' he says and leans over the bar so he can speak quietly, 'a couple of weeks back you stumbled through some story about pretending to be a kid on social media to catch a perv for your sister. Remember?'

The glass stalls just shy of my mouth while my mind races for exactly what I told him. Must have been drunk. Very, very drunk. I take another large swallow. 'No. Why?'

He jerks his chin towards the booth by the window. 'Owen reckons one of his mates showed him a picture of some girl he met on Facebook. Said she looks like a younger version of you. A *much* younger version.'

'One of his mates, huh?' I know Owen is keen to become a client. I shudder as I consider the tattered flanno, the jeans that are held together by beer stains and the beard that— well, I'm not sure how long some of those leftovers have lived there. 'Let's just say if this mate starts sending dick pics to photoshopped twelve-year-old me, he might get more than he bargained for.'

Tom laughs but he's looking at me with a weird intensity. 'What?'

'I have trouble picturing you as the superhero type.'

'Because I'm not!' I answer, appalled. 'I was helping Bailee out.'

'Ah, I see.' His smile gleams with humour. 'You thinking of signing up as a child protection officer like your sister? Interesting career change.'

'Ha. No.' Then, because he's still looking at me with curiosity, I sigh and wiggle my finger at my glass for him to top it up. If I have to make conversation, I may as well squeeze in one more drink. 'When Bailee started work last year she got a lot of grunt cases. One guy was stalking this kid online and I offered to help out, that's all. A few years back I developed some interesting computer skills working for this guy—doesn't matter. Anyway.' I smile a little in satisfaction at the memory. 'We made up a fake child profile with Photoshop to trick the guy into nailing his own arse. And it worked too well. She reeled in six of the bastards.'

I shrug like it's no big deal. He doesn't need to know just how much of my time it's begun to take up. Or why. 'Keep it to yourself, okay? I don't know why in hell I told you, but I don't want to ruin my reputation.' I swallow the extra shot and get to my feet. If I get my butt into gear, I'll still make it home on time. 'I need to call a taxi.'

'You told me because I'm one of the few people on this planet you like.' My surprised expression inspires a cheeky grin and a wink. 'You told me that too.'

'God, how drunk was I?'

He laughs. 'I'm surprised you didn't drag yourself out on all fours.' He glances outside. 'There's a taxi pulling up now. I called it for Travis. Take it. I'll call him another one.'

I glance across to old Travis's favourite booth. Every time I see him his hair is a shade whiter and yet he's still the only person I know who can drink more than me and keep his legs under him. He's looking relaxed with his back to the door and half a glass of something amber in his hand as he chats to a mate. I reach across the bar for Tom and plant a noisy kiss on his mouth. 'Thanks.'

'You are *so* welcome.'

Pleasantly dizzy, I smile over my shoulder then step outside into the blustering winds. The main street is littered with people, mostly older teens arriving in town for a night out. A girl dressed in marginally more than me almost knocks into me as she laughs and stumbles past with a couple of boys. Further down the road, towards the waterfront, I hear a commotion from a larger group of already inebriated partygoers waiting for the nightclub to open at the local leagues club. There's few other options—a couple of pubs, a wine bar—but the younger crowd are all headed in the same direction. Gosford might only be an hour or so north of the city, but its nightlife options are dismally limited. I shiver. My little red dress is no match for the sudden drop in temperature but it's tight, so at least it doesn't blow up anywhere it shouldn't. It's been hot for a week and the change was expected, but I'm glad the taxi is sitting waiting as the rain starts to spit down.

I climb in and give the driver the address, lean back against the smooth vinyl seat and stare blindly out the window as we cruise through the quiet suburbs towards home. I'm tired. I hadn't realised quite how tired. But I still have work to do, just a different sort. I open my phone. I can't *believe* I told Tom I stalked perverts on Facebook. I never talk to anyone but Bailee about that. Then again, other than Tom or my sister, who do I talk to? Tom's right. I don't like many people, so the list is short. My messages come up. Two of the three paedos I've been stringing along have replied. One wants to know if I've seen a dick before, the other wants a photo of me naked.

I hiss out a breath. I'm more than aware of what to expect from this particular brand of lowlife, but the anger still hits me, every time. These sickos think they're talking to a twelve-year-old. Someone's little girl. The perversion of it, the disregard for anything but seeing through their own fucked-up fantasies at the expense of the kids they target, makes my stomach do its usual long roll.

The taxi sweeps in off the road and pulls up outside my townhouse. The rain has become a steady deluge. 'Thanks.' I throw some money at the driver and hurry inside, turn on the computer and pull off the heels and the dress, before sliding on my comfy old dressing gown. The black material is tattered and frayed and leaning towards threadbare, but I can't stand to part with it. I wrap it tightly around me and sit. A glance at my screen tells me it's nine forty-five. Not bad.

I open my Tor browser, my VPN and check the network connection to Doc's computer. *Yes.* He's online. He has no idea I'm tracking his movements through the spyware I attached to his computer via a file share a couple of weeks back. Doc, as he's known, is Bailee's latest target. She's been attempting to track him down since one of her young clients admitted he's been bribing local street kids with alcohol and drugs to perform sexual acts at parties. None of them are willing to go to the cops. I found him, and this forum, three weeks ago. Well, I sort of found him. I found him *online*, but right now his identity is still a big question mark because no one goes by their real names on the dark web. Right now he's chatting to Rocketman69, another forum member, about his latest video upload. I haven't watched it. I don't want or need to. I know I'm about to find out more than I want to know about it from reading this thread.

Rocketman69: She's a sweetheart this one.

Doc: I reckon. I generally like them younger. But she's cute for fourteen.

My stomach does another sick turn. 'Oh yeah, just keep digging that pit, arsehole,' I mutter, and I mentally will him to bring up the party they've been talking about for days. I desperately want to be able to give Bailee a location, but they never mention one. Because they're talking filth, I turn on the television. I don't want to watch anything, I only need a solid link back to normality.

I yawn. The idea of a warm bed has my eyes drooping. But I'm not going anywhere. I'm latching on to Doc like a pitbull to a postman's arse until I get what I want.

Rocketman69: You partying tomorrow night?

Doc: I think so. Having trouble with the wife.

Rocketman69: Weren't you getting rid of her?

Doc: Gotta play it right so I keep the kid. Just about got everyone convinced she's lost the plot. You going?

'Oh, you keep getting better and better.' I hope whoever the wife is, she'll be able to get the kid and get the hell out once Bailee has this evidence.

Rocketman69: If I can get there on time.

Doc: Need a faster car mate?

Rocketman69: Ha. The car's not the problem.

A picture of a hotted-up cherry-red Commodore appears.

Doc: You think? No wonder you're always late. Take a look.

A few seconds pass and another photo pops up. This one of a sleek black Porsche.

Doc: Something else I want to hold on to.

Rocketman69: Nice.

There's a few more comments before they sign off. I'm pissed off I still don't have any more details on these parties. I screenshot a picture of both cars then take a better look at Doc's.

The photo isn't recent. It's been taken in daylight, and why would someone leave a car like that *outside* the garage? I'm guessing this is an ego shot from when it was new. I immediately look for a number plate but the angle's not showing it. Looks like the picture has been taken from above, perhaps a second storey. On the other side of the street—in the far corner of the shot—I can see the backs of a couple of kids lugging bags. Their heads and shoulders are cut off from the photo.

I record every detail I can see. From the reflection in the car's windows it looks like the house Doc lives in is white or cream. There's a neat little pebble garden on either side of the drive showing off bird of paradise plants. I can see part of another car parked across the street and a sandstone fence with iron windows dripping in hot pink bougainvillea. No visible street numbers.

I send Bailee a text to see if she's still up. She's used to me calling at all hours and calls me straight back.

'Forget it,' she tells me. 'My client changed her story. Said she made it up.'

'Seriously? Because I have him.'

'You've found the Doc guy?'

'Only online so far.'

'You're a genius, you know that, right?'

'Just stubborn.'

'Do you have a name?'

'Not yet. I can only see what he sees. I know there's some sort of custody issue going on and he's on a mission to make his wife seem crazy. Also that he drives a rather stunning black Porsche. I don't suppose that helps?'

'Not really,' Bailee says after a thoughtful pause.

'If he'd do some online banking or something that would help, but I have an idea he keeps this particular little setup just for this purpose, which makes sense. I'll have to keep working on it.'

There was a long, audible sigh down the line. 'Without a name and address, an active complaint or any physical evidence to pass on to the cops, they're not going to be able to investigate.'

'Of course not,' I agree with a hint of contempt.

'Thanks anyway, though. I'll have another go at convincing Janie to talk.'

I end the call, annoyed. If the kid has suddenly changed her story she's been pressured—or worse. And unless I do all the work the cops should be doing, nothing will be done about it. The Porsche is still front and centre of the screen.

Am I going to let this bastard scare a kid into shutting up just because the cops are useless?

'Pfft, not likely. Not when I'm this close.'

I'll find the car, and then I'll find him. I take another look at the photo and it occurs to me to wonder what school uniform those kids are wearing. I get up, grab my bottle of JD from the pantry and sit back down to find out.

CHAPTER TWO

Saturday, March 6

Detective Inspector Rachael Langley took a sip from her water bottle and wriggled her toes in her heeled shoes. They were aching, and the tight bun she'd fixed at the base of her skull wasn't doing her head any favours, either. She was dressed in one of her appropriate navy skirt suits, flattering enough and suitable for the warm conditions, but in a straight-down-the-line no-nonsense cut that no one could claim was anything other than professional. She'd perfected the image over her twenty-two years on the force. A woman didn't make inspector or earn the respect of her team by adding soft touches to her appearance. Nothing but hard work and a thick skin got you anywhere, and if people were a little scared of you, even better.

But it was fast approaching seven thirty and the end of a thirteen-hour shift for the State Crime Command's Homicide Unit. She wanted to strip off the facade and fall into a hot bath, preferably with a glass of wine and a good book. Soak her feet, eat chocolate. Hide from what was about to begin.

Her feelings about the work she'd done on the Spider case were complex. Seeing it all hashed out in a prime-time television documentary was going to be uncomfortable. She was a long-time cop who liked catching the bad guys, not one who enjoyed the spotlight.

'You sure you don't want a glass of sparkly?' Homicide Commander Superintendent Ed O'Hanlon asked, standing beside her in front of the big screen. 'I bought it for you, not every other freeloader in here.'

'I don't drink in front of my colleagues, you know that,' she said but smiled gratefully. 'Now, if I could just go home.'

'Oh come on, look how many of those colleagues have stuck around to watch.'

There were thirty-two. She knew because she'd counted them. And she had a suspicion it was as much about the wine and canapés Ed had put on as the documentary that was keeping them back after shift.

'Sit down. Enjoy your moment.' Ed gestured to the desk chairs that had been arranged around the screen as someone announced the show was starting.

Resigned to the fact there was no escaping the next sixty or so minutes, Rachael sat next to Ed and waited as the large screen shifted from darkness to light, to reveal a network television studio complete with a smiling, middle-aged presenter.

'Good evening and welcome. Tonight, on the twentieth anniversary of the death of Thomas Biddle's first victim, we take a look into the Spider case and how one young, newly appointed detective constable brought down not only a child killer but an entire network of paedophilia and abuse. I'm Stanley Dennis. Welcome to *Detective Insider*.'

Clapping and whistles quietened around her as the image on screen moved to that of a little girl of around four years of age dancing and singing for a home video. Rachael's voiceover begins. 'My name is Detective Inspector Rachael Langley, and after more than two decades in the police force, this case remains the worst I've ever had to deal with.'

Cue music, dark and staccato, as newspaper headlines flash on screen: SHOCKING DEATH OF SEVEN-YEAR-OLD GOSFORD GIRL. A FAIRYTALE KILLING? SICK FANTASY OR PURE EVIL? Short clips of news reports from solemn-faced newsreaders recounting the horrors of the crime followed.

Rachael felt Ed's fingers creep into her hand, clasp it. She squeezed them back then let go. Seeing these images again made her want to hold on, but it wasn't an appropriate time or place to be holding hands with the boss.

Back to the studio and the host stood beside one of the less-shocking crime scene photos. A pink teddy bear's head, battered and dirty, poking an ear and an eye out from the earth.

'Thomas Biddle,' Stanley said, 'AKA the Spider, preyed on countless children until his capture in 2003. His movements first came to light in 1995, when he joined what was quickly becoming one of the largest dark web paedophile rings in the country. From his home on the Central Coast— an area renowned for its relaxed coastal lifestyle, beautiful beaches, boutique shopping and stunning bushland—Biddle encouraged other members to attend intimate get-togethers, creating opportunities for and sometimes participated in the sexual abuse of these members' children, the videos of which were shared online in a pay-per-view system. By 1998, these videos were becoming more and more violent, until in 2001, when, under the alias of the Spider, Biddle abducted and killed his first victim, Jennifer Holland, posting video of the horrific crime on a new website he called the Spider's Web.'

An elderly woman appeared on screen, her face drawn, tears soaking a tissue held close to her face. 'Jenny was such a beautiful little girl. Always so bright and happy, until my daughter died and Jenny was left in the care of her stepfather. She was a different child after that. I suspected something was up and I reported him to the authorities, applied for custody. But these things take so long. There wasn't enough time. About a week after I got the ball rolling, Jenny was murdered.' The woman's voice choked and her image faded back to the studio, where Rachael now sat with Stanley.

'The video of Jennifer acting out the role of Cinderella before being murdered was posted to the Spider's Web. It became so profitable Biddle produced two more—he murdered Ella Frazer and Tia Brown—prior to his capture in 2003 by the now Detective Inspector Rachael Langley, who joins us tonight. Welcome, inspector.'

'Thanks, Stan.'

'Inspector, your work on the Spider case has been lauded by police both in Australia and overseas. You've continued to receive accolades throughout your twenty-two years on the force for outstanding work on many other high-profile cases. What is it about the Spider case that stands out as the worst you've had to deal with?'

'This case is the closest I've come to true evil. Biddle made a fortune from video sharing, but his enjoyment came from the pain and suffering he could inflict on children. The spotlight, the attention that came from that was also very appealing to him. He liked to think he was smarter than everyone else, so he'd leave clues for the police to follow. It was one big game to him. He thrived on being the centre of attention, on outsmarting the authorities.'

'How do you think he got away with the murders for so long?'

'No one knew who the Spider was. On the surface, Thomas Biddle was simply a member of the online community. While Biddle was building connections to source victims, other members believed his only interest was in making videos and, from those, making money for the participants. Besides, even if the abusive parents had held any suspicion Biddle was responsible for the murders, they weren't about to go to police with that information, because what Biddle had on them would have sent them to prison.'

'What can you tell us about these videos?'

'Biddle based his videos on fairytales. The children were forced to act out scenes from a story in which the ending had been altered to allow the villain to win. After death, the children were posed carefully in locations reflecting the theme.'

'And there were intricately designed wings found on each victim, regardless of the costume?'

'Yes. The wings reflected those described in Mary Howitt's poem "The Spider and the Fly".'

The camera returned to Stan. 'We're going to take a look at each victim and learn how Inspector Langley finally captured the Spider. But coming up after the break, we'll hear from Biddle's brother Robert about Biddle's early life and what he thinks turned his brother into a monster.'

An hour later, Rachael stretched in her seat as the show rolled towards its close.

'After an intensive investigation spanning two years,' Stan told the audience, 'Inspector Langley's sheer refusal to let go of a simple hunch finally led police to Biddle. And just in time. He was caught at the house of potential victim number four. Could you tell us about that, inspector?'

'Correct. Both the mother and father of Biddle's chosen fourth victim were methamphetamine addicts and though the father was the perpetrator of the abuse, the mother was complicit. They'd both been members of Biddle's group and making money off their videos for a couple of years by the time he attempted to abduct their youngest daughter. A tip-off from a school teacher and a follow-up with an older child living in the house led to the Spider's capture.'

'Those children's names were never released to the media due the sensitive nature of what happened?'

'That's correct.'

'We do know, of course, that the younger child was safely placed in care. Was the older child ever found?'

'Unfortunately by the time we arrived, she'd taken her sister to a neighbour's house and fled. Every attempt was made to find her.' On screen, the frustration leached into Rachael's voice, her face. 'I can only hope that, after what she went through, she's found peace.'

'As I'm sure we all do. Detective Inspector Rachael Langley, thanks for joining us tonight.'

The show wrapped up and the credits rolled. Thank goodness. Rachael got to her feet and thanked her colleagues as they clapped and congratulated her. It seemed everyone had something to say. The documentary had been well done; she wouldn't have agreed to participate had she had any doubts as to the seriousness of the journalism involved, but though she was smiling, inside that familiar feeling of helplessness had risen to the surface. Sensing her thoughts, Ed invited everyone to take some leftovers and began to pack away.

'You know,' he said when they finally extricated themselves, 'you're quite inspiring.'

'Ha.'

'Seriously. You could retire from the field and teach.'

'Retire? Teach? I'm only forty-eight! I'm not done with the field yet.'

They reached his car and he unlocked it, popping the boot. 'You commanded the child protection unit for seven years, now you're in your third year as a top cop in homicide. What else are you hoping to conquer?'

'The world?' she suggested. She tossed in her bag, grimaced at the kink in her neck and rubbed it. 'Something— anything else that will take the spotlight off the Spider case.'

He dropped his briefcase in then turned her around, pressed his thumbs into the base of her neck and worked them in circles. Her eyes closed and she groaned in gratitude. 'It'll never go away. You're famous for it.'

'I see it as my biggest mistake.'

'I know. But no one else does.'

'I should have listened to my gut. I could have saved her.'

'You were an inexperienced detective and did *exactly* what you should have done—and that was to follow orders.' He turned her to face him. 'You caught a monster. So you're just going to have to soak up the accolades for the rest of your life and stop blaming yourself for the rest of it.'

'Hmm.'

'Goodnight superintendent, inspector,' a detective called out as she reached her car parked not too far from Ed's. Rachael immediately stepped away from Ed.

'Goodnight.' She sent a slightly embarrassed wave and climbed into the car. Damn it, they had to be more careful.

She couldn't help the yawn that burst from her.

Ed smiled. 'Long day. I heard you're close to making arrests on your latest case.'

'Sure, boss, but you know how these criminal organisations are. It's like fighting Hydras: every time you chop the head off one, several more seem to rise up to take its place.' She swore under her breath. 'I hate these shoes.' She kicked one off, then the other.

'But you looked so good walking around in them.'

'Cut it out,' she groaned with a smile. 'I need food, not compliments. My stomach's been growling so loud I'm surprised you couldn't all hear it through the program.'

He chuckled. 'How does Italian and a nice bottle of red at your favourite restaurant sound?'

'Like heaven.'

'Then let's get going. We'll make a reservation on the way.'

*

It *was* heaven. Her favourite restaurant, candlelight, quiet music and, of course, Ed. She picked up her glass and took a sip of smooth, fruity merlot while she studied him. He had a good face: strong lines and clean shaven. His dark hair was short and neat and sprinkled with grey, and he filled out a suit very nicely with a physique some twenty-somethings would envy due to his strictly disciplined workout regime. But what had really drawn her to him was the innate empathy he had for others, his strong sense of fairness and a sense of humour that more than thirty years as a cop hadn't managed to sour.

And as usual, he'd known exactly what she'd needed tonight. In the year since they'd started seeing each other, he'd managed to do that a lot. It was against every professional code in their current positions to be seeing each other, but she didn't care. He was the one personal thing she'd put ahead of the job in her whole career and she wasn't giving him up.

'What's that look about?' Ed asked, reaching across the table for her hand.

'I'm thinking about all the ways you spoil me.'

His eyes twinkled then heated. 'It's probably better I don't think too much about how I'd like to continue to do that until we get back to my place.'

'Mine's closer.'

'I can work with that.'

Her smile widened as she took the last bite of her arancini entree. 'Mmm, yum. We should have started us earlier. Then I wouldn't have gone so long without you introducing me to this restaurant.'

'We could have started us eighteen months and one week earlier. Because in case you've forgotten, that's exactly how long it took me to convince you that you were entitled to a personal life.'

'With the boss,' she said, taking another sip of wine. 'Who knew I had it in me?'

'Certainly not Finn. I'm still not sure he's forgiven me.'

She smiled. 'Of course he has. He reminds me of you.'

Ed pulled a face. 'I'm not sure I want to remind you of your nephew.'

'I mean as a cop. He's idealistic and compassionate. Yet everything has to be done completely by the book. No grey areas.'

'Better hope he finds a woman to make him stretch the rules one day then. It's really the only way to learn.'

She laughed but shook her head. 'I don't think that'll happen. His divorce has been rough on him, but he still cares for Vivienne. The bitch. I honestly don't know why. And he misses Ava so much. Visits every second weekend aren't enough. He would have been at work with us tonight but it's Ava's birthday and he was calling round to see her.'

'Vivienne will soon get sick of having to stay home every other weekend with Ava. You wait, she'll be throwing the kid at him at every opportunity in no time.'

'I hope so.' She placed her wine down as her pasta was placed in front of her. She breathed it in. 'Smells divine.'

'Are you going to inhale it or eat it?' Ed teased, then thanked the waiter for his gnocchi.

She savoured the first mouthful, relishing the flavours of ricotta and black truffle as they exploded inside her mouth, then groaned when her phone rang. 'Damn,' she muttered and took it out of her bag. The number wasn't familiar. 'Who could that be?'

'If you don't know, it doesn't matter,' Ed decided and took the phone from her fingers.

'Hey!' The phone stopped ringing before she could snatch it back.

'Don't pretend you wanted to answer it,' he said. 'Because we both know you didn't.'

She pulled a face at him but it slid into a grin. He was right. Besides, if it was important, whoever it was would leave a message. 'It wasn't a saved contact.'

'Then it was obviously an overseas telemarketer trying to sell you solar panels.'

She chuckled. 'You don't know that. It could be about a case.'

'More likely,' he admitted with a sigh. 'It's always about a case.'

She took another sip of her wine. 'Isn't that what your ex-wife always used to complain about?'

'Ouch. Low blow, inspector.'

The phone rang again and, ignoring his muttered curse, she plucked it from his hand. Same number. Still grinning, she answered. 'Rachael Langley.'

'Hello, Rachael.' She didn't recognise the voice, and something about the intimate tone instantly prickled the back of her neck and had the smile dropping from her lips. Her eyes clashed with Ed's.

'I'm sorry, who is this?'

'I enjoyed watching you tonight.' The voice was deep, the tone precise, the man behind them in no hurry to get the words out. 'I wanted to thank you. It was … quite flattering.'

Flattering? That threw her. 'You were flattered by my work on the Spider case?' she said to keep Ed in the loop. Ed's look became quizzical. She shrugged.

'You got one detail wrong though, and it's a big one, I'm afraid.'

Who *was* this? The guy had to be some sort of nutcase. How the hell did he get her number? She wondered whether or not to simply hang up, but something—maybe cop intuition—had her probing further. 'A big mistake? Why don't you tell me about it?'

'You never caught the Spider.'

'I'm not sure where you got your information.' She wished they were somewhere more private so she could put this man on speaker, let Ed in on the conversation. 'But that's not true. Biddle has been in prison for seventeen years.'

'Biddle!' The caller laughed humourlessly. 'Biddle wasn't the Spider. Biddle was a no one. A minor league friend of Winter. A fuckwit who never deserved the credit for my works of art.'

The niggle of sick churning she'd felt in her stomach since the beginning of this conversation kicked up several notches. '*Yours?*' Her eyes hit Ed's again, harder this time. 'Are you telling me you're the Spider?'

Ed huffed. 'Someone's messing with you,' he warned under his breath and signalled for her to cut the call. In return she shook her head and lifted a finger.

'I don't know why you've called, or how you got my number,' she told the caller, 'but I don't believe you and I'm—'

'I'm glad.' Again, the tone turned intimate. 'I'm going to enjoy proving it to you.'

Some of the colour must have left her face because Ed reached for the phone. 'Hand it over,' he said quietly.

She almost relinquished it, then slapped it back to her ear. 'Wait. If you're the Spider, where have you been for eighteen years?'

'Around. The web can be a very dark place. Lots of corners to hide in. Lots of ... flies to catch. I had to put away the fairytales but I've kept busy enough.'

Flies to catch. She felt her heart rate bump up. 'Then why call? Why are you talking to me?'

'What can I say? Tonight was nostalgic. I'm inspired, Rachael. Thank you. You were a worthy adversary all those years ago.' His voice cooled several degrees. 'But I beat you. How do you think you'll fare this time?'

She realised her hand was shaking when the phone bumped against her jaw as she almost dropped it. 'I still don't believe you,' she hissed into the phone, 'but whatever you think you've got planned, just try me!'

'You're sounding a little flustered, Rachael. I'll let you go. For now. I've got a date with Ariel. How long, do you think, will it take you to find her? Longer than it took me to find you? The trick is to not be predictable. Maybe change restaurants from time to time. Enjoy your pasta.'

The line went dead. She spun around in her chair, again, her gaze darting around the restaurant, desperate for some sign, some idea of who she was looking for.

'He's here,' she told Ed.

'What? Where?'

'I don't know. He just ...' She slid her eyes over every man in sight. Could that be him there? Or there? Or that guy outside? Maybe him, or him ...?

'Rachael, are you sure?'

'He knew what I had on my plate!' She pushed up from her chair to take a better look around. No one was paying attention. No one was on their phone. She dodged tables of couples and waitstaff on her way out to the street to look around outside. The footpath was littered with pedestrians, all moving, most hurrying along, some strolling, chatting with friends. But no one watching. No one was standing still.

'Rachael.' Ed came up beside her and looked around much as she was.

'He was here!'

'So you said.' He kept his voice low and rubbed his hands up and down her arms. 'Come on, it's not like you to get this shaken up. Come back inside and tell me exactly what he said.'

'He said he was the Spider,' she told him, still watching for any sign of anyone taking too much interest.

'And that's ridiculous,' Ed said. 'It's just some kook looking for attention, someone who saw the show and wants to see if he can rattle you.'

'But that's just it,' she said quietly. 'I'm not so sure it was. He said he's going to kill someone. Tonight.'

CHAPTER THREE

I'm pretty damn sure I shouldn't do this.

I stare out over the ocean through the windscreen of my car, flipping the thumb drive around and around in my left hand as I take a swig from my hip flask with my right and ponder what I'm about to do. I looked up almost every school on the coast before I figured out the children in the photo were wearing Terrigal Public School's uniform. That was followed by three hours of street scrolling on Google Maps—fanning out from the school to find the right driveway. After that, a quick stroll past the house and a check of the mail got me a name. Jonathan Davies. I went home again, looked him up. He's hot. I mean, he posed for some professional man's magazine as poster boy for keeping fit and I had a good look. He's fucked in the head but there's not much wrong with the rest of him.

So, name and address. Tick. Add in the screenshots of the forum conversation and maybe the police might be persuaded to knock on his door. But I want solid proof of what he's been doing with those kids to give to Bailee. I need access to his computer before he gets a whiff that the cops are on to him.

Another drink and I begin to feel steadier as the nerves I've spent all evening refusing to acknowledge sink further back in my consciousness.

I can do this. The nerves are stupid. It's not like I haven't broken into a house before. I know he's at that party tonight and the wife and kid have moved out. He and his arsehole friends were talking about it earlier. This is my best chance.

I turn on the ignition and get moving. Up the main road, turn left. Every house in this street looks like a prop for a luxe property magazine. But then again, this is Terrigal. The coastal holiday hub of the Central Coast has a distinct cosmopolitan feel with trendy, high-end shopping and fine dining. It's roughly twenty minutes from my little dump in the worst part of an otherwise pretty suburb, and yet a world apart. I don't tend to visit much. I spot the dazzling bougainvillea a few houses up in my headlights and slow further. And there it is. *The* house. Despite the not two but three storeys of elegance, it looks anything but extraordinary in this neighbourhood. The aura of in-your-face wealth makes me uncomfortable.

In most circumstances my very ordinary car would do anything but attract attention, but in this street it's out of place enough to have some snooty old bag calling the cops, even in the dark. I'd intended on one last drive past before parking around the corner, but there's a party on a couple of doors down. The street is dotted with cars of all kinds, so I park under a tree that still somewhat prevents the glare of the streetlight showing my car off and sit for several minutes. Watching.

The garage is closed, so I can't tell if there's a car in there. And the house is all dark. I watch for several minutes but no lights go on or off. I wait a bit longer. My fingers resume fiddling with the thumb drive. Flip. Flip. Flip.

One more drink.

My phone rings, startling me. 'Yeah?'

'Hey, it's me,' Bailee says. 'I wanted to apologise again for last night. You went to so much trouble. I should have told you sooner that she'd pulled the plug.'

'No big deal, but, look, I have to go. Can I call you back?'

'Ah yeah, sure. Where are you? Sounds like a party.'

'Kinda. Bye.'

I hang up fast, because the less she knows the better, then I hold off on getting out until three loud, drunken teens have stumbled past. They call out something disgusting to a couple making out on the back of a parked ute. The guy flips them the finger and gets back to swallowing his girlfriend's tongue.

I open the door and slide out. Close it quietly. I try and wander across the road casually until I reach the lawn, then I duck into the darkness and lunge for a gate by the side of the house. It's locked but easy enough to slip over. I find myself in a courtyard with a lap pool surrounded by shiny white pavers and glass fencing, raised gardens of mondo grass and more birds of paradise, and some fancy red plant that cascades from wall-mounted pots. The ocean looms in the background. The moon is rising over it, leaving a glittering silver trail on the water. The lulling rhythm of crashing waves is a constant.

Fuck you, universe. Why do arseholes get to live like this?

I turn my back on it and go to the expanse of glass windows and doors that make up the back of the house. A sensor light springs to life.

Shit. I move to the shadows.

The back doors are—thankfully—fitted with a traditional lock. I can pick one of those in my sleep. At least, I used to be able to.

After several nervous minutes wondering how I could have so badly lost my touch, I hear the click I've been waiting for and the door slides quietly open. I freeze. Wait. No alarm trips. I take a few steps then repeat. Freeze. Wait. Nothing. I can't see any sign of an alarm on the wall, so I'm guessing I'm safe. Now what?

One of the best things about suburbia is that nothing is ever perfectly dark. There's always a light source from somewhere, even if it's faint. As my eyes adjust I look around for places I'm likely to spot a laptop. I decide to start upstairs so I take the wide stairs—are these floors actually marble?—two at a time. At the top I turn right and look into the first room beside the staircase. 'Hey Siri, turn on the torch,' I whisper, then nearly jump out of my skin when Siri's voice booms, 'It's on.'

I turn down the damn volume, then shine the torch around and, bingo, it's a generously sized office. A laptop sits perfectly centred on a large, gleaming desk.

'Excellent.' I slide quickly into the office chair and—wow, comfortable—get to work on bypassing the password, which I manage to achieve much faster than I did the door.

A quick look at its contents tells me this is not the computer I'm looking for, but I wasn't really expecting it to be.

I know there's got to be a second laptop. But where? Hoping it's somewhere in the office, I start opening drawers, cupboard, containers, and after too much time has elapsed, I find a smaller laptop behind the top row of books on the bookshelf. It's a relic. An IBM Thinkpad. It has to be close to twenty years old. Maybe this isn't what I'm looking for, but when I open it up, it has some charge in it, so it's been used recently. There's a reason this thing was hidden.

At first glance there's not much to see. It's running Windows 98. Everything is so old it's kinda cool. But there's nothing much on here other than an Outlook program that desperately wants to update.

I take a peek anyway and am confronted with emails dating back close to the suspected couple of decades. Most are video links to cloud files and the titles say it all. This is the correct laptop all right. So now I'm wondering what else I've missed. I click on a file called 'The Farm', which paves the way for dozens more subfolders. And the world opens up.

I skim through records related to whatever farm he seems to own, another containing Excel charts of crypto credits and debits and another with links or instructions on how to reach a number of illegal sites. The rest are labelled with girls' names and dates. Starting with the most recent additions, I click on 'Kelli' and ew. A girl, maybe ten or eleven. In the shower, getting dressed, undressed. I can usually keep my emotions pretty level but it hits me hard. His daughter? The one Davies wants to keep when he gets rid of his wife? I click on another file and see some girl nowhere near old enough doing something she shouldn't even know about let alone be performing. 'Got ya! You're done, arsehole,' I say happily and begin copying the hard drive.

The download takes time and I'm tapping my fingers as I wait.

Voices carry from the street outside, arguing. I hope no one starts throwing punches down there. The cops being called is the last thing I need.

The download completes. I take out the drive and close everything down then stash the laptop back in its hiding spot. Mission accomplished. Another arsehole who's gonna get what he deserves.

A door bangs downstairs.

My heart slams into my ribs. My breathing stops as I struggle to listen.

'Well, I'm really sorry to have called and cut short your night, Jon,' a female voice snaps, 'but I thought saving our marriage might be more important to you than beers with the boys! I can't exactly have this out with you while Kelli's here, can I?'

Lights go on. The cool hue of them surges upstairs to dimly touch the white walls of the second-storey hall.

'I don't want to save our marriage, Charmaine! Go back to your sister's, take a pill—take a bottle of them—and get over it!'

'Fine! But you're not having Kelli. She stays with me!'

There's a laugh and it's down-to-the-bone mean. 'Everyone knows how batshit crazy you are. I *will* get custody.'

'Everyone *thinks* I'm batshit crazy thanks to you is what you mean! You've been spreading that shit around for months, haven't you? Undermining me with our friends and family, making me look stupid, forgetful, unhinged. You won't get away with it!'

'I already have!' There's thundering up the stairs then, 'Where are you going?'

'To pack Kelli's things! I'm picking her up from that sleepover and she's coming back with me. First thing tomorrow I'm contacting my lawyer.'

'You can't. *Our* lawyer's already working for me.'

'Then I'll get a better one!'

'With what? You have none of your own money!'

'I'll figure it out! You're not having her!'

There's nowhere to hide. I should have closed the door. But too quickly she's right there. Slim, jeans, black tee, cropped blonde hair. She stops to lean heavily on the wall and swipes uselessly at the tears streaming down her face. She looks exhausted, defeated. Then she looks up and her eyes are dark, round and startled. I realise she probably can't make out more than a dark shadow and is about to scream so I step forward. My finger instinctively goes to my lips, but she's not cooperating.

'Who are you? The new lover? He's replaced me already?'

'Your husband's a fucking paedophile,' I hiss. 'No. I'm not a new lover.'

'A *what*? Who *are* you?'

'You really need to be quiet.'

'Who are you talking to?' Davies's voice gets louder as he comes up the stairs.

My stomach dives again. I might have been able to talk my way out of it with this woman. But *him*?

Three loud bangs on the front door have me flinching. The footsteps on the stairs recede.

'Who are you?' the woman demands again. 'You have no right to be in this house! I'm calling—'

I go for the best chance I have. 'I'm someone who believes you. Someone who knows you're not nuts and that your husband wants everyone to think you are so he can get custody of your daughter.'

There's a long, thoughtful pause then, 'How do you know that?' I detect the hint of a tremble in her voice this time and hope I'm winning.

'I told you.'

'You told me my husband is a paedophile.'

'And I can prove it.'

She walks further into the room and eyes me suspiciously through tear-dampened lashes. 'If he's touched our daughter, I'll kill him!'

'What are you doing here?' Davies asks someone. We stop to listen.

'You left the party early.' Another male voice. 'Thought I'd drop by and make sure you were all set for my special event.'

Now what? This is just getting more and more complicated.

'I can't talk about this right now. I have a problem to sort out,' Davies said.

'So will we, unless we have a deal.'

'Last time was a bloody nightmare! I'm not putting my job on the line like that again.'

'If you want to keep that job, you don't have a choice.'

'Look, my wife's upstairs.' Davies sounds pissed off. Urgent. 'You need to go.'

'Oh right, the wife you've made out is crazy, yes?'

'Would you shut up! And as for the rest, if I go down, so do you. Got it? Now piss off!'

Again, Davies is coming up the stairs. Charmaine is standing in the doorway like a statue. I haven't felt this sort of bone-deep fear for years, but it's come back with a serious surge of adrenaline. I grab Charmaine and pull her back against the near wall. I don't even dare blink as he marches right past. Another light goes on. This one brightly illuminates the hallway and spills into the office.

I hear his curse from somewhere down the hall. 'Charmaine! Where the hell did you go?'

He's coming back. *Shit.* He's opening and closing doors as he goes, checking each room. Even holding my breath seems to make too much noise.

'I told you to go!' Davies says from right outside the office.

'I don't take orders, Doc. You're sure I can't change your mind?'

'You can't.' Davies walks past the door to the man at the top of the stairs. 'I'm sorry, but I got you in, that's it. I'm done taking chances.'

'Yeah, I'm afraid you are. You think you can threaten me and get away with it?'

'What are you—' There's a kind of dull thud that doesn't make much sense.

'Guess that crazy wife of yours finally had enough,' the stranger says. 'You set this up for me perfectly, you fucking idiot.'

There was a wheeze I'm guessing comes from Davies that might have been words.

'Bye, Doc.' The sound of someone tumbling down the stairs rumbles like thunder before the house falls into complete silence. A moment later the stranger's footsteps move down the stairs. 'No thanks necessary, Mrs Davies,' he calls on the way. A few more hurried footsteps, then red and blue flickers like disco lights on the walls as the door opens and closes quietly.

'Hey you! Got any beer?' It's a teenager's voice. Slurred. Far off. Everything inside seems silent, but the noise outside is picking up, making it difficult to be sure. A rowdy crowd, some sharply barked orders. A minute passes. Two.

I think Charmaine and I have fallen into some sort of state of utter disbelief because we're frozen, staring at each other.

Did he really leave? I have to check. I inch out of the study and slowly turn my head around the corner to look down the stairs. The breath I didn't realise I was holding whooshes out when no one kills me. The flashing cop lights are right across the street. More excitement flares up. A glass shatters. More yelling.

'I think he's gone,' I tell Charmaine. 'Must have got frightened off by the cops.'

Davies hasn't gone any further than the bottom of the stairs. A kitchen knife is sticking out of his chest, blood is pooling around him. His eyes are wide and staring, his mouth open as though still working on his last words.

Charmaine steps around me. 'Oh my God!' She's down the stairs in seconds with a disjointed kind of stumbling gait. 'Jon? Jon! Wake up. Oh, God.' Her hands are everywhere, looking for signs of life, shaking him. She clasps the knife.

'You probably shouldn't touch—that.'

But she's pulled it out and now her hands are covering the wound, applying pressure. She's still frantically demanding he wake up.

I walk down the stairs more slowly. My legs are jelly. 'I don't think that's going to help.'

'He's not breathing!'

'Probably because he's dead.'

Her head snaps up and she looks at me like I'm the antichrist for not caring, but seriously? I'm not at my best just now. The sound of the blood pounding in my ears is still louder than the chaos outside. My thoughts are jumbled. And, hold on a sec … there's a comfortable paunch, grey hair. 'Are you sure that's him?'

'Of course I'm sure! I recognise my own husband!'

'He doesn't look much like he did in the magazine pictures.'

'The what? The … That was twenty years ago!'

'Oh, shame.'

She blinks. Stares. '*Shame?* You think *that's* the shame? What kind of a lunatic are you?' Her eyes are wide, her face has absolutely no colour left and she's covered in her husband's blood. But underneath all that is an attractive young woman. Maybe a forty that would get away with thirty. Dead guy looks like he's pushing sixty, but considering what he's into, a young bride fits, I suppose.

Her eyes have gone back to Davies. 'I can't believe this,' she whispers, more to him than to me. 'I can't believe any of this. How could this happen?'

'You're kneeling in blood.'

She stumbles up and back, stares down at her bloodied knees, her hands. They shake, much like her voice. 'What *the hell*? Just … *what*?'

She's about to lose it. I know the feeling. But—'Not yet!' I manage to say, hands out, palms up as though sheer will can hold her collapse off. 'You should get help. Go get the cops or something.'

'Are you gonna tell them what happened?' she asks incredulously.

'Who me? I don't do cops.' I'm already backing towards the back door.

She sits—falls—heavily onto the bottom step. The trembling is out of control and her voice is rising. 'They're going to think I did this. He's been making me out to be a crazy woman. You heard the other guy.' She pushes back to her feet and clutches at her hair, begins to pace. 'He wanted a divorce. Fine. He wanted our daughter. Not fine. I guess that's when it started. Quiet words with friends and family over his concern for my mental state, talking to a shrink about the problems he's having with his crazy wife, making a police report that I had a substance abuse problem and had threatened him several times. Then yesterday I find a legal letter petitioning for full custody of Kelli.' She takes a deep breath, then another. 'He works with the police all the time and he's been telling them this shit. I'm screwed.'

'Here.' I hand over the thumb drive. 'This proves what an arsehole he was. It has some pretty revolting stuff on it. Give it to the cops.'

She lifts her hand to take it, then sharply recoils as though it might burn her. 'I can't use that! Don't you see? That's perfect motive!'

'But—'

'Yes, officer, I swear,' she cuts in, her earlier shrillness returning. 'This random stranger broke into my house, overheard me fighting bitterly with my husband over divorce and custody issues and presented me with the news my husband is a paedophile and out to make me look crazy. Yes, I can understand why you might think that would be enough to send me over the edge. But no, I didn't actually do anything, because believe it or not, at that moment, random stranger number two wandered in off the street and killed Jon with my kitchen knife. Yes, that's right, while a bunch of cops were outside. No, sorry, I didn't see him and can't describe him. No again, I don't know him and didn't ask him to kill Jon for me. And actually,'—she directs at me as she drags her fingers across her eyes—'it's probably better that you don't stick around because all you can add is that he called out before leaving to let me know no thanks were necessary.'

'True,' I reply, all too happy to resume my exit.

There's a humourless laugh before she flops back down on the bottom stair and stares out the window. 'I may as well hold out my hands for the cuffs.'

I really need to get out of here, but I can't seem to take the steps. Damn it, damn it, *damn* it! Why do I care?

'There's got to be another way.'

'Sure. You broke into my house. My best chance would be to run out there right now screaming that you did it.'

I glance outside and wonder if I'd stand a chance at escape if she did. Probably not. 'I get it, I really do. But I'm not the one covered in blood with my fingerprints all over the murder weapon,' I point out.

She looks back at me; a small streak of blood smears her hairline. 'I wouldn't do that. I didn't mean it.' The tears start again, great long lines of them. 'My daughter … God. She's going to grow up without me. She's going to believe I killed her father.'

And there's another little girl that will be fucked up forever. And that's, I suppose, why I care. But what can I do? Another long minute passes while I think about that.

Charmaine stands, starts towards the front door. 'May as well get it over and done with.'

I take another reluctant look at Davies. 'I don't think we can clean up all this blood,' I say loudly enough to have her stopping in her tracks to look back at me.

'What?'

'It's everywhere. And if the TV cop shows are anything to go by, they'll find evidence of it anyway. But without a body ...'

She starts back towards me. Her red, swollen eyes narrow in confusion. 'What are you saying?'

I bend down and put the drive in Davies's shirt pocket. He's dead. He won't be hurting anymore kids and after this, I can't have anything to do with investigating this group. The further out of it I stay, the better. 'Who knows you're here?'

'Just my sister.'

'Will she lie for you?'

She stares off into space for a moment, thoughtful. 'Yes. He has most people convinced I've lost the plot but not Veronica. She knows what he's like. She'd lie for me.'

'Okay. Then this is what we're gonna do.'

CHAPTER FOUR

Sunday, March 7

Rachael sat by the window of her ninth-storey apartment, her tired eyes blurring over the framed picture in her hands. The big hairy spider with gnarled legs and dripping fangs had the face of man, its expression all the more menacing because it carried the smile of a paedophile who'd made a career out of hurting little girls and exploiting them online.

A ten-year-old shouldn't have been able to replicate the features of that monster with this kind of precision. But this face had been seared into that child's mind by who knew how many horrifying encounters. Encounters she should never have had to endure.

And I couldn't save her, Rachael thought. *I couldn't save her, but I did get the Spider. I caught the monster. Didn't I?*

So many mistakes, so many regrets. Right from the first moment her sister Kayla, a teacher at a local primary school,

first tried to get her attention. All too readily the memory
drifts in.

'I'm telling you, Rach. She needs help!'

Rachael stared at the impossibly large pile of paperwork
on her desk and tried to concentrate on her sister's words
over the phone, even as the case in front of her pulled at her
attention. 'Lots of kids need help, Kayla. If you report it to
your local—'

'I'm reporting it to you! You're a detective now, right?
Abused children are supposed to be your thing. I have an
abused child in my class.'

'You think. And maybe you're right,' she added. 'But I've
only just made detective and I've already been invited in on
the Spider case. If I can help crack this, it'll make my career.
Kayla, this guy is the worst of the worst.'

'She's tiny,' Kayla pressed on. 'She looks closer to seven
or eight than ten. She's withdrawn, anxious, has no
friends and so much as raise your voice in her presence
and she cowers like a mouse. But she's so sweet and she
puts on this stoic little face and tries to be brave. She has
bruises all the time. I've repeatedly tried to pin the mother
down and she never returns my calls or emails, never
shows up.'

'I get that, but—' Out of the corner of her eye, she saw
Sanders, the lead detective, approach. 'Meeting in five,'
he told her. Shit. She hadn't finished preparing her ideas.
'Look, I'll make a note, pass on your concerns, okay? It's the
best I can do.'

'Rach—'

'Gotta go. Bye!' She ended the call and swore under her
breath. Damn it, she would have thought her sister would

be more understanding. Of course she'd like to help, but there were other people who could look into it. She had to make a good impression in this case. The Spider was her priority. He had to be stopped.

She reached for her notepad. What had she done with her pen? The desk was a mess. She shuffled everything around, tried to tidy just enough to find what she was looking for without losing what she needed on top.

'Detective Langley, are you coming?' Sanders called, this time from the doorway to the meeting room.

'Yes, of course.' She'd figure out who could best handle it later. 'Right away.'

By the time she'd gotten out of her chair, the pile of paperwork had again imploded into mayhem, and her sister, and the student, had been forgotten.

'Hey. What are you doing up so early?' Ed's voice was still sleep-filled as he appeared from the bedroom in a pair of grey boxers and a white tee and headed for the coffee machine. They'd begun leaving small necessities at each other's places several months ago, but she was starting to think Ed had more clothes at her place than at his own. She wasn't sure yet how she felt about that.

'I couldn't sleep,' she admitted. 'Didn't want to wake you by tossing and turning.'

With the coffee underway, he came over and bent down to kiss her. Then his eyes went to the picture. 'I didn't think you ever took that off the wall at the office.'

'I have to get it reframed. It fell a few days ago and broke.' She ran her fingers over the corner she'd taped back together. 'I'm beginning to think it could be an omen.'

'What do you mean? Is this about that crazy guy on the phone last night?' Ed took the picture and placed it on the coffee table, then took her hands in his. 'It was some-one after attention. Don't drag all this back up again. Stop punishing yourself. It's been eighteen years, Rach. Let it go.'

'What if I did get it wrong? What if we all did? If that "crazy guy" really is the Spider, then Biddle was telling the truth all along and we stuffed up.'

'No one stuffed up. We're going to look into that phone number today. Find out who I get to beat up for doing this to you.'

She managed a smile. 'I hope you're right.'

'I am.' He tugged her to her feet. 'Come and join me on the balcony for coffee. Then maybe when the café opens we could wander down the street, grab a nice long, lazy Sunday breakfast?'

'You took me out last night.'

'And look how that turned out. I still owe you a relaxing meal.'

She leant into him as he pulled her closer. 'I might be persuaded.'

'Then I think we should start with a shower, don't you?' he murmured against her mouth.

Her phone rang, jolting them. Anxiety clawed at her immediately.

Ed picked up the phone to check the number before handing it to her. 'It's work.'

'Right.' The tension eased and her shoulders dropped. This was silly. Ed was right: she was letting some random idiot get to her. 'Rachael Langley,' she answered.

'Sorry for the early Sunday call, inspector,' the familiar voice of Detective Sergeant Barbara Wills replied. 'But you left a request last night to be notified of any possible child homicide reports.'

Her breath halted, making her 'Yes' strangely weak.

'There's been a report of one just come in. Gosford area. Local detectives are on scene and forensics are en route.'

Rachael dropped back down to the lounge, legs giving way underneath her. 'A child homicide on the coast?' she asked weakly. 'Any other details?'

'Not at this stage.'

'Let Detective Sergeant Carson know, would you? He's close by. Ask him if he's in a position to attend.'

'Yes, of course, inspector.'

'Thank you.'

Ed poured a coffee and handed it to her. 'That's terrible. Poor kid.'

Her mind was racing. 'A dead child in Gosford, Ed. Possible homicide.'

'I heard. Finn will look into it.'

Why wasn't he getting it? 'Ed. A dead child. Gosford. That phone call last night. The caller was looking forward to proving me wrong. He's done this!'

Ed put his coffee down and placed his hands on her shoulders. 'Let's not jump to conclusions,' he said calmly.

But she couldn't help it. The caller had said he'd show her, and now this. The Spider had operated in the same area as the victim had been located this morning. She strode back to the table to pick up the picture of the Spider, her mind spinning back to the little girl who'd drawn it. The hole that had been in Rachael's heart since that day ached. 'I never got the chance to ask her if Biddle was the man she drew in this picture. But it is him, isn't it? It looks like him.'

'It does.'

'He was *there*. At the house. We found all those videos, clear records of the abuse he carried out against his victims on his computer. Everything pointed to Biddle being the Spider. Everything.' She looked up. 'How could I be wrong? How could I have let him take another child?'

*

Mosquitoes bothered Detective Sergeant Finn Carson's face as he moved carefully around a photographer. He felt the slide and squelch of his shoe as it sank in a solid inch of black mud, then looked down with a curse before watching where he took his next step. The creek's shoreline was a tangle of mangroves littered with rubbish: McDonalds, KFC, beer bottles, an old mattress. Several black rubbish bags close to bursting looked like recent additions to the makeshift tip.

'Don't remember asking for assistance from you mob.'

The voice was disparaging and familiar. Turner. Crap. They hadn't been on the best of terms since Finn had scored the promotion to homicide Turner had believed should have been his, and it sounded like he was still holding the grudge.

'Morning.' Finn took another couple of careful steps towards the scene. 'I got a call to come down here. Check it out.'

'Oh, yeah? That was fast.'

'What have you got?'

Turner stepped aside with a sour expression. 'Doc?'

Finn had the greeting on the tip of his tongue when he noticed the forensic pathologist in charge wasn't the 'Doc' he'd been expecting. The man was younger, thinner and had blond hair poking out from under its cover. The stranger straightened, stepped around the victim and over a mangrove branch to speak to him.

'I'm estimating she's been dead around four to six hours. Probable strangulation. We'll of course know more after the autopsy and tox analysis.'

The body wasn't easy to look at. Children never were. The girl's body was face up and had been carefully laid out between the mangroves as though she was sleeping. Auburn hair streamed out from a pretty, freckled face, dragging with the current and tangling with debris. She was dressed in a mermaid costume that sparkled, even in the low light. Her hands had been placed on her stomach and held a child's plastic bucket filled with sea life toys. Fishing line ensured they didn't slip. Delicately beaded wings framed her shoulders. Though her eyes were closed and a peaceful expression etched her face, the signs of abuse stood out vividly against her pale skin.

His stomach lurched because this looked too much like something else. Like the work of another unfathomable monster he'd revisited on prime-time television last night. No wonder Rachael had wanted him to check this one out. He was surprised she wasn't here herself.

He shoved his hands into his pockets to protect them from the hungry insects. Christ. What was she, eleven? Twelve? Only a little older than Ava. He had the irrational urge to take his jacket off and wrap her inside it. To protect her somehow, though it was already too late. She had no business being in the water on a warm autumn morning. Barely 7am. She should be tucked up in bed, waking up to the smell of pancakes, looking forward to weekend sport or a family outing. Not this. Anything but this.

Finn dragged his thoughts from the perverted cruelty of it and forced himself to think like a cop. His gaze bounced from the victim to the snaking creek bordered by thick mangrove swamp and the light traffic on the bridge that separated Erina from East Gosford; the handful of houses tucked in by the road on the eastern side. Why here? Even the scene was uncomfortably like one he'd studied more than any other, in which the killer had placed the bodies where he knew they'd be found quickly, before his 'works of art' could be destroyed by time and the elements.

'Who found her?' he asked Turner.

'A father and son out for an early morning fish. I've taken a statement, got a couple of my guys going door to door looking for any witnesses.'

'Any traffic cameras in this area?' Finn asked, looking around.

'Not where we need them.'

'Let's find out what's on this road closer to town anyway. Both directions. If we get any leads, we might need footage from further afield.'

'You think she was dumped here or travelled?' Turner looked out over the water.

Finn stared for a moment, unsure whether Turner was testing him or if he genuinely believed there was a chance the girl had floated like that on the tide and somehow caught herself up in a perfect pose among the twisted mangroves.

Aside from anything else, Turner had worked the Spider case with Rachael.

'If she'd travelled, she'd be face down.' He smacked at a bug by his ear. 'This body's been placed exactly how they wanted us to find her. The killer put her here.'

'Well, well,' Turner said, 'maybe it wasn't just being the boss's nephew that got you the job.'

'Not the time, Turner,' Finn barked. He didn't need this crap. If Turner possessed one ounce of empathy his mind would be too full of what had happened to this child to be picking old fights. 'We need an ID.'

'I'll get right on to that,' Turner said with mock enthusiasm. 'That is, assuming you want the help? From your presence, I suspect that Rachael's bringing her whole team in on this.'

'I'll report back to Rachael and, yes, I'm sure she'll want to pull together her team as quickly as possible. As for help, if you can make some space available for us at the station, I'd appreciate it.'

Turner nodded curtly. 'I'll make space for *us*. You're not keeping me out of this. It's my turf, my case.'

'That's up to Rachael.'

Turner sneered, looking like he had something else to say. Instead, he simply started back through the mud to the road.

Finn sighed in resignation. Of all the detectives in all the world ...

'Got a fan there,' the pathologist noted.

'Yeah. Who are you, anyway? Where's Davies?'

'I'm—' He paused in the act of stretching out a hand and withdrew it, removed a glove before again offering the handshake. 'Steven Van Zettan. Jonathan is on personal leave for a couple of weeks. Something about a marriage separation.'

'Do you know what you're doing?'

Van Zettan's brows rose. 'I believe I have enough experience to—'

'I'm sorry,' Finn blurted before the man could finish. He rubbed at the tension building behind his eyes. 'That sounded rude.'

'I've been getting the third degree from Detective Constable Turner since he arrived. Thought it must just be the culture around here.'

'It's not. But that one puts my back up.'

'Can't imagine why,' Van Zettan said with a smile.

Finn managed one back before another look at the victim had it dropping, silenced by a churning grief for the child he'd never met and a ferocious fury for whoever was responsible. 'I just want you to tell me you're the best damn forensic pathologist that ever lived. That you're not going to miss anything. Because we need to get the person who did this. No mistakes.'

'Understood.' There were several heavy seconds of silence, then, 'My daughter Jessie is sixteen. What's been done to this girl ...' He shook his head sadly.

'My Ava's ten.' His fury grew as he thought of his daughter, who he'd had to drag out of bed and return to her mother so early in order to be here.

'I won't make a mistake, detective. I want this guy in prison as much as you do.'

'How long until we can get her out of the water?'

'I've done all I can from here. We'll bring her up shortly.'

As though on cue, two more forensics officers appeared with a body bag.

Finn stepped back. *I'll get him, sweetheart,* he silently told her. *I'll get the piece of shit who did this to you. I promise.*

He made his way back up the track towards the road, the weight of the girl's murder hanging over him like a heavy cloak. He appreciated Van Zettan's sentiment, but the kind of person who could do that to a child didn't deserve a jail cell, he deserved a bullet.

There was a flurry of movement and sound as he approached the other vehicles. Normally a clearing with a lonely bus stop, this morning the roadside space was a car-park. Cops, forensics—and the media had arrived. Turner's officers were keeping them from encroaching any closer on the scene.

Finn climbed into his car, ignoring the questions launched at him by hungry reporters. He took out his phone and called Rachael. She answered on the first ring.

'Finn! What have you found out?'

'We've got a female victim approximately eleven to thirteen years of age. Been dead maybe six to eight hours.'

'Any signs of sexual assault?'

'Can't tell yet, but she's got some bruising. Especially around the throat. She's, ah, wearing a dress-up costume.'

He heard Rachael's sharp indrawn breath. 'The Little Mermaid?' she asked.

'Well, it's *a* mermaid,' he said.

'Oh, God. He said he had a date with Ariel. Wings, Finn. Are there wings on her back?'

'Yeah. Yeah, they're there. Rachael, what's going on?'

'I'll explain when I get there. I'm on my way. See you soon.'

He heard the line drop out, put down his phone. A dead child posed peacefully in a fairytale costume, wings on her back. The Spider was in prison. So what the hell was this? Some sicko who saw the show last night and decided to experiment?

As he stared thoughtfully into space he noticed an old man in grey trackpants and polo shirt hanging back by the road with a black dog. The man seemed undecided about whether to approach the scene or not. His gut told him that the man's movements meant more than general curiosity so he got out of the car. Rather than manoeuvre past the media, he caught the man's eye, waved him over, and instructed a young officer to let him through.

'Good morning,' he said. 'I'm Detective Sergeant Finn Carson. I saw you standing over there. It looked like you might have had something to say.'

'Well, maybe I do,' the old man agreed. 'Though I'm not sure if it's got anything to do with why you blokes are all here. I'm Noel McMahon. I live over the bridge there.'

'On the water?'

'Yep. Been there fifteen years. I'm always calling in about the illegal dumping that goes on down here. I'm sure most of you blokes are probably sick of hearing from me.'

'There is a lot of rubbish down there,' Finn said.

'Ends up on my bit of the creek sometimes. Found a needle once. It's not that I don't have better things to do than go around dobbing on people, but it's not safe for the grandkids, you know?'

'I understand completely. You wouldn't happen to have seen anyone dumping down here last night, would you?'

'No, but I have a camera I keep pointed in this direction. It doesn't pick much up unfortunately. It's a bit far away. But you blokes managed to get a number plate off it once and booked a dumper. I'm not sure if it caught anything last night. I was just over there wondering whether to say anything or go home first and have a look.'

'I'd be very interested to see the footage.'

Noel scratched his head. 'Not sure how to copy it.'

'No problem. I'll send someone back home with you to collect it.'

Noel looked relieved. 'Well, yes, that will work.'

'Appreciate it.' Then, 'Turner! I need one of your men.'

*

By the time Finn arrived at Gosford Police Station, Turner was hovering near reception with a constable named Harvey and a smug expression on his sour face. 'I have some officers cleaning up level one. As you'd probably remember from your time here as a lowly local detective, there's a large space, some private offices. It's not technically ours anymore, the police bank let the lease lapse a couple of years back, but I'm sure Rachael can wrangle something. She'll be familiar with the space. It was used on the original Spider case.'

So he was thinking about it. 'No one's saying this is related, Turner.'

'Personally, I would have said there was little doubt.' Turner smirked. 'I was imagining the look on Rachael's face when she discovered she wasn't the perfect cop everyone thought she was. But,' he continued before Finn could reply, 'then I discovered who the victim is and I've changed my mind. Maybe her stepfather saw the television last night, liked Biddle's idea ... can't be sure on that, but otherwise this looks relatively straightforward. We're not going to need a homicide squad for this piece of shit. This is our victim.'

Finn took the offered photo of a smiling school girl with a long auburn ponytail and shy, dark eyes. 'Yeah, that could be her. We'll have to verify that, of course.'

'Her name's Summer Edgely. Would have been thirteen next Tuesday. History with the Family and Community Services. Numerous allegations of abuse by the stepfather, Tyson Brewer. Brewer's known to us as a brawling drunk with a record of inappropriate behaviour towards Summer. The family had previously been referred to Community Services, but Summer's circumstances never quite met the risk of significant harm threshold so the family were offered the usual basic support and referrals. They didn't take them up.'

'The mother?'

'Refused to believe any of the allegations,' he said with a shrug. 'Said Summer was a drama queen looking for attention. Thought she'd run off. I'm guessing she'll have to believe it now.'

'And live with it,' Finn said with a nod. '*If* it's proven the stepfather is responsible.'

'If?' Turner said with a snide grin and roll of the eyes to the other constable. 'Care to make a wager, detective? Because guess who's gonna be right?'

'I don't bet on murdered children,' Finn said. 'And I don't guess. We'll work out what happened to Summer and who did it using actual police work.'

Turner huffed out a humourless laugh. 'I think I'll go bring in the parents. Wrap this up fast before the media carry on too much.'

'We need one of them to formally identify Summer's body before we start thinking about interrogating grieving parents.'

'Grieving, my arse. But fine. I'll take Wilcox and inform them. Get them out to ID her then bring them in.'

Finn remained silent as Turner and Wilcox headed out the front doors.

'Detective Carson?'

Finn turned his attention to the young officer manning the desk.

She smiled. 'Can I get you a coffee? I'll show you around if you like.'

'Thank you,' he said, 'but I know my way around. I used to be stationed here.'

'Oh, I see. I'm Constable Debbie Reynolds. I haven't been here long.'

'How have you found working here?'

'I like it. It was my first choice for a posting when I graduated last year so I was lucky to get it. Is Inspector Langley really coming up here to run the investigation?'

'She'll be here any minute. Why?'

Debbie shrugged and smiled again with a trace of embarrassment. 'She's someone I admire. She was great on the telly last night, don't you think? I joined in the hope of becoming a detective. I'd love to meet her.'

'You will, soon enough.' And he'd have to make a note to mention to Rachael how well she'd come across on the program. He knew she hated the spotlight.

As they made their way through the station to the break room, Debbie's step faltered. 'Also,' she began hesitantly, 'you should probably know Turner has been mouthing off a bit, so don't be surprised if some of the officers are a bit standoffish to begin with.'

Finn stopped in his tracks, brow raised. 'What has he been saying?'

'That you screw over your colleagues to climb the ladder. That you get promotions you don't deserve because your aunty is Inspector Langley. That if any of us end up assisting with the case, to go to him with anything we find rather than you, so you don't steal the credit.'

'Steal the credit?' he said with a dry laugh. 'He always did think of cases as competitions rather than collaborative investigations. If he still can't figure out what screwed him, it was that, not me. Regardless, I expect full cooperation without prejudice from anyone invited into this investigation or they're out.'

'Of course,' Debbie replied seriously and stepped into the break room, heading for the coffee machine.

'Constable Reynolds?' he said, sending her a crooked smile. 'Thanks for telling me.'

Her face split into a grin. 'You're welcome. Please call me Debbie. How do you like your coffee?'

CHAPTER FIVE

My brain is telling me I have to move, my body is threatening all kinds of retribution if I dare try. Jonathan Davies. Boot. Shit. What had I been *thinking*? I've done some pretty crazy crap before but this one surprises even me.

I fumble for my phone and squint at the time. Ten o'clock. Several message alerts come up. One of Bailee's arseholes is looking for a meet up, Henry wants to confirm his Tuesday appointment and shit—Bailee. I forgot to call her back her last night. I send her a short apology and reassure her I'm fine. You'd think by now she'd realise I'm unreliable, but she still believes I've met some terrible fate every time I don't call her back.

My long-cold coffee is still sitting beside me so I take a sip. It stays down. Just—my stomach protests alarmingly. I need to keep this guy on the hook so I tell him I'll get back to him when I can sneak out. I hear the roar of a car speeding down the street. It drags my attention back to the outside world and what's waiting for me. I know this is not going to end well. I gingerly get to my feet, poke myself in the eye as I shove on my sunglasses and stagger through my front door. Flies bother my face as I squint through my glasses to the central driveway separating my row of town-houses from the ones opposite. No one seems to be about.

I cast a quick glance at my next-door neighbours' place just to be sure. I avoid the Parkhursts the way others might avoid an unflushed hospital toilet. Their place is as old and boring as everyone else's, but they lord it over our dismal little community like royalty and hate me with a passion. Probably because I go out of my way to annoy them whenever I can be bothered. I like to think of it as cheap therapy.

My '99 model Civic is sitting in its little parking space by my front door. I picked it up cheap almost five years ago and it's been nothing but reliable. I'm quite fond of it, but I wonder if it might have to go now that it's had a body in it. I approach the boot, hoping to hell last night might have been nothing more than a wild, JD- and pot-induced hallucination. I know it's not, but the way I got into both when I finally made it home last night means I have to check to be sure. Besides, the idea of seeing that body again is freaking me out and I have to be able to look at it and touch it and get rid of it. Hopefully it's still properly wrapped up in that blanket.

I unlock the boot, preparing myself. I've seen dead bodies before. When you grow up on the streets, you expect to come across them from time to time. And well, it hasn't been that long since I put this one in here. Waiting out the cops, sneaking my car into Doc's garage then getting his ridiculously heavy and awkward body into my boot had seemed to take forever. The lid pops open. I'm pretty confident I can—Nope! God! No!

What hits me is as bad as it gets. I blindly scramble to get the boot shut again as my eyes burn and water. The resulting fumbled *Bang* reverberates painfully up my arms. The wrenching cough as I stagger away is almost enough to send my stomach hurtling up through my throat.

How can a body smell that bad that fast? My already impossible hangover kicks up several notches.

'Lexi, dear? Is everything all right?'

Oh, not now! I turn around and try to smile. I get an impression of my sixty-nine-year-old neighbour-across-the-driveway's ample form in black tights and a loud KISS T-shirt but my eyes are still purging themselves, my lungs are singed and I'm going to throw up.

'Morning, Dawny,' I manage to say, though my voice comes out weak and thready. I cough again, but I think it's the sight of tears streaming down my face that has her hurrying closer, limping on her dodgy 'I don't have the time for a replacement' knee.

'What on earth has happened?'

'Just, um … allergies.' I clear my throat and give myself a mental pat on the back for quick thinking. But Dawny's nose screws up.

'Oh dear, I think it's a bit more serious than allergies.'

My excuse hadn't covered the lingering odour, and from the look on Dawny's face, she not only smells it, she assumes it's coming from me.

Despite everything else bothering me, I object to that. Honestly? Never, *ever*, even on the worst of days, am

I physically capable of producing that kind of stink. I'm offended but stuck. I can't exactly explain, so I swipe at my eyes, smile, though it's tight, and press on. 'Do you need something?'

'Well ...' Dawny seems to be rethinking whatever had brought her out here, and I entertain a small glimmer of hope she might leave me alone. She likes to chat. Rumour has it she did a decent stint of prison time in the eighties, and though no one seems to know what for, her preference for dressing like a street kid combined with the holier-than-thou moral code in our judgemental little plot means the neighbours tend to avoid her. Of course that makes her lonely, so when she corners you, you're toast. 'I got up this morning about my normal time, you know, I'm sure I've told you I like to be up by nine. I don't like to sleep any later or I can't sleep at night. Then I have a second supper and I end up with terrible indigestion. Oh, it's been bad lately. I—'

'I can't help your indigestion, Dawny,' I cut in. I'm going to be sick and I know how this goes: there's a point to her story, but it gets lost in a thousand detours. If I wait it out, she'll go on and on in her slow all-the-time-in-the-world manner, repeat herself three times and forget what she's come to say. Then she'll want to come back and tell me later. 'You need to talk to the chemist.'

'Oh, yes. I'll get around to it. That's not the problem. But it has been bad and—'

I can feel my mouth watering as it does just before I lose whatever's in my stomach. A hot flush washes over me, my head is spinning. 'What's the problem, Dawny?'

'Oh, I was watching television. I suppose you saw that terrible news of that young girl found dead in the creek?

Just awful. So I turned it off and went to get a nice hot cup of tea. Well, it'd just boiled when the lights went out. Now I can't make them work. In the kitchen I mean, and I thought you might be able to take a look. I haven't changed the globes in a while but when—'

'Maybe later, okay?'

'I'd really appreciate it. Thank you, Lexi, dear. They—'

'No problem.' I *really* have to get inside. 'I'm just gonna ...' I point to my front door, start walking.

'Of course, of course. You go on back inside and do what you need to do.' Her nose screws up again. 'Perhaps see a doctor.'

The smell isn't me! I want to yell at her, but I can't, and I don't have time, anyway. I'm too busy avoiding obstacles as I plough my way through my lounge and kitchen to the bathroom. The relief is enormous, but the purge intensifies the pounding in my head.

I clean myself up and go back out to the kitchen. I need to take something to help but I don't want to risk it on an empty stomach, so I nibble cautiously at a piece of stale bread while I sit and stare out the window. My eyes land on my car and—Dawny, still hovering, a frown on her lined face as she inspects the boot. Shit.

I throw open the front door. 'What are you doing?'

Dawny drags her attention from the car, but she seems slightly more vague than usual. 'Oh, nothing. Just waiting. It's a lovely day to be outside, isn't it?'

Panic crawls up my spine because her eyes have already gone back to the boot and it's anything but a lovely day to stand in the sun. 'I said *later*, Dawny. I'll take a look later. As in not yet.'

'Yes, yes, of course. No problem, dear.' She smiles and nods, then waves a hand before limping back across the drive to her place. The fact I get rid of her so easily only makes me more nervous. She couldn't possibly have seen anything, could she?

I close the door and sit back down at my kitchen table, let my head fall into my hands. What am I going to do?

Come on, Lexi. Think.

I've seen enough TV to know there are plenty of methods of getting rid of a dead body. The weighing-it-down-in-the-water option is my clear favourite, and all the nearby bodies of water I can think of drift through my mind before I'm forced to dismiss the idea. I'd need deep water. Even if I manage to find a suitable public wharf, I have no idea how I'd stealthily drag an enormous body out to the end of one, weigh it down and dump it.

Burying it doesn't sound a lot easier. I'm not exactly a fit and strong Amazonian. At best I'd end up with a shallow grave that wasn't worth the effort. Maybe I could drive out to the end of some godforsaken fire trail and dump it behind a fallen tree in a patch of scrub or something?

That sounds easy so I hold on to it for a moment. But from what I've seen on the news, those are generally the bodies people stumble across by accident.

I can feel myself slowly starting to panic. This is not the simple solution I thought it would be last night.

I'm desperate enough to consult Google, and my stomach is kind of behaving, so I swallow down some chemist-brand paracetamol and move to the lounge room, open my laptop and type in *best way to dispose of a body*. The first hit I get claims to have ten options for me. Hopeful, I click on it and wonder how many people have done what I'm doing right now. What kind of demand could there be for this sort of information, anyway?

The first thing I see is someone shoving the remains of a body into what I think might be a woodchipper. Ha. Nope. There's got to be a better option. Burial. Already ruled out. Reusing a grave. Still burial. Burning … hmm. I'll admit the idea is less than appealing, but I read on. I couldn't pull it off as a backyard barbecue by the sounds of it, but maybe dumping the body in the bush *and* burning it might work. Added bonus: destruction of prints and DNA. Teeth are still an issue. The author suggests removing them. Ha again, but I keep that in mind as I look at the remaining options. No, they're all way beyond my capabilities and—ew, pigs. Really? My stomach starts to roll again.

I sigh and stare back out the window. No sign of Dawny this time. Is she inside calling the cops? The idea is probably ridiculous, though I'm not so sure the Parkhursts wouldn't, should they venture outside this morning and smell anything suspicious. How long do I have until that stink escapes the boot?

I get back to my feet and rub my fingers above my eyes where the headache refuses to dissipate. I'm going to have to go with the dump and burn—the teeth will have to stay. Then all that's left to do is hope to hell no one ever finds him.

CHAPTER SIX

'How many times do I have to fucking tell ya! I never touched the lying little bitch!' Tyson Brewer leant threateningly over the interview table and snarled at Finn. Though it was edging towards too cold in the interview room, Brewer's flannelette shirt was unbuttoned, showing off a faded blue singlet sporting large perspiration stains. His thick greying hair was a spiky, sweaty mess. Specks of dark dust had invaded the crow's feet that fanned out from his reddened eyes, making the lines appear deeper. When he scowled, those eyes slitted into an expression that was pure violence. He was a bricklayer by trade and had a heavy-set physique to show for it. His thick, beefy hands would have had no trouble creating the bruising Finn had seen on Summer and he doubted very much the man had kept them off his wife, either. As for grieving, Finn had seen no sign of any.

'Nice way to talk about your dead daughter.'

Brewer sat back in his chair, shrugged and muttered, 'Not my kid. Anita's.'

Finn felt his own hands want to curl into fists. 'Who you'd raised, if you could call it that, for the last three years.'

'That's right!' Brewer again bounced in his seat and pushed a fat finger at Finn's face. 'Raised, fed, kept a roof over her head. Even paid for her school stuff. All she ever did to repay me was make me life hell.'

'Right. By doing what exactly?' Finn read from the file he had in front of him. 'Falling into your fists? Getting in the way of the video cameras you had hidden in her bathroom? Listening to threats to post said videos on her Facebook account if she didn't complete housework? For not lying at school—and so having food and warm clothing withheld from her—when she was asked about injuries she'd suffered from your so-called discipline?'

Turner stepped quietly into the room and took a seat beside Finn.

'Ah, that's bullshit.' Brewer sniffed loudly, a thick, snotty sound that was followed by a large swallow and a swipe of his nose along his forearm. 'Never proven. Half of that crap was Summer trying to get sympathy from the teachers, the other half came from Anita this one time when she had the shits with me about cheating on her. Payback.'

'Wow, you've really been victimised by the women and children in your life, Mr Brewer,' Turner said. 'Better find some alibis for the last forty-eight hours so the police can start feeling sorry for you.'

Brewster stood, eyes bulging with anger. 'You can't speak to me like that! I told ya friend here I never touched her! She was always taking off. Had some street kid friends we couldn't keep her away from. Why don't ya go find them!'

'We'll get to it,' Finn promised. 'Sit down, Mr Brewer. We're not done.'

Brewer's eyes darted around the room as though he'd briefly forgotten where he was. 'I'll sit, but I'm not saying nothing else until I get a lawyer.'

'You're not under arrest,' Finn reminded him.

'Yet,' Turner muttered.

'I said I want a lawyer.'

'Fine.' Turner sighed loudly, got to his feet.

Finn followed Turner out and closed the door behind them. 'Legal Aid's not coming in for this.'

'I reckon he's thinking he's already fried. May as well have admitted it right there and then.'

'He could be innocent,' Finn pointed out. 'Let's not get ahead of ourselves.'

Turner's sneer increased. 'Regardless of whether or not he murdered Summer, he made her short life hell, didn't he?'

'That doesn't make him a murderer,' Finn said with a heavy sigh. 'What did the mother have to say?'

'She's upset, not making a lot of sense. But she maintains Brewer couldn't be responsible. All she's worried about is protecting the bastard.'

'It happens. In a way, Anita is as much a victim as Summer.'

'I'm sorry but I disagree.'

'Did you manage to find out when she last saw her?'

'Said it could have been Friday.'

'Could have been?'

'She's not sure. She said Summer often ran off. That she'd always come back when she was ready. Apparently, she'd been doing it more and more lately.'

'And Brewer mentioned something about street kids she was friendly with.'

'Yeah, yeah. But it's hard to look far past that bastard in there right now.'

Brewer called out for a cigarette break. When no one answered, he raised his voice. Demanded again.

Finn stuck his head back around the door to find Brewer gnawing at the skin on the side of his thumb. 'How about keeping it down for a minute?'

'Fuck you. I need a cigarette! Is me lawyer coming or am I walking?'

'We can't let him walk,' Turner growled.

Finn agreed he should probably hold him until Rachael arrived. 'If he doesn't want to answer our questions and verify his whereabouts last night, we may need to give him a reason to need that lawyer.'

'Damn straight.' Turner slipped back into the room, left the door ajar. 'Mr Brewer, we're going to ask you one more time. Where were you last night between the hours of ten pm and five am?'

'Screwing your mother.' He shoved Turner as he made for the door.

'*Now* you're under arrest,' Turner said. 'You do not have to say anything, but failing to do so when questioned may harm your defence.'

Dual footsteps moving fast along the corridor drew Finn's attention over the racket Brewer was making as Turner read him his rights. Rachael was barrelling down the corridor, Debbie struggling to keep up. 'That lift is ridiculous,' Rachael said to Debbie. 'So slow.'

'Which is why we take it to come up but use the stairs to go back down.' Debbie puffed a little as she spoke.

Rachael spotted Finn, smiled, then shifted her gaze as Turner reappeared. To her credit her eyes only flickered slightly when she noted who he was; a barely imperceptible moment of unhappy recognition.

'Finn, Detective Turner,' she said.

'Inspector,' they replied.

'You're wasting your time here,' Turner told her. 'It's under control.'

'Is it?' Her attention was drawn to the interview room where Brewer had resumed his yelling. 'Who's that?'

'Tyson Brewer. The victim's stepfather,' Finn said.

'A real piece of work,' Turner added. 'Plenty of assault charges and claims of abuse against him towards the victim.'

Rachael looked Brewer over, tipped her head to the side in thought as Brewer yelled, 'You bastards can't do this!' before again demanding his cigarette.

'He's not the killer, but he probably did abuse the victim,' she said.

'Oh, what are you, psychic now?' Turner snapped, 'You can't possibly know that!'

Finn figured otherwise. If Rachael said it out loud, she was pretty damn sure.

'And if you're thinking you're walking in here and taking the credit for Brew—'

'Cool your jets, Turner,' Rachael cut in. 'We'll need a warrant to search his house. On top of checking—in case I'm wrong—for evidence associated with Summer's murder, we need to look for evidence of Brewer's involvement in a paedophile ring of any sort, either in person or online. Also check if he's a member of any groups or clubs that hold regular meetings, parties or get-togethers. If he is, ensure they're not cover groups for illegal activity. Is his browser history wiped? Does he have a Tor browser and a VPN to cover up his movements?'

'Yes, your majesty,' Turner said, wide-eyed.

'Inspector will do,' Rachael shot back.

Brewer's yelling was now accompanied by the banging of his chair on the floor.

'Oh, for heaven's sake.' Rachael walked around Finn and Turner to the doorway. 'Mr Brewer, Inspector Langley, lovely to meet you. I assure you that your behaviour will dramatically slow down my colleagues' responses to your various requests. You should know we intend on doing a thorough search of your property, after which time, if we're satisfied of your innocence, we will be able to let you go. However, we can legally hold you under arrest for six hours and will do so for the pure pleasure we'll derive from that if you continue to deliberately piss us off.'

Brewer scowled and opened his mouth but Rachael cut him off with a lift of her index finger and an 'Uh-uh. These are not idle threats, Mr Brewer. And if six hours isn't enough incentive to shut up, I'm sure I'll find something or other during that search I can charge you with in order to extend your stay with us further. Do we understand each other?'

Brewer closed his mouth, sneered, spat at the floor and looked away silently.

'Thank you, Mr Brewer. We appreciate your cooperation.'

Finn covered a grin at the way Debbie stared, mouth slightly agape.

Rachael turned back around. 'Is the autopsy sorted?'

'Tomorrow morning, first thing,' he said. 'Davies is on leave. We've got a new guy—Van Zettan.'

Rachael's face lit with recognition. 'Steven, excellent. He's just back from spending a few years running the show in New York. Brilliant man.'

'And humble apparently.'

'What makes you say that?'

'I gave him the third degree. He said he was new, that's all. Didn't elaborate.'

'It won't hurt to have his eyes on this. A fresh perspective. But we may also need to consult Davies due to his work on the Spider case. Do we know when he'll be back?'

'Two weeks,' Turner said. 'It's apparently a bit of a delicate situation. One of the forensics guys was saying it's all around the lab that he's going through a marriage breakup with a crazy wife. Having all sorts of problems.'

'With Charmaine?' Rachael said with a frown. 'I've met her on a couple of occasions and she's always seemed very grounded. Sensible. Still, the breakdown of a marriage would be very difficult.'

Finn caught the sideways glance. Yes, marriage breakdowns were very difficult, but he didn't need to be thinking about that right now, or for Turner to find out about it. Rachael moved on.

'I've pulled together a joint homicide and child abuse strike force,' Rachael continued. 'Everyone will be here shortly. Those who live on the northern end of the city might choose to commute; others who live further out may not be able to. I need to sort accommodation for any who need to make use of it. Suggestions?' she asked Turner.

'How many?' Turner asked.

'Ten detectives including myself and Finn to start, about that again in analysts. I expect that number to grow.'

'Grow? They're all coming in tonight? And we don't even know for sure there was any sexual assault. You've already got them on a strike force?'

'Everyone will be here tonight or first thing in the morning. I expect the entire team will be assembled by 8:30am Monday.'

'The Waterview and The Palms are the closest motels,' Turner decided. 'Debbie, would you mind making a couple of calls?'

Debbie nodded. 'Of course. I'll sort it.'

'Thank you,' Rachael said.

Turner inclined his head, then returned to the interview room where Brewer was still waiting.

'Turner hasn't changed,' Finn said. 'I'm surprised he's taking instructions.'

'It won't last,' she said, drawing a laugh out of him. 'He had it in his head I was going to boot him off the case. When I didn't, it threw him. Thanks for this morning. I appreciate you getting there so quickly. And I'm sorry to have messed up your weekend with Ava.'

'Goes without saying and shit happens, but what aren't you telling us?'

'I'll get to that.' Then to Debbie, 'Where have you put us?'

Debbie blinked, her expression remaining blank long enough to put a frown on Rachael's face.

'You do have space assigned to this strike force?'

'Yes, sorry, of course. It's upstairs. I'll show you.'

'Excellent. I have some things to collect from my car.' She moved off again, the tap, tap, tap of her steps light as she hurried away.

When Debbie didn't immediately move, Finn glanced at her and noticed the furrowed brow. 'Everything all right?'

'I want to be her when I grow up. Is she always like that?'

'Efficient? You don't get to where she's gotten by standing still.'

'Right. Of course.'

'And on that note, you'd best catch up. I'm guessing she'll have a lot of stuff to bring in.'

'Right. Of course.'

He gestured for her to get going. Rachael was a power-house, but even for Rachael, this investigation appeared to be surging ahead in questionably fast leaps and bounds. She'd known about the costume before Finn could tell her and she had already organised a strike force. What did she know that he didn't?

CHAPTER SEVEN

Rachael dropped the last of her things by the doorway. The area assigned to the strike force was a familiar space: a well-lit rectangular room with tables and chairs stacked up along the back of it. Windows ran almost the length of one side, and she caught glimpses of Brisbane Water and the mountains beyond through the branches of one of the old fig trees that bordered the park across the road. Some things had changed in the last eighteen years, others hadn't.

'Can I help you with anything else, inspector?' Debbie asked, appearing behind her.

'Thank you. We'll need more pinboards and we should begin setting these tables up. Did I spot an Officeworks as we came in? I'll need copious amounts of Post-it notes, whiteboards, markers and magnets.'

'Yes,' Debbie confirmed. 'If you'd like to write me a list, I'd be happy to run over for you and collect whatever you need.'

'Constable Reynolds,' Turner said from the doorway. 'You're supposed to be back on front desk.'

'Yes, sir, I'm assisting.'

'You have your own duties to perform.'

Debbie looked at Rachael, clearly uncomfortable. 'Sorry, inspector. I'd be happy to run that errand during my break.'

Rachael smiled. 'Thank you, Debbie. I'll sort it.'

Debbie nodded then, with a strained glance at Turner, hurried away. As Rachael watched her rush off, she noticed a couple more constables in the hallway. Their smirks disappeared when they caught her staring. Turner's fan club, she gathered. She should have known the truce wouldn't last long.

She let her smile drop into the kind of resting bitch face she reserved for the most aggravating adversaries. She knew from many years of practice and experience it was effective. 'Let's have it,' she said to Turner. 'And be done with it. Because if you undermine me during this investigation, I—'

'Undermine you?' he asked with exaggerated surprise. 'I wouldn't dream of it, inspector. You have my full professional support.'

'Then what was that about?'

'Oh, you know how it is,' he said. 'Young officers like Debbie tend to find themselves in awe of people like you. They bounce around like excited little puppies trying to be helpful. I'm making sure she doesn't get too carried away until she figures out how it really works.'

'And how's that?

'Oh, come on,' he said conspiratorially, with a quick grin back at the spectators. 'A lucky break in a high-profile case, a willing superior to sleep with.'

She kept her expression unchanged. She knew he was looking to get a rise out of her and she damn well wasn't going to bite. 'Be careful, Turner. I won't tolerate another outburst like that.'

His face transformed from smug to bitter in seconds. 'Meaning what? If you try and take me off this case, I'll take this as far as it can go. You'll get no cooperation from the other police—'

'Your work on the Spider case could be valuable to this investigation, but step out of line again and that's exactly what I'll do. As for Reynolds, I could use her.' She smiled coldly. 'I'm putting her on the strike force.'

The red flush extended from his neck to his cheeks. 'You really think you can walk in here and take over?'

'Yes. You're in charge of Brewer. Organise that warrant, do the search and make sure you follow up those points I made with you earlier. You can go now.' She looked past him. 'As can you,' she told the other two.

They hesitated, obviously wanting to see what Turner would do. She, too, wondered if he'd have the balls to say or do anything really stupid. But she doubted it.

Then Finn appeared. 'Rach, sorry, am I interrupting?'

Rachael refused to break Turner's stare. After another moment of tense silence, Turner walked out without a word. Everything inside her sighed with relief. She might have perfected the art of it, but she hated confrontation. If there was any other way to handle Turner, she'd take it but she knew from experience he'd take any opportunity to undermine her position with the other officers. And he was right. She was on his turf.

'Sorry, Finn, what can I do for you?'

'What was that about?'

'Same old Turner. What's up?'

'I was hoping you might have time to run me through what you already know about this case.'

'Of course. Feel like a walk? I'd like to find a decent coffee shop I can frequent while I'm up here.'

'I know just the place.'

They took the stairs to the ground floor and headed for the front doors. Rachael spotted Debbie behind reception. 'Hang on, Finn.' She approached the desk. 'Debbie?'

'Inspector. Sorry again about before.'

'There's no reason for you to apologise. I've spoken to Detective Turner. If you'd like to be involved with the strike force, I could use you.'

Debbie's face lit up. 'Really? Are you sure? I mean, yes, please! That would be amazing!'

'Don't get too excited. It'll be a lot of running around after coffees and lunches, shuffling paperwork, filing and sorting, and freeing up the detectives' time by taking care of some of the more mundane tasks.'

'I can't tell you how much I would love a chance to experience being part of a homicide investigation. I'll take whatever opportunity I can get. No job will be too mundane. Honestly.'

'We'll see how you feel about that after the first few days.'

'Thanks, inspector. Truly.'

Rachael smiled again before joining Finn at the door. 'Shall we?'

'I think you made her year,' Finn said as they wandered down the road.

'I like her. She's enthusiastic. Helpful.'

'But enough of both to put a probationary constable on the strike force?'

'How else is she going to learn? Besides, I need a local cop.'

'What about Turner?'

'I haven't booted him out. Yet. But he probably shouldn't have kicked off our last conversation with his belligerent views on my validity as an inspector and my sex life.'

Finn expelled a frustrated breath. 'Son of a bitch.'

Rachael noted the momentary tightening of the jaw and closing of the fists with amusement. 'Finn, I told you I can handle it.'

'You shouldn't have to. How long has it been since the Spider case? You made the right call, he made the wrong one. You got a promotion, he didn't. That's as cut and dried as it gets.'

'Yes, and fast forward several years and he applied for your job, and you got it.'

'You didn't get me that spot.'

'You're missing the point. Turner's incapable of seeing any truth other than his own. No one will ever convince him that I reached my position by putting in a lot of honest, hard work or that you earned your place in homicide for the same reason. All he sees is that he's constantly overlooked and that the system is unjust, that it's someone else's fault. But he can be nasty, Finn. And calculating. He holds grudges. Be careful.'

'I think I can handle it,' Finn promised dryly.

'Hey, that place looks cute,' she said of a trendy-looking sandstone building.

Finn chuckled. 'Yeah, it's a cocktail bar. It's actually a fantastic cocktail bar. But it's not open and you want coffee. We're going this way.'

'Right. So let me tell you what I know. I received a phone call last night.' She filled him in as they collected their coffees and wandered back to the station at a comfortable pace.

'You think he's telling the truth? Is there even a chance?'

'It was a solid conviction.' She chewed her lip. 'I don't want to believe we were wrong, but it needs to be explored.'

'How would some random nutcase get your mobile number?'

'I don't know.'

She saw a possibility dawn on his face. 'You don't think the call came from a cop?'

'It's something I've been considering.'

'How could someone who spends years training to defend the public and uphold the law be that person?'

She shrugged. 'We know criminals are occasionally drawn to law enforcement, just as paedophiles are to childcare positions and pyromaniacs to firefighting, and, of course, perpetrators are often drawn to crime scenes. In lieu of a crime scene, an event that perpetuates the crime would be the next best thing. Assuming he's the narcissist I believe he is, he'd be on the lookout for anything related to the crimes he committed.' She sipped her coffee, frowning with worry. 'That was one thing that always bugged me about Biddle. I couldn't understand why a man with the personality we profiled would deny his work once captured.'

'He was also profiled as highly intelligent. That intelligence overcame his ego long enough to see him through the trial. Someone's copied him. It's as simple as that. What does Ed think of all this?'

'Ed's thinking copycat.' They waited for the road outside the station to clear, then crossed. 'But copycat or not, I need to set my team up so we're ready to catch the bastard as soon as we get a lead. I don't want him getting a chance to strike again.'

They reached the station doors and she stopped. 'Why don't you go home. I'm going to play around with our space for a while. Make sure I'm ready for tomorrow morning.'

Debbie came racing out. 'Inspector. I'm on break. Do you have that list of supplies you need?'

'I'm afraid I haven't had a chance to get that together yet.'

'Why don't you text it to me?' Finn offered. 'I'll go with Debbie to collect everything then I'll come back and help you set it all up.'

'Thanks, Finn.'

'Back soon,' he promised.

Rachael went upstairs and looked around the empty room. The first time she'd been in this room it had all been so overwhelming. She visualised it how it had looked before, how it would again once she had it how it needed to be: bustling with busy people and equipment and walls spilling with pinned photos and maps and evidence. To the left of the door, one wall was already mounted with a pinboard. A few old tacks, some bent, were stuck around the edges. She preferred to use whiteboards and magnets, or if using a pinboard, to equip them with brightly coloured plastic pins that were simple to push in and pull out. But they'd used those gold thumbtacks during the Spider case. She had a fleeting memory of trying to dig them out when they'd been pushed too hard into the board. She shook her head. It was silly the things that popped up in her memory sometimes.

What if I got it wrong? The thought had been playing in her mind since last night, torturing her since the young girl's discovery this morning. If she let it, she knew it could paralyse her with doubts and guilt, prevent her from thinking clearly, from doing what needed to be done.

She dragged out a folding table and set it up, lifted her boxes of files onto it and opened the first one. She'd kept it all. Every little piece of paper that had littered the walls on that case. And now she was back, but she wasn't the rookie cop anymore.

'Detective Langley, are you coming?'

'Yes, of course. Right away.'

The room was crammed with detectives and other police staff. Some were sitting, while others stood in whatever space they could find. A pinboard running the length of one wall was littered with notes and pictures, maps and evidence that, so far, had gotten them nowhere. But it was what sat in the centre of the board that held the attention of the room. The three photographs were almost mesmerisingly beautiful. The little girls looked peaceful in death: a stark contrast to the horror of the sick roleplay they'd been forced to participate in.

The first, seven-year-old Jennifer Holland, was draped in a vibrant red cape, her dark braids falling over her shoulders towards the bed of yellow daisies she'd been so carefully placed on. Dappled sunlight filtered down from willow branches, one beam of warm light perfectly illuminating her young face. Her hands had been placed on her chest, holding a small basket of berries.

Victim two was six-year-old Ella Frazer. Her costume was a sparkling satin and lace ballgown delicately beaded and glittering so brightly the photo was hazed with light. A tiara had been placed in her loose blonde curls, a transparent slipper in her little hands. Her flower bed had been lavender.

Victim three. Tia Brown had been found yesterday. The eight-year-old had been wearing a simple dress with a blue bodice, puffed sleeves and a long, yellow skirt. A red bow sat in her hair. In her hands was a book of fairytales, her bed was white wisteria.

All posed, sleeping in flowers, all characters from a fairytale, but each also wore a set of little silver wings with pearl beading.

The media had soon begun to refer to the monster behind the murders as The Storyteller, but the killer had had other ideas. 'I am the Spider,' had read the anonymous message that had come through to the station.

It had been Rachael who had immediately made the correlation between the silver and pearl wings and Mary Howitt's 1829 poem. It, too, was pinned to the board for all to see and remember, in case more clues they hadn't yet figured out sat within.

'Good morning, everyone,' Detective Inspector Matthew Sanders said loudly over the general noise and conversation of the room. 'We've had confirmation from Community Services that Tia's family was on their watchlist.' A fresh round of murmurs echoes through the room. 'That's three for three. All our victims had been prior victims of family abuse. Why?'

'Could just be coincidence,' came from the corner of the room. 'Child abuse is much more prolific than most people imagine.'

'Coincidence is unlikely, Detective Turner, but I suppose it's possible.' Sanders didn't look impressed.

'Could the Spider be someone within Community Services?' another asked. 'Perhaps he knows the families, the children?'

'Check it out,' Sanders said. 'Anyone else?'

'They're already broken,' Rachael murmured, almost to herself.

'What was that, Detective Langley?

'Sorry.' She cleared her throat and raised her voice. 'These girls were already used to the abuse. They most likely didn't know anything else. The Spider needs victims who will play the part, act out his fantasies. That's got to be easier with these sorts of victims.'

'You may have a point. But how is he finding them?'

She had a theory on that too. 'What if the abusers of these children were part of an established paedophile ring? I'd like to search for any ties the victims' families may have, then look into local families in the DOCS system for our next potential victim based on that information. It might put us a step ahead.'

Turner sniggered. 'See you sometime next decade.'

She knew it would be a mammoth task, but she didn't mind hard work.

'Got a better idea, Turner?' Sanders asked, sending the other young detective back in his seat.

'No, sir.'

'Do it,' Sanders told Rachael. 'Any progress on where the costumes came from?'

'The materials are all reasonably common, but the only place we've been able to find the beads used on the wings is from an online store in Sydney. We have them checking their records.'

'Excellent.' He turned to another team member. 'How are we going on locating the source of the flowers?'

'We think he's sourcing them from multiple florists. No one we can find has sold those flowers in the amounts necessary.'

'So we've gotten nowhere? Contact Davies again. How can we not be getting a trace of evidence off any of these bodies?'

The thought of Jonathan Davies returned Rachael to the present. She took out her phone, which reminded her she hadn't messaged Finn, so she did that before calling Davies on his mobile. It went straight to voicemail so she left a message and asked him to call her as soon as he received it, then went back to unpacking. She was sad to hear of his marriage breakup. She wasn't particularly close to the couple but they were friendly enough and had seemed, despite their age difference, to have suited each other, always laughing and smiling at the few functions she'd seen them together.

Her eyes fell on a blue sheet of paper and, with a long breath, she lifted her original copy of the poem from the box. *Will you walk into my parlour? said the spider to the fly.* An icy chill raced through her veins. Because she didn't want to walk into that world.

Not again.

CHAPTER EIGHT

A bit more research later and I have a list of supplies I'm going to need to pull this whole covering-up-evidence thing off. I think about driving to Woolies but decide against it. It's already warming up and I don't want the car anywhere near curious noses, so the cleaning supplies will have to wait. That extra research also gave me a good idea of why the body already stinks so much and I realise my mistake in wrapping it in a rug rather than something plastic and waterproof. I doubt the putrid odour will ever completely go away.

The servo down the road should stock what I need for phase one, so I head out on foot. I notice Dawny's face plastered to her window as I walk past; I grit my teeth and attempt a smile. No, she couldn't have seen anything. She was probably hoping I was on my way over there to solve her lighting issue. This is why I generally avoid being nice to people. They develop annoying as hell expectations.

The servo isn't particularly busy, but I'm uncomfortable about what I'm buying. Guilt? No. I'm just cleaning up. Prominent pathologist or not, Jonathan Davies got what was coming to him. Disgust burns in my chest and I snarl, realising too late I'm facing some poor innocent teen with a Gatorade in hand trying to get by me. He stutters out an apology. Oops.

I feel conspicuous. An itch at the back of my neck makes me think everyone knows what I'm up to. That scene in *Fifty Shades of Grey* comes to mind: the one where the fucked-in-the-head rapist-slash-romantic hero purchases masking tape, cable ties and a length of rope and convinces the twit serving him that it's a turn-on. I peek around the shelves to check out the *Bride of Chucky* lookalike manning the register and decide I'm not pulling off a light flirtation. Besides, all I really need is a container of diesel, a new ciga-rette lighter—just in case—and some rubber gloves. I'd kill for a mask, but I don't see any.

A few minutes later everything's gone down without a hitch, except I didn't really think through getting the diesel home. It's heavy. Really heavy. I switch hands several times as I walk the cracked concrete pavement, and the heat of the morning has perspiration running down my back. About halfway home I kind of grunt a bit as I adjust my grip for the tenth time and the diesel almost slips from my sweaty fingers. A woman hosing her nature strip gives me an odd smile and looks questioningly at the fuel container.

'Morning,' I mutter self-consciously. *Just preparing to burn a body.* I turn up the driveway into my row of townhouses, struggle on. I'm so keen to get home I'm almost in front of my neighbours' place before I see her.

Fuck. Miriam Parkhurst, back from tennis in her little white skirt and top and Nike sun visor. She was probably attractive enough in her day, but her pathetic attempt at wearing clothes designed for twentysomethings just shows off her sagging everything. She stops unpacking her car to look at me with much the same expression I'm pretty sure I'm wearing. Complete loathing.

'What are you up to now?' she asks suspiciously.

'Car ran out of petrol,' I puff, staggering on.

'That's a lot of petrol.'

Nosey old bitch. 'Yeah, the rest is for my new motorbike.'

Her mouth turns even more sour. 'Motorbike?' The word is delivered with pure horror.

I want to laugh. Too perfect. But I keep my expression neutral, keep walking. 'The muffler's screwed so it roars like a bitch, but I got it cheap. Gonna practise riding it up and down the driveway till I get the hang of it.' Because she doesn't look quite horrified enough, I add, 'At night. When it cools down. So quite late.'

'You're going to ride a motorbike up and down this drive-way late at night?' she calls at my back as I keep moving.

'Or early in the mornings. Maybe both. Bye, Miriam.'

It's only a few more steps to my front door but when I risk a glance back, Miriam has already run back inside to no doubt complain to her equally annoying husband. I drop the container and every muscle in my body groans with relief. My brief chat with Miriam was a pleasant distraction but I'm back on task. I have to get this done. I toss the little plastic bag with the lighter and gloves on the front seat then wrestle the diesel into the back. I really wish I had that mask. I try not to breathe as I get in the driver's side and start the car.

I'm pretty sure my best bet is going to be Ourimbah State Forest. It's close by and there's a track that, according to Google, looks okay for my car: one long trail with lots of smaller ones running off it. I'll drive out into the middle of it, pick one of those smaller trails at random and it'll be done.

I set off on the Old Pacific Highway, make the correct turn into Palmdale Road. There's barely any traffic and the trip doesn't take long. I'm a little nervous when Palmdale Road becomes narrow, dirt and mostly one lane. I hear the diesel sloshing around in its container. I was kind of hoping this was as bad as it was going to get and I'm not even on the track yet. If I get my car stuck out here, I'm screwed. The land around the road opens up momentarily and I see a cluster of cars parked tightly together. Strange. Bushwalkers? That could be a problem. I know I'm close to the track. But then the forest engulfs me again and I have to watch the road.

As I make it around the corner I have to slam on my brakes. A group of mountain bike riders are blocking the entrance to the track. The guy in front is having a cigarette. A couple more are eating fancy-looking energy bars while three more fuss over a bike. The smoker watches me with interest for a few seconds, looks the car over, then wanders towards me.

'You looking for someone, babe?' he asks.

Babe? It could be my bad mood, my headache, or perhaps my innate distrust of men who spend more time talking to my boobs than my face, but I'm not impressed. 'That's not really any of your business, is it? Do you think you could move? Please?'

His eyebrows go up. 'Not for a few minutes. Gotta change a tyre, fix a few things up.'

'A few minutes? This is why people don't like you,' I say. A few minutes may as well be hours. I can't breathe in this car. I am far from feeling better.

'People don't like me?' He turns back to ask the question.

Oh, what the hell: I have *a few minutes* to kill. 'Cyclists! It's bad enough when you twats ride two or three abreast on the road and refuse to move your arses over. Six of you completely blocking the track holding a personal I-love-lycra party? You've got to be shitting me.'

Most of my frustration comes from the knowledge I'm screwed. They've had a really good look at me and my car and they're on their way up there too. This is a waste of time.

While they all exchange glances that make me want to feed them their own tightly packed testicles, I manoeuvre the car back out onto the road.

'Nice meeting you,' the smoker says.

'Yeah, yeah. Go hold your next party in traffic, *babe*.'

I send him my worst smile then drive away, a bit surprised I bothered snapping at them. I don't usually go out of my way to antagonise people, unless it's the Parkhursts, so I blame my rapidly deteriorating temper on the universe for not making this easier on me.

Now what? I pull over as soon as I see space and snatch my phone from the passenger seat. I didn't search up another option. This one looked as good as it got. I study the map. There does seem to be another way up there. Old Maitland Road. It's not far.

Back out onto the main road and off I go again. I reach the next entry point only to find a locked gate. Damn. Another possible entrance is filled with roadworks and states local traffic only. I stare at the sky and silently scream to whoever might be listening that they've got to be shitting me. Okay, I see another one. I drive a little further, only to find another locked gate.

Every nasty word I can come up with flows from my mouth. Gates? I didn't think of this. I'm not the bushwalking type so how would I know? All I can do is limp back to base and think of something else. Besides, I'm beyond queasy. I *need* to get out. At least the weather's turned cooler. From the looks of the cloud rolling in, it might even rain. Great for the dead smell, not so good for the supposed upcoming bonfire.

As I pull into my driveway and get out, I stare at the scrub behind my place. For the hundredth time I think of how perfect the thick wall of jungle would be for hiding a body. The problem is, I couldn't penetrate it far enough to get him in. And well, nosey neighbours.

'Lexi, dear!'

Speaking of … 'Yes, Dawny?' I ask tiredly.

'I found some globes in the cupboard, in case the ones in the kitchen have blown. Could be that simple.'

I'm gonna have to look at this thing, or she's never gonna leave me alone. A slightly less pissed-off part of me acknowledges it'll be dark soon and she probably needs the light to see. And no one else gives a shit. 'On my way, Dawny.'

I lock my car, check nothing's oozing out of it and decide most of what I can still smell is what's been burned into my nostrils over the past waste of an hour and a half. I'll deal with Dawny, get her off my back, then look elsewhere. Maybe Strickland State Forest.

Almost an hour later, Dawny exclaims, 'I can't tell you how wonderful it is to be able to see in my kitchen again. You're a gem, Lexi, and so clever!'

'Don't mention it, Dawny, it was nothing.' It wasn't nothing. It was hope-the-hell-for-the-best fiddling with loose wires. It's not like I'm an electrician. The fact I didn't electrocute myself surprises me.

I take another scoop of lemon meringue pie. Upside to probable near-death experience: Dawny's cooking. 'This is so good.'

'You should take the rest home. It might put some meat on your bones. In my day, women *ate*. None of us were obese, either. Most of the diets these days seem like rubbish to me. All the young ones paying for those fancy shakes or believing bacon and eggs will make you skinny! Some caveman diet or something.'

'It's called Paleo, I think,' I manage to fit in as she takes a breath.

'Is it? Well, they're all higgledy-piggledy to me. Make no sense at all, really. I reckon people come up with these things to keep you fat on purpose. There's no profit in making people better, is there?'

I open my mouth to respond but I'm too slow.

'Just like those drug companies, I say. Customers not cures. I must admit though, I did have a go at the wine and eggs diet one of the fancy magazines published back in the seventies. For a laugh. I've never had a problem with my weight. Ended up off my scone, so it wasn't all bad, but I wasn't any lighter at the end of it.'

I've kind of zoned out by this point. I'm enjoying my pie knowing I don't really need to add anything to the conversation. It's kind of pleasant.

Then Dawny swallows down another mouthful of pie and taps a serviette to her lips. 'Now,' she says and leans in conspiratorially, eyes gleaming with fun. 'Why don't you tell me what's in your boot?'

I stare for a moment, both surprised and unsure what to say. I think briefly about professing innocence, but she's smelled it, worked out I've put something in there, so I'm pretty sure that's a waste of time. My mind scrambles for an explanation. 'Okay, look, um … you got me. I hit a dog. Someone's dog. It died and I didn't want the argument, so I thought I'd get rid of it.'

Dawny's brow goes up and she smiles knowingly. 'And a garbage bag and a Cleanaway bin wouldn't do? I did notice you lugging home that fuel can.'

I cringe, but left with no choice, I barrel on with my story. 'This was a big, nasty dog, Dawny. I was going to take him up to the state forest but there were locked gates and road-works and cyclists …'

'So he's still in your car? Well, that's probably a good thing.' She nods to herself while I consider if I really want to ask her why. 'Not so good for the car, of course, but burning bodies beyond recognition isn't as easy as you might think.'

'Huh?' I'm confused. Does she really believe it's a dog or does she know it's a person? It certainly sounds like she knows it's a person. On closer inspection, she's wearing per-haps the shrewdest look I've ever seen on her face. But if she knows it's a person, why isn't she freaking out? I wait, doing a bit of my own freaking out, while Dawny slowly savours another mouthful of pie.

'I'll admit,' she says after swallowing, 'I did wonder about whether or not I should ask. But then I said to myself, well,

Lexi is a good girl, there must be a good reason for all this. She's always doing me favours. Maybe I can do her one.' Dawny washes down the last of her pie with remnants of her tea. 'I did some time, you know.'

This was it. She was about to tell me she was some sort of granny serial killer. 'Oh?'

'Mmm. I was sure the Parkhursts would have warned you about me. Before they got it in their head to start warning people about you, anyway.' She gets up and limps towards the hallway. 'You know they've got you pegged as a drug dealer? That's what they told Frank next door, anyhow.'

'Oh well, I find it difficult to care.' Why isn't she calling the police? Maybe that's what she's gone to do. I jump up to follow her. 'Where are you going?'

'To turn on my little chest freezer. I suppose rigor's set in?'

'Rigor?' What the? I picture the rusty old shell of a freezer that has sat on her back patio forever and feel as though I've entered the twilight zone. I need a drink. A joint. Something. Apparently, it was the sweet old ladies you had to worry about. 'Dawny, it's probably better you don't get involved.'

'Too late,' she calls over her shoulder. 'This is the most excitement I've had in years. Boil the kettle again, would you? It's not quite dark outside. Better have another slice of pie and wait it out. We don't need the damn Parkhursts poking their noses in.' She stops suddenly, turns. 'It's not Old Don Parkhurst is it?'

'No, Dawny. It's not Don.'

She looks disappointed. 'Ah well, never mind.'

CHAPTER NINE

Monday, March 8

Rachael waited patiently for the room to settle. The previously bare space was now filled with overflowing boards and tables loaded with computers and equipment. There was a constant drone of voices as the team of detectives and analysts set themselves up and prepared for the days and weeks ahead, punctuated by the occasional scrape and drag of furniture and snapping of cases.

Deciding she needed to be seen, Rachael stepped to the front of the room and looked pointedly around. As one by one everyone noticed her waiting, the noise died down. Finn walked in as silence finally descended and smiled briefly before finding a seat.

'I'd like to thank you all for arriving so promptly,' she began. 'I realise most of you are used to packing up at the drop of a hat to assist in out-of-area cases but I also understand it's not easy, especially for those of you with families. You should know up front that I believe this will be a long investigation that is unlikely to end in only one homicide. Being that we are less than a couple of hours from home, many of you might wish to commute rather than stay in the accommodation we've made available and, of course, that's an option available to you.'

As she ran through all the preliminaries, Rachael looked around the room with satisfaction. She'd picked this team incredibly wisely, and there was a good mix of older detectives who'd worked on the Spider case and fresh, younger faces chosen for their experience on other cases. Her analysts were, in her opinion, the best in the business and had spread themselves and their resources out along the back of the room, ready to begin. 'So I'll turn you over to Detective Sergeant Finn Carson for a quick briefing on the homicide and then I'll take up a few more moments of your time before we get stuck into it. Finn?'

'Thank you, inspector.' Finn walked to the front of the room and stood beside Summer Edgely's smiling face. 'The body of twelve-year-old Summer Edgely was discovered in Erina Creek at approximately 6am yesterday by a father and son on a routine fishing trip.' He pointed to an area on a map. 'She was lying face up in the mangroves at the base of the Punt Bridge, wearing a Little Mermaid costume. The pathologist on scene was Professor Steven Van Zettan, who concluded Summer had been dead six to eight hours, and placed in the water shortly after death. Summer had multiple bruises and abrasions and the suspected cause of death is strangulation, but we'll know more after the autopsy which is set for 10am.

'We found some reasonably fresh tyre marks in the mud that suggest the killer has left the road at the bus stop here,' he said, using the wrong end of a pen to trace the route, 'driven through this clearing and parked about twelve feet from the shoreline before carrying the victim down to the water. Evidence has been taken of these tyre tracks as well as a set of heavy footprints leading to her location. There was also what appeared to be fresh garbage at the scene, which may or may not be relevant. The black garbage bags held food scraps, used syringes, alcohol containers and cigarette butts. A local by the name of Noel McMahon who lives on the opposite side of the creek keeps surveillance on the area and we have video footage showing a dark-coloured van arriving, then leaving the scene a few minutes later. Unfortunately, the footage is very dark and grainy so nothing much to go on, but we're looking into whether the content can be improved.

'It's worth noting that Summer's family was known to Community Services and claims of inappropriate behaviour towards Summer by her stepfather were under investigation at the time of her death. Mr Brewer and Summer's mother, Anita Lightfoot, are both denying any involvement in her murder. Hopefully I'll have more for you shortly. Rachael?'

Rachael smiled at Finn and, instead of moving back to the front of the room, directed everyone's attention to the side wall. 'I've seen many of you glancing over here since coming in this morning. You're no doubt wondering why I have evidence from an old, closed case taking up so much room on the boards. The case, as those of you who worked on it will recognise, is that of Thomas Biddle, aka the Spider.'

'Good work on the telly, inspector!' Detective Sergeant Alec Claxton, one of her more experienced detectives, called out with a wink. There were a few other flattering comments and a spattering of claps before she managed to silence them with a lift of her hand.

'Thank you, but you may have to reserve judgement on my work on that case.' She tried to keep her expression cool, calm. 'Because at approximately nine thirty on Saturday evening, after that show had aired, I received phone call from a POI claiming to be the Spider. That man knew ahead of time about our victim, Summer Edgely, and mentioned to me during the phone call that he had a date with Ariel.'

'No way!' Claxton declared, his face darkening. 'We have the Spider.'

'We worked for years to put that guy away,' Detective Constable Annalise Rayburn, a year off retirement, added. 'So who is this guy?'

'I wish I knew. For what it's worth, I believe we put the correct guy away. There's already one small inconsistency between cases. Summer was twelve, while the victims in the Spider case were in the six to eight years age bracket.'

'A copycat?' Rayburn suggested.

'That's my belief at this stage. I want you to take this information into consideration when working on this case, but don't let it blind you to other possibilities. By their very nature a copycat will do their best to imitate the original serial killer but can deviate accidentally or otherwise in methodology due to a lack of information, ability or resources. We don't want to miss anything by being too glued to this.

'For those who remember the case, use this to refresh your memories; the rest of you, take a good look. If the case stays true to form, a video will turn up somewhere on the dark web. The videos from the original case will be accessible to you for comparison but for those who haven't seen them, I warn you, they're extremely upsetting. The camera follows the progress of the girls in several scenes. Biddle roleplays with them from behind the camera and his voice is altered. Even when the villain "wins" we never see enough to positively identify him, which is one of the reasons he proved so difficult to catch. Questions?'

'Did we get a match on the phone number?'

'It was a burner phone. Nothing we can use.'

'That's the drawing they showed on the crime show, isn't it?' one of her analysts asked, pointing to the picture in the frame Ed had managed to tack back together.

'That's the first image I ever saw of the Spider.'

'This guy who's claiming to be the Spider … what's he been doing all these years and why start again now?' Rayburn asked.

'Our POI claims to have been inspired after watching the documentary.'

'So we've got you to thank,' Turner said from the doorway.

'You're all class, Turner,' Finn said.

'I thought you might like to know the media is out front,' Turner said. 'And Brewer's coughing up alibis all over the place for the last few days. He worked Monday through Saturday— already verified—and spent the majority of every night at the pub. Plenty of people vouch for him being there. Nothing incriminating on his phone or laptop. Oh, and the doorknock and search we carried out didn't turn anything up.'

'Thanks, Turner,' Rachael said before again addressing the group. 'A note about the media: I'll deal with them at all times. No one else is to give them anything, okay?'

There was a round of agreement.

'Okay. We've got a long list of interviews to get through. Let's get to work.'

As her team scattered, she noticed Debbie staring quietly at the board dedicated to the Spider case. 'Constable?'

Debbie looked startled, then embarrassed, smiled slightly. 'Sorry.'

'Are you all right?'

Debbie's gaze dropped. 'No, not exactly,' she admitted. 'I'm sorry. I can't quite believe some of this stuff.'

'I wouldn't want you on my team if you weren't at least a little affected by it,' Rachael said.

'Really? I thought in this job you were supposed to be able to shelve the emotion and concentrate on the facts.'

'It's a balancing act. You've got to care enough to let it push you to go places you'd rather not go in order to solve the crime, but you've also got to be able to sleep at night.'

'How does that work?'

'When I figure it out, I'll let you know. Debbie, if it gets too much—'

The constable's head shot up with a jerk. A battle light came into her eyes. 'No, I need to see this through. I feel like I have this rock lodged in my chest and it's not going to go away until it's all over.'

Rachael knew that feeling; knew it could be both energising and draining. It would keep her going or burn her out.

'Whenever you start to feel overwhelmed, talk to me,' she said. 'I won't think you're weak, I won't take you off the team,' she said with a smile that warmed kindly when Debbie looked embarrassed.

'Debbie, someone called Megan has a delivery for you downstairs,' Finn said, joining them.

'Right. Thanks.' Then she said, with a grateful smile at Rachael, 'Excuse me, inspector.'

'So, you are attending the autopsy this morning?' Finn asked.

Rachael checked the time. 'Yes, of course. I'm just going to find something to snack on. I forgot to order breakfast for the room last night.'

'I have a spare room,' Finn reminded her. 'I'm sure Ava wouldn't mind sharing it with you over the weekend if we're all here that long.'

'You barely get enough time with your daughter as it is. I'm not intruding on that any more than I already have.'

'Rubbish. She'd love to spend time with you. You're the cool aunt.'

'*Great* aunt, more precisely.' She shuddered. 'That sounds so old!'

'You'll never be old. Why don't you go get a proper breakfast? I can handle the autopsy.'

'No, but thanks. I always go. And I need to know if there are any more similarities between Summer Edgely and Biddle's victims.'

'Anything in particular?'

'One thing,' she admitted. 'Just one detail that wasn't shared with the public. I'm hanging on it not being found.'

'What was it?'

'Here we go.' Debbie appeared back with a coffee in a large, brightly patterned reusable travel cup. She'd written *Inspector* on it in permanent ink. 'Flat white on skim, correct?'

'You're off to a good start,' Rachael said gratefully. 'I was ready to kill for one of these. You didn't mention you were psychic.'

'Call it woman's intuition. The cup's a gift. Save the planet and all that.' She handed Finn another cup, this one devoid of pink and gold flowery embellishments. 'And a tall black for you. I hope neither of you are on any kind of strict diet because the pastries are to die for. I got you a selection.' Debbie brandished a large paper bag before setting it down on the desk.

'Nope.' Finn dived straight in and pulled out a mini chocolate croissant. 'How did you manage this?' He groaned as the pastry melted in his mouth. 'Can we take her back with us when we're done here?' he asked Rachael.

'Don't tease,' Debbie said, before taking a sip of her own coffee and pulling a happy face. 'Or I'll be counting on it.'

Rachael selected an apricot danish. 'Are you aiming to be a detective?'

'That's why I joined the force. What would you like me to do today? Should I run around now and take orders from everyone else for coffees first? I have a menu. The café will deliver whatever we want as many times a day as we want, as long as the bill is at least fifty bucks.'

'That'd be nice of you. Sure, introduce yourself to everyone, make the offer.'

'Will do.'

'I'd also like you to contact Community Services for me. Organise for everything they have on Summer Edgely to be sent over. If they baulk at it, let me know.'

Debbie's face split into a grin. 'Right away.'

'Real police work,' Finn said. 'You've got a fan.'

'She wants to make detective and she doesn't mind running coffee duty to get her feet wet. I like that, so we'll see what she's got ... other than eyes for you.'

'What?' he scoffed. 'Get out.' Then more seriously he said, 'Do you really think Community Services is going to be able to add much to what we know?

'They do their best.' She sipped her coffee as Marjorie Holmes sprang to mind. She'd be retired by now, had been somewhere in her early to mid-fifties when Rachael had first met her.

The desk of the Community Services office was old and scratched, the computer about as ready to retire as the woman controlling it. There was a mix of young and old workers in the cubicles surrounding them, all sporting looks somewhere between frazzled and bored. Rachael had been told to see Marjorie. She had the seniority, the experience. But explaining her mission to Marjorie had been met with frustration and a strong sense she wasn't going to get very far.

'You want all of them?' Marjorie checked with one cocked eyebrow visible over the rim of her desktop computer.

'Yes, please.'

'You don't want to narrow it down at all?'

'I thought I had.'

'I'll email them across,' Marjorie said with a heavy sigh. 'Might take a while, though.'

'Thanks. Would you happen to know if any stand out?'

'Stand out? Stand out how?'

'The potential victims we're looking for have most likely had videos of them shared. They may have suffered abuse at the hands of more than one perpetrator.'

'I couldn't tell you. I know that sounds awful, but you'll see why when I send all these files across. There's a lot still waiting to be investigated.'

'This can't be an easy job.'

'Too many kids, not enough of us,' Marjorie said. Her eyes shone with genuine sadness. 'Not enough funding and when we need them, not enough foster carers. A lot of times we have to prioritise the youngest kids. By the time they're older, they'll be lucky to see us. The unfortunate truth is the less serious claims sometimes take too long to be seen to. We work hard, we care, but the task is monumental.'

Rachael thought about Kayla's student. 'So what would happen if a teacher reported a suspected case?'

'We'd look into it, of course. Is there any proof?'

'I don't think so. Some bruising perhaps and she's quite small for her age. Withdrawn.'

'Has the child said anything?'

'No. She's scared of getting into trouble.'

'There's your biggest barrier right there. It would help us, and consequently that child, if you could get her to tell you what's going on. If she does, that expedites the process. We could move much more quickly.'

'Okay, I'll keep that in mind. Thank you.'

Rachael saw herself out. Overloaded caseworkers, too many kids in the system. No wonder Kayla had called her. She probably already knew this. She got into the car, pausing on the driveway to the main road. Her finger hesitated on the indicator.

She should turn right, back to the station. She didn't have time to go chasing up random cases, she reminded herself, then made a left turn. She'd take one look. Spend ten minutes at the school, see the student, see what she thought.

Hopefully Kayla was wrong and the child was fine. Rachael wasn't sure how she'd know that just by looking, but if nothing else, it might stop a war with her sister.

She made it to the local primary school at lunch time. Kids ran around outside with sandwiches or ice blocks from the canteen, an assortment of balls and skipping ropes, and in the quad a pair of cute twins played hopscotch on one of the painted decals. It looked like a good space, a happy place with happy kids. Good start.

She found Kayla in a brightly decorated classroom, tidying up from some sort of craft explosion. 'Hey.'

Kayla looked up, the surprise in her eyes followed by a warm smile. 'Rach! What are you doing here?'

'I came to talk to you about this kid you're worried about,' she said, following her sister's lead and picking up offcuts of coloured paper from the floor.

Kayla stopped, straightened, stared as though she'd grown another head. 'Really?'

'Yeah, why?'

'Because I thought once you hung up, you'd completely forget and we'd have an argument in about six months' time as to whether I actually ever mentioned her to you or not.'

Because it was so close to the truth, Rachael screwed her papers into a tight ball and bounced them off her sister's forehead. 'And yet here I am.'

'Yes, you are.' Kayla's smile dimmed. 'I'm glad, but I don't know if she'll talk to you.'

'Rach.'

'Sorry, what?'

'I was talking to you.'

'Million miles away, sorry. What did you say?'

'I said thanks to this traffic we're late.'

She looked around, noticed he was pulling into the car-park at the back of the Forensic Medicine and Coroners Court Complex. 'Steven will catch us up.'

Van Zettan was already looking over X-rays and narrating his findings when they reached the examination room. Summer Edgely's body was laid out on the table in the cold, clinical room and as yet appeared untouched. 'Sorry to interrupt,' Rachael said.

Van Zettan held up a hand, kept talking. 'There is a clear fracture to the hyoid bone. No further fractures apparent in X-rays.'

He turned and smiled. 'Rachael! And Detective … Carson, wasn't it?'

'That's right. Nice to see you again.'

'Likewise. I'm just getting started.'

'A fractured hyoid is suggestive of strangulation as probable cause of death, right?' Rachael said.

'Along with the petechial haemorrhaging and the bruising to the throat, I'd say yes. But she could have more to tell us when we open her up.'

Rachael stepped closer to Summer's body. Immense sadness filled her for the child who'd only just begun her life before having it taken so violently from her. Thin purple lines darkened her wrists. 'Her hands were holding a bucket of toys. Were they held together with clear fishing line?'

'Yes. That's right. How did you know?'

'It's consistent with an old case I worked on.'

'Ah, of course. Thomas Biddle.'

'You're familiar with the details?'

'Isn't everyone? I caught the documentary. It was well done.'

'I was hoping you might familiarise yourself with the details of those post-mortems. I'm interested in any inconsistencies you might find between this victim and the previous ones.'

'I see. And yes, I'll pull the records, crossmatch everything. All toxicology results are taking several weeks to get back at present, but I'll do what I can to hurry them through. Right. Shall I continue?'

Rachael nodded, stood back with Finn and watched Van Zettan work. The careful, methodical process wasn't new to Rachael but she was waiting for one thing in particular. If it was absent, she was going to give one big sigh of relief, but if it was there, if that one detail that was never released to the press was present ... Her eyes still slid from the body to the collection of tools on the tray as Van Zettan checked for and found signs of sexual assault.

They swung back to the pathologist when he said, 'There's something here.'

'What is it?'

Van Zettan held a condom with a pair of forceps. It was stuffed with what looked like a roll of paper and tied twice at the end.

'Damn it!' Rachael breathed.

'This is the thing you were worried about,' Finn said. It wasn't really a question.

'The chance this is the work of a copycat just dropped significantly.'

Van Zettan put the evidence into a container and continued. Rachael knew she'd have to wait until it had been

swabbed before she'd have any chance of getting whatever
was in there out.

As Summer was systematically taken apart, Rachael had
to remind herself several times that what Van Zettan was
working on was just a body. An empty shell. That the little girl who'd resided in it was long gone. Her mind kept
returning to the piece of paper. She felt antsy and began to
fidget, shifting her weight from one foot to the other.

'Why don't you step out and get some fresh air?' Finn
suggested.

She shook her head. 'I'm fine.' But she wasn't fine. Not
even close. *Does this mean I put the wrong man away? Is
this my fault? Is what happened to Summer my fault?* Did it
even matter what that note said? The mere fact it was there
changed everything.

'Almost there,' Van Zettan commented. 'Then we'll open
it up.'

By the time the note was removed and unrolled, Rachael
was feeling light-headed enough that the words had her
head spinning.

Do you believe me now, Rachael?

She took in the words, took a couple of quick steps back,
bent and put her hands to her knees.

'Hey, sit down,' Finn instructed, guiding her to a stool.

'I'm okay.' But inside she was screaming. Why did this
bastard have to make this personal? Wasn't what he'd done
to this girl bad enough without making her feel responsible
for it?

Van Zettan's face was sombre. 'Let me see if we can get
anything off this paper. I'll get back to you as soon as possible with this and the preliminary tox results.'

'Thanks,' Finn said.

'Yeah, thanks, Steven,' Rachael said.

Finn put a hand on Rachael's elbow and she allowed him to guide her back outside.

It was … quite flattering.

I'm inspired, Rachael.

Do you believe me now, Rachael?

'Damn it!' The words burst from her.

'Okay, I know what's going through your head,' Finn said. 'And you know damn well you're being stupid. This doesn't prove anything. Whoever we're dealing with could have inside knowledge from Biddle himself or someone else.'

'He did this to prove himself to me.'

'No, he did it because he's a son of a bitch paedophile child murderer. None of this is your fault.'

'He certainly wants me to think it is.'

'Yep. He does. He's entertaining himself with this shit. He thinks he's clever. The smarter he thinks he is, the more likely he'll be to make a mistake. Come on, let's get back.'

They got in the car. 'His whole MO seems to be as much about getting your attention as anything else,' Finn said. 'Why?'

'How should I know?'

'Come on, Rach, you're not thinking. Profile this guy.'

She thought about it. 'Okay … At a guess … he's a narcissistic arsehole who thrives on the spotlight.'

'That's a start. How does that fit with the Spider?'

'Pretty perfectly. If he is the Spider, he's probably pissed that the credit for his work was taken by Biddle. Seeing that credit stolen on national television might have been too much.'

'Okay, yet Summer was twelve when his previous victims had all been much younger. Why?'

'Maybe this was a last-minute decision. He saw the documentary, had something to prove and not enough time to prepare. He had to take who he could get. Summer had run away. She would have been an easy target.'

'I guess that's possible. But that would mean he knocked up that costume pretty fast.'

'Okay, good point. Perhaps that doesn't work. Finn, there's a small chance he got this detail elsewhere. I still don't want to think we put the wrong man away, but I think now we have to take the theory more seriously. This guy has intimate knowledge of the case and he's making it personal. Apart from anything else, why would a copycat be targeting me? He's showing off, Finn. And I don't think he's going to stop.'

CHAPTER TEN

It's full sun outside when I open my eyes. The hangover is there, like a dull velvet hammer bothering my right temple. Yesterday was pretty full-on and I'm honestly glad it's over. My nose scrunches up as I catch a whiff of the chemical mix of cleaning agents I used on my car. I scrubbed myself until I was red raw in the shower last night but a lingering remnant of grossness that could be bleach and something else clings to me.

Without being vain, I like to think of myself as a bit of a tough arse. I don't baulk at much and since I began helping Bailee out I deal with what most people would consider vile, evil and disgusting on pretty much a daily basis. So it's a little humbling to realise a senior citizen with a dodgy knee and a talent for making pies can manipulate a big, stinking body into a chest freezer and feel nothing more than a genuine sense of achievement, while my stomach lurches in all directions, close to passing out. I grimace. I've been put in my place by an elderly Nigella Lawson and I'm having an identity crisis.

I get myself a coffee, turn on the telly in time, I hope, for the last of the morning news. As it flicks to life on the screen I reach for my phone and notice the arsehole I've been stringing along has replied. He's sent me a larger than life photo of his red-pubed genitals and wants to see my breasts. I tell him I'll show him in person if he meets me by the public toilet block at a nearby park tomorrow after school. Then I open my laptop and bundle up all the evidence I have on him so I can send it to Bailee. She'll sort it. My only regret is that I can't be there for the meet and greet. I can't imagine anything could be much more satisfying. I like seeing arseholes get what they deserve. On the rare occasions that actually happens.

From what I can see, the cops are mostly too hamstrung by rules and regulations and laws that favour predators over victims to do what needs to be done. Being governed by a system that lets monsters walk on technicalities and allows weak judges to pass down pathetic sentences makes for unreliable outcomes. All those back-breaking investigations and dangerous arrests they do every day. For what?

As though to back up my inner rant, Constable Luke McGraw's image stares hollow-eyed back at me from the next news story. I don't like cops, but I feel for this one. He's on suspension after using what advocates for a sadistic killer of two toddlers are calling unnecessary force. He put a boot in after the feral bastard threatened to come after his kids next. Oh no. How terrible. He'd kicked the legs out from under the monster, called him a nasty name. I'd be surprised if the bastard even bruised. Now the constable was awaiting his own version of a trial.

'What a joke.' I flick the television off again in disgust and hit send on the email to Bailee. I don't know how they do it. Put their lives on the line day in, day out. Be polite to animals. Be abused, attacked and, if they step out of line, have one human reaction or make the slightest mistake, just once, the people they put their life on the line for, those people they're protecting, will abuse and attack them too.

No wonder so many of them are arseholes.

A knock on my door has me closing everything down and checking my window. Bailee waves at me so I let her in.

'Where have you been?' she demands, coming in with daughter Lucy on her hip. Kai comes running in behind them flying a plastic plane and making swooshing noises.

'Around, why?'

'It's like you dropped off the planet for a few days. Here. I desperately need a coffee.' She pushes Lucy at me and it's either take her or she'll be on the floor, so I hold on tight.

'Letsi!' Lucy announces, pointing a tiny finger at my nose. She's got Bailee's colouring and is so damn cute with her fair curls, big green eyes and twin dimples.

'It's not Letsi, it's Lexi!' Kai corrects Lucy. 'Aunty Lexi, look at my plane!'

'It's very cool.'

'And I got a *PJ Masks* T-shirt, look!'

As I take care to give the T-shirt the appropriate amount of attention, Bailee helps herself to mugs and coffee, grabs the milk from the fridge. 'Kai had a dummy spit this morning over the shirt being in the wash. He wanted to show you. And when my darling son gets an idea in his head he doesn't let it go. We would have been here an hour earlier but it had to be washed.' She chews on her lip. 'I'm not sure it's completely dry.' She flicks on the kettle and sighs heavily, leans back against the counter. 'But I caved and let him wear it.'

I tickle Lucy and she lets out a delighted squeal. 'How else would a smartarse child psychologist in training handle it?' I taunt.

'Aunty Lexi said arse!' Kai sings out with a huge grin.

Bailee narrows her eyes at me but smiles. 'So what's your go?'

'My go?' I stop playing the tickling game to shoot a questioning look at my sister. 'I have no go. What's your go? It's Monday. Don't you work?'

'I'm working Saturdays so I have Mondays off. Which you knew about because I told you when we organised this. You forgot we were coming, didn't you?'

Ah shit. 'I've been busy,' I mumble in apology.

'Thought so. I saw you through the window as we arrived, talking to your computer.'

'I don't talk to my computer.'

Bailee pours the water into the mugs and takes them to my kitchen table. 'You do when you're onto something … or someone.'

'Well we're obviously not going to talk about that now, are we?' I remind her with a look at the kids.

'And I don't need children underfoot while I have my coffee.' Bailee takes Lucy from my arms. 'Who wants to watch *PJ Masks*?'

'Me!' Kai runs and skids onto the mat in front of my television, ready. Bailee lowers Lucy next to him. A moment later the show's theme song is blaring through the house and Bailee is sitting, breathing in her too-hot coffee with an expression more suited to a decent snort of cocaine.

'So who've you got in your sights?'

'I've just sent him to you. That perv I hooked through my fake Facebook account. Honestly, moron, how many kids even use Facebook anymore? He's meeting me at the park for a look at my breasts tomorrow arvo. I've got his name, ISP and residential address, details of our online conversations and one whopping big picture of his less than impressive—' I look up and clear my throat. I'm never sure when the kids are nearby. 'Microphallus.'

'Excellent. I'll get it sorted. Thanks.' Bailee risks a hot sip and grimaces. 'You know, you've got a real talent for this stuff. If you did this legitimately and worked with the police, imagine what you could do with the sorts of help and resources they have.'

I realise I'm looking at the roof when I notice a new cob-web attached to my ceiling light. Honestly, beating my head against a brick wall would be less painful than having this conversation again. Bailee is set on remodelling me into the semblance of something that fits within acceptable society, whatever that is, and was born with the same stubborn tenacity I was. 'I don't like cops or rules, I'm not a team player and even if I had some sort of cataclysmic breakdown and decided I was, they're more likely to throw me in jail than give me a job if I put myself in their way.'

Bailee sends me a look that has me shrinking in my seat. It must work wonders with the kids. 'I've already told you I can talk to—'

'I'll catch monsters my way, thanks.'

'Do you really catch *monsters*, Aunty Lexi?' Kai asks from the doorway, eyes wide.

Intent on making full use of the distraction, I pounce on it; I turn around and get up, creep towards him with a mock-menacing grin. 'Yep, especially little ones who like *PJ Masks* and sneak out into the kitchen.' He screams happily and runs, glancing back over his shoulder to make sure I'm still chasing. Lucy has no idea what's going on but joins in anyway, her high-pitched squeal deafening.

'Right, I think it's time to go,' Bailee calls out over the ensuing chaos.

It's not that I'm not relieved to get back to work but as it's the shortest visit in history I wonder if something else is going on. 'You're leaving already?'

'*We* are. I promised the kids we'd go to the beach. There won't be many more days left that are warm enough. You're coming.'

'You haven't had your coffee you so desperately needed.'

'It's crap coffee, Lex. We'll do a drive thru.'

Before I can utter a lame excuse, Kai is tugging on my arm and bouncing urgently. 'Come on, Aunty Lexi! Pleeeee-ase? You're way more fun than Mummy.'

'Beats, beats!' Lucy calls out, toddling in at a run.

'It's bea-*ch*,' Kai corrects her.

I really need to get back to my computer. But Kai, the four-year-old professional heartstring tugger, is doing his puppy-eyes thing and Lucy's lit up like a Christmas tree. It shits me to admit it, but I'm toast. 'Okay, okay. But only for an hour or so.' Besides, maybe a dip in the ocean will rid me of the last of the lingering death-smell that's clung to me all morning.

*

I suppose it's not so bad, sitting in the shallow water on a warm afternoon playing silly games with kids. As I have no intention of ever having any of my own children, I figure I may as well enjoy Bailee's every now and again. Lucy and I build a very wet sandcastle with a bucket. As it slumps and collapses, Kai runs in and jumps on it, yelling, 'Into the night, to save the day!' Lucy screams in protest. Starts to cry. Yeah, it's fun, I remind myself.

A couple of guys with paddle boards who've been sunbaking nearby wake up at the noise. One looks over and slides his sunglasses down over his eyes and I'm not sure the glare he's experiencing isn't coming off me. I don't get out in the sun all that much. I dare him to complain with a direct stare, but he smiles and settles back down. Not all men are arseholes.

Bailee tosses the two brightly coloured beachballs she's been hugging across the shallow water and both kids scamper after them. 'You're still brooding over something,' she says. 'Is it about that Doc guy? Did you get any further with him?'

'No,' I lie, because what else can I say? The story of how his body came to be in my neighbour's chest freezer might not go down so well. 'Just stuck on the guy I sent you today.'

Kai tosses his ball at me and I catch it. I toss the beachball further than Bailee, up the beach rather than in the water. I'd feel pretty bad if one of Bailee's kids drowned while we're discussing saving other people's.

'I was thinking it might be worth handing over what you found out about Doc after all. Maybe someone might have a chance to look into it.'

'I really don't think I have anything useful.'

Bailee's shoulders slumped. 'What kind of party could an old guy take a young girl to without looking suspicious?'

'I couldn't say.' At the sound of my phone I stretch back to reach for it. 'Yeah?'

'Lexi, dear, it's Dawny.'

'Dawny, ah … hold on.' I stand up and walk away to put some distance between me and Bailee, just in case. 'Is everything okay?'

'Not exactly, dear. I'm here with the police.'

My stomach plunges but before I can react further she continues. 'Bit of an incident. Actually it was quite exciting. Oh—don't panic. It's nothing life or *death*.' The emphasis on death has me catching my breath. That had to be code for nothing to do with Doc, didn't it? So what the hell was going on?

'Then what is it?'

'I'm afraid your car's been stolen. A few of those tragic-looking emo types drove it away right under my nose about ten minutes ago! Can you believe it?'

A million questions race through my head but the one regarding the plausibility of kids randomly hijacking my car on a Monday in broad daylight in the driveway of the town-house furthest from the road in the complex was a straight up no-brainer. 'No, Dawny. I really can't.'

CHAPTER ELEVEN

Tuesday, March 9

Rachael stood in front of the room full of reporters and searched out familiar and unfamiliar faces. As usual there was the mix of the steady and stone-faced, along with the impatient and highly strung. Both could be deadly. A couple of them looked like they'd skipped school to be there. But then, the older she got, the younger everyone else seemed to be.

She was introduced, so she stepped forward. Collected her thoughts. 'Good morning. At 6:15am on Sunday the seventh of March, the body of twelve-year-old Summer Edgely was discovered by fishermen in mangroves on the bank of Erina Creek in the vicinity of the Punt Bridge. Summer had been dead between six and eight hours and was clothed in a mermaid costume. We believe the body did not drift to this location, but that it was purposefully placed there. There is vehicle access to that area and tyre prints and footprints suggest the body was driven close by then carried to the location. A crime scene was immediately declared in the vicinity and an extensive forensic examination of the scene was undertaken. A post-mortem carried out yesterday has ruled strangulation as cause of death. We have conducted enquiries with residents and would like to speak to anyone who was in the area around the Punt Bridge at East Gosford on Saturday evening or early Sunday morning, and anyone who may have seen any people or vehicles that appeared suspicious or out of place in that vicinity should also contact us. A major incident room has been established here at Gosford Police Station, where a strike force will investigate Summer's death in cooperation with local detectives.'

'Inspector, can the fishermen be ruled out as suspects?' one reporter immediately fired off.

'Yes. The fishermen who discovered the body have been interviewed and excluded from our investigation.'

'Inspector, do you find it strange that the morning after the documentary on the Spider airs on television, a child is murdered and posed in a fairytale costume?'

'This certainly appears to be a copycat murder.'

'Inspector, is it true that right after the documentary aired, a man claiming to be the Spider called you personally to tell you you'd made a mistake and to expect a murder?'

Rachael's blood turned to ice. Where had that come from? One of the younger reporters. An unfamiliar face. Tall, beanpole thin, neat brown hair, black-rimmed glasses. A checked, collared shirt. Young and inexperienced, if she was reading him right. But he was waiting for an answer, his face almost apologetic but keen. She knew any hesitation would prove too long, that the slightest sign of fear on her features would give away the truth to the more experienced reporters. She rallied herself. 'We were aware the program would bring a number of crank callers out and we're dealing with those calls as we receive them.'

Everyone threw questions at her at once and Rachael spoke over them. 'I have no more details for you at this time. Thank you.'

But the room had gone into a frenzy. She squeezed through the reporters, dodging microphones and more questions as she made for the door of the room that had been temporarily set aside for the media.

'Inspector.' Debbie followed her through the door and out into the hall.

'Who was that?' Rachael asked. 'I need to know who that reporter was.'

'I'll find out,' Debbie said.

She snagged Debbie's arm. 'Quietly, okay? I don't want the rest of the media out there to think he's got us in a panic.'

She got in the lift, and Finn slid through the doors before they could shut. His face reflected fury. 'Where the hell did he get that information from?'

'I don't know. I expected some questions about the Spider murders due to the obvious case similarities, but no one knew about that phone call except us, Ed and the strike force.'

'We've got a leak.'

'I need to speak to the team. Debbie's going to find out who the reporter is. I'll speak to him privately.'

'This is not going to go away. The media are going to be all over this. It's going to cause the public to panic.'

'I know.' The lift doors opened and she charged towards the strike force room. As she appeared, everyone paused with an air of expectation and waited silently for her to speak.

'Well?' she asked. 'Anyone?'

The room remained silent. Some officers shifted uncomfortably in their seats, others glanced around. No one spoke, so she pinned them with a serious glare before speaking.

'Here's the thing. It's not that difficult to make a mistake. Sometimes we take the job home with us. We're tempted to talk to partners, family, close friends. We don't mean to let things slip. They just kind of come out. Especially in high-stress situations, if we've had a bit too much to drink or we have a particularly nosey significant other. And sometimes those people tell other people and so on and so forth and before you know it, the media are onto it. Happens to the best of us. So if this sounds like you, you need to gather up your courage and let me know. Let me know you've made a mistake. And you need to let me know by the end of day. You're my team and I value every single one of you. This is your chance. You will still have a career, we will work it out.

'If you don't come forward and I have to find you, things will look very different. I need to be able to trust my team. We need to be able to trust each other. This is not news to any of you. This is the sort of lecture I give graduates just coming out of the academy. If I discover a team member has deliberately leaked information to the press I will boot you out on your arse and make sure everyone sees you heading for the shit pile as you sail through the door of unemployment. Clear?

'I'm going downstairs now to talk to the reporter who picked up that piece of juicy information. I will get an answer. If I have to, I will trace his phone records, his emails, his movements for the past three days and find the answer for myself. You know I can and I will. That's all.'

As she turned around, the room erupted with chatter.

Debbie was waiting in the doorway. 'I know I'm the newest, least-known member of the team but I swear I would never do that.'

'Then there's nothing for you to worry about,' Rachael assured her. Besides, she was pretty damn sure Debbie wouldn't do something as stupid as threaten her new position on this strike force. The opportunity meant too much to her and she was taking it seriously. 'Did you get the name of the reporter?'

'Yeah, he's a freelance. Name's Rick Burrow. He's waiting in your office.'

'Thanks, Deb.' She looked at Finn. 'I don't suppose you told anyone?'

Finn pulled a face she'd been seeing since he was a kid. It clearly read, *seriously?*

'Want to talk to this reporter with me?'

'You bet.'

In the interview room, Rick Burrow was pacing nervously. He sat when they entered then, as though not sure on protocol, stood, hunched over, waiting for Rachael to take a seat first.

'Mr Burrow. As you know, I'm Inspector Rachael Langley. This is Detective Finn Carson. Please, sit down.'

'Thanks. Um … Am I in trouble?'

Rachael took her seat. 'No. No, of course not.' Then she waited while Finn ducked out then came back with a third chair and sat. 'We just need to ask you a few questions.'

'Oh, okay. Sure.'

Rachael linked her fingers in front of her on her desk and pinned him with a no-nonsense stare. 'Where did you get your information from?'

'I, um—to be honest, it kind of turned up out of nowhere.'

She considered him in a heavy silence for several seconds. 'Hmm. Mr Burrow, someone out there is pretending to be the Spider. Often, perpetrators of crimes enjoy involving themselves in their own cases and as there's a very short list of people privy to whatever prank calls we receive, you're now officially a suspect in regards to Summer Edgely's murder.'

She watched the colour leach from his face. 'Wh-what?'

'That being the case, you're going to need to do better than "It turned up out of nowhere".'

He lifted both hands in a wait-a-minute gesture. 'What I meant was, I—I don't actually know who sent me the info or why. See, I only finished uni a few months ago and when I approached all the newspapers about a job none of them were really interested in hiring. But a couple of them said to bring them some stories and if they were any good, they'd purchase them. So, I've been chasing stories for months, chasing police, chasing ambulances, but I haven't gotten anywhere. I set up a website, advertised online for stories. I know that sounds a bit crazy but I figure there's got to be people out there that have stories to tell and maybe no one will give them the chance, r-right?' he stammered, his eyes darting between Finn and Rachael. 'Sorry, I'm probably rambling. Get to the point, right?'

'Take your time,' Rachael said. 'Would you like some water?'

'Oh. No, thanks. So the thing is, I got a ton of replies and most of the stories were, frankly, really terrible.' He managed a laugh. 'I spent more time trying to let people down gently than actually writing anything I would have a shot at selling. I was so sure I was never going to get anywhere that I changed my job at the service station from part time to full time and did nothing about stories or the website for a couple of months. And then I got an email out of the blue yesterday afternoon saying I should be here at this time and ask you that question this morning. I can show you the email.' He pulled it up on his phone and handed it over.

Rachael read it, frowned. Nothing requesting money for the information, no name attached, and the sort of email address she knew would lead nowhere. She checked the time it was sent. Around the same time the press conference had been announced. She passed it to Finn. 'We'll make a copy of this for our records.'

Finn nodded, then said to Burrow, 'Would you mind telling us your whereabouts on Saturday night through to Sunday morning?'

'Oh, sure, of course. My girlfriend and I met some friends at the movies Saturday night then she and I went back to my place. She stayed over, probably left around one on Sunday afternoon. I would be happy to give you her name and number to verify.'

'Thank you,' Finn said.

'So is that it? Can I go?'

'We appreciate your assistance,' Rachael added. 'Please let us know if you receive any more emails from this person.'

'Okay.' Then more hesitantly, he said, 'So, um … is there anything I can use? For a story? Sorry, I …' He trailed off at her stern look.

She thought about it. She was going to assume the sender chose this young man because he was more likely to blindly do as asked. More experienced reporters would have wanted to know the source, replied with more questions, complicated the process. They likely would have approached her before the media release, hoping to get the jump on the story in case she was going to run with it today anyway.

Whoever this was wanted to create hype by dropping that piece of information in front of all the cameras and associated media. They wanted to cause chaos. But for her personally or the investigation? Either way, here was a malleable young man looking for a story and she needed to shut it down before the public went into meltdown.

Rachael caught Finn's frown and knew he had to be wondering what she was thinking when the short answer to Burrow's question should have been no.

'So here's the deal. When all those other reporters who were here today attempt to contact you over where you got your information, you're going to tell them you were guessing. It was simply a hunch you were hoping might pay off.'

'And in return?' When Finn coughed, Burrow's face burned with more embarrassment. 'I didn't mean that the way it came out. I just meant ...'

'You should record this, Mr Burrow.'

Burrow opened the voice recorder on his phone and once it was on, she began. 'We receive crank calls about cases every day. There was always going to be some fallout from my appearance on the *Detective Insider* documentary. We can't be sure yet why Summer Edgely was murdered, but we're looking into the theory she was dressed and posed as she was because the killer was looking for attention. Men who kill children tend to be impulsive, with lower intelligence, and they often suffer from mental illness. We believe it likely our person of interest is an unstable, insecure personality who feels powerless in his

day-to-day life and craves the same sort of notoriety Thomas
Biddle received on the television program. We have a number
of leads we're currently chasing up and we're confident we'll
soon have the perpetrator in custody.' She reached over and
stopped the recording. 'There's just one stipulation here. You
make sure to quote those words as mine. Don't state your
own opinion or come to your own conclusions about this guy.
Remain impartial and simply report the story. Okay?'

'You've got it! Thank you, inspector. I'll make sure I let
you know if I get any more emails.' He was champing at the
bit to get going.

'It was nice to meet you, Mr Burrow. I hope the story sells
for you.'

'Are you kidding? An exclusive with the lead detective on
the homicide of Summer Edgely? Thanks again.'

She watched him all but dance from the room and sighed.

'What are you doing?' Finn asked, as she knew he would.

'I'm trying to shut down a mass public panic.'

Finn got to his feet. 'It was more than that.'

'I want to piss this guy off. Smash his ego. I want him to
contact me again.'

'And what have you always told me about playing with
fire?'

She got up, walked with him back out of the room. 'I'll
have my incoming calls monitored so that if and when he
calls we can get a location on him.'

'All right. Let's hope it works.'

'There's something else. Going by the time on that email,
our POI knew about the press conference almost as soon as
it was arranged.'

'Once the media get hold of something it's out there.
But ... you're still worried we could be dealing with a cop.'

'It's got to be that or someone connected to the media. At the very least, we know we've got a leak. I just hope that's all we've got.'

Finn dragged a hand over his face. 'Which means we're going to have to watch our team as closely as our POI. That's not fun.'

She checked the time. 'And the day's only going to get better. You ready to go see Biddle?'

'Can't wait.'

'I'll go and get my stuff, meet you at the car.' Rachael went back to the strike force room, which immediately quietened. She hated that this issue had driven a wedge between a generally cohesive group. 'Okay, listen up. The tip-off came through via email. Unless I have confirmation by tonight of where the leak came from, I'll be chasing that up tomorrow. Right now, Detective Carson and I are off to talk to Biddle.'

'You're going to the supermax in Goulburn?' Claxton asked.

'No. Due to the prostate cancer, he's been transferred to the hospital in Long Bay prison, and is receiving treatment at the Prince of Wales Hospital.'

'Gotta love that these monsters get all this free treatment,' Claxton muttered.

'Not gonna argue with you there.'

'Before you go,' Claxton said, 'can I have a quiet word?'

'Of course.' She met him outside the door.

'I've been looking into the costume Summer was wearing. The wings are authentic,' he said, face grim. 'Same pattern and design as those used on the Spider's first three victims, same beads and, if my search is anything to go by, they're now impossible to buy anywhere, so he's had them stashed. Costume also appears to be homemade. You can't buy that anywhere, but you can get a pattern for it from Spotlight.'

Rachael stared at the floor, nodded slowly. 'Maybe I was wrong about Biddle.'

'If you were, we all were.'

'I appreciate that. But this is on me.'

'Oh—sorry!' Debbie said, charging through the door and almost running into Rachael. 'I wanted to make sure I caught you before you left.'

'I'll let you get back to it,' Claxton said.

'Thanks.' Then, 'What is it, Debbie?'

'I chased the department for Summer's file. It looked like we were going to have some trouble accessing it without going through all the hoops but then Summer's caseworker got involved. She's collating everything to bring over herself. She was pretty annoyed she hadn't been contacted sooner and is hoping to speak to someone when she arrives.'

'Sure. I'll let Detective Rayburn know. Who is the caseworker?'

'Ah ... someone Kensington. Sorry, I'll go check.'

She stared at Debbie as the world seemed to shrink into a long, narrow tunnel. 'Bailee Kensington?'

'Yeah. You know her?'

'Ah, yes. I do.' And how could that be a coincidence? First her, now Bailee? Was this monster going to drag everyone back in? She needed to be the one to talk to Bailee, but she couldn't. Not yet. She needed to see Biddle. To demand an answer. Have something to give to Bailee when she broke the news.

'Change of plan,' she told Debbie. 'Please call Mrs Kensington and delay her. Tell her I'll see her late this afternoon. Five o'clock.'

CHAPTER TWELVE

Thomas Biddle sat opposite Rachael and Finn in the claustrophobic, overly warm space of the Long Bay Correctional Centre interview room, the notorious child killer now only a shell of the man Rachael remembered, had studied, had expected to find. Biddle's eyes were still as small, still as black and still as soulless as before, but the lines on his face had become sagging grooves, and the hard physique had weakened with age and illness. The cancer was eating him alive and she couldn't have felt less sympathy.

He still chilled her to the bone. There was something about some people, evil people. They had an energy that seemed to reach out and envelop you, dragging you into their empty, black, airless space until you want—need—nothing more than to escape. To breathe. To feel warm again.

It looked like Finn felt it too. She could almost see the tension radiating from him. Both of them had been silent most of the journey, preoccupied with their own thoughts. Now he was staring at Biddle as if the man was a cockroach he wanted to step on, to drive into the ground under the ball of his shoe.

'Looking sick, Biddle,' she said while her stomach twisted at the way his eyes roamed over her like a long-lost lover's. 'The lifestyle in here must suit you.'

For a long moment she wasn't sure he was going to respond. Then finally, 'It's seems like forever since I've seen a woman. Even an old one. It's been too long, Rachael.' Biddle's eyes slowly detached themselves from Rachael's face to move to Finn's with cold disinterest. 'Who are you?'

'Detective Finn Carson,' Finn replied. 'And you can call her inspector. We're here because someone's taking the credit for all your hard work. Pretending to be the Spider.'

Biddle lifted his shoulders to his ears, dropped them and sat back in his chair. 'I told you lot all along it wasn't me. I was never the Spider.'

Rachael leant her elbows on the table, her expression puzzled interest. 'You were always so proud of yourself online. I can't fathom why you refused to take credit for your work after being captured.'

The grooves in his cheeks deepened and spread on a sneer. 'Not exactly a capture to be proud of, was it, Rachael?'

'That's inspector,' Finn corrected again.

'Without your planted evidence, you would never have had a case.'

'I caught you at the scene, you bastard. Who planted you there?'

'And the costumes? The materials? All that money I was supposed to have made? Now what did I do with that? And having hidden it all so well, why would I haphazardly bury the teddy bear in the backyard? Seems a bit silly for a smart man, Rachael, doesn't it?'

'And the recorded evidence we have of you molesting children?' Finn asked. 'Did the police make that up, too?'

He chuckled. 'I'm not denying I liked a bit of underage porn or that on a couple of occasions I participated in some. I was involved in that group. I admitted that. But I've paid for that, haven't I?' He looked at Rachael as he said it.

Yes, he'd done the eighteen years he'd received for that on top of his three life sentences for murder. If it wasn't for his crimes as the Spider, he'd be out on the street. But even if this man, this evil, soulless predator, wasn't a killer, even if she'd got that wrong, the idea of this man walking free was abominable.

'No. I don't think you can ever fully pay for what you did,' she said. 'But if you want to start making amends you could tell us who you spoke to about the murders.'

'I can't tell you what I don't know!' Frustration leaked into Biddle's tone as he put his head in his hands. 'I'll talk about what I did. I'll relive it as often as you like.' And that smirk returned. 'But I didn't kill those girls, Rachael. I liked 'em better alive.'

Another twist in her gut, another chill down her spine. 'You'll rot before you get out of here.'

'Maybe,' he acknowledged, once again sagging back in his chair. 'I remember the good old days, though.' He stared off into space. 'Drinking, drugs, parties … the old gang. Guess the Spider was in on those.'

'If it really wasn't you,' Finn said, 'it's in your best interests to help us find him.'

'Bit beyond me these days, I suppose,' Biddle said, ignoring Finn's remark. 'But the idea of going someplace, maybe to the country ... now that would be nice. I could find a quiet farmhouse with a big fireplace, put my feet up in front of the telly with a bourbon or two. Got those special entertainment platforms available these days, right?' he said, eyes returning to Rachael's. 'Foxtel, Netflix. Youtube ...'

Was there a fleeting glimmer in those tired eyes?

She pounced on it. 'What do you know?'

He shifted in his seat, seemed to sag. 'I have to lie down.'

'I don't believe you. Answer the question!'

'Guard!' Biddle called weakly. Then, 'Bye, Rachael. I do hope you find the Spider.'

'Let's go,' Finn said. 'I'm sick of breathing the same air as this piece of shit anyway.'

So was Rachael, so she stood and followed Finn to the door.

'Oh, one more thing,' Biddle called to their backs. 'Did you ever have kids, Rachael? Daughters? Granddaughters? I'd love to see some photos. Nothing good to jack off to in here.'

She stalked back in and leant across the desk. 'I should have let you bleed out!'

His grin was enormous. 'Why didn't you?'

'And let you miss out on all of this?'

Finn tried again. 'Rachael, let's go.'

For a moment longer all she could do was stare into the monster's eyes with hatred. Then she turned on her heel and walked out.

They were driving away from the prison before either spoke again.

'Well? What do you think?' Finn asked.

'I don't know. The man is a disgusting excuse for a human being at the best of times. I want to say there's a chance he's thrown a clue in there somewhere, but I'm not sure there's enough of him left to pull off his old games.' She stared out over the tree-studded nature strip that separated the prison from the main road and the residential suburbs beyond. 'If he knows anything at all, he's dangled something in front of our faces. We just need to see it.'

As the journey dragged on, Rachael pondered what they knew, what they needed to tackle next. All the while, Biddle's comments rolled around in her mind. Was there something in what he'd said, something she was missing? When a text came through she glanced at it, noticed it was from Van Zettan.

'Anything important?' Finn asked.

'A couple of preliminary findings from Summer's tox screen. She had drugs and alcohol in her system.'

'The original Spider victims didn't have alcohol in their systems, did they?'

'No. So there's another discrepancy in MO.' She saw the station come into view and heard the click of the indicator as Finn drove off the street. 'Drinking, drugs, parties!'

'Sorry?' Finn parked, turned off the car.

Rachael didn't move. There was something here she needed to process. 'Biddle said he missed the drinking, drugs and parties. That he guessed the Spider had attended the parties too. Now Van Zettan's telling us Summer had drugs and alcohol in her system.'

'You think our POI picked Summer up at a party? She was only twelve.'

'His group used to run their own parties.'

'So ... there's a new group? How would Biddle know that?'

'I don't know. I'm thinking out loud. But I do think he's given us that clue after all.' She got out of the car and waited for Finn to follow, then went inside.

'Assuming he has,' Finn said. 'Where do we even start looking?'

'He said the parties were a bit beyond him.'

'So? Are you sure you're not reading too much into this?'

She hit the elevator button. 'No, wait. Instead … instead he wanted to put his feet up. Watch television.'

'Yeah, what was it, Foxtel, Netflix …?'

Rachael gave up on the lift and hit the stairs. 'And then he paused and said, "Youtube".' She chewed on her lip as she made level one and walked into her office, turning the comment over in her mind. 'That doesn't really fit, does it? Youtube is a video-sharing service.' She opened her computer and brought up the site. 'What am I looking for?'

'What about you start with Summer's name?'

She typed it in. 'Nothing.'

'The poem. "The Spider and the Fly"?'

She typed it in, shook her head. 'Just a bunch of animations related to the original poem. Nothing here. What about …' She typed in 'Rachael', scrolled through the drop-down menu and caught her breath. 'Finn.'

He placed a hand on her shoulder as he read the title.

Do you believe me now, Rachael?

She felt her fingers shake as she made herself select it.

She watched the video through once, did her best to hold back the emotion as snippets of Summer Edgely's last moments flashed on screen. Her eyes lifted to Finn's. She swallowed once to make sure her voice was steady, then forced herself to think out loud. 'I'm going to get someone from cyber crimes to look at this and have the video removed from the web. It's already had several views.'

'Of course.'

'We need to find out if there's any more copies out there. I don't want this video turning up on the evening news or being shared around on social media if it's within our powers to stop it. But everyone in our team needs to see this.'

A tap on the door had them both looking up. Debbie.

'Is everything all right?' Debbie asked.

'Not exactly. What's up?' Finn asked.

'Bailee Kensington is here.'

God, she wasn't looking forward to this, Rachael thought. 'Show her in, please.'

'I'll take care of it,' Finn said, but Rachael stopped him.

'No, Finn. It's fine.'

'Rachael, give yourself a minute.'

'Finn, Bailee Kensington used to be Bailee Winter.' She saw the understanding come over his face, then the questions flood in. 'I don't know how it fits yet, but it can't be coincidence, can it?'

'Inspector.'

Rachael looked up, saw Bailee behind Debbie and smiled in greeting. 'Bailee, Hi. Please come in.'

'Rachael,' Bailee said, returning the smile, and stepped straight in for a brief hug. 'It's lovely to see you. Though I wish it was under different circumstances. Someone should have called me on Sunday.'

'I understand why you feel that way,' she said, rounding the desk to her seat and gesturing for Bailee to sit opposite. 'But there's some details to the case we needed time to get sorted first. Things you need to know.'

Bailee's eyes flashed hot. 'Was it that arsehole of a stepfather, Tyson Brewer?'

'We don't think so.' Rachael hesitated, her smile turning grim. 'The man who did this is claiming to be the Spider.'

Bailee's face was no less stunned than she'd expected it to be. 'That's impossible!'

'Summer was found wearing a costume, posed like the other girls.'

'I know but—'

'The man who did this has been in contact. He told me I got it wrong. That I put the wrong man in prison.'

Bailee was shaking her head. 'You don't honestly believe that?'

'Our POI knew an intimate detail of the murders that was never released, used the same rare materials to create the costume. Maybe Biddle somehow shared those details with our POI,' she added quickly. 'We're looking into that possibility. But we also have to look into the possibility that the Spider is still out there.'

'Listen, Brewer's a real piece of work,' Bailee objected. 'He'd kill Summer and dress her up like that just because he thought it was funny.'

'Bailee, we've looked into Brewer and we don't believe he's responsible.'

Bailee's hands hit Rachael's desk hard. 'Biddle is the Spider! I don't believe this. *You* can't believe this! You found that evidence buried in his backyard!'

Rachael understood the anger and disbelief, but it was important for all of them that she kept calm. Much calmer than she felt. 'I haven't decided what I believe yet. What's important right now is that other girls in your caseload might be in danger. I'm going to need a list of every girl on your books.'

Bailee's anger was replaced with shock. 'You think the killer chose Summer because she was one of mine?'

'I don't think we can rule that out.'

'But if we're really going to entertain the idea that Biddle wasn't the Spider, why would this other guy come after my clients?'

'Once Biddle was caught we were able to access and dismantle the paedophile ring. Regardless of who the Spider was, he'd been choosing his victims from that pool. When it all collapsed and police were crawling all over everyone involved, he would have wanted to distance himself from it all and then he effectively would have had to start from scratch. I'm guessing at this stage, but perhaps he's holding a grudge against anyone who'd had involvement in that. Or maybe he's ready to jump back into the limelight again and thinks tying it back to us will glean more immediate interest, give him more credibility. I don't know, Bailee. But I'm throwing everything I can at this.'

'Is there a video?'

Rachael hesitated. That was enough for Bailee to pounce.

'I want to see it.'

'It's not a good idea,' Finn said, as much to Rachael as Bailee.

Bailee's expression darkened. 'Summer was *my* responsibility. No doubt you're talking to everyone who even remotely had anything to do with her. I guarantee I know more about her than her parents and most of her friends did. I might see or hear something or someone I recognise. I need to see it. *You* need me to see it.'

'Show her,' Rachael told Finn, getting to her feet. 'While I get it copied and taken down.'

*

'I'm still not sure showing Bailee the video was a good idea,' Finn said as he steered the car into his daughter's school's carpark.

'She's not going to talk to the press, but I do think she's going to put pressure on the right people for answers.'

The tidy carpark, with its neatly painted lines and pretty rows of fig trees was close to empty at this time of evening, just a light scattering of cars awaiting the end of band practice. Finn pulled in close to the wide double gates. 'She shouldn't be long.'

Rachael settled into her seat and watched a few kids in the adjoining junior school playground doing after-school sport. It was a vastly different playground to the one belonging to the little school Kayla had worked at. The school at which she'd first met Lexi Winter.

Kayla stepped out of the classroom with Rachael and scanned the playground. Kids, a crazy tumble of them fighting for a soccer ball, whizzed past in a blur of sound and movement.

'Give me a sec,' Kayla said, her eyes pinned on a girl sitting on the sidelines by herself.

That can't be her, Rachael thought. The girl Kayla was talking about was ten. This one was too small, surely? The girl hunched a bit lower when she noticed them staring, almost melting into the background. Kayla walked over, said something. The girl's gaze darted across. A one-shouldered shrug followed. Kayla stood, waved Rachael over and met her halfway. 'Want me to stay?'

'No, I'll speak to her alone.' It was in the back of Rachael's mind the girl didn't look strong enough to handle both of them at once.

She smiled as she approached and sat down on the wooden bench beside Lexi, noted the shadowed eyes that skittered from place to place but refused to land anywhere. Her forearms were raw from scratching. Long welts made by nervous fingers marred pale skin and the occasional bruise. As Rachael sat, the girl tucked a sketchpad she'd been drawing in under her leg.

'Hey Lexi, my name is Rachael. It's nice to meet you.'

When Lexi said nothing, she tried something else. 'What are you drawing?' In response the notebook was shoved further under her leg. 'Did Kay—Mrs Carson mention that I'm a police officer?'

The smallest of nods.

'My job is to keep people safe and to look after people who might need a bit of help.'

Lexi's head jerked slightly, her frown seeming to suggest that whatever she'd been told about police, that hadn't been the tone of the conversation.

What was she supposed to do now? The child clearly didn't want to talk. Another change of tack. 'I see you have a bruise on your arm there, where you've been scratching.' Rachael pointed to it and the girl did her best to shift away. Rachael considered asking her how she got it but doubted she'd tell her. Instead, she tried yet something else. 'I'm helping another little girl at the moment who has a bruise on her arm just like that one.' When Lexi's eyes shifted slightly in her direction, she pressed on. 'Do you want to know how she got hers?'

A tiny shrug.

Acknowledging she was probably crossing a line but suddenly desperate to get answers, needing to help, Rachael continued. 'This little girl had—has to sometimes do things at home that she doesn't want to do. Things that sometimes leave bruises.'

Those big blue eyes were still cautious, but they slid up to make contact with Rachael's. 'Like what?' Not much more than a whisper.

'Things she's not supposed to talk about.'

Another pause, but she could see the little girl was thinking this time. 'Like make videos?'

Rachael's breath hitched. 'Yeah,' she said, hoping Lexi would elaborate, 'like make videos. Will you let me help you, Lexi?'

Lexi seemed to be considering that, then abruptly jumped to her feet and snatched up her notebook. 'I'm not allowed to talk to police.'

'Why not?'

'Police are liars and pigs and they shoot little bitches like me!' She ran away.

Rachael stayed where she was, too stunned to move. The desperate fury in Lexi's face, in her tone, in her words was heartbreaking. What sort of parents teach a child those terrible things about police? Parents who don't want their child talking to or trusting police, she acknowledged. Parents who have something to hide.

'Are you thinking about the video?' Finn asked. 'You've gone quiet.'

'Not exactly. But between the video and seeing Bailee again … it's brought back some memories.'

'She's not what I imagined at all. She's so young and so together. How does that happen after you've been raised by meth addicts and groomed by a paedophile?'

'She was still very young when we got her out, and I believe her sister sheltered her from what she could. She was also very lucky to get the most fabulous foster home with two of the nicest, most giving people I've ever met. She doesn't remember a lot of the time before that.'

'Blocked it out?'

'The human brain is very good at protecting itself.' Because she needed to think about something else for a while, she asked, 'How's Ava enjoying band practice?'

'She's taken to it better than I thought she would.'

'How come you're allowed to pick her up?'

'Viv's got something on this arvo. I don't mind. It's another chance to see her.'

'You miss her.'

'I do. There she is.'

They spotted Ava wave and leave a group of girls walking out to awaiting cars.

'I swear she's grown a foot taller this month.'

'Not quite,' he said, but there was no arguing that at ten, his daughter was fast looking more of a young woman than a child. She had her mother's mousy brown hair and tall, slim figure but the big wide smile and green eyes were all Finn's. That smile spread in genuine pleasure when she saw them.

'Someone's happy to see you,' he said.

The door was yanked open and a guitar case tossed in. 'Hi Dad! Aunty Rach! Hi!'

'Hi Ava. How's my not-so-little niece?'

'I'm a vocal diva,' she said with a grin and a spin, 'and my guitar's not bad either.'

'If you do say so yourself,' Finn teased.

Ava got in and closed the door. 'It was just band practice tonight but Mr Totness wants me to have private lessons. Says I'm a star in the making! But ...' She hesitated. 'Mum's complaining about money again so ...'

Rachael and Finn exchange glances. 'I don't have an objection to private lessons if it's something you really want,' Finn said, already wondering what it was going to cost him, 'as long as you stick—'

'I know, I know. I have to stick to it for at least a year and practise hard. Sure, Dad.'

'Then okay. I'll cover it,' he said. Somehow. He was already paying rent on an apartment so Viv could have the house, paying child support and picking up all the other bits and pieces along the way. It didn't leave a lot, but he'd find it. He noticed Rachael's probing gaze a moment before she spoke.

'You know what?' she said. 'Consider it an Aunty Rachael treat. I'm all for supporting a future diva.'

'Thanks!'

'Welcome, and on that theme, who's up for something special for dinner, my treat?'

'You don't have to pay for everything,' he objected. 'I can afford it.'

'I can't for the life of me figure out how,' she replied. 'Besides, I'd like to treat everyone. Humour me.'

'Not going to say no to that,' he said. 'Thanks, Rach.'

CHAPTER THIRTEEN

'How about you tell me what really happened to my car?'
My hands are on my hips and my tone is as stern as I can
make it, but Dawny's not budging. She's sitting at her
kitchen table with a cup of tea and a *That's Life!* magazine,
working on a giant crossword and talking around in circles.

'It's often better to just accept that these things occur.
Youth these days … nothing better to do than go around
pinching stuff and stirring up trouble. Bring in compulsory
military service, that's what I say.' She pressed her pencil
down on a square and stared into space. 'A five-letter word
for a fern leaf. Ah … frond.' She jotted it down.

'I need my car!' I say. 'I can't walk everywhere, I hate public transport and cabs are expensive.'

'Better get another one. Car, I mean. That'd be my advice.
You won't be getting yours back.'

'So you do know more than you're saying!'

'It's not a bad thing, you know. You never could have gotten that car all the way clean. Bound to have been some evidence left behind. Now there's none.' She lifts her eyes to smile happily at me. 'I had this car once. A little Datsun 120Y. Well, one of my lady friends puked in the back after a big night. The stink made my eyes run every time I got in. Nothing could shift it. Once I decided the damn smell was gonna outlast religion, I had to get rid of it. Best thing in the end, really.'

'My insurance doesn't cover theft! I can't afford a new one.'

Dawny's face drops into a worried frown. 'Oh dear, well, that could be a problem.'

'You think?'

'We really do need one quite quickly. Leave it with me.'

I'm immediately suspicious. 'Why do *we* need one?'

'Well, you just said so yourself, didn't you?'

'Dawny.'

Her gaze returns to her puzzle. 'Hmm. What's a five-letter word for believe in?'

'Seriously? I don't know …' Stupidly, I think about it. 'Trust?'

'Ah, now that's a nice thing to have in a person!' she says with another smile beamed in my direction. 'How about you work on that? Now, I have to tell you, you don't look yourself, dear. You're a little worked up. Not good for the complexion. Wait there.' She disappears then returns with a shopping list and a handful of cash. 'I need a few things. Be a dear and get them for me would you? And maybe ask the chemist, if you wouldn't mind, about what's best for indigestion? Thanks for that. You look like you need an outing. You're welcome.'

I smile sweetly as agitation burns in my throat. 'I don't have a car!'

'Neither do I. And the bus is so difficult to get into with my dodgy knee.' She returns my sweet smile and mine becomes a grimace.

'Okay. Fine. I'll … deal with it.'

'Thank you.'

I leave, muttering to myself in annoyance as I make my way home, but once back inside my own house, I go to Coles Online and start an order of what she needs, beginning with the antacid. I'm churning through the rest of the list when I come across: *salt – bulk bags. Many. Maybe try the pool shop.*

'Huh?' I finish the order and go back across the drive.

Before I can reach Dawny's front door, Don Parkhurst bursts from his like a small angry hippo while Miriam watches from the doorway, her nose even higher than usual.

'Stop right there, Lexi!'

My whole body sags. 'Look, don't bust your pacemaker. I'm not getting the bike, okay?'

'You've killed our lawn!'

'I—um.' This was not what I was expecting. He's standing over his precious couple of metres of turf, tapping his foot. His brow is lifted, his finger pointing at the yellow grass as though I might miss it. 'It's not dead, it's just … turned a nice autumn colour.' I try harder on that smile, don't quite pull it off.

'It was all that bleach you used on your car. You parked it on the lawn and spread it everywhere!'

'I parked it on my lawn, Don. I can't help that yours is beside it.'

'Why not wash it on the drive?' Miriam called out from the doorway.

I stare at them bug-eyed in mock disbelief. 'Because then it goes down the drain. I could kill a dolphin! What is wrong with you two? You don't care about our marine life?'

They're clearly unsure if I'm serious. They should know better: my hose doesn't reach that far.

'You're going to have to replace the turf!' Don says in a no-nonsense matter.

'Okay, sure, Don. Whatever you say.'

'Today! And you're going to have to lay it.'

I snigger. 'Sorry, Don, I'll stick to people. Anything else is too kinky for me.'

'I—I meant ...'

'Got a spare two-fifty? Come visit. But you want to play games with grass, you're on your own.'

Don, clearly flustered, shakes his head, throws a dismissive hand in the air and turns on his heel. He needn't have worried. I wouldn't touch him for ten times that amount. Well, maybe for ten times.

I hear Miriam console her husband. 'She's just a tramp. We'll call the police.'

'Good luck getting them out over some burnt lawn, stupid old bat,' I mutter. But with the Parkhursts out of the way, I'm back on track. I reach Dawny's door and bang on it. 'Dawny?'

It opens. Dawny smiles, lets me in. 'Yes, dear?'

'Your groceries, complete with Gaviscon, will be here tomorrow between two and seven. Except the salt. Why do you need so much salt?'

'To dry out our friend,' she says as though I'm mildly dull. 'And kill the smell.'

I almost don't want to ask but, 'But *our friend* is in the freezer.'

'Let's just say it's for eventually. Now, never you mind about the details, dear. But while I've got you …'

When I leave Dawny's I'm exhausted. I flop on my lounge, stare at the roof and enjoy the silence. How can the woman talk so much and still not say what I need to hear? What the hell has she done with my car and who the hell did she get to do it? Also, I'd really like to know why she went to prison. The woman knows too much.

I check my phone and notice the time. Shit. Dawny really does dissolve an afternoon. Henry's birthday party is in a couple of hours. I couldn't feel less like dressing up and playing girlfriend but I need the money and I'll admit I'm curious about the investment manager. I drag myself back to my feet. What the hell am I going to wear?

*

Three hours later I'm well into my role. I tried to dress more conservatively than usual. The dress is black and mid-thigh, my breasts are mostly covered. It's a bit too scoopy at the back for a casual-banker thing but it's the best I can do. Besides, stuffy Miss Investment Manager's eyes practically fell out of her head when I walked in and planted one on Henry, so I'm pretty sure I had the effect he was hoping for. I wonder if I should bolt early, give Stuffy some time alone with Henry. But do I really want them getting together? I need that $250 a week. I probably shouldn't have pushed Henry to ask her out, but then again, I haven't been making the best choices recently.

'Another champagne?' Henry asks in my ear.

'Ah, sure. Thanks.' It's okay. I'm not huge on wine, sparkly or otherwise, but he's sprung for the expensive stuff so I try and appreciate it. And it does take the edge off the situation. I'm bored. And I can tell Stuffy is working up the courage to talk to me. I can hardly wait.

Almost as soon as I think it, she sidles up beside me. 'So, Lexi, what do you do for a living?'

I shrug. 'I mostly live off my investments these days.' The answer rolls smoothly off my tongue. I've been using that one since I began escorting, figuring that if I consider my clients my investments, it's not that far from the truth. But I do realise the implications in this case. I have to hope she's not going to quiz me too hard.

Diamond teardrops glitter from her ears as she swishes her dyed blonde curls and gives me her best smile. 'Oh, is that how you and Henry met? Through the bank? I'm the new branch investment manager you know.'

'Yes, I know.'

Her eyes light up and she touches a hand to the matching silver and diamond necklace. 'Henry mentioned me?'

I struggle for several silent seconds against the grimace desperately attempting to hijack my face. I mean what is this, high school? 'Sure did,' I say in a mock conspiratorial tone that is wasted because she's too keen on what I have to say to notice the sarcasm. 'I've heard rave reviews. Henry was so pleased with the advice you gave him.'

She turns a comical shade of pink, her eyes glowing. 'He really is the sweetest man. You're very lucky.'

I watch her closely, but I don't detect anything in her face, tone or words that isn't completely genuine. Maybe she really is into him. And those diamonds she's deliberately flashing don't look fake. Maybe she isn't a greedy, money-hungry gold-digger. Maybe she's even his one chance at happiness.

Ugh, here we go. I must me mad. 'Well, actually,'—I lean in slightly, lower my voice—'Henry and I aren't really working out.'

'You're not?'

'No, see. Henry wants a wife to dote on. Someone to travel with and spoil and I'm afraid I'm not ready for all that. I wish someone else would come along. It would make it so much easier to let him down if he had another love interest. Know what I mean?'

Not only did she know what I mean, I could see the cogs turning in her brain, figuring out how she was going to slide right on in there and fill the position. I hope I'm right about these two, because my rent is about to become a whole lot more difficult to meet.

'Oh, so I wouldn't be stepping on toes if I ...'

'Asked him out? Go ahead.' My phone pings. It's been doing that for the past fifteen minutes and no one ever needs to contact me that badly. I'm starting to worry. 'Excuse me.' I begin to back away from the party. Maybe the Parkhursts really did manage to get a cop interested in talking to me about the yellow lawn. Can't get one to investigate a paedophile but a burnt lawn ... I need to know, so I head over to see Tom and check my messages. They're from Bailee.

Call me
Lexi, call me back.
Where are you? It's urgent. Call me!
FFS, Lexi, call me back!!

'So is it a double or a double double?' Tom asks from behind the bar.

'The last one.'

'Got it. And you're not leaving without one of our finest nachos tonight.'

'I need this to kick in first.' I throw back half my drink. 'Thanks.'

With a flash of a grin he moves away to serve another customer. I call Bailee back. She answers on the first ring.

'About time.'

'While I'm generally free to spend my days sitting at home staring at my phone in case you call, occasionally I do have to—'

'Lexi,' she cuts me off. 'Where are you?'

'With a client. You okay?' I hear the heavy sigh that kind of trembles out and she spares me the 'you're so much better than that' lecture for a change. Now I'm really worried.

'Are you home now?'

'Not yet. I'm still at the bar.'

'Of course you are,' she replies and she sounds tired. 'Drunk?'

'Working on it.'

Another sigh. 'Okay, look, I know that's your best coping mechanism for doing what you do but I need—'

'Spare me, okay?' I take another long swallow of my JD. I hate having that psychological shit thrown at me. Whether she's right or wrong, I don't particularly care. 'What's up? I thought it was urgent.'

'It is, but I don't want to tell you over the phone or when you've been drinking.'

'Kind of out of options for the time being. And it's urgent, right? So spill it.'

There's a long pause. 'It's bad. And I'm not going to tell you all of it while you're drunk in a pub, but there's this video I need you to look at as quickly as possible.'

'Um ... What kind of bad?' If there was CCTV anywhere near Jonathan Davies's house, I'm stuffed. 'Not anything to do with me bad?'

'Why, what have you done?' Her tone sharpens.

'Nothing. Sorry, go on.'

'It was made by someone claiming to be the Spider and the girl is dead.'

Okay, I'll admit that gives me a kick. But ... 'The Spider? That's not possible.'

'That's what I said. I need you to look at it though, because whoever's done it needs to be found. The police are on it but I thought you might be able to get more info through all those contacts you've made on the dark web.'

'I doubt it. But okay. I'll check it out when I get home. Make some enquiries.'

'Go home now.'

I glance back at Henry. He's talking to Stuffy. 'I'll do what I can.' I'm talking to myself; Bailee's hung up so I head back over. Stuffy looks disappointed when I pull Henry aside.

'This is looking good. Asked her out yet?'

'That would hardly be appropriate with you on my arm,' he reminds me.

'No problem. I'll cut out and give you guys some alone time.'

'But we haven't ...' His eyes go to the door to the stairs.

'Might be your best chance. Strike while the iron's hot and all those other for-good-reason clichés right?'

He debates that while I try not to look like I'm desperate to rush off. 'I guess I should pay you then.'

I kiss him on the cheek and whisper, 'Not now. She's not taking her eyes off you. Good luck.' Then I send Stuffy a wave and a wink and hurry off before Henry has a chance to change his mind.

I wave down a taxi and once on my way, I click on the video Bailee has sent and prepare myself to concentrate on details. The camera jostles around. The cameraman is outside. The sky is dark, no visible moon, but I can make out the silhouettes of treetops in the distant background, over a green Colorbond fence. The backyard is well lit, and the footage settles on a paved pool area. Herringbone-patterned terracotta pavers. A kidney-shaped in-ground pool. Light blue lining with lights. A simple black rail fence in front. A white plastic table and single chair in the far-right corner and a thin line of garden the length of the back fence filled with some sort of decorative grass. There's a splashing sound, and a girl I'm guessing hasn't quite reached her teens comes into view. Red hair to below the shoulders, a smattering of freckles, pale skin. She swims to the pool steps and shows off a shiny green and blue costume. She's smiling, but sluggishly. Something's wrong. The camera follows her progress, zooming in on her face. 'Hey Ariel,' a male voice calls out. 'Come out of the water. I know you want me.'

The girl frowns a little, as though trying to remember something, then shakes her head. 'King Triton won't let me.' She's drugged, or drunk. Something.

'Ah, but I am a human prince. Come play with me.'

'What kind of sick shit …' I mutter, earning a curious glance from the taxi driver in the rear-vision mirror.

The girl slides onto the edge of the pool, her legs snug in a mermaid tail. A large male hand reaches for hers. The video dims in and out and now Ariel is tied to a small bed with a Little Mermaid doona set. She's struggling, but half-heartedly. 'I can't stay, prince. I must return to the sea.' She's slurring her words now.

The shadow of her captor slides over her before the dark figure blocks the view. The lower part of a face appears, jolting me with its sudden closeness to the camera. A Cheshire Cat grin with white teeth, one chipped incisor, a dark, stubbled jawline. Then his back as he approaches the bed and kneels over this victim holding Triton's spear. He slides it over her. 'Are you going to sing for me, Ariel?'

I swallow the bile that rises to the back of my throat. I want to reach through the screen and attack him, defend her somehow. I hate that I can't. That whatever he's about to do has already been done. Two large hands wrap around her throat. My breath is coming fast and shallow, my hands are shaking. But that's it. The video ends.

It takes the remaining few minutes of the taxi ride to pull myself back together. I have an idea I know what this is and once inside, I call Bailee. 'It's a teaser video for something called rough 'n' snuff and the videos pull big money. It's rape and murder for entertainment. The victims are not always kids but the paedos are catching on to the profit potential and more content's becoming available.' And just in case she thinks I'm going to watch it again: 'I wouldn't even know how to begin to dismantle this, Bailee. That's one for your guys.'

'I don't expect you to take on the whole industry. I thought maybe you could help find *this* one.'

'This could have been uploaded from anywhere. Just because someone's got a mermaid fetish doesn't mean this has anything to do with the Spider. Most of these videos are European.'

'Not this one.' I hear her drag in a breath, the emotion thick in her voice. 'The victim was found floating in Erina Creek on Saturday morning.'

My stomach flips. 'The kid from the news?'

'Her name was Summer. She was twelve years old.'

'Damn it.'

'She was one of mine.' I hear the tremor in Bailee's voice. 'I'd been trying to get her placed in care for two years.'

'Oh Bailee, I'm so sorry.'

'Apparently it's the same format as the other videos the Spider made. Just a shorter version.'

'Biddle's in prison.'

'This guy ... He called Rachael. Told her she got the wrong man.'

My mind is shouting, no, no, *no*. 'You've spoken to Rachael?'

'She's up here on the coast working the case. There's a whole strike force on this.'

The silence stretches on and I feel the weight of it like a wrecking ball on my conscience.

'Lexi, say something.'

I don't know what to say. I feel like I've been hit by a truck. I scramble for the face on the video. The Cheshire grin. That couldn't be the Spider. The Spider was Biddle and Biddle is in prison. Exactly where he deserves to be. As close to hell as possible.

'That is *not* the Spider. That grinning dipshit is someone else.'

'Whoever he is, he killed Summer.' There's a sniff. Damn it. She's crying. 'Can you help?'

'I want to I just … I don't know how. This is not some idiot who's going to want to talk to me on Facebook. And I doubt he's stupid enough to leave anything traceable on that video. I'll take a better look, see if anything stands out, but that's about all I can do.'

'Thanks, Lexi. And if you need any extra resources—'

I hang up. I'm in no mood to hear about how I should be working with the police. The idea is as ridiculous as it was yesterday and last week and every other time she's brought it up. I stop pacing my lounge room and drop down onto the lounge, hit play on the video again and pause it on Summer. That poor kid. A beautiful young girl with no future and a horrific end. Anything I do from here on in will be too little, too late for her. The reason I help Bailee is so the kids these arseholes abuse can have a second chance. A future. But I can't change things for Summer. Nothing I do will bring her back. I skip forward, see that smug, grinning mouth. *Who are you? The Spider?* No. Biddle's the Spider. I still remember the stupid poem.

'Do you like rhymes?' Mr Biddle asked Bailee.

We're in bed. Bailee had a nightmare so she's crawled in with me. He shouldn't be up here. I don't know where Mummy and Daddy are and I don't know what to do. Bailee giggles, nods. She's only five. She didn't even go to school this year. Mummy says she doesn't have to go until she's six. Bailee doesn't know anything much.

Mr Biddle's always nice and friendly to Bailee. He brings her presents, says she's special. I don't know why. I do know he buys the videos Daddy makes with me. Sometimes I have to make them with Mr Biddle, too. I hate them both. Then they take the drugs together and watch the videos. I hear him tell Daddy I'm getting too old. I wish Daddy would listen, that maybe he'd stop. But I worry about Bailee. I don't like the way Mr Biddle looks at her.

Like he's looking now.

He holds his arms out to get her to sit on his lap but when she moves I grab hold of her pyjamas and keep her next to me. He shifts closer, talks low.

'Will you walk into my parlour? said the spider to the fly; 'Tis the prettiest little parlour that ever you did spy. The way into my parlour is up a winding stair, And I have many pretty things to shew when you are there.'

'What kind of things?' Bailee asks.

'Ah, you wait and see, little fly,' he says. 'One day I'll show you. We'll make it a special event.'

I sit up with a jolt. *Special event*. I've heard that recently. Doc's killer had talked about a special event.

I think about that, then flop back down and shake my head. Nah, it's silly to assume something Biddle said eighteen years ago has any relevance to anything going on today. I can almost dismiss it, except between Bailee's local partythrowing paedo ring, the sick fairytale video and the dead child, it's like history is repeating itself. And Summer's body had turned up the morning after that special event was to be held. Coincidence?

I struggle to bring to mind the conversation between Davies and his killer. And it hits me. Davies's killer had said *his* special event. Was the man who killed Davies also Summer Edgely's killer? The man claiming to be the Spider?

I get up and head for my bottle of JD. So much for leaving anything to do with Jonathan Davies well and truly alone. Instead, it seems I've managed to put myself right into the middle of it.

CHAPTER FOURTEEN

Wednesday, March 10

Rachael stared at the emails crowding her inbox until they began to blur on the screen. She put some serious thought into deleting each and every single one of them. At this moment, nothing outside of this case seemed important. Other cases, online orders, bills and dental reminders were part of a whole other reality and could wait. Would have to wait, because she couldn't deal with anything else. There was simply no room left. Every part of her was filled with the Spider. With Summer Edgely. With Thomas Biddle.

Her finger hovered over the delete button on an email from a wine subscription promising a delivery. Her phone rang and her hand instead skimmed over the keyboard to pick up the phone. 'Rachael Langley.'

'Good morning, Rachael. It's Steven Van Zettan. I wanted to let you know I attempted to pull the lab results from the victims of the Spider case.'

She could tell from his tone the day was about to become more complicated. 'And?'

'They're missing.'

'That's odd. Which ones?'

Finn poked his head around the door. She motioned for him to wait.

'All of them. I've tried calling Jonathan to find out what could possibly have happened, but he isn't returning my calls. Seems he's intent on guarding his last few days off. It's most inconvenient. Could you have someone send me the relevant files from the police database?'

'Yes, of course. Thanks, Steven.'

She dropped her phone on the desk and sighed. 'Morning, Finn.'

Finn came in and sat. 'What was that about?'

'The lab results from the files of the Spider's victims are all missing.'

'All of them?'

'And Jonathan's still refusing to call anyone back.'

'I can't imagine it's all that different to being a cop. Once you answer the phone, you're back at work, leave or no leave. Did you see Rick Burrow's article in the morning paper?'

'Not yet. I had every intention of chasing that up next. Why?'

'Want another headache?'

'Ha. I live for them.'

'Then you'll love this.' Finn handed her the newspaper folded to the page containing the story.

ATTENTION-SEEKING IMPOSTER WILL SOON BE IN CUSTODY.

'Well, he got his wish. He's published.'

'Rather stunning debut. It's full of derogatory comments about our POI's intelligence. It reads like an opinion piece and it's as inflammatory as hell.'

'Idiot,' she murmured, scanning the story. 'I specifically told him to stick to the facts and quote me.'

'He's goaded him. And a man like this is likely to have an ego that won't stand for it.'

'I need to talk him.' She got up as Debbie walked in.

'Inspector,' Debbie said. 'Mrs Kensington is here with Isabella Jacobs and her mother. She says you should talk to Isabella. They're waiting downstairs.'

'Thanks. Any idea why?'

'Isabella was Summer Edgely's best friend. Apparently she was too scared to talk to the police initially but admitted afterwards to her parents that she knew more than she was saying. Mrs Kensington convinced them both to come in.'

'She's a star.'

'It's funny, I've never seen Bailee spelled that way. And now I've seen it twice. From the Spider case and now this caseworker.'

'Because they're the same person.'

Debbie's eyes widened. 'This Bailee is Bailee Winter?'

'I'm sorry, I should have made that clear.'

'Oh, no problem. So ... any word on the sister?'

'No. They haven't been in contact.'

'Are we sure?'

'Why?'

'To solve the mystery of what happened to her. It'd be nice to find her, right? To know what happened?'

'Yes, of course,' Rachael said feeling slightly impatient. 'But just now ...'

'Right,' Debbie said, back on track. 'I'll bring them up.'

'Great. Could you also go through the files we have from the original Spider case and see if we have any paper copies of the lab results for each victim? If so, send them over to Dr Van Zettan, please. And contact Rick Burrow and ask him to drop in this morning. I need to speak to him. Tell him it's urgent.'

'No problem. Oh, Jim was hoping to see you when you have a sec.'

'Who's Jim?' Finn asked.

'I'll introduce you.' She led him into the strike force room and gestured to the back, where the team seemed to have miraculously made space for three more large monitors attached to computers and assorted other equipment. The top of a head of red hair could be seen sticking out from above the central monitor. 'Jim Hudson is a digital forensics specialist who's recently joined the Cyber Crimes unit. He's had the video of Summer since last night.' She led Finn through the busy room.

'Jim,' Rachael said.

The man looked up through heavy glasses. 'Inspector, hey.'

'Jim Hudson, meet Detective Sergeant Finn Carson. How are you progressing?'

'I'm in the process of trying to recover deleted metadata from the video,' Jim said with a nod acknowledging Rachael's introduction.

'Any luck?' Finn asked.

'These guys aren't amateurs. I'd say they've done this sort of thing many times. I'm scanning for evidence of ties to an established organisation within the dark web while I work.'

'What kind of evidence?'

'Teasers are used by web hosts to sell content. You view the teaser, buy the full video and the host rakes in tons of money, generally in crypto.'

'So why not promote it on the dark web?' Finn asked.

'They would have, but this is about extra publicity. Say you're a run-of-the-mill paedophile looking for new content. This teaser gets some hype through either traditional media or social media. It gets your attention, you want to see more. You track it down and bingo, new customers.'

'So if we wanted to buy the full video, where do we go?' Rachael asked, coming closer to perch on the edge of the desk.

'Well, that's the thing I don't quite get. There should be an ID embedded on the video so customers can identify the publisher. They're generally hidden in plain sight. It could be anything, from something as obvious as a watermark to an item deliberately displayed in the video.'

'Item?'

'Yeah, so if the host site is, say, Teddy Bear's Den, they might put the same teddy bear in each video. But this one appears to be frustratingly devoid of any identifying markers.'

'So what next?'

'There'll be chatter about it on the dark web. I'm setting up a program to scan across a number of sites to see what I can find out.'

'Great. How did you go enhancing the security footage from the dump site?'

'Not fabulous.' Jim pulled up some grainy black-and-white stills from the video. 'This is the best shot we have of the driver. It's still not much more than a hazy blob.'

'Damn.'

'I'll keep working on it.'

'Thanks,' Rachael said.

'Nice to meet you. Good luck,' Finn said.

'Yeah, thanks, man.'

Finn's lips twitched as he followed Rachael back to her office. '"Thanks, man"?'

'He's a nice kid.'

'Hey, we need all the help we can get. Especially with all that computer stuff. Good to have him.'

'The teaser video is interesting. I thought it was a personal dig at me. A "See, I told you it was me and look at what I can get away with".'

'Maybe it was both. He wanted to dig at you and sell his video at the same time. He might need the cash.'

'The Spider successfully ran his own website before. There's nothing to say this guy's not doing the same thing. Do you want to sit in on this interview with Bailee and Summer's friend?'

Finn shook his head. 'Give me a yell if you need me, but I have a few calls from the public to chase up regarding sightings of Summer just prior to her death.'

'Great.' Rachael walked into her office and put a reassuring smile on her face. 'Hi Bailee, Mrs Jacobs. Hi Izzy. Can I get anyone anything to drink? A coffee? A soft drink?'

'No, thanks. We're fine,' Mrs Jacobs said. She looked uncomfortable, upset. Her fingers were twisting in her lap and she kept shooting her daughter distressed looks. Izzy, long brown hair hanging flat along her cheeks and her T-shirt suggesting she was a fan of someone called Melanie Martinez, wore the hunched and somehow defiant stillness coupled with the bored expression kids her age managed to pull off with little effort.

'So Izzy, Bailee said that after the police spoke to you, you remembered something else that might help us?'

Izzy gave a reluctant nod but didn't look up. A nudge from her mother and a sharp look finally had her making eye contact with Rachael. Briefly. 'Um, yeah, maybe.'

'That's great. And really brave. It can be a bit scary coming in here.'

As she'd thought it might, the comment got Izzy's attention. A look of rebellion came into the teen's eyes. 'It's not that, it's …' A shrug and she looked back at the floor. 'I'm not supposed to say anything. I'll get into trouble.'

'From who?'

'All of them!'

'Them?' Rachael prompted. 'We should be able to help with that, once we know what we're dealing with. And I'll say it again, it's brave. It would have been much easier not to help. Summer's lucky to have had a friend like you.'

Izzy laughed humourlessly. 'She wasn't enough of a friend to listen, was she? She wasn't enough of a friend not to dump me to go to some stupid party!'

Rachael saw Bailee stiffen as something flickered in her eyes. At the same time, she noted the tears that had welled in Izzy's eyes and decided to press on.

'Summer went to a party without you?'

'Lots of them! I told her not to go! She wouldn't listen!' Almost yelling now, Izzy dragged in an unsteady breath and dropped her eyes again. Her chin wobbled.

'A really good friend. You did what you could, Izzy. None of this is your fault. Can you tell me about this party?'

Her shoulders lifted in another shrug. 'Not really. Summer used to come to my place nearly every weekend to get away from her stupid pretend dad. Sometimes she'd crash for a few days when it got really bad.'

'We thought it was better for Summer to stay with us than be out on the street,' Izzy's mother added. 'We never mentioned it, though, because we didn't want any trouble from that horrible man Tyson Brewer.'

'That was very kind of you,' Rachael said.

Izzy sniffed loudly and Rachael reached across the desk and handed her a tissue.

'But then Summer started going to these parties on Saturday nights,' Izzy continued. 'She said there were lots of other kids and the guys that ran the parties gave out free food and drinks. Alcohol. She said I should come.'

'Okay. Then what happened?' Rachael asked.

Izzy glanced nervously at her mother. 'I snuck out with Summer last Saturday night. We went to this place in Gosford and there were some other kids already hanging around. They were dressed like they were heaps older than us. I said I didn't think it was a very nice place for a party, but Summer said we just had to wait there to be picked up by ten. That someone would turn up and take us all to the party. I got a bit worried because I didn't want to be driven off somewhere, but everyone else seemed cool with it and they'd done it before and it had been fine, so I hung around. Then this black van turned up and everyone cheered and started piling in. There were cans of mixed drinks and bottles of beer and stuff, and everyone was grabbing something as they found a spot on the floor to sit. Summer did too. I … I almost got in but I … I chickened out. I said I'd changed my mind. I didn't want to go. I told Summer not to go. All the others were like "Come on, hurry up, you're wasting time", and then when I refused they were booing me and calling me a baby. Telling me to go home, get lost.

'Summer begged me to get in but then the guy who'd driven up slid the door shut and told me to fuck off. That if I said anything everyone's gonna hate me, and that he was gonna come find me, that my life would be over, did I understand? So I nodded and said I did and the van left. I had to walk home by myself in the dark.'

'That was a smart decision, Izzy. Was that the last time you saw Summer?'

Izzy nodded.

'Do you remember where the pick-up point was?'

'Yeah, but it changes every week. When I went with her it was on the corner by the train station.'

'What about these other kids? You didn't recognise any of them?'

'No.'

'Do you think you could describe the driver of the van?'

'Maybe. And I tried to remember the number plate, because, well, because Summer got in. It was FGH and one of the numbers was a 7.'

'Izzy, you're an amazing young lady. We're going to get to work on that while I get you started with a sketch artist, okay?'

Another shrug. 'I could try.'

'Thank you, Izzy. Mrs Jacobs, thank you for bringing Izzy in.'

Mrs Jacobs hugged herself as she stood. 'If she'd gotten in that van ... It's bad enough, losing Summer. She was becoming like a daughter to us. But to think I could have lost them both is too hard to contemplate.'

'You've raised a smart daughter. Bailee, would you mind waiting with them while I get the ball rolling?'

'Not at all.'

Rachael strode back into the strike force room. 'Okay, Debbie, can you contact whatever sketch artist you regularly use up here? I need them ASAP. Everyone else,' she said over the top of the general work noise, 'we're looking for a black van, rego FGH with the number 7 in it somewhere. I also need CCTV of Gosford train station and the surrounding area between nine thirty and ten thirty on the night of Summer's murder. We're looking for a small gathering of young people waiting for a pick-up in said black van, which contained one male driver. The driver got out to assist the group into the van. We also need to find anyone else who might have witnessed any of this, so target train station personnel, bus or taxi drivers.'

'All this from Summer's friend?' Finn asked appearing beside her.

'She said Summer was attending regular parties put on by older men who supply food and alcohol to attendees. When Izzy refused to get into the van she was threatened, told to keep her mouth shut.'

'Lucky decision.'

'Yeah. The pick-up location changes each week so we'll have to hope we get enough from the previous one to get somewhere.'

'Sketch artist will be here shortly, inspector.'

'Fabulous.'

'No black vans listed with that rego, inspector,' Claxton called out. 'But we do have a set of plates that could be a match recorded as stolen.'

Rachael blew out a frustrated breath. 'Of course.' On top of recently learning that the email address used to send Burrow his instructions was a dead end, she'd expected no less.

'Debbie, would you mind taking Izzy and Mrs Jacobs some water and asking Bailee to come and see me?'

'Right away.'

'Bailee's certainly proving to be valuable,' Finn said.

'Yeah. And I think she's about to give us a bit more,' she said and waited for Bailee to come in. When she did, Bailee spoke before Rachael could ask.

'I think the parties Izzy is referring to have come up on my radar before. I have another client who initially came to me with the information that some of the local girls, mainly street kids, were being bribed with alcohol and drugs to perform sexual acts at weekly parties. I began looking into it but then she returned and said she'd made it up. I had the clear impression she was lying and that someone had convinced her to shut up, but I couldn't budge her so I had nothing to go on.'

'Someone else who was threatened into shutting up. We're going to need to speak to her,' Finn said.

'She's taken off. Told her friends she was staying with her boyfriend.'

'If you can pass on her details, we'll chase that one up,' Rachael said. 'Would you help us with something?'

'Anything.'

'We need to know if any more of your clients have heard of or have been attending these parties and where they're getting their invitations. As Izzy's just proven, I don't think they're comfortable talking to police. Could you try and find out for me?'

'Yeah, yeah, of course, I'll get on it.'

'Keeping her busy,' Finn said as they watched her head down the stairs.

'She's one small step away from deciding Summer's death is her fault. I don't want to give that thought time to grow and fester. She needs to be part of the solution.'

CHAPTER FIFTEEN

'Hello, sweetie!' the old lady says as I get off the bus. She always says hello. She lives in a little house behind the church and looks after the gardens and stuff. I smile, sort of, and look down at the ground as I walk past as fast as I can. I'm not allowed to talk to strangers. I want to cross the road and grab an orange from the orchard, but she's watching, so I keep going. It takes a long time to walk to the end of our road and my stomach is aching.

I finally reach the house and pause, listening for a minute before going in. Are Mummy and Daddy home? Mummy's shoes are there, the strappy ones she always wears, right by Daddy's big boots. I take off my shoes and leave them neatly by the door, then I quietly go inside. Are they happy? Mad? Are they having a conversation that I shouldn't walk in on? I can't hear anything so I sneak to the fridge in the laundry. There'd been twenty-two beers in the fridge this morning and now there's only seventeen. When Daddy gets home and drinks I have to be more careful not to upset him. Up to three is generally okay, four to eight is the worst, more than that and he gets lazy. Can't be bothered with me. Still no noise. I wonder where Bailee is and if Mummy's asleep. I step lightly but she's in the kitchen stirring a can of tomato soup into a pot. Bailee is sitting at the table colouring in.

'I'm home,' I tell Mummy.

'You're late,' Daddy snaps.

I jump a little. I didn't see him sitting in the next room, but he's getting up, coming into the kitchen. Mummy turns off the stove and one look at the cold expression on her face has the hairs on the back of my neck prickling.

'Nice colouring, Bailee, darlin',' Daddy says and ruffles her hair. Daddy's nice to Bailee. She's his kid, not a second-hand one like me. I can smell the beer on him as he turns to me. 'You gonna tell me why you're late?'

I look from Mummy to Daddy. I can feel that mood the house gets when something bad is going on. It makes me feel sick. 'The bus was a bit late.'

'Oh, right. I thought you might have been caught up telling tales to the teacher.' He and Mummy look at each other and my mind is racing trying to think of what I told Mrs Carson. But I didn't tell her anything. The police lady came, but I didn't tell her anything. Not really.

'I didn't!'

He walks around to the cupboard behind me, pulls his gun off the shelf. My ponytail is ripped back painfully, the hard cold metal presses into my throat. 'What did you say, you little bitch?'

Terror rips through me. 'Nothing!'

'I don't believe you! One of them social workers came to the house today. Said they were investigating a complaint.'

'I didn't say anything, I promise!' My head feels like it's on fire. The gun hurts my throat. Tears spring to my eyes.

'Oh, you're making her cry, Daddy,' my mother taunts, her eyes mean.

'I'll make her do more than cry if the damn authorities ever turn up here again.' Somehow he manages to shake me without his grip on my hair or the pressure of the gun loosening. 'What have I told you about talking to pigs?'

'That they've got guns and they shoot little bitches like me.'

'You talk to them social workers, they'll tell the pigs. Got it?' He shifts and the gun presses impossibly harder into my throat. I can't breathe. 'If I ever find out you talked to them, I'll shoot ya myself.'

The pressure releases and I drag in a breath. Then he points the gun at my eye, jerks it back like he's shooting me.

'I said, got it?'

'Yes.' I can barely control my shaking legs, can barely stand up.

'Yes, what!'

'Yes, Daddy!'

'Get upstairs.'

I slip around him and go to my room. Ted is on the bed so I pick up the tattered bear and hug him, lie down and stare tearily into his black plastic eyes. I know what's coming next. Maybe after I can have some soup. Maybe.

I hear the footsteps coming up the stairs and then he's there. The snarl turns to a smile as he unbuttons his jeans.

*

I sit up, dragging air into my starving lungs. I'm a mess, wet with perspiration and tears, my hair tangled wildly around my face. I pull it from my eyes and realise my hands aren't steady. I should have known the dreams would come back. But that's all they are now. They can't hurt me. My head is pounding, so I stagger out to the kitchen in search of pain-killers and have to make a pitstop as I lose what's left of last night's dinner.

We don't talk to pigs. They shoot people. They've got guns just like mine and they shoot little bitches like you, got it?

'Yeah, *Daddy*, I've got it.' I went to bed thinking about the Spider—so dear Daddy and all that shit has come back to haunt me. 'Hope you're rotting in Hell, arsehole.'

I drag my hands through my damp hair and grimace as I snag a finger in a tight tangle. I silently hope dear old Mummy's there too. I never found out what happened to her and if Bailee knows, she hasn't mentioned it. A quick check of my phone tells me it's after ten. I have to leave for a lunch date with my pretend boyfriend and his elderly mother in two hours. I get up and head for the shower, turn the spray to hot and attempt to scrub the memories of my stepfather and Biddle from my skin.

I haven't had the dreams for years and I don't enjoy them. I want to forget it, forget the whole thing. I should never have gotten involved in the first place. What happened to Summer is terrible, but I'm not a cop. This is their job. It's just ... how can they be so *stupid*? How can they doubt that Biddle's the Spider just because someone else copies one of his murders and claims the title?

And what if ... what if they catch this other guy and let Biddle go?

When I'm done, I shut off the burning water, put the scrubbing brush back on the soap holder. My towel scrapes across my stinging skin as I attempt to wipe away what didn't wash off. That feeling, the one that seems to live under the skin where no amount of soap or scrubbing or scraping can reach. I know I can't eradicate it but the ritual of trying to remains.

No, they wouldn't ever let Biddle out. Would they?

I throw on my dressing gown and hurry to my computer, bring up the video Bailee sent. I need to prove to myself this guy is not the Spider. First and most obvious, the Spider didn't release teaser videos. This guy has, but it could be argued that he's simply keeping up with the market. He wants to sell, he needs to send people to him and this is what they do these days, so I can't rely on that.

What else? The Spider watermarked his content from before it was popular to do so. It was more about ego than copyright. He wouldn't change the distinctive stamp he used. I go back to the teaser video and start working through it. Over and over, frame by frame. There's nothing here. Nothing. Of course there isn't. Because it's not him.

But then there it is. The Spider. I stare at it for a long time, my heart in my throat.

Just a copycat, I tell myself with an edge of desperation. *Just a really good copycat.*

*

I'm back home a little after three. Leon's mother is full-on exuberant and spent most of lunch pushing for a wedding that's never going to happen. He should just tell her. 'Guess what, Mum? I'm gay.' Five words he's sure will break her heart. Instead he throws me a grand a month to make her happy, to let her think I'm the love of his life because she's dying and he figures she never has to know otherwise.

I'm going to pour myself a drink and put my feet up for a while. Enjoy the quiet. Try and pretend this thing with Biddle and Summer and the pretend Spider and the dream hasn't been playing on my mind all day. Maybe I'll make it a double.

But as my butt hits the lounge, Bailee calls out from the front door. 'Lexi!'

'Shit.' I get up again with a groan and move to the door to open it.

Bailee strides in. 'I called you, like, six times. Where have you been?'

'You did? Oh, my phone's on silent. I was working. Leon's weekly lunch with his mum.'

'He's still pretending?'

'Yeah. It's easy money. I follow him around staring at him adoringly, eat a home-cooked meal and everyone's happy. I would have called you back when I saw you'd called. I only just got in.'

Bailee flops onto the lounge. 'I wanted to talk to you in person anyway.'

'Sounds ominous.'

'Kind of. Turns out we need to find Doc after all.'

I sit back down beside her. 'I thought we'd had this conversation.'

'Everything's changed. We now know Summer was attending parties put on by a bunch of old pervs. These men pick the kids up and drive them to the parties and drop them back afterwards. Summer took off last week to attend one and it was the last time anyone saw her. The Spider has to have taken her from that party. Lex, maybe Doc is the Spider.'

'Doc is not the Spider, Bailee.'

'How could you possibly know that?' Before I can open my mouth to answer she barrels on. 'I didn't want to believe it either but it's the same. It's exactly the same! Some guy sets himself up under an alias with a group of paedo scumbags so he can scope out and pluck his victims right out from under their noses. Then there's the identical elements to the murder—the video, the costume—and Rachael said … she said there was another detail that was never released, a terrible one, that this guy has gotten right. Lex, even if he's not the Spider, he's just as dangerous and to find him, we need to find this group. And the best way to do that is to find Doc, right?'

I press my fingers to my eyes and attempt to crush the frustration. 'I can't give you anything to help the police until I can prove this guy is a fake.'

'Why not?'

'Because Biddle can't be allowed to get out of prison! If I help catch this other guy and they decide he was the Spider all along, they're gonna let Biddle out. And I want him to rot in there. He deserves to be where he is. I won't help him to be released. I just won't.'

'Is that what this is about?' Bailee's hand covers mine while her face floods with sympathy.

'Kind of,' I answer carefully. Because it's easier to let her believe that's all it is. And it's a legit excuse. I don't intend to ever help Biddle become a free man.

'I blocked so much of it out, and I know you didn't, that you carry all that around with you all the time. But there are bits I remember. And I get it's hard going there again. I'm not asking you to. Just give Rachael what you have on Doc. They'll figure it out. For what it's worth, Rachael doesn't want to be wrong about Biddle either. She's not going to concede she was without absolute proof.'

'I'll get to the truth faster.'

Bailee's lips purse and her disappointment shows in her eyes. 'I have to go pick up the kids from daycare. I'll talk to you tomorrow.' She gets up, then hesitates at the door. 'This is not just about who is or isn't the Spider. Summer's dead, and there'll be another victim. We need to stop this as fast as we can.'

I watch her go then grab the bottle of JD to refill my glass. Maybe I should have told her the truth. The idea brings a wry smile to my lips. *Hey, guess what? I do know Doc and I know exactly where to find him! Let's wander across the drive and I'll introduce the two of you. He might not have a lot to say though ...*

I pour myself a drink and down it in three mouthfuls, then pour another.

I'm not going to give Bailee the info she wants on Davies. The second she goes back to the station with it, the police are going to head over there, find him missing, find all that blood and start asking her questions about who tipped her off. They're going to start wondering if the person who told her had anything to do with Davies's disappearance. And they're going to start hassling Charmaine. I don't have much faith she won't crack under pressure, and her story, as we already agreed, would never stand up. I need to figure out who the murderer really is before that happens.

I take my drink to the computer, sit and stare at the blank screen. Davies's killer had been at a party with him before murdering him, which means he's got to be part of that group. And if Summer's murder was his special event, then he's got to be the one calling himself the Spider.

It should be simple enough. I just need to get on to that site, run through all the members in a process of elimination until I figure out which one he is. The spyware I infected his computer with allowed me to see Davies log in to the site several times and I know how, but it's a risk. If the so-called Spider is online when I enter, he's going to know I can't really be Doc. Maybe they all know he's dead.

What the hell.

I double-check that all my internet security is running, then I log in and reach the homepage. There are several recent forum threads, and I don't have to look any further to see the explosion of chatter about the Spider's latest video. There are several links to it on the threads. For some it's next level, for others it brings back memories. All seem to think the hundred-dollar viewing cost is substantial— these arseholes are the epitome of cheap and nasty—and someone is wondering if Summer Edgely is one of the new girls that had recently started attending parties. I click on that particular thread. Someone called Tumbleseed is sure she gave him a blow job, another thinks that, nah, the girl he remembers was taller, her hair darker. Another member argues the girl at the parties was definitely Summer, because she'd told him her name before allegedly doing something I have trouble believing he's not making up as he goes along. I skim through their speculation on whether Summer was taken from the party or she got back in whatever van they're talking about at the end of the night. No one seems to be sure.

So okay, Summer was probably there, but these particular arseholes know nothing about who the Spider is or what he'd had planned. I click on a link to another thread as a chat window pops up.

Rocketman69: Hey, Doc. Was beginning to wonder what happened to you.

I take a breath and prepare to play Doc, calling to mind any relevant personal info I can recall about Rocketman69 to smooth over the conversation while I read a bit more. I manage to fool him for about fifteen minutes while I note down the members I can find along with any scraps of information they let slip about themselves. I'm making slow but steady progress when a new chat screen pops up.

Victor Rheus: Who are you?

'Oh, right, Vic-tor-ri-ous. Funny.' But this guy is onto me, and that's not funny. He knows I'm not Davies. I forgo my members search. As no one else has blinked an eye at my presence, I'm guessing my hunt for the so-called Spider has been much easier than I thought it was going to be. So now what?

My fingers hover over the keyboard, ready to shut down. I've discovered what I wanted to know. I have a screen name. I still haven't got a clue who he is, what he looks like or where he lives, but I can hardly ask him outright. My best bet would be to jump back on later when Victor's gone, see if he gives anything away about himself in the threads like Davies had. My finger twitches. I hesitate. Because what if he thinks the cops are onto the group and the site shuts down? What if I can't find it again? The adrenaline is pumping through me while time ticks on. I refuse to believe that this guy is anything other than a phoney using Biddle's alias.

He's no Spider but he's still a child rapist and a murderer, and I need to get him on both Davies's and Summer's murders. If I can do that, Charmaine is off the hook. And as long as no one ever figures out I took the body, so am I. It's ambitious. 'And probably stupid,' I warn myself out loud. But maybe I'll get some sleep, some work done without Summer's petrified face—or Biddle's sleazy one—haunting me.

My fingers resume their hovering while I think of something to say. I need to become a member of this group. It's the only way I'm going to get all the information I need.

Doc: Okay, you got me. I'm not Doc. I'm a good mate of his. But, man, he's gonna be pissed that I told you. He said it's the one thing I wasn't supposed to do.

Victor Rheus: You're lying.

Doc: I'm just looking for him, okay? I can't reach him and I was hoping someone might know where he is.

Victor Rheus: By pretending to be Doc?

Doc: Maybe I just wanted to take a look at a couple of the videos first. I knew you guys would kick me off once you found out I wasn't him. He shared some party videos with me and said he'd help get me in. Now he's not answering his phone. Not answering his door.

There's an extended pause before another message comes through.

Victor Rheus: Doc wouldn't have shared party videos.

Doc: Yeah, he did. Along with some other pretty epic shit.

Victor Rheus: Like what?

I think back to what was on Davies's computer.

Doc: Vintage Spider stuff.

Victor Rheus: Bullshit.

I pull up my videos. I want to offer to send him one with a nasty little RAT attached, but this guy's way too jumpy to be giving out email addresses. Instead I attach a photo to a new thread. Tell him to go look. A moment later he's back.

Victor Rheus: Where'd you get that?

Doc: He has them saved on a laptop.

He leaves the chat without answering and I'm worried I've blown it. Rocketman69 is still waiting for a response so I get back to him before leaving. I'll pop back in later, hope Victor looks me up.

As I stretch back in my seat and contemplate my probable insanity, my phone rings and I answer it distractedly. 'Yeah?'

'This is Constable McGinley from Woy Woy police. I'm calling to let you know we've located your car.'

I sit up straight in my chair, not sure whether to be relieved or very nervous. 'Really?'

'It was dumped on a back road at Kincumber. We've gone over it for prints and it's ready for collection.'

'Ah, okay. Great. Where do I pick it up?'

I get the information I need and end the call, then I'm straight over to Dawny's. There's a car in the drive, which is strange. Dawny never has friends over. I almost don't knock but I want to know.

'Well?' I ask when she answers the door. 'How did you do it this time?'

'Do what, dear?'

'My car has been found.'

'Has it? Wonderful! Let's go get it.' Before I can object, Dawny's clutching her handbag. 'Have you called a taxi?'

'I can't get it until tomorrow.'

'Oh, well. Is everything all right?' Her gaze sweeps over my face. 'You sound a bit snappy.'

'Actually . . .' I almost tell her about Bailee, about the situation, because who else can I talk to about it? But there's a noise from inside that sounds a bit like a cough and she cuts me off.

'Tell me tomorrow, dear, when we pick up your car. My show's about to start on the telly. I do like *The Chaser*, don't you? Bye-bye now.'

'Sure, Dawny,' I tell the door. 'See ya.'

'Strange, strange, strange,' I mutter as I head back inside. I heave out a tired breath and acknowledge that the whole day, really, has been strange. And because I'm in all this up to my eyeballs now, I jump back online and use the link I found on the forum site to pull up the full version of Summer's video.

A moment later, I'm welcomed to the Spider's Web.

CHAPTER SIXTEEN

Finn glanced at the time as Rachael walked past, stifled a yawn. Almost five. 'Hey, you want a coffee?'

She smiled. 'Yeah. That would be ...' Her phone rang. She checked the number. He saw the surge of nerves and knew a moment before she announced it to the room. 'This is our guy! Everyone ready?'

Finn held his breath while Jim sprang to action and the rest of the room dropped into deathly silence. Rachael was white, her phone clasped in a death grip. On Jim's nod, she answered the call, hit speaker.

'This is Detective Inspector Langley.'

'I caught the morning headline.'

'Which one?'

There was a low chuckle. 'Let's not play games.'

'But the Spider loves to play games. Always did.'

'And you were never one to lie to the public. I guess we've both changed. As for this rude little reporter and his nasty words, what are we going to do about that?'

'They weren't his words, they were mine. He was supposed to quote me.'

'Yours? Rachael, you disappoint me. Why would you do that?'

'Because I knew your ego wouldn't stand for it. That you'd call. And I wanted to talk to you again.'

'Nicely played. But you don't really believe those things you said.'

'Which ones? That you're desperate for attention, that you suffer from a mental illness or that you're mildly stupid?'

His sharply indrawn breath was audible. 'It's important to remain polite. It's a reflection on oneself. Speaks of character.'

'You really want to speak to me about character?'

'I'll do more than that.' In the background a door squeaks open. Humming. Muffled bursts of it in differing tones. 'I'm sure you've got a location on me by now. I have something to take care of before you arrive. Oh, and Rachael, I hope our little chat was worth it.'

The phone line went dead.

'He's in Wyong,' Jim called out. '142 West Hammond St. Residential address belonging to ... wait. That's Rick Burrow's home address.'

'Contact Wyong police,' Finn said. 'Let's get people there now and eyes on traffic cams.' Rachael's hand gripped his sleeve when he would have moved. 'What's wrong?'

'You heard that humming sound in the background? I think our POI had someone with him, maybe gagged.'

Strain marred her features. 'Debbie did you get hold of Rick Burrow earlier?'

'He didn't pick up. I left a message.'

'Let's go,' Finn said.

'We're already too late,' Rachael whispered, voice taut.

'Claxton! Send an ambulance out to that address along with the police,' Finn called over his shoulder and grabbed his keys. 'Rachael, let's go!'

*

When they pulled up outside the modest weatherboard house a grim-faced officer appeared, his badge claiming him to be Constable Willis. 'He's gone,' he told them solemnly. 'House is clear, victim is in the kitchen. Just a warning. It's not pretty.'

'Thank you,' Finn said, then, when Rachael ploughed ahead: 'No, you don't. Wait for me.'

'Who's the boss?' she reminded him, but the fact she let him enter the house first spoke of how upset she was. She was going to blame herself and there was nothing he could say to talk her out of it.

He stepped inside, through a small lounge room and past another officer towards the kitchen. He saw the blood first, the body as he rounded the corner. He'd seen something like this only once before. A rage killing that had left the secret boyfriend of a married woman almost unrecognisable. This was worse. He felt as though he'd stepped onto the set of some B-grade slasher movie. Rick Burrow's upper torso had been destroyed. Around what was left of his neck was a message.

I NEEDED A LESSON IN MANNERS.

'Oh my God,' Rachael said in a voice that cracked at the edges.

'You don't need to be in here.'

'Finn.' And there it was, the 'don't mess with me' tone.

'What? You don't.'

He saw the deep breath, watched her expression turn from shock back to homicide detective.

'Are forensics on their way?' she asked the officer inside.

'About a half-hour off.'

'We need to establish a crime scene, talk to neighbours, see if anyone saw anything.'

'I'll take care of it,' Finn said as he followed her back outside to the sound of sirens. He called Jim. 'Anything on that phone?'

'It's off again. No luck. Hold on.' The phone was muffled while Jim spoke to someone else.

'I don't have all day, Jim,' Finn reminded him mildly after a minute had passed.

'Sorry, detective. Superintendent O'Hanlon was on the other line. Homicide's being flooded with calls.'

'What about?'

'It seems like every news outlet in the country has been sent one of the emails I'm sending you now.'

'Rach!' Finn called and gestured her over. 'Ed said we need to see this. It's just been sent to the media.'

The email came through on his phone. 'It's from the same untraceable email address that sent Rick the tip-off,' Rachael noted.

Attached was a video, which opened to show Rick Burrow bound to the chair, gag down around his neck. Fear held his eyes wide and reddened his face, soaked his collar with sweat. His mouth shook. 'The Spider would like everyone to know that Rachael Langley got it wrong,' he said, words tumbling out in a trembling mess while his eyes tracked as though reading from a script. 'The Spider is still free and he killed Summer Edgely. There'll be more girls, more victims. And I was rude and nasty for writing those lies in the newspaper.' A flash of the Cheshire Cat grin from the video of Summer, then the camera was back on Burrow. His already wide eyes turned to saucers. 'No, please! I'm sorry. I—' The camera went black while the sounds of a man being murdered filled the room.

'Christ,' Finn said. He put the phone in his pocket and walked away. He needed a minute. 'I wonder why he spared us the vision?'

'He wanted to ensure he wasn't seen on camera,' Rachael replied.

'And that video has just done the rounds. We thought the fallout from the paper was going to be big.'

'I have to talk to Ed,' Rachael said, 'and get back to the station, deal with this.'

'Yeah,' he said. 'Take the car, I'll wait for Van Zettan.'

*

By the time Finn was able to disentangle himself for the evening he was ready for a beer and sleep—provided he'd be able to close his eyes without seeing the ruined body of Burrow behind them long enough to pass out. He made it to his apartment a little after seven. It wasn't a flash place, but it was the best he could afford after the divorce and comfortable enough, with a small balcony that had a partial view over Brisbane Water. Somewhere to breathe. Maybe he'd sit out there with that pre-bed beer and be grateful he was alive.

He unlocked his door and went in. Tossed his wallet and phone on the kitchen bench.

'Dad?'

He spun, knocking his wallet from its resting place. 'Ava! What are you doing here?'

She stood in her bedroom doorway with a small backpack over her shoulder, the spare key to his apartment in one hand, an iPad in the other.

'Are you okay? Where's your mother?'

Ava looked sheepish. 'I got Tabitha's mum to drop me off.'

'But your mum knows you're here, right?

Ava's mouth twisted into a grimace. 'Not ... exactly.'

Oh hell. 'She'll be frantic.'

The grimace crumpled. He knew that look well. She was angry, but also close to tears. 'No, she won't. She and Chris Wilson's dad Louis went out.' The way she pronounced Louis left him in no doubt Louis was the latest love interest, and he could feel himself getting pissed off. He was pretty sure he wasn't going to like what he was about to hear.

'And ...'

'And Louis is coming back to stay the night afterwards— again—and it's always weird. Mum said if I didn't like it I could stay at Tabitha's but her big brother picks on me and the bed is uncomfortable. So I got a ride here this arvo thinking I could stay with you but I didn't realise how long you were going to be.'

He sighed heavily. 'Why didn't you call me?'

'You said I could come over whenever I wanted! Besides, I didn't have my phone.'

The phone that had cost him a fortune. 'Why not? Av, it's there so if there's an emergency you can use it.'

'Mum had to borrow it cause hers broke.'

He couldn't believe this! Anger rose in his chest, making the words come out more harshly than they should have. 'She took your phone?'

Ava nodded silently as tears trickled down her cheeks.

What was Vivienne thinking? With a silent curse, he stepped close and wrapped her in a hug.

Ava squeezed him back, sniffed. 'Can I stay with you just for tonight? I hate it at home.'

'Of course you can stay here. You're staying here.'

'Thanks, Dad.' She stepped back, face teary, but smiling. 'I'm starving.'

He needed to call Vivienne, let her know. And did he even have any food in the fridge suitable for dinner? 'Why don't you jump online, order us pizza?'

Ava's eyes lit up. 'Yes, please!'

He walked out of the apartment and dialled Ava's phone. Vivienne answered just as he was about to hang up.

'What, Finn?'

'I thought you might like to know where your daughter is.'

'What? She's at Tabitha's. What are you on about?'

'She's here. She's staying with me tonight.'

'Like hell she is! It's a school night!'

'And yet Tabitha's place is okay?' he shot back. 'She doesn't want to be there, and she damn well needs better from her mother than to be palmed off on a school friend so you can go out partying with your latest fling!'

There was a loaded silence, deadly quiet, before Vivienne's voice came through. 'Don't you dare judge me! You were never home. And I never knew when you would be—or if you'd come home at all. You put the job first. That's why we split!'

'Yes, that's right, it's all my fault.' He felt his temper spike another notch. 'And going to work to support my family while you were at home with our daughter is a lot different from going out partying!'

'I'm not partying!' There was a pause then a quiet sigh. 'It's a school fundraiser, for heaven's sake. And I'm allowed to have a personal life, Finn. Ava's got her nose out of joint because she doesn't like Louis, but he's not a fling. I gave her the option of staying at Tabitha's so she'd be supervised while I was out and I'd have a chance to talk to her about all this tomorrow when he wasn't around.'

'Okay.' He pressed his fingers to his eyes, told himself to calm down. 'Okay. Maybe I overreacted.'

'You're working that case, aren't you?' Vivienne said quietly. 'That dead kid in the water. I saw Rachael on the telly.'

'Yeah. Summer.'

There was a sigh. 'Look, keep Ava there tonight. I'll collect her in the morning.'

'She has her uniform. I'll drop her at school and tell her you'll pick her up. But could you give her back her phone?'

'Fine. And yes, I'll give it back. I took it because I knew I could call her on Tabitha's mother's phone while I was out, but I was worried if she needed me at the function she wouldn't be able to contact me because she dropped mine a few days ago. It's in getting the screen repaired.'

'I really overreacted,' he admitted.

'It's fine. Bye, Finn.'

'Dad?' he heard through the crack in the door.

He ended the call. 'Out here, sweetie,' he said as casually as he could. 'I just had to let your mum know you're okay.'

'Oh.' The smile became hesitant. 'What did she say?'

'She's happy for you to stay tonight. She's going to talk to you about Louis tomorrow.'

Ava looked relieved, then a scowl that nearly made it to her face when he mentioned Louis was wrangled into a small smile. 'Okay then. I ordered the pizza and thickshakes.'

'Then I guess we'd better check out Netflix and find ourselves a movie.'

CHAPTER SEVENTEEN

Thursday, March 11

Rachael sat at her desk, elbows bent, her hands holding up her head as she stared at a pile of paperwork. A knock on the door had her lifting her eyes from the words swimming in front of them. A moment of pleasure shimmied through her. 'Ed!'

'I called by your motel on my way in, then when you weren't there wondered where else would you be at this time of the morning.'

'I like to get in before the rush. And I don't suppose you missed the chaos outside the station? Media have been beating the doors down since half-past six.'

'I noticed. Here, I bought us these.' Ed held up a brown paper bag. 'Toasties from down the street.'

'Thanks, what are you doing here?'

'Thought you could use the support.'

'I'm fine.'

'I'm gathering you've seen the news this morning?'

'No. I'm making a new habit of avoiding it.'

'Then you won't want to see these.'

Ed dropped three morning papers down in front of her. THE SPIDER RETURNS, DYING MAN INNOCENT? and REPORTER PAYS THE ULTIMATE PRICE were plastered across the front pages.

'Let me guess,' she said. 'They're all about how I put the wrong man away and now it's my fault Summer and Burrow are dead.'

'Not this one.' Ed tapped on THE SPIDER RETURNS. 'It raises questions. This guy's not making any sensationalist claims or going for the cops-are-crap angle. To be honest, it's not a bad article.'

'And the other ones?'

'One nasty claim about a police cover-up threatening the lives of everyone's daughters, while going for the injustice angle with a picture of Biddle looking three parts dead in a hospital bed. The other all about responsible journalism.'

'He was a whole lot less than three parts dead when we saw him. Older, tired, maybe a bit drawn, but would I trust him not to run the hundred-yard dash if an opportunity to escape presented itself? No. And has everyone forgotten he's a child predator?' Rachael rubbed at the beginnings of a headache. 'But I get it. It's out there and it's going to be a shit fight from here on in.'

'And ... I'm afraid I have some more bad news.'

'Don't say the court ban's been lifted on the media using that video?'

'No. They can use what he said, but the video is out of the question.'

'Then I'm almost too afraid to ask, but go on.'

'Biddle's lawyers have lodged an appeal against his conviction.'

'Well, they didn't waste any time.'

'It's premature. Even if it's granted, you know how hard it is to get a conviction overturned.'

'But you're worried. Why?'

'You know me too well. I've had our fabulous premier on the phone demanding answers. He won his seat on promises of law and order. I think he'd like nothing more than to discover a miscarriage of justice and be in charge of seeing it resolved while getting a dangerous child killer off the street. He's already making promises to rush the appeal through, should it be granted.'

'I can't worry about dickheads on power trips. I have to focus on finding this guy.'

'And how's that going?'

Rachael sighed. 'A group of older men have been putting on parties for underage girls. Mostly street kids by the sound of it. Alcohol, drugs, food, transport. And they've been going on for who knows how long. The kids get picked up and dropped off at a location that changes each week. They're plied with drugs and alcohol and encouraged to … play to the crowd, if you like. Summer was going regularly. She was last seen heading off to the latest one.'

'So you think the Spider has infiltrated this group and is using it to choose his victims.'

'It looks like it. Though Summer was a client of Bailee Kensington's, which is a pretty big coincidence.'

'Could be. And the only way you're going to know if he's targeting Bailee's clients, or if one of Bailee's clients just happened to be at the party, is when he takes his next victim.'

'You've hit the shittiest nail on the head. The next party will be held this weekend and we don't have a clue how to stop it. Our POI has told us he's going to strike again and I can't stop him. I'm going on camera at nine to warn the public, plead with kids not to go to the parties, for all the good that will do. And Bailee's informing all her clients.'

He walked around behind her, circled his thumbs into her shoulders. 'Rach, if you feel too connected to this case, perhaps someone else should take over.'

'Who? And no, I don't want anyone else taking over. I think the connection I have with this POI might prove valuable. We've established a dialogue. We don't want to lose that. Until I'm booted off this case, I'm sticking.'

'No one's booting you off the case.'

'Not yet. Wait until everyone's had a chance to decide I'm incompetent. I was sure, Ed. I was so damn sure Biddle was the Spider. But now I'm second-guessing everything.'

'What really bugs you and has all along is that Biddle never truly fit the profile. He should have proudly taken credit for his work, but he didn't admit to anything.'

'He did to his victims.'

'Scared little girls?'

'Why would Lexi draw him like a spider unless he'd admitted who he was?'

'I can't talk to you,' Lexi said from the same spot on the same bench in the playground. 'I got in trouble last time.'

Rachael felt the guilt like a hot poker. She wasn't sure why she thought the department could investigate quietly without the parents having a chance to take it out on their daughter. She'd been so sure there was a case against them she hadn't thought it would be a problem.

'I'm sorry you got in trouble. I want to help you.'

'No, you don't.' Lexi's eyes were devastatingly bleak. 'You don't even want to be here.'

'That's not true. What makes you say that?'

'You keep looking at your watch and you don't sit still. Either you don't want to be here or you have to be somewhere else more important.'

'I do have to be somewhere else, but you know why I'm not there? Because I think talking to you is more important.'

That was met with a long, assessing look that would have done any detective proud. 'But your boss doesn't think so.'

'You're a very observant, very perceptive young lady.'

Lexi's eyes refocus on the ground. 'That's how come Mrs Carson says I can draw good pictures.'

'I bet you can. You had a sketchbook with you last time I was here. Mrs Carson said you like to draw.'

Lexi looked at her out of the corner of her eye. 'Do you really shoot people?'

'No, I've never had to shoot anyone.'

'You don't look like a pig.'

She smiled. 'Do your parents think the police are pigs?'

'My daddy said so.'

'And he told you we lie and shoot people.'

A nod.

'That's because your daddy doesn't want you to talk to me.' She struggled to say the word 'daddy' without contempt leaching into her voice. Her heart was breaking for this little girl. Rachael had to get her away. Had to make her safe. 'Lexi, I can help you. But you need to tell me what he's doing, tell me about the videos. If you do that, I can take you somewhere safe, right now.'

Lexi's pale face crumpled. 'I can't.'

'Why not?'

'I have to look after Bailee. And he said you can't prove anything. And if I go and you can't prove it and I have to go back, he'll kill me with his gun and then no one will look after Bailee.'

What was it with this guy and guns? The anger she felt towards this bastard was only outdone by the anguish she felt for the child. She wanted to tell her she wouldn't have to go back, but after last time, could she be sure? Not without proof. 'Lexi, do you think you could safely bring one of Daddy's videos to school and give it to Mrs Carson without him knowing?'

Lexi shook her head, eyes panicked. 'No!'

'Okay, okay, forget that,' she said quickly. 'Do you know where he keeps them?'

'He sells them to Mr Biddle.'

She filed the name away to run checks on when she got back to the station. 'Who's Mr Biddle?'

'The man that helps him make the videos.' The bell rang and Lexi looked around nervously. 'I have to go. I can't be late for the bus.'

'Okay.' Rachael scrambled for anything else she could think of that might persuade Lexi to give her something else to work with. 'Lexi, you're really good at drawing pictures, right? Would you draw me a picture of Mr Biddle?'

Lexi hesitated then nodded. 'Bye,' she said before running away.

'Lexi was a brave little girl,' Ed said, sensing her thoughts, 'but she was only a little girl. A man reciting a spider poem to her would have been enough to have her seeing him that way. Drawing him that way. Biddle admitted he was part of that group, that he was fascinated with the Spider, that he told the girls about the poem. They weren't the only kids involved to have heard it.'

'What are you saying?'

'With all the building evidence, I think we unfortunately might have been outplayed. But look, we all agreed at the time. The courts convicted him. I promise you, there's going to be no comeback on you over this.'

'That's bullshit and we both know it.'

'No official comeback. Biddle's still a monster, Rach. Come on, eat your breakfast.'

Debbie appeared at the door. 'Morning, inspector. Oh, I didn't realise you had company.'

'Debbie, this is Superintendent Ed O'Hanlon.'

'Very nice to meet you, sir.' To Rachael, she said, 'I was going to take your breakfast order but ...'

'All sorted, thanks.'

'Okay. Also, CCTV footage has come in overnight from the time and location Summer went missing. Jim's just arrived to take a look and Bailee Kensington is here to drop in the information you were after on Janie Miller.'

'Great, Debbie. Thank you. I'll be out in sec. Ask Bailee to hang around. I'd like her to look at the CCTV footage with us.'

'Yes, inspector.'

'Picked up a little protégé, have you?' Ed asked when Debbie left.

'She has the makings of a good detective, that one. Come and I'll introduce you to Bailee.'

'Sure but.' Ed held up half a toastie. 'One bite. At least. Or I'm barricading the door.'

She snatched the toastie with a grin and took a bite, took it with her as she left her office. 'Morning, Bailee,' she said.

Bailee looked up from her phone. 'Rachael, hi.'

'This is Superintendent Ed O'Hanlon.'

'Hi.' Bailee shook his hand.

'It's lovely to meet you, Bailee. We appreciate your assistance with this case.'

'Anything I can do.'

'Do you have a few minutes?' Rachael asked.

'Of course. Debbie said something about CCTV?'

'Yep, follow me.'

Jim already had the footage on screen as they approached. 'What have we got?' Rachael asked him.

'A group of nine girls hanging by the corner of the station. I believe that's Summer there, and Izzy's behind her.'

Rachael looked closer at the grainy black-and-white images. 'I agree. Bailee, can you take a look at this and tell me if you recognise anyone else?'

'Of course.' Bailee moved closer and said nothing for several seconds, then slowly shook her head. 'I can't be absolutely sure because of the quality, but I don't recognise them from this. They're not mine.'

'Morning,' Finn said, entering the room.

'Morning,' Rachael said. 'We're going over the footage from the party pick-up.' Then to Jim she said, 'Play on.'

Jim hit the button.

'Here comes the van,' Rachael noted.

'There's some sort of design on the front there,' Ed said, trying to make it out. 'Looks like flames, maybe?'

A thin man with broad shoulders jumped out of the driver's seat. He was wearing a dark hoodie and it was impossible to see his face. A streetlight reflecting off the windscreen wasn't helping with vision quality. He went around behind the van, and a few seconds later he was back in the driver's seat. Then the van was pulling away and Izzy was left standing alone on the roadside. She looked around as though nervous before walking away, hands in pockets, her head swinging from side to side as she checked for any threats.

'We can't get a good look at our POI,' Rachael said, disappointed. 'But the plates are visible. They match Izzy's account. What about later? Do we see them come back?'

Jim sped through the footage and then stopped, rewound. Played. 'There it is. Just after two.'

Rachael watched a group of girls get out of the van. Counted them. 'They're all there except Summer.'

'Jim, can you make the pattern on the van any clearer?' Bailee asked.

'Possibly, but it'll take me some time. Interesting though ...' He flicked open another window. 'I've been working on the footage the old guy gave you from where Summer's body was found.' He showed them a dark, pixellated image of a vehicle. 'We knew it was a van. Dark coloured. But here, where we can make out a figure carrying something, a car goes over the bridge and the headlights partially illuminate the area and ...' He stops the footage. 'I thought this was a weird reflection from tree branches on the hood but it could be the same pattern we're seeing on this footage from the station. Flames, perhaps.'

'You think it's the same van?' Rachael asked.

'Could be.'

'Black van, purple flames.' Bailee dragged in a breath and raked her fingers through her hair, held them there for a moment. Then she turned to Rachael. 'Sounds a lot like Cody Ellis's van.'

Rachael felt a surge of hope. They needed a decent break. 'Who's Cody Ellis?'

'Cody is Janie Miller's boyfriend.'

'The Janie that reported the parties?'

'Yes.'

Rachael walked to the far side of the room and pulled Izzy's sketch from the board. 'Bailee, could this be Cody?'

Bailee walked over and took the sketch, studied it. 'It's possible ... Yes, I think so.'

'Where can we find him?' Rachael asked.

'Wait. Cody wouldn't have had anything to do with Summer's murder.' Bailee's face screwed up in confusion. She stared at the floor while she held some sort of internal debate. 'He's troubled, yes, but he's a pushover. One of those kids that goes along to get along. It gets him in trouble. Quite a bit, sure. But for stupid stuff. Petty theft, a bit of vandalism. He's everyone's scapegoat. A follower, not a leader.'

'Maybe you don't know him as well as you think you do.'

Bailee's eyes flashed. 'As part of the support network we offer the kids on our books, we have meet-ups, fish and chips on the waterfront or the occasional movie on cheap day.

It gets the kids together, so they can talk, offer each other support, know they're not alone in what they're going through. We've found it also encourages them to talk to us, be more upfront about what's really going on at home. Cody often comes along with Janie. He's not a bad kid.'

'Was Summer part of this group?'

'She came sometimes. Probably more often than not.'

'I wonder if Cody could be issuing invitations,' Rachael said to Finn. 'If he has access to the at-risk girls and develops a friendly relationship with them it would be straightfoward to pick the right ones for the parties.'

'No one I spoke to mentioned that,' Bailee said. 'But maybe they've been warned to keep quiet too.'

'One way to find out,' Finn said. 'Where can we find him?'

'Not sure. Let me make a phone call.'

While Bailee went off to do that, Rachael looked at Finn. 'Get held up this morning?'

He filled her in on Ava and Vivienne. 'I feel like a dick for being so fast to overreact.'

'Ava's always been a daddy's girl. She's not going to appreciate another man hanging around.'

Finn nodded. 'I guess I was unfair to Viv.'

'Give yourself a break. This case is getting to all of us. And as for Vivienne, she would have known Ava would have been happier at your place last night. But for some reason she's so threatened by the relationship you two have that she'd rather discourage it. She's also living in your house for nothing while you're paying her full child support, as well as for the majority of Ava's stuff. Viv only needs to work part time while I honestly don't know how you can afford to live. I hardly think you're the king of unfair.'

'It's so she can be home for Ava. You raised me after Mum died. You know how hard it is.'

'And making ends meet wasn't always easy. A lot of single parents do it tough. Really tough. I just don't happen to think Viv is one of them. And I have to say it, I can't see her as P&F material.'

'Might be the new boyfriend—the father of some kid at school.'

Bailee reappeared. 'I have Cody's mother's address. He often parks the van in the backyard. There's alley access off the main street.'

'Let's start there then,' Rachael said.

'I'm coming with you,' Bailee said.

'Stay here,' Rachael said. 'We're going to bring him in for a chat.'

'But—'

'If you want to do something, maybe find him some legal help.'

'Are we sure he's going to need legal? If he cooperates …'

'Yes, Bailee, he's going to need a lawyer.'

'Okay. I'll contact Legal Aid. They have a children's legal service.'

'Children's?' Finn asked.

'He's only sixteen,' Bailee said almost defensively.

'I can feel sorry for this guy too,' Rachael said, 'but I feel a lot sorrier for Summer. For Izzy, who we just saw walking home at night on her own and who could just as easily have met a similar fate as Summer before making it back.'

'I know,' Bailee said. 'I agree, I … some of these kids, they never have a chance.'

'And yet look at you,' Rachael reminded her. 'Let's go, Finn.'

*

Lynda Ellis's house was an untidy fibro box set on a quarter-acre block on the edge of town. Tall grass fought for space with thistles, a pile of large garbage bags, and other assorted rubbish in the front yard, which was framed by a simple roll top wire fence. Rachael led the way along a narrow, overgrown concrete path and stepped up onto the tiny front porch to knock on the door.

'Are we sure someone lives here?' Finn asked. But the drag of the door opening brought his attention back from the roof, which looked ready to fall in on them.

A spindly woman with sagging skin and sharp eyes looked them up and down. 'Cops?' she guessed, clearing her throat when it rasped.

'Yes, hello,' Rachael said. 'I'm Detective Inspector Rachael Langley and this is Detective Sergeant Finn Carson. Are you Mrs Ellis?'

'I'm her. What's he been up to then?'

'Would you mind if we came in? We were hoping Cody might be home.'

'Doesn't live in the house. Tells me he can't stand the smell from the dog or the noise from the telly. Might be out the back though. Parks his van there most nights. I know that's here, so he probably is too. Hold on, I'll have a look.' As she moved away she grabbed the remote to the television and clicked off the noise.

Rachael looked around the kitchen and lounge area while a small mixed-breed dog, grey and stiff from age, sniffed at their shoes with a half-hearted wag of its tail.

'Hey, buddy.' Finn gave the dog a light pat, which Rachael thought was brave considering it really did stink.

Two pantry doors hung open, revealing empty shelves. A little fridge hummed loudly in the corner.

'Yeah, he's here,' Mrs Ellis confirmed and yanked open a glass sliding door to an equally depressing backyard. In it sat the black van from the CCTV. One side appeared to be open. 'Oi! Codes!'

'What?' a voice called back. A moment later a head appeared out of the open door. Cody's eyes rested on Rachael and Finn and he stilled.

'Cops wanna talk to ya!'

Sensing he was going to bolt, Rachael stepped around Mrs Ellis and out onto the long grass. 'Hi Cody,' she said with a friendly smile. 'I'm Detective Inspector Rachael Langley and this is Detective Sergeant Finn Carson. Could we have a quick chat with you?'

'What about?'

'We're talking to everyone who knew Summer Edgely. Hoping someone might have seen or heard something that could help us with the investigation. Only take a minute.'

'I didn't know her.'

'She was in Bailee Kensington's youth group. You were there sometimes, right?' She was within two steps of him now and Finn was right beside her.

'Yeah but I didn't ... I mean I knew who she was but I didn't ... hold on ...'

He stepped back inside the van, turned away from them for a second before turning back, one arm hidden from sight. 'I didn't know her. I can't help ya.'

'What's behind your back, Cody?' Rachael asked.

'Nothin'. I said I can't help ya!'

'Cody, show me your hands.'

'Fuck this,' Cody said, holding out a knife in a trembling hand. 'I said I can't help ya!'

He pushed past her so hard and fast, Rachael sat on her butt on the damp grass. She looked up to see Cody climbing over the back fence.

Finn was at her side in a second. 'Rachael, are you—'

'Get after him!' she instructed, glad Cody hadn't lunged with the knife rather than his free hand. As Finn followed Cody, she dusted off her hands and requested backup on the radio.

'I'm so sorry.' Mrs Ellis's voice sounded behind her as Rachael swept at the grass on her suit.

'It's not your fault, Mrs Ellis, I'm fine.' Mrs Ellis looked at that moment so sad, so helpless, that Rachael's heart went out to her. 'I really am fine, he just panicked.'

'Can I ask what he's done?'

'Just gotten himself in a bit of trouble.'

'Always doing that. Thought I raised him right. Did my best. But there was never much here for him to do, so he was always out on the street looking for fun, you know? Kept getting in the way of the wrong people.'

'Why don't you go inside and sit down while I help Finn find him? Then we can sort all this out.'

Mrs Ellis nodded. 'Right then. I'll be inside. I-I'll wait.'

Rachael went after Finn, only to find him coming back in. 'Lost him. Went over a fence and that was that.'

Rachael grinned. 'Getting old?'

'I'm not sixteen with the leaping skills of an antelope that's for sure.'

'We'll get a few patrols around, keep a lookout. In the meantime, I'm calling for this van to be towed to be examined for evidence.' Her face fell. 'Best go ask Mrs Ellis a few more questions about her son. Ask her if there's anywhere he's likely to turn up. Poor thing. I feel so damn sorry for her.'

'Yeah, me too.' Finn stared back at the house. 'It looks like life's been tough enough.'

CHAPTER EIGHTEEN

I'm staring at the car in disbelief. This is not mine. Oh, it's the same make and model, same colour, but it is absolutely not my car.

'Everything all right?' the police officer asks me.

'Um. Yeah. I guess I just ... didn't expect to see it again.'

'You're lucky. Mostly once they're gone, they're gone, or found burnt out or written off. There was another one of these reported stolen yesterday.'

'Another blue Civic?' My eyes slide to Dawny.

'Yeah. They're quite a common car on the road. Makes them easier targets. I guess perhaps they didn't like the condition of yours and found a better one.'

'I can't for the life of me understand why,' I reply as I look at the beaten-up exterior. There's some stupid fluffy animal hanging from the rear-view mirror and I have never ever on purpose listened to the radio station advertised on the mostly peeled off and faded out bumper sticker.

'It's a bad idea to leave your key in it though, even if the car is in your driveway.'

'I didn't—' But there the key is, in the ignition. On an unfamiliar pink lips keyring. 'Oops. Must have.'

'Well, I just need to you to sign it out and it's all yours.'

'Thanks.'

Dawny and I hop in a few minutes later and, to my surprise, the car starts and the engine runs smoothly. I leave the lot and steer the car towards home, silently preparing for the oncoming battle of wills. When I'm reasonably sure I'm ready, I begin.

'Whose car is this, Dawny?' I ask nicely.

'According to the rego plates and engine number, it's yours,' she says, flicking at the dust on the dash.

'I see.' I wonder if it's actually worth the effort of asking or better to go bang my head against a wall and hope the answers materialise behind my eyelids.

When I've pondered that for a few moments, I decide it's worth the effort. 'Just how extensive is the criminal network at your disposal?'

Dawny's 'Ha!' is short, sharp and amused. 'No need to be dramatic! And I know what you're thinking. I didn't have anything to do with stealing anyone's car.'

I can't help the glare of disbelief. 'I beg to differ.'

'I mean the one that cop was talking about. And this one doesn't have any traces of any crimes having been committed in it if things ever get sticky. You're welcome.'

That drags a smile out of me. 'I am grateful, Dawny. But I'm worried I'm going to get myself into more trouble by trying to avoid any.'

'Well don't be. Desmond is a pro at this sort of thing. It was quite nice having a reason to catch up with him.'

Uh oh. 'Wait. Who is Desmond?'

'Desmond? Oh, a bit of a blast from the past. We used to sleep together on occasion.'

'And was it his car that was in your driveway last night?'

'Well, yes, actually. Why?' Dawny asks, suddenly fascinated with the scenery.

'Because you couldn't wait to get rid of me. You've never ever rushed me out the door like that.'

'Oh, don't be so sensitive, dear. You're always welcome.'

'I knew you were up to something.' I smile slowly. 'Any reason I'm not allowed to meet Desmond?'

Dawny thinks about that for several moments before answering. 'He's a private person.'

'Okay, so how much did you tell this private person about what happened?'

'Oh, he doesn't need details, dear. Just a job to do.'

'You never cease to amaze me, Dawny.'

'Oh, stop! Quick!'

'Huh?' At the urgency in Dawny's voice I lean hard on the brake and dive off the road. 'What?' I ask a little breathlessly.

'Over there, that garden centre. They have a sale on.'

I'm lost for words. My mouth tries forming a few before I actually get anywhere. 'Garden centre? I thought there was some sort of emergency!'

'There is, now you come to mention it.'

How much more of this can I take? 'There's an emergency and you just ... forgot?' I almost don't want to ask. 'What is it?'

Dawny's look is sheepish. 'We have a slight problem with the freezer.'

Shit. 'What kind of problem?'

'Went off sometime during the night. Been going off and on for a few days. But this time I think it's carked it for good. Won't go back on.'

'Wait, is this why you wanted to salt? You said it was for eventually.'

'Right you are. As in when the freezer eventually died for good. Just wasn't as much eventually about it as I would have liked. But don't you worry. Desmond got us salt. It occurred to me some good old blood and bone might be the thing to be scattering around when we open that freezer. In case he's thawed and is a bit on the nose. You know what the Parkhursts are like. Besides, I need some pansies. Got any money on you?'

*

As I unload the fourth bag of blood and bone from the boot onto Dawny's driveway, my phone pings. It's Bailee.

Seen the news?

Before I can respond, another ping.

Never mind. I'm coming over.

Because of the news? Or to pressure me into helping with Summer's murder? I've been working on it, but I'm not getting far. Not yet. Perhaps the half-bottle of JD last night hadn't helped with clarity, but its numbing properties sure as hell helped with having to watch that video frame by frame, over and over and over. And Victor hasn't been back online, so my bid for membership hasn't progressed at all.

'You just about done on that phone, dear?' Dawny asks. She's sitting on a chair by the front door, sipping her tea.

'Yeah, sorry.' I lower my voice. 'You know, Dawny, I can't believe you somehow managed to get me a car with a boot that doesn't smell repulsive and then we put this stuff in it.'

'Blood and bone's the only thing that will mask the smell when we open that freezer,' she whispers back, copying yet somehow mocking my hushed tone.

She's good. Almost too good. 'Dawny.' I straighten and dust off my hands. 'What did you go to jail for?'

She smiles into her tea. 'Took you a while to get around to asking.'

'I generally mind my own business.'

'That's a good philosophy.'

'Right. Got it. Are we doing this now?'

Dawny hands me a shovel. It looks old enough to break if I blow on it too hard. 'Just a small circle by the driveway, about the size of a car tyre. I'll plant my pansies in it. Mix the soil with some of this, the rest can be sprinkled over the lawn and watered in.'

The old brown car I saw last night pulls in and Dawny's face brightens. 'Well, it's about time!' she calls to the man who gets out. He's about my height, but if possible he's even scrawnier than me and maybe a few years older than Dawny. He doesn't move like an old guy though, and those scrawny arms have definite sinew. He's wearing smart tan pants and a crisp checkered shirt. I can see the edge of an old tattoo under one short sleeve. He's clean shaven and his hair is neatly styled. He places a hat over it that I think is called a fedora. The first thought that comes to mind is 'gangster'.

He looks around slowly and I almost expect he'll pull out a Tommy gun at the first sign of trouble.

Apparently satisfied he's not about to be assassinated, he nods at Dawny. Then his sharp eyes land on me. 'You the hooker?' he asks and looks me up and down more with suspicion than any sort of appreciation.

'Ah …'

'Is that how we speak to friends, Desmond?' Dawny asks. Then, 'Lexi, meet Desmond.'

What do I say, exactly: It's a pleasure? Nice to meet you? It's neither of those things, exactly. Al Capone is kind of freaking me out. I settle for 'Hi'.

He nods and then stares at me.

'I'll, ah, get started on that garden for you, Dawny.'

'Thank you, dear.'

'Got your salt,' Desmond tells Dawny. He lifts the boot and starts throwing it onto the lawn.

'Wonderful! Now, Desmond, I've made a pie. It might be nicer to eat it before the task ahead, wouldn't you agree? Oh dear. Too late.'

I turn around at her disappointment and see the Parkhursts charging over.

'We saw you unloading the gardening supplies and thought you must have actually been going to fix the disaster you made of our lawn. Is that the case?' Don asks me.

'Oh sure,' I say with enthusiasm. 'I'll get right on that.'

'Good.'

'What is with the salt?' Miriam asks, nose screwed up as though it was the pool salt sitting beside the newly unloaded blood and bone that was the offensive stuff.

'Who is this lovely lady?' Desmond asks in a voice as smooth as silk. I blink in surprise at the change in him. He gives a kind of welcoming bow.

'Ohhh, I'm Miriam.'

'A beautiful name for a beautiful lady. Call me Desmond.' He extends a hand as though to shake, then pulls hers to his lips and kisses it.

Miriam blushes.

'And you, sir?' Desmond asks.

'Would prefer you let go of my wife's hand,' Don replies tersely.

'Oh.' Desmond smiles at Miriam then releases it with a flourish. 'I apologise. It's not every day one meets someone so lovely. Tell me,' he asks Miriam while I trap flies with my mouth, 'is the Marilyn look deliberate?

I'm going to throw up. But Miriam is patting her hair and lapping it up like she's lost whatever brain she had. Don is also flushed, but for an entirely different reason.

'I'd be glad to come and look at whatever problem there is with your lawn, Miriam. I'm quite the accomplished gardener.'

'Oh, that's very kind of you, Desmond.'

'No need,' Don says, taking Miriam's arm and steering her away. 'I'm sure Lexi has it under control.'

'Goodbye, Desmond!' Miriam calls with a wave as they hit their driveway. As they walk away, I see Miriam duck her head to the side. 'That was so rude!' she hisses to Don.

'So she saw the salt,' I say, because no one seems to care.

Dawny chuckles. 'All she's gonna worry about for the next week at least is how to style her hair more like Marilyn Monroe.'

Desmond scratches his head, frowns. 'Meant Manson, but whatever.'

The snigger bursts from my lips.

'You are the hooker, though, eh?' he asks me.

'I'm an escort.'

Desmond nods, his mouth forming a silent 'Ah'. Then, 'Got a spare few minutes later to escort me somewhere private?'

'Desmond, do you want to eat this pie or end up in it?' Dawny threatens.

He grumbles but follows her inside.

I'm not a menial labour type so it takes probably longer than it should to dig the tyre-sized hole in Dawny's lawn. I dump the pile of leftover green grass on the Parkhurst's dead patch. They told me I had to replace it. They didn't say with what.

Spreading blood and bone around is not fun and I don't do a great job. It ends up scattered around in clumps, some too big, some too small. But the stink is the same so I figure that will do. I chuck a bit on the Parkhursts' clump of grass too. Hopefully the stink will waft through their window for days.

I'm finishing off when Dawny and Desmond come back out.

'We're going round to take care of the freezer,' Dawny tells me. 'Go wash up if you like, help yourself to some pie.'

'Thanks.'

Desmond is inspecting my work. 'You're a shit gardener,' he tells me.

'I am, aren't I?' I flash him a smile and I almost get one back.

'You're a good hooker though, eh?'

'Desmond!' Dawny exclaims.

He tips his hat at me and I think I actually detect a hint of humour. A flash on his finger hits the light.

'You're married?' I ask before thinking.

He's looking at me funny and I'm not sure whether he thinks the question is stupid or I am for daring to ask it.

'He is,' Dawny says. 'To Catherine Delaney.'

I'm getting a vibe I should probably shut up, so 'Oh' is all I say.

'Never heard of Catherine Delaney?' Dawny asks as though astounded.

Shit. Wrong response. Now what? 'Ah ...'

'Unbelievable,' Desmond says and, with a shake of his head, he walks towards the salt, lifts the bag and heads around the back—to the freezer, I suppose.

'She was quite the accomplished killer,' Dawny tells me. 'Until they caught her.'

'I see. And you were ... friends?'

'Very close. She's a bit of an expert at disposing of bodies.'

Explains a few things. 'And yet she went to prison?'

Dawny's eyes gleamed with fun. 'They only found the last one, dear.'

Desmond collects another bag of salt and I'm still getting the look. He disappears again as Bailee drives in.

'Hi Dawny,' she says once she's out of the car. 'Getting up to mischief?'

'Oh, you have no idea.' Dawny checks with me. 'Has she?'

'No!' I blurt, then say more calmly, 'I can't imagine she does.'

'Goodo, then. Bailee, this is my friend Desmond.' Dawny introduces Desmond as he appears for his third bag.

Desmond kisses Bailee's hand. 'You a hooker too?'

'Huh? Oh. No.'

'Pity.'

Bailee really doesn't cover her distress very well. 'Um.' She looks for help.

'Ah, Dawny, I'll be back shortly to help with the next bit, okay?'

'Don't be long, dear!'

I lead Bailee to my place and go inside, get a water and hope I can rinse the taste of blood and bone from the back of my throat. 'So, what's up?' I ask before she can start quizzing me on the *Twilight Zone* episode happening over the way.

'A couple of things. One, I can't believe you didn't see the news. That reporter. The one who wrote the front-page story on the Spider being a copycat.'

'Well, someone agrees with me.'

'Yeah, he's dead. The Spider—real or otherwise—shredded him beyond recognition yesterday after making him read a statement saying he was wrong and rude and that this guy is the real Spider and he's going to take another girl soon.'

'Oh, shit.'

'No kidding!' Bailey's eyes bulge into twin saucers.

'What was two?'

'Huh?'

'You said one, blah blah dead reporter, so I'm expecting a two.'

'Right. A teen I know. Cody Ellis. Not one of mine but the boyfriend of the girl who first mentioned the parties to me. He's got a few issues but at heart I would have said he's a good guy. It looks like he's been transporting girls to and from those parties. We think his van was at the site where Summer's body was found.'

'Oh, shit,' I say again.

Bailee throws her arms out in frustration. 'I'm sure he's just gotten in over his head. He's very easily led. Rachael and Finn have gone to find him. I had to organise legal help for him.'

'Wow, what a sweetie. If you see him first, don't go playing Supernanny, all right? Walk the other way.'

'Lexi, that's not helpful.'

'I am being helpful!' I argue. 'I've known plenty of kids like that. They don't mean to get in trouble, they don't mean to cause a fuss, they don't mean to stab someone during a robbery or push someone in front of a bus while they're running from police or any of those horrible, terrible things. But it happens anyway, and you know what they'll tell you? It's never their fault, bad shit just happens to them. Good people die around them. Trust me.'

'I would have thought you of all people would have been more understanding.'

I freeze. Stare. 'Really?'

Bailee sighs and sits. 'Sorry. I didn't actually think that through. And now is probably a really bad time to ask if you've gotten anywhere with the Spider stuff?'

'I've been looking at the video,' I say tightly before deciding to let it go. 'The problem is all the data has been stripped. I've noted some basic observations, some details, but it's taking time.'

'Rachael's team is already on that,' Bailee says with more frustration. 'She has the best cyber guys in the country on it.'

'Yeah, but have they found the website yet? Downloaded the full video?'

'The website? You found the website and the full video?' Bailee asks in disbelief.

'Yeah.'

'That's huge.'

'Yeah. Hooray. The Spider's Web is back.'

'With everything happening so fast, I don't think Jim has even had a serious go at finding that yet. But Rachael assumed the Spider would bring the site back.'

'He's not the Spider and who's Jim?'

Bailee's brow lifts. 'The guy that's doing the job you should be doing. Should I see the video before I—'

'Absolutely not.' Movement catches my eye through the window and I see Dawny waving at me. I plaster a smile on my face and wave back. 'I have to finish up with Dawny but I'll send the details across to you tonight.' I'd already decided to share the Spider's Web info with Bailee. It gives nothing away on Jonathan Davies and will hopefully prove to be a distraction from his group long enough for me to do some more digging. 'Tell this Jim guy he can reach the site with the instructions I'll attach but he'll have to create an account and pay a fee to watch the video.'

'Thanks, Lex. How should I say I stumbled across this information?'

'I don't know. What do you always say?'

'It varies. But ... would it really be the end of the world to talk to Rachael for five minutes?'

'Oh please, not again.'

'You can always walk away if you don't like what she has to say.' She rushed on: 'But if you do. If you just see her and say hi, I think, I think you could work with her. Forgive her.'

Apparently former attempts to hit this on the head have been nowhere near forceful enough. So I spell it out. 'I'm not you, Bailee. I'm not the sort of person that can have any sort of working relationship with the cops. And honestly—not that I care—but I think I might be a bit of a disappointment. Rachael might think she wants to find me. She doesn't.'

'What are you talking about?'

'You have two kids, a husband, and you've started a psychology degree while juggling a career in child welfare. Your whole life screams overachiever. That's what I'm talking about.'

'I'm all of those things because you saved me,' she says quietly.

'Oh, cut it out.'

'No, I won't. You put me first. So did Rachael. Now I have a husband that does the same thing. I've had every chance you haven't. Besides, child one came with the husband so I can't take the credit there, and Rach helped me get my job. I *know* she'd help you too. She'd love the chance to be able to. She's never forgiven herself.'

'So you keep saying. The problem is, I do illegal shit. All the time. Even what I did to find the site and dig my way in was illegal, okay? I don't feel like explaining all that to the cops. And one thing will inevitably lead to another and they'll figure out I've been your source on all the other cases. That's bad news for you, right? Imagine if those arseholes have their charges dropped because we went about collecting evidence against them the wrong way?'

I see that one hit home but she frowns and shakes her head. 'I doubt—'

'Look, I'm handing you the website, the video. I'm sure Rachael and the other cops will figure it all out and save the day. In the meantime, I'll potter around back here and if I get anything else worth sharing, I'll hand it over. But I'm not talking to that woman and I really need to get back to Dawny. Okay?'

'Okay! Okay,' Bailee says before opening the door. 'Lex … Thanks.'

I wish I could believe this will be the end of it. But I very much doubt it. I say goodbye and am almost out the door when my computer pings. I pounce on it. I've left the chatroom open hoping Victor would get back to me and a quick check shows he has.

Victor Rheus: There's no videos on Doc's laptop.

He must have gone back after our last chat and taken it. I briefly wonder how he managed to get into the computer to check but it doesn't matter. Right now he thinks I've lied. I have to change that.

Doc: Then you picked up the wrong one.

I ponder if I can wrangle a membership in return for telling him where to find it. But yet again, he logs off, and is gone.

CHAPTER NINETEEN

Friday, March 12

'More stimulating reading from the press today,' Finn said, dropping into a chair. 'Honestly, we should just ask the reporters who did it. They're always so sure they know more than we do.'

'Nature of the game.'

'And the public seem to have more faith in the headlines than they do the official reports.'

'Sensationalism sells.'

He shot her an unappreciative stare. 'I want to bang heads together and you're being calmly philosophical. You know they're blaming us for Rick Burrow's murder?'

'I'm blaming us for Rick Burrow's murder,' Rachael told him. 'I knew he was inexperienced and desperate for a good story. My mistake was in believing he knew how to follow instructions. But no, he wanted more sensationalism, because, again, that's the nature of the game.'

'Speaking of Burrow, no useful forensic evidence was found at his home. There are a number of fingerprints but nothing came up for them in our system. They're probably not related to the case.'

'All that mess and nothing?' She stared into space. 'We always wondered how no forensic evidence was ever found in the original case. I suppose this is another crack in our case against this new POI being a copycat.'

'It's a lot easier these days for people to be aware of how to conceal evidence. He'll make a mistake. They always do. Eventually.' Finn got to his feet and drained his coffee.

'I have a report back on Cody Ellis's van,' Rachael said. 'Plenty of forensic evidence there including dozens of fingerprints. No matches to anyone on file, but that's not unexpected.'

'Are you still happy for me to head off and track him down this morning?'

'Yes, please. I've got Jim familiarising himself with every traffic cam around Gosford and working out major routes where we could use extra surveillance. We don't know what vehicle will be picking up kids tomorrow so we're going to have to hope the extra patrols Turner's organising will spot whatever group or groups of kids are hanging around on street corners looking like they're waiting to be picked up.'

'You're going to let them get in and follow them?'

'Not if I can help it. I'm happy to take the chance at chasing down the driver, but I don't want to do it with a vehicle full of kids. There were no seats or seatbelts in Cody's van, but there were glass bottles of alcohol. I don't have any confidence the next vehicle will be any safer. A chase like that could end in tragedy.'

'Yeah, look, I've got Ava this weekend, so I'll have to try and swap it so I can help.'

'Finn, I'm sorry. I know you need that time with her.'

'I can't let someone else's kid die so mine can sleep at my place instead of her mother's. Ava's old enough, she'll understand.'

'And Viv?'

He sighed heavily. 'Viv will remind me what a shitty father I am and then tell me it's fine.' He shrugged helplessly and kind of laughed. 'It's routine.'

'I wish there was some other way. Bailee, hi,' Rachael said when Bailee knocked on the door. 'What are you doing back here?'

'Has Jim discovered the Spider's Web yet?'

Rachael shook her head. 'Jim's been working on finding Cody Ellis. You mean the website?'

'Yep. I have the information on how to find it here and the video is on it. The full version. Apparently you have to pay in crypto to see it, though.'

'Then let's get that sorted,' Rachael said, surging to her feet.

*

The atmosphere in the strike force room was heavy, filled with an oppressive sadness and an overwhelming sense of helplessness left over from watching Summer's murder that had played out on screen in front of them. Before breaking the silence, Rachael took time to ensure she was steady, that her voice wouldn't shake, that the tears that sat behind her eyes remained there. Lodged in her chest was enough raw anger to push her through it. To lead. She just needed to rally it. Seeing the devastation, the fatigue, the defeat on the faces of her colleagues helped her bring it to the surface.

'We all knew this was going to be a tough case,' she said. 'This video wasn't comfortable for any of us to watch. All those emotions you're feeling are normal. You want to cry, cry. You want to smash something, smash it. But then you need to channel what's left into drive and motivation. Because we all know what we just saw happen to Summer is going to happen to someone else's little girl unless we catch this bastard. We need to remain focused. Let's get back to work.' Then to Jim she said, 'You do nothing else until you find something on this video to help us catch this guy.'

'Yes, inspector.'

She placed a hand briefly on Jim's shoulder because he looked like he needed someone else's strength, then he took a breath and nodded and she saw some of his normal self return.

'Bailee, my office?' When Finn sent her an enquiring glance, she nodded that he was free to follow.

'Are you going to be okay?' she asked Bailee when she sat opposite Rachael, swiping at a stray tear.

Bailee nodded. 'I knew it was bad. He's sick. No sane person could do that. Now I get why you said the Spider case is the closest you've ever come to true evil.'

'You said someone sent you this information?'

Bailee pulled herself together. 'Yep. This person has managed to uncover paedophiles online before.'

'Does this person have a name?'

Bailee hesitated. 'Yes, but they would prefer to remain anonymous.'

'Why?' Finn asked.

Bailee shrugged. 'That's just how we work.'

'Does this person have any other details on the Spider?' Rachael asked. 'Anything else that could help us?'

'Not yet. Finding content on the dark web is one thing, finding the person behind it is another.'

'And this source has the skills to do that?'

Again, Bailee hesitated. 'Potentially.'

'What about the parties, anything on those?'

'Doc was found on a paedophile site. He's the guy Janie was talking about. The one I mentioned who's been coercing girls into behaving inappropriately at parties. My source got as far as figuring out he's local, um ... said something about him trying to make his wife come across as crazy so he could get custody of his child, and that he owns a black Porsche ... I think that was all. Oh, and that he's using a separate computer for all that stuff, which is why it's so difficult to track him down. I think the forum he's associated with is where the information on the Spider's Web came from.'

Rachael frowned and thought about what Bailee had told her. She didn't like where her thoughts were leading.

'What is it?' Finn asked. 'Finding this site is a great new lead. Who knows what Jim will be able to glean from it?'

'Yes it's great but that's not the lead I'm thinking about.' She pulled out her phone and called Jonathan Davies. The call rang out. 'This is probably ridiculous,' she said, but she was already getting to her feet.

'What is?'

'A man going by the name Doc who lives locally and owns a black Porsche. Going through custody issues.'

'The only Doc I know is our forensic path— No way,' Finn scoffed. 'Jonathan's not going to be wrapped up in any of that.'

'Regardless, I think it's time we find him, don't you?'

Finn's expression turned grim. 'I'll drive.'

'Bailee, get in touch with your source, make sure you have all the available information on Doc.'

'Of course.'

'And Bailee, well done.'

*

In the car, Finn's finger hovered over the ignition then dropped to his lap and he turned to face her. 'You don't really think Jon's a paedophile do you? How long have we known this guy?'

'A couple of decades, but not well enough to be able to say without doubt he couldn't do something like this. I'm worried about the fact that, on top of this new evidence, there are files missing from the Spider case.'

'Whoa. You've gone from Jon being an aboveboard, respected forensic pathologist to a potential paedophile to someone deliberately interfering with evidence to aid a child serial killer? Rach, slow down.'

'I'm just putting all the pieces together. I know we can't be certain of anything yet. I really hope I'm wrong. But we can't not go there, Finn. We need to keep an open mind. If Jon is involved in a paedophile group that is somehow involved with the Spider, we can't assume that it's not all connected and hasn't been for a very long time. Let's go.'

The trip to Terrigal passed in relative silence. Even after Finn pulled the car up outside the impressive home, Rachael sat a moment longer, preparing herself to talk to Jon. To bring up the impossible.

'You ready?' Finn eventually asked.

'Yeah. We'll ask him to come down to the station from the get-go. If the daughter is here, we'll have to contact Charmaine to come and collect her. No mention of any suspicions until we're back. We're going to have to handle this very carefully.'

'Got it.'

They got out of the car and approached the three storeys of glass and modern lines that spoke of an expensive architect and comfortable wealth.

'Have you been here before?' Finn asked.

'Twice. For a wedding and a fiftieth.' She rang the doorbell.

While she waited for an answer, Finn wandered away. 'Rach!'

His voice had her spinning, stepping quickly around him to see a broken window. Looking through it, she saw a haphazard blood stain that trailed down the stairs and along the floor.

She went back to the door, banged on it urgently this time. 'Police!'

Nothing.

She tried again, then said to Finn, 'Call it in.'

*

Jonathan Davies's once quiet property quickly transformed into a frantic crime scene. An officer guarded the front and taped off onlookers and media while police and forensics spilled out from the house into the perfectly tidy strip of front yard, stepping cautiously over the manicured lawn as they searched for evidence. Inside the garage yet more forensic analysts crawled around, marking and photographing evidence.

From her vantage point in the foyer, Rachael watched it all unfold as she managed the scene and waited for Van Zettan to speak to her. When he caught her eye, she took it as her signal and approached, careful to avoid disturbing anything.

'Well, what can you tell me?' she asked.

Van Zettan straightened and pressed a hand into his lower back. 'Looks like the victim was attacked at the top of the stairs and has fallen or been pushed, tumbled to the bottom then dragged out to the garage. From looking at the blood, I'd say it could have happened a week or so ago, but without a body it's impossible to be precise on timing.'

'So we're looking for a body, not a live victim?'

'I'm leaning towards a homicide. Unless the victim received immediate medical attention it's unlikely he or she could have survived having lost this amount of blood.'

'Okay. Thanks, Steven.'

She went upstairs to look around, found Finn in the office. A stack of books had been removed from a shelf and an older style laptop was clenched in his hand. 'Bailee's source was right,' he said. 'I found the stashed computer. It's password protected so I'll get Jim to figure out how to get into it.'

'Okay.'

'I think there should be another computer here. There's a charger cord on the desk plugged into the wall but it's not attached to anything and it doesn't fit this computer.'

'Maybe whoever broke in took it, looking for what you just found.'

'Anyone get in touch with the wife?' Finn asked.

'She's on her way to the station. Daughter has been with her this week. Neither have been in contact with Davies for several days. Because I know her, I think you should be the one to interview her.'

'You know as well as I do the statistics point to her involvement in all this.'

'She wouldn't need to break in,' Rachael pointed out.

'She could have gotten someone else to do it.'

'Or this could be about a break-in gone wrong. Or about the Spider. Too early to tell.'

Finn ran his hand over his head. 'For the little girl's sake, I hope she hasn't discovered what Jon was allegedly up to and done something desperate.'

'Yeah. Me too. I'll organise a doorknock, see if anyone saw or heard anything.'

Finn nodded then at the sound of his phone ducked out of the room to answer it.

She followed him out and paused in the hallway. It was lined with framed pictures of Davies, Charmaine and their daughter. Holidays, family portraits, a shot from every year of Kelli's school life. Among them was a collection of pictures that looked to have been drawn by a child: simplistic recreations of pastel-coloured butterflies and spotted toadstools and sunshine. The images had her thoughts moving back to the picture that took pride of place on the wall above her desk.

'She drew you a picture,' Kayla said into the phone. 'You need to see it.'

'Okay, great, she said she would. I just have to finish up something here and then I can—'

'Would you listen?' Kayla insisted. 'I said to her, "What's this? A spider?"'

'And she said "No, he's *the* spider."'

'I'll head back,' Finn was saying. 'I've got a car going to pick up Mrs Davies so I'll get that interview underway.'

'Great. See you later.' Rachael took one last long look at the framed pictures. Some kids drew fairytales. Others drew nightmares. How long would it have been before Kelli's drawings had become dark and menacing? She still didn't want to believe Davies could be wrapped up in all this. But something had gone very wrong here. She needed to find out who this latest source of Bailee's was. See what else they could uncover.

A screeching of tyres outside the window drew her attention to the road below.

Finn, laptop in hand, was crossing the road. Almost before she could process what was happening he was tossed up and over the bonnet of a speeding car. The laptop flew through the air in one direction as his body was travelled in the other. The car slammed to a stop as police rushed towards the scene. The driver reversed onto the kerb, their door opened, closed, and the car took off with another screech of wheels. As the car made the turn towards the main road, an arm appeared from the window. There was a flash of steel and Rachael's stomach lurched again. Gun.

Bullets rained out in quick succession, forcing her officers to the ground and giving the car a decent head start. Two of her officers climbed into a squad car and pursued with lights and sirens.

It wasn't until that moment that Rachael realised she was still frozen to the spot.

She ran downstairs, yelling directions into her radio as the process took over. By the time she got outside, Finn was sitting up, leaning against a forensic van and protesting an officer's best attempt at first aid to the side of his pale, damp face where a cloth was slowing a stream of blood.

'I'm fine.'

'You're not fine!' Rachael said, bending down beside him.

'I need a car.'

'Finn, it's under control.' She could hear another officer's radio, hear all the right communications back and forth. 'You're going to the hospital. Did you get a look at the driver?'

'I didn't see anything. He took the laptop.'

'I'm guessing now he has both. Someone's trying to hide something and for the risk he just took, it has to be big.'

'I need to get after him.' He shifted as though to stand, grimaced and gave up. He might have been running on adrenaline, but he was slurring his words and his face was devoid of colour and dotted with perspiration.

'Absolutely not. You're getting your head looked at.'

'Inspector.'

She squinted up to see Turner hovering. 'What are you doing here?'

'Came to see if I could help. Or I can take Finn to the hospital?'

'We've got medics on the way so not necessary. But I've got units out looking for the car that ran into him. Another car on the road would be helpful.'

'No problem.'

His apparent decision to play nice was noted but there wasn't time to think too much about it as an ambulance appeared. 'Here's your ride,' she told Finn. Then, because she was needed on the radio, 'Make sure he gets in,' she told the officer beside him. She needed to get back to the station. It would be easier to coordinate from there.

'Inspector,' Debbie said, catching Rachael as she entered the strike force room. 'Did you get the car?'

'No,' she replied, rubbing at the headache bothering her forehead.

'Mrs Davies is still waiting. She's been here quite some time now.'

Damn it, she'd forgotten about Charmaine. 'Thanks, Debbie.' Finn wouldn't be doing that interview now. She just hoped he was going to be okay—wanted to get over to the hospital to check. 'I'm going to need to get someone to talk to her. Claxton maybe.'

'Claxton's just left. Should I call him back in?'

'No. I'll find someone else. Thanks. Why don't you head off, too?'

'Thanks. Have a good night.'

'You too.' Rachael caught sight of Turner hanging by the doorway as she turned for her office.

'Inspector,' he said. 'Do you have a minute?'

'Ah, maybe one. What's up?'

'I'd like to be in charge of investigating Jonathan Davies's disappearance.'

'That man is crucial to our case. He's the only POI we know of who could have direct links to the parties and potentially even the Spider.'

'I know that. So give me a couple of your guys to assist and we'll take care of it while you get on with the rest of the investigation.'

She considered him, considered his proposal. 'Why should I do that?'

'Because I've finished organising the patrols for tomorrow night and I need something to do.'

'I was going to have you look into Janie Miller's disappearance. We believe she's taken off of her own volition but she has evidence pertaining to this case that could be important.'

His mouth twisted. 'Sounds more like something Debbie could manage.'

'Debbie isn't a detective.'

'So send one with her. She could use the experience.' He lifted both hands, palms out in defence against the flash of anger she knew had jumped onto her face. 'Hold on. Look, I know I shouldn't have said what I said when you arrived and I completely deserved your professionally delivered fuck-off. But I have the experience to take some of the load off your other detectives. I can investigate this while they focus on your POI, on tomorrow night's activities, on the website. Hell, if nothing else, it'll keep me out of your way.'

It made sense. She needed all the resources she could get and his attitude seemed to have done a 180-degree turn for the better. And she needed someone to talk to Charmaine.

'All right. Thanks. Take Fulton and McGrugan. I need you to start by interviewing Charmaine Davies. Debbie said she's here.'

'Yeah, thanks,' he said. 'I'll do that.'

'Don't let me down, Turner.'

CHAPTER TWENTY

Saturday, March 13

Why hasn't Victor gotten back to me? 'Arsehole,' I say to the screen. At least the website's still up. He must have found the second laptop and my credibility is still intact. So what's his go? He can't be planning to let me pose as Doc forever. My phone buzzes and I check it. Henry. He cancelled on me last night. He never cancels. He's hoping to catch up for a chat. Interesting.

An annoying tapping breaks my concentration and I look around only to find a waving Dawny at the window, so I put down the phone and get up to open the door. 'Morning.'

'Have you seen the television?'

I frown. 'Not yet. Why?'

'That man in my freezer. They're saying he's missing. There's grave concerns for his welfare.'

Had to happen eventually. 'I'd say they're warranted, wouldn't you?'

'I have to admit he was much prettier alive than dead. Who'd have believed he was fifty-four! Didn't look a day over forty, I say. And a good-looking one at that.'

'You should have seen him twenty years ago.'

'That poor wife looked distraught though, didn't she? That did give me a moment.'

I guess the idea that the less she knows the better is pretty redundant at this stage and I know she's curious. 'Dawny, the guy was a paedophile. He was systematically destroying his wife's credibility to make her look incompetent so he could get sole custody of his daughter for his own sick enjoyment. His wife was distraught at the time. But it was a stressful situation. I bet lying to the cops is another one.'

Dawny's mouth formed an O and she was completely silent for possibly the longest moment since I've known her. Then her mouth closed on a tight line and her head nodded. 'I knew there had to be a good reason you killed him. I have to say I wouldn't have had a bad moment if I'd done it myself.'

'I didn't kill him. I just happened to be there to help cover it up after some other guy did. Because of the bullshit he'd heaped on his wife no one would have believed she didn't do it and she most likely would have gone to jail and left her daughter without a parent. I thought the simplest solution was to help her get rid of the evidence.'

'And get rid of it we will.' Dawny patted my hand. 'You're a good girl, Lexi. I'm going to bake you a pie. Apple or lemon meringue?'

'Apple,' I say. 'Although ...'

Dawny grins. 'You make your mind up and let me know.'

'Are you sure you have time? How's your houseguest?'

'Houseguest?'

I pull a face. 'Dawny are you going to tell me it was just Desmond's car that stayed over last night?'

A smile crept onto her face. 'It's been a while. Poor Desmond. It's nice to have him round again. Hadn't spoken to him for years before this! Wasn't sure I could find him, to be honest. But a bit of calling around and he turned up. Would do pretty much anything for me. Been a bit lonely, I think.'

'And what about the crazy, murdering wife?'

'Pfft. Don't worry dear. Catherine'll be the first to tell ya all men are born with a dumb stick and wherever it points a man follows—and there's no reasoning with them because they can't use their brain once all the blood's run south.'

'Charming.' I say, then I think about a few of the clients I've had over the years and revise my sarcasm. 'Though not always inaccurate, I suppose.'

Dawny cackles. 'Don't know why she ever got married again after she killed her first husband.'

'She ...' I actually press my hand to my forehead to stop it from spinning and wonder whether she makes at least some of this stuff up. 'And how did you come to be sleeping with a murderer's husband?'

'The first time? We were smoking some pot and—well, everyone knows about weed dick, so it should have gone south, not north. But there you have it. Anyway, whatever will be will be, I always say. Fate and all that.'

Bailee pulls up. Again. I'm pretty sure I've seen her more in the last week than I have in the last year. I'm also pretty sure she's supposed to be working today, so I'm guessing whatever she's here for is important and probably to do with the website.

'Got time for a coffee?' she says as she locks her car.

'Well, then, that's my cue,' Dawny says. 'You can fill me in a bit more later. Lovely to see you, Bailee. Bye-bye.'

'Bye, Dawny.' I open the door wider and Bailee steps past me into the house. 'So it's not that I'm not happy to see you, but why are you here?'

'I have some good news.'

'I'm up for some of that.' I flick the switch on the kettle. 'What is it?'

'Turns out your useless information on Doc wasn't so useless after all.'

Everything stops. Even the breath halts in my throat. This is not good news. This is why they found him, I gather, which means they know Jonathon Davies was Doc. 'What I gave you was information on the Spider's Web.'

'Yeah, but before that when you were looking for Doc, you mentioned about him being a local guy having marriage issues and the car and the rest of it.'

I stare at her, realising my mistake and somehow blaming her for it. 'And you passed that on.'

'Turns out that's all they needed.' Her smugly upbeat tone isn't helping my devolving mood. 'The guy was on the news this morning. Did you see it? It's Jonathan Davies. He's a forensic pathologist who works with the cops all the time. Rachael and Finn both knew him! They went to pick him up to talk to him but when they got there he was gone and it looks like something horrible might have happened to him. Hard to care, right? But then— What?' she asks, her eyes moving over my face like she's suddenly realised I'm not sharing her excitement.

'Not what, *why*?' I complain. 'Why couldn't you stick to what I said I was prepared to share!'

Bailee's taken aback by my outburst. 'What's the big deal? You didn't say not to mention it.'

I sit heavily in my chair. 'So … what happened?'

'The new forensic guy they got in thinks he's probably dead. Finn found the second laptop you mentioned but—'

Next time Bailee tells me she's got good news, I'm locking the door. 'I never mentioned a second laptop.'

'Yes, you did. You said he must have a second one because he never did any banking or anything on the one you were remote viewing.'

'And the wife?' I ask weakly.

'Wife? Oh, you mean Jonathan Davies's wife? She's been questioned by one of the detectives. Rachael couldn't do it because she knows her a bit I think, and Finn was going to but, like I was about to say, he was taking the laptop in to be searched when this nutcase ran into him with his car and grabbed it. Then the guy took off, shooting at police.'

Well, there's an update. I guess Victor needed help to find it. At least now Charmaine won't be their only suspect. The game has shifted and I need time to think. To figure out what that means. What to do next.

'Why are you annoyed?'

I sigh heavily. 'Because I told you to leave Doc out of it and you didn't.'

'Yeah and come to think of it, you've been really quite adamant about it, haven't you? And now you're genuinely pissed off because they found him. You know more than you're saying.'

Her tone pisses me off as much as anything else. The implied *how dare you*. 'Yes, I do! You know they're going to blame the wife, right? I was going to make sure she wasn't put through the ringer, she wasn't separated from her daughter, that everyone who had already decided she was a lunatic because of what her arsehole husband did trying to get custody of the kid didn't get a chance to crucify her. But thanks to you and your helpfulness, that's all very possibly stuffed. And when the easiest way for the cops to close this case is to lock her up for a murder she didn't commit, the kid's stuffed too. I told you I'd help my way, but you knew better. So well done, Bailee! Excellent work!'

I don't think I've ever let her have it before. But while I expect her to act all crestfallen and sad, I'm wrong. Her eyes fire back as hot as mine.

'How do you know the wife is innocent?'

'I just do! And I'm not going to tell you all of it. Ever. Because like I've tried to explain before, I live on one side of the law and you live on the other.' I'm pissed off enough to add, 'I shouldn't have ever come back into your life.'

'But you did. And you've helped bring charges against more than a dozen paedophiles. And if I stuffed up it's because you couldn't be honest with me. And that law rubbish is just an excuse to keep yourself in a comfortable hole. I know what you went through but—'

'Oh, please. You weren't even there when I was in that room with BJ and Biddle. They never touched you.'

'I wasn't there? I was *there*, Lexi. A foot away on the other side of that wall. I remember the way the one spring in your bed always squeaked. I remember the bastard's growly voice: "Whose little girl are ya?"' She mimicked, too close to the truth.

'Shut up, Bailee.' I suddenly have the overwhelming need for a drink so I snag my bottle of JD and swig a shot straight from the bottle.

'Then you'd have to say, "Daddy's little girl."'

'I said shut up!'

'"Who's little girl are ya? Daddy's little girl. Whose little girl are ya? Daddy's little girl." Over and over and over and over and I'd cover my ears and squeeze my eyes shut and I wished as hard as I could that bastard would fall down dead but he never did! Not until—'

I slam the bottle down on the table and the crack it makes has me grimacing for my furniture. 'I was protecting you from it all, from knowing.'

'Yeah, you did. But I was five, not stupid. Would you put that away?' She waves at my JD. 'It's ten in the morning.'

'You told everyone you didn't remember anything.'

'I told everyone I remembered bits and pieces. Like one day when I watched through the door. I was so scared. I didn't want to look but I was frozen. I couldn't look away. Then at the end he turned off the video and said you had to try harder or the money would stop and it would be all your fault. Did you want to be the reason I ended up on the street with no food to eat?'

Everything inside me wants to collapse in a pitiful crying jag but I hold my breath so nothing can escape and start the flood. 'He liked to use that one,' I manage to say.

'So then I decided it was my fault. Even when the counsellors tried to make me believe otherwise, I refused to. Oh no. What he did to you was so I could have food to eat and somewhere to live. And then you'd gone and that was my fault too.'

'That was *not* your fault! None of that was ever your fault!'

'You put up with the abuse for so long. Then Biddle came after me and you stopped putting up with it. You stopped all of it.'

'I had no choice.'

'You did have a choice. You chose to protect me.'

'Of course I did!'

'Then stop yelling at me and let me help you!' Bailee's phone starts blaring. 'Damn it!' Then, 'Yes?' Her face changes, softens, her tone evens out. 'Hey, Cody. Take it easy. Yes, of course I'll come in with you. Where are you? I'll meet you. How about the park near the station? See you soon.' She ended the call and smiled, drew in a long, noisy breath. When she speaks it's quieter, calmer. 'I'm sorry if I've stuffed up. I didn't mean to.'

'I know,' I say in the same milder tone. 'I'm sorry I yelled.'

'Forget it. I have to go meet someone.'

'Yeah that Cody kid. I heard. Let me get changed.'

Bailee looks genuinely confused. 'Why?'

'Because I'm not letting you go off alone to meet some fugitive who's been taxiing girls to their deaths. What is wrong with you?'

'Don't you start yelling again! I don't need protecting anymore.'

I take one more drink. 'Of course you do. Let's go.'

*

'There he is,' Bailee said and pointed to the far end of the park. The skinny guy with the untidy hair was pacing, looking more like an addict needing a hit than the innocent kid Bailee had been carrying on about all the way over here.

'Cody!' Bailee calls out.

His head jerks up and he hurries over. 'I need you to tell them I'd never be involved in Summer's murder,' he blurts. 'I just wouldn't.'

'I know that,' Bailee says steadily. 'So tell me what happened.'

'They came to ask questions and I could tell they wanted to blame me.' Cody walks around in a big circle, his hands waving furiously. 'I got scared so I grabbed my pocketknife and I was just going to run away but the lady cop was in the way. I knocked her over as I ran. But I didn't mean it. I wasn't gonna hurt anyone.'

'I believe you,' Bailee tells him.

'I don't,' I say. 'What are you on?'

'Lexi!'

'No, I'm serious,' I tell Bailee, then say to Cody, 'If you're gonna drag Bailee into this, you little shit, you have to be honest. What have you taken?'

He stares at me consideringly for several moments before his shoulders drop. 'I've got a bit of an ice addiction. I'm gonna kick it,' he says to Bailee. 'I swear.'

'Were you high when the cops came to see you?' I ask.

'Nah. Nup,' he answers, but he doesn't meet my eyes. Then he turns back to Bailee, and again with the pleading look. 'I need to get this sorted. I'm not a murderer.'

'I'm pretty sure they know that,' Bailee says. 'But you did transport kids to those parties.'

'So? They're mostly street kids. They've got nothing. I take 'em up for a night out, that's all. They have a good time, have a feed, a few drinks and party. And the guys give 'em stuff they need like hairbrushes, toothpaste, deodorant, sometimes even clothes, blankets. And they don't have to do nothin' they don't want! So the old pervs get a wank out of it. What's wrong with that?'

'They're providing drugs and alcohol to children in return for sexual gratification,' Bailee says. 'What's not wrong with that?'

'They don't do nothin' they don't want! And none of them guys are killers. They're not gonna murder anyone.'

'Summer had been drugged.'

He scratches at his face. 'Don't know nothing about that.'

'And the dumping her in the creek part?' I ask. 'Your van, wasn't it?'

From the look on his face I have to wonder if he's as harmless as he professes to be. 'I never did that! I just get paid to clean up after the parties. Two hundred bucks. I clean up and toss some bags of rubbish away and I don't say nothin'. That's it.'

'That's all the police need to hear,' Bailee says.

'I told him I wasn't doing it no more, anyway. Not since they found that girl's body where I put the rubbish. I was, like, set up.'

'Wait, who? Who did you tell?' I ask. A feeling of dread washes over me.

'The one that pays me. I told him just before I called Bailee that I'm going to the cops to tell 'em it's not my fault.'

Up until then I hadn't wanted to call him stupid, but there it was, on the tip of my tongue. 'Was that Victor?'

He looks confused, then his eyes widen on Bailee. 'How's she know? She work with Victor?'

'No, of course not,' Bailee says, but he's already backing up. 'I don't want no part of this. Whatever this is.'

'Cody, she's not working for Victor,' Bailee says again.

'Seriously not,' I say. 'He's an arsehole. I want to catch him. But do you really think it was a good idea to tell him you were coming here now to dob him in?'

Cody's looking around, starting to sweat. 'Nup, changed my mind. Don't want to talk to anyone. Gonna get outta here.' He's rushing, not looking. He steps back onto the road. A car blares its horn and narrowly misses him.

Bailee lunges towards him, opens her mouth to say something, but a sharp crack beats her to it.

Cody lifts his hands from his stomach and then he's falling. I see blood but it takes me a couple of seconds to make sense of what's happening.

Gunshot? I turn at the sound of rubber on tarmac. As though in slow motion, I see a car coming up the road. An arm is extended and in the hand is a gun. I see Bailee go down beside Cody.

The world turns to chaos. Police are swarming from the station on the other side of the road, pedestrians are screaming and yelling. I get moving. I'm within a couple of metres of Bailee and Cody when I notice the car has stopped a few metres ahead and the gun has changed target. My stomach sinks as I think it's pointed at me but, no, it's off to the left. I hear someone come up on that side of me and lunge at whoever it is as a second shot fires. It splinters the trunk of an old fig behind us before either of us hit the ground. Another screech of tyres and the car is gone.

My elbow stings where it connected with the road, and everything else aches from tackling whoever is under me.

I scramble off the woman I've just brought down without so much as a glance and rush to Bailee. She's fine but staring at Cody in shock. His abdomen is like a bloody swimming pool and he's either passed out or died, I'm not sure.

'Son of a bitch, it's the same damn car!' I hear from somewhere on the road behind me. 'Rach, are you all right?'

'We need an ambulance!' the woman says as she brushes me aside and after a quick check begins CPR.

Did he say Rach? As in Rachael? I stagger back, incapable of anything much but staring. The woman isn't wearing a uniform and I can only see her profile, but is it? Then she turns her head to shout more instructions and I get a better look at her face.

Everything seems to stop. The noise, the chaos, the flashing lights, the cop cars crawling past us on the road to give chase while others block it off to general traffic all fade as everything floods back. All of it. I'm ten years old again. I'm living in hell and the intensity of the memory is overwhelming.

For what could have been minutes or seconds, I'm stuck, staring at a cop that promises to save me. But never does.

I get shuffled further back out of the way as more cops surround Bailee and Cody. Someone, a big guy with broad shoulders and a calm voice, guides Bailee back as an ambulance arrives. He looks like he's been hit by a truck. Bruising extends from one side of his face to down below his collar and a red line mars his forehead. He's moving stiffly but steadily. And he obviously knows Bailee. *Maybe that's Finn*, pops into my head out of nowhere. The guy that got hit by the car.

I'm shaking. I don't know what from. The shooting? Rachael? All of it? I need to get out of here.

'Excuse me, miss? Are you hurt?'

I look blankly at a young officer with a lot of blonde hair and a kind smile. 'What? Oh, no. I'm fine.'

Bailee is coming towards me. She's a mess. The ambulance takes off and she grips my hand with her stained one. Tears tumble down her cheeks. 'I think he's dead. I think Cody's dead!'

'Come inside,' the policewoman says. 'Let me get you both a cup of tea and when you're up to it, you can tell me what happened. Okay?'

Bailee nods and grips my hand tighter but my feet are frozen to the spot. I look back to where Rachael had been but she's coming back across the road with Finn in tow. A smile masks the flustered strain when she looks at me. Probably because I just saved her life, but even that wavers as she gets closer.

Bailee wipes her tears from her face with her forearm and sniffs. Kind of steps almost in front of me as though defending me. 'Ah ... Rachael, I should ...'

Rachael stops a few feet in front of us.

Another cop jogs over. 'Excuse me, inspector.'

Rachael holds up her hand and stares at me intently as the one I think is Finn catches up. I'm not sure whether she can't quite place me or she has and she can't quite believe it.

'Lexi?' Her voice is barely audible. I don't know how I expected her to feel about seeing me again, but it wasn't overwhelmed and that's how she sounds. It makes me more uncomfortable. I held a grudge against a larger-than-life authority figure for so many years and looking at her like this, just an ordinary woman who seems to be as lost for words as I am, doesn't fit with that. I'm not sure what to do with it.

'Yeah, hi.'

'I can't believe … Where have you been? Are you all right?'

'Around. Surviving. Doing fine, thanks.'

'You just turned back up and saved my life.'

I hear the disbelief and shrug. 'It was a reflex. No big deal.' And honestly, can I just get out of here? I look around. Is it too much to hope an escape hatch might magically appear in the road?

'Would you come inside? I'd like to talk to you.'

'I'd rather not. Nothing personal, but I'm not big on cops.'

Rachael looks disappointed but whatever. I'm having enough trouble dealing myself.

'See ya.' I manage four decent strides away before she calls out.

'You know the Spider's back? We should at least talk about that.'

That has me turning back. 'Biddle is the Spider. And Bailee tells me you're thinking you got it wrong. You didn't get that wrong, Rachael. *That's* the part you got right!' I take two angry steps back towards her. 'You let them let him out and you're as useless to me now as you were back then!'

'Lexi!' Bailee gasps.

'That's enough,' probably-Finn growls. 'Rachael puts away monsters every day.'

'Yeah, yeah.' I flick him a cold glance before returning my attention to Rachael. 'And who do you think handed you the last one?'

'What?' Rachael's confused gaze bounces between me and Bailee.

'Davies was a paedophile and a liar and his wife had nothing to do with what happened to him,' I tell her.

Two full beats of silence before the cop who'd approached at the beginning of our reunion tries again. 'I'm sorry, inspector, but ... '

I use the interruption to get out of there. *I need a drink* is all I can think as I do my best to make my departure look as though I don't want to run for my life. I didn't know it was possible to feel claustrophobic outside. I can't breathe. I continue on down the road, hear Bailee calling as she catches up.

'Hey, wait up.'

'I need a drink.'

'I'll have one with you.'

That surprises me—Bailee barely touches the stuff—until I remember she just saw a guy shot on the street.

'Sorry about Cody.'

'They were still working on him when they put him in the ambulance.'

'Oh. Well, good.' Maybe he'd get to tell his side of the story after all.

I walk past two hotels in favour of reaching Tom's. It's a hike, but Bailee doesn't complain. And at least it's quiet when we get in there.

'Ladies,' Tom says. 'Starting early?'

'Two double shots of JD.' It comes out part plead, part demand, and I dare Bailee with my eyes to amend the order. Today is not the day for one of her prissy little single shots with Diet Coke. When she doesn't object, I slide one of the drinks in front of her.

Bailee eyes the glass with concern. 'We're going to have to go back after these. They're going to want witness statements, I think.'

'Solid no.' I take a sip. 'You already got your wish. I spoke to Rachael.'

'Yes, you did.'

Another sip, a moment to enjoy the warmth of it hitting the back of my throat, then a wry smile. 'Go as well as you planned?'

'I don't know why,' Bailee says dryly, 'but I expected it to be a bit less dramatic.'

'I don't know why, but so did I.'

Bailee chuckles into her glass. 'You're pissed off because you had to play hero. You, Miss Wrong-Side-of-the-Law, saved the life of a police inspector.'

'Possibly. Only possibly. And I didn't do it on purpose,' I mumble into my drink before downing the rest of it. 'I didn't know who I was tackling.'

'I don't think it's going to make any difference. They're probably going to want to give you a bravery award or something.'

'You're enjoying this.'

Bailee shakes her head. 'I think it's shock. I'll probably fall apart in a minute.'

'Then are you going to drink that or wreck it by crying into it?'

Bailee takes a tiny sip and shudders. Then surprises me by taking a mouthful. Her face screws up but she gets it down. 'That might hold the breakdown off a bit longer.'

'Is there something you're waiting for?'

'The story!' she says, wide-eyed. 'Mrs Davies, the pathologist. I want all of it.' She takes another decent mouthful of JD as though she already knows this story's going to be easier to take if she's half smashed.

'No deal.'

She points what's left of her drink at me. 'Did you kill him?'

'What? No!'

Bailees eyes narrow and I'm pretty sure the JD's already doing its job. 'So how do you know Mrs Davies didn't?'

'I'm not having this conversation with you.'

Bailee waves at Tom. 'Better get us a refill.' Then says to me, 'You are having this conversation with me. Every hero needs a sidekick.'

'Oh, Bailee, you're in for a bitter disappointment.'

CHAPTER TWENTY-ONE

Sunday, March 14

Rachael looked around at the tired faces of her team and stifled a yawn of her own. The incident with Cody yesterday, followed by a long evening searching fruitlessly for any sign of a van and groups of kids, had everyone feeling drained. With Cody out of the picture, she hoped the party hadn't gone ahead. Maybe they needed more time to organise an alternative vehicle, or they'd decided to lay low until things calmed down. But she knew there was a chance they'd missed them. That another victim might already have been taken. And that's why most of her team was back here early on a Sunday morning. Because no one wanted to take time off while something like that could be happening.

'We've got plenty of footage of the shooting,' Jim said, showing them an image from a video. 'But nothing in particular of any help. The car is the same one used in the incident outside Davies's house. It's a stolen vehicle with stolen plates. The driver had a cap and sunglasses, a long-sleeved shirt with a hoodie up under the cap.'

'Our POI doesn't mind taking risks,' she said, taking a sip of the coffee that was now only mildly warm. 'But following this I'm guessing we'll find the car dumped somewhere, probably burnt out.' She stopped talking to huff when Finn appeared in the doorway. 'Is it really so impossible for you to take a day off?'

'Everyone else keeps turning up.'

'Not everyone else was hit by a car one day, almost involved in a drive-by shooting the next. Go home and rest, Finn.'

'Where are we with Davies?' he asked, ignoring her request and finding a seat.

Rachael shook her head in frustration but looked at Turner for the response.

'I interviewed Mrs Davies, who claims she hadn't seen Mr Davies since the weekend before his disappearance. Since Mr and Mrs Davies separated she has been living with her sister. Mr Davies had picked up Kelli from school on the Friday afternoon, then taken her to a birthday party sleepover with a friend on the Saturday night. That's the last time anyone appears to have seen him.'

'Lucky she wasn't there when Davies was taken,' Debbie said.

'Luck or planning?' Finn said. 'Whoever attacked him could have had prior knowledge of their movements.'

'Which brings me back to Charmaine Davies,' Turner continued. 'Jonathan Davies had filed for divorce and was seeking full custody of his daughter. He claimed his wife had a substance abuse problem and had been behaving irresponsibly, had made threats to harm him when he'd brought up the idea of her seeking help. He'd been worried for his daughter's safety as well as his own. Mrs Davies's sister has verified Mrs Davies was at her home on the night of his disappearance, but I'm not convinced she's telling the truth. I'll be looking into that further.'

'See if you can find any evidence of that alleged substance abuse or any of the other claims he'd made, especially those against his safety,' Rachael said. 'Was Mrs Davies aware of the hidden laptop?'

'She claims not.'

'Was she aware of his association with any online pae-dophilia sites? If she believed he wanted custody of Kelli for the purpose of abusing her that could be enough to push her to commit murder, whether or not she really was unstable.'

'She didn't run me over for that laptop,' Finn said. 'I didn't see much but I know it wasn't a woman.'

'I think it's safe to assume whoever took it is involved in some way with the group running the parties and wants to hide any evidence. That included keeping Cody Ellis from talking. We know our POI doesn't have any problem killing as a means to an end. We also know he knew Davies, or at least where he lived, so although we may not yet be able to rule out Mrs Davies, this guy is at the top of my list as our murderer.'

'And a lot of this supposition is based on Davies being a member a group we know very little about, that apparently ran a website we haven't seen,' Finn said. 'Until we get a look at it, we can't even be sure that information is correct.'

'Bailee's source discovered the website after looking into claims by one of Bailee's clients, Janie Miller, who it now appears would rather hide from police than talk to us,' Rachael said.

'And if yesterday's comments are anything to go by, Bailee's sister Lexi is that source,' Finn said.

'Wait,' Turner said. 'You're talking about Lexi Winter? You found her?'

'She was with Bailee bringing Cody Ellis to the station yesterday,' Rachael said. 'Bailee will be in this morning to provide more details. There simply wasn't time yesterday with the operation we ran last night.'

'And Lexi Winter discovered all this information?' Turner asked.

'I'll know more once I've spoken to Bailee. Let's get to work.'

'I'm not sure we should have let Lexi walk away yesterday,' Finn said as everyone went back to their respective spaces.

'What could we have held her on? She'd just possibly saved my life. And look.' Rachael waved a hand towards the lift. 'Bailee's just walked in. Let's see where we are after I talk to her.'

'Right. I might call the hospital, see how Cody Ellis is doing.'

'Would you mind giving his mum a call, too? Just a check up?'

'Yeah. Yeah, I'll see how she's doing.'

'Thanks.' Then, 'Bailee! Hi. Thanks for being prompt.'

'No problem. Hi Finn.'

'Bailee. I'll leave you ladies to it.'

Rachael gestured for Bailee to follow her into her office. 'You look a little pale. Are you all right?'

'I don't do well on spirits. Long story.'

'Take a seat. I have some Panadol around here somewhere.'

'I've already taken enough to knock out an elephant, but thanks anyway.' Bailee sat and closed her eyes for a moment before opening them with a squint that spoke of a stunning headache. 'Rachael, I'm sorry I didn't tell you I've been in contact with Lexi. She wasn't keen on the idea.'

She might not like it but she understood, so she nodded. 'Go on.'

'She's been helping with several cases I've been working. It started when I was having trouble with a case last year.'

'Wait. Could you start right at the beginning for me? When you first saw her again?'

'Okay.' Bailee sighed and pulled a water bottle from her bag, took a sip. 'I was sixteen, and it was only for a moment. Cassie, my foster mum, and I were going out to lunch for my birthday. I saw Lexi standing on the corner. She smiled a little then stepped out of view and we were gone. I didn't *know* it was Lexi, but something niggled at me and after a while I forgot about it. Then a few months later, on Christmas morning, she walked past the front window of our house. When I looked up, she glanced away and hurried on. I got up and went outside but she was already gone. The thing was, I was five the last time I'd seen her and I'd blocked so much of my old life out. But something inside me recognised her. I wanted to believe it was Lexi, but I also didn't dare to. But every birthday and every Christmas I'd catch a glimpse of her.'

'She was keeping an eye on you.'

'Yeah. And then two years ago, just after I'd gotten engaged, I'd taken Kai out for a play in the park at the end of our street. He was two years old. I was talking to another mother. Her little girl and Kai were playing in the sand-pit and I took my eyes off him for maybe thirty seconds, a minute, and I heard some commotion, looked up and Kai was gone. He'd wandered over towards the toilet block and a guy had approached him. And there was Lexi, Kai in her arms, hurling abuse at this guy who was yelling back, calling her a psycho. Seeing her expression, hearing her voice, watching her protect Kai ... I knew. God, I got over there and put my arms around both of them and started crying.'

'And the guy?'

'I don't know. He said he saw a toddler wandering off by himself and thought he should turn him around. He was probably telling the truth. I never saw him again.'

'But that's when you finally spoke to Lexi.'

'She was all cool about it and I was a mess. I wanted her to come home with me but she wouldn't, just said she'd check in from time to time for a chat if I wanted. She was glad I was doing well. She knew everything I'd been up to. All of it. But she only gave me little bits about herself. Rach, it's taken all this time to get a phone number then finally an address. To feel like we can properly reconnect. I've spoken to her about talking to you, but I couldn't force it. I wanted to tell you.'

'But she asked you not to. I understand. If there was any other way I wouldn't be pushing now. But I need to know everything Lexi knows so I can try and prevent another murder. If she doesn't want to talk to me, I'd be happy to have someone else talk to her. If she doesn't want to come in here, I can have someone meet her wherever she likes.'

Bailee didn't look confident. 'I'll run it by her.'

'Do you know how she came by the information on Jonathan Davies?'

'I can't ...'

At her hesitation, Rachael sent her a smile she hoped read reassurance. 'Nothing we talk about is going to get her into trouble. This conversation is strictly in confidence.'

'She's really good with computers. Like freakishly good. She said she did some dodgy job for a while that involved hacking or something. She's had to do what she's had to do to survive.'

'No judgement.'

'So she's been helping me build evidence against lowlifes. I know that it's against all the rules. I know I shouldn't discuss cases. It was only meant to be one particularly bad one, but it just kind of flowed from there. I don't want to lose my job over all this, but if I do, I'm not sorry those guys have been caught.'

'I told you this conversation is in confidence,' Rachael reassured her.

'Thank you. Also, I still haven't heard from Janie. Her parents are getting worried. I thought she was just dodging us, but I also thought she was with Cody.'

'We'll start a more serious search. Now, I need to know everything Cody told you.'

'He wanted to come in, explain.'

Rachael listened, took some notes, and when she had everything she needed, she stood. 'Thanks, Bailee. I'll get started on finding Janie and I'll hope to hear from Lexi shortly.'

Bailee nodded and got to her feet. 'You know this thing with Lexi isn't only about you. We were raised not to trust or speak to any cops. Lexi still kind of lives by that.'

Rachael managed a smile. 'Because cops lie and shoot little girls. I remember.'

'Compounded by several years on the streets, doing what she needed to do to survive. But she's a good person. Even if she doesn't know it. She'll help. She'll work with you. I know she will.'

'That would be handy,' Rachael said. Nice even, to be able to work with Lexi.

But would Lexi ever be able to forgive her?

*

Rachael popped a piece of steaming fish into her mouth and looked out past the beach to the ocean. The sun was setting in brilliant hues over the surf and the air had a touch of cool to it that was pleasant. Finn and Ava were searching for shells and Ava's pockets were full, so Finn was balancing a load in his hands. 'This was a nice idea,' she told Ed. 'I'm glad you came down.'

'If I don't make you take a break, you'll work seven days a week.'

'We all are. At least Finn got to spend a couple of hours this afternoon with Ava. He's missing so much. We all just want to catch this bastard.'

'And you've been holding off talking to me about the case until Ava was busy, and now she is, so spill.'

'I suppose I should get you up to speed. We've learnt quite a bit more about the parties from what Cody told Bailee. We know these men are luring vulnerable kids in by providing them with the basics they need to survive. Combine a desperation for basic life essentials, peer pressure, drugs and alcohol and what chance have these kids got against these types of predators?'

'And you're sure Davies was involved?'

'As sure as I can be at this point. It all fits. And with the lab work missing from the reports on the original case, along with Steven's surprise at the lack of detail in Davies's reports, I have to wonder if he has been involved directly with the Spider as well.'

'You're going to need some serious proof to make that one fly. So, who'd want him to disappear? If the Spider had such a useful ally on side, surely he wouldn't have had anything to do with it?'

'Turner's looking at Charmaine.'

'Ah, Turner.' He chuckled. 'How's that going?'

'He was a complete arse when I first arrived but that's settled down. We're tolerating each other.'

'And Ellis?'

'The longer it takes him to wake up, the worse the prognosis. It's a case of wait and see.'

Ed brushed the sand from his hands. 'You could have been in the same position. I still can't get my head around Lexi Winter reappearing and knocking you south of that bullet.'

'And the rest. All those bastards she's helped put away.'

'Child victim turned vigilante. If the media get a whiff of that she'll never hear the end of it. I'd love to meet her.'

'She doesn't want a bar of me, and it sounds like she may have come across some of this information illegally. She's hardly going to come forward to help if it's going to get her into trouble.' She smiled at Ava as she jogged back with her shells, Finn approaching more slowly behind her.

'You should talk to the attorney-general,' Ed said. 'This is an important, high-profile investigation. I think you'd have a strong case for immunity from prosecution if Lexi's information is valuable enough to warrant it. Don't go making her any promises though until it's granted.'

'Aunty Rach, look at these,' Ava said, spilling the shells onto her towel.

'I like the little purple-coloured one,' Rachael said.

'Nah, the big pink one's more impressive,' Ed said.

'I think I agree with Ed,' Ava said. 'Here, you can have the purple one. Who's Lexi?'

'But wait, there's more,' Finn said and put his handful with the rest. 'Lexi is just someone to do with work,' he told Ava.

'Yeah,' Ed said. Then to Finn, 'Isn't it great she's turned up?'

Finn shrugged. 'I'm reserving judgement. She's not exactly friendly.'

'Why not?' Ava asked.

'I tried to help her when she was a little girl like you, but I couldn't.'

Ava rolled her eyes. 'I'm not little, Aunty Rach. I'm ten.'

'I can't imagine it's easy for her,' Ed said. 'Perhaps she might be more likely to talk to an intermediary.'

'I mentioned that to Bailee,' Rachael said. 'But who?' She exchanged glances with Ed before they both turned to Finn.

Finn pulled a face. 'Is this *request* coming from my aunt and her, ah, friend or my boss and my boss's boss?'

'That's funny,' Ava said with a giggle. 'You should talk to her, Dad. You need to talk to more girls. Is she pretty?'

'What? No!' Finn said.

'That's harsh!' Rachael objected. Then to Ava with a gleam of humour, 'And yes, she is.'

'I meant—fine.' Finn sighed. 'I'll talk to Bailee, see what she can set up.'

'Great,' Ed said with a laugh. 'And the sooner the better by the sounds of it.'

'I've got to get Ava back home soon,' Finn said with a pretend frown at his daughter. 'I'll call Bailee after that.'

'Oh, can we have one more look for good shells before we go?' Ava begged. 'We didn't go that way.' She pointed to the other side of the beach. 'Please, Dad? I want to make a necklace!'

'Sure,' Finn said. 'Ten more minutes.'

*

'Sorry again about this weekend, sweetie,' Finn told Ava as they approached the house.

'That's okay. This arvo was much more fun than sitting around with Mum and her new boyfriend.' Her attitude-loaded voice had Finn struggling not to smile.

'You still don't like him?'

'Not really. I mean, he's nice to me and everything but ... he's nowhere near as cool as you.'

He had to admit that felt good to hear. 'Just be nice to him for your mum, all right?'

'Yeah, yeah.'

He pulled up outside the house. He wished Viv would keep the gardens up a bit better, but he supposed she probably didn't have the time. They'd been his mother's pride and joy. Rachael had kept the place after his mother's death instead of selling it, which would have helped much more with the bills. But she'd said it was his to keep, so she'd rented it out for the extra cash she'd often so desperately needed, because Rachael had refused to see him go without anything. He'd never be able to repay her for everything she'd done for him. The idea he might have had to sell it after the divorce had been gut-wrenching, so he'd offered the place to Viv while Ava was growing up to delay the possibility. In the meantime, the veranda could do with a paint. Once this case was over he'd drop round, see to it. Maybe he'd tidy the garden up while he was at it.

'Thanks, Dad.' Ava leant over and hugged him.

'Don't forget your shells,' he said and reached into the back to hand them to her.

The door banged and he looked back to the house to see Viv on the front veranda. The new guy had come out behind her and stood there staring, one arm possessively around Viv's shoulders, the other on the veranda railing. And okay, no matter how reasonable, it did grate on him. Just a bit.

'Love ya.' He kissed Ava on the temple and watched her gather her things before climbing out of the car. With a wave at Viv, he pulled away.

He felt ridiculously lonely.

'Just tired,' he told himself. 'Hell of a week.' He should drive by Bailee's place, see if she was home. She was probably more likely to talk to him about Lexi face-to-face than over the phone.

When he got there the lights were on and he could hear children squealing and laughing inside. So yeah, home.

A man he assumed was Bailee's husband opened the door, carrying a cute little girl with tired eyes. 'Can I help you?'

'Hi, I'm Detective Finn Carson. A friend of Bailee's. Is she around?'

'Ah, sure. Mike, hi. Bailee's not here, hence the riot. She had to race off to chase up something with work. With all the Spider stuff going on she's missed a bit of time at the office.'

'Okay, never mind,' he said. 'I'm actually looking for Lexi.'

Mike looked him up and down again. This time suspiciously. 'I don't know where she is.'

'Could you hazard a guess?'

'Sure, but I'm not going to get myself into trouble with Bailee by talking to police about her sister.'

'She isn't in any trouble. We're trying to liaise with her. She has some information we need to help solve a case.'

Mike considered that while Finn gave him his best 'trust me' smile. 'Look, I don't know where she is. To be honest, we don't really get along.'

Finn couldn't help the small chuckle. 'I doubt that's your fault.'

'Yeah, well, she is what she is. Right now, she's probably in a hotel room with a client somewhere.'

'A ... as in she's a prostitute?'

'Bailee will say escort. Whatever.'

His thoughts exactly. 'I really want to get this sorted for Rachael. Can I at least have her number?'

'No, sorry. I don't have it.' The little girl rubbed her eyes and grizzled, her face falling. She started to cry. 'She's tired. I need to put her to bed.'

Because Mike hadn't quite shut the door in his face, Finn tried one more time. 'I just need to talk to her. It could save a child's life.'

Mike bounced the girl gently. 'Bailee won't do anything to risk her new-found relationship with her sister. She's worried Lexi will disappear from her life again. I'm not giving you a home address, but if it's that urgent, you might want to head down to Gosford. She spends a lot of time at one of the pubs there. Um … Tom's Joint.'

'Thanks. Really appreciate it.' He jogged back to the car. He knew where the pub was. And hell, he wouldn't mind a beer.

CHAPTER TWENTY-TWO

'So you see, I think we might really have a chance,' Henry tells me over drinks at a back booth at Tom's. 'And I've got you to thank for that. Isn't it funny how these things turn out?'

'Yeah, it's funny,' I agree, because I guess it really is a bit of a joke. I'm my own worst enemy. 'I'm happy for you. I really am.' If I say it out loud, there's a chance I can make myself believe it.

'Thanks, Lexi. I'll miss you. After all this time, you're like family.'

'Aw, get outta here.' I finish the drink he bought me and shift as though I have to go. 'The last thing you want is to get caught talking to me. Good luck.'

Henry stands and smiles down at me all nostalgic for a few quiet seconds. Then he nods and walks out.

'And that's the end of that,' I mutter. I now officially can't afford to live and Henry's right. We've both got me to thank. I get up from the table and head for my regular spot at the bar. Sit.

'So that's really the end of Henry?' Tom asks me. 'I think I'll miss the big marshmallow.'

'Yeah, well, who knows? It might not work out.'

'True. He could be back before you know it.'

'I'm gonna have to find a new client. In fact, you'd better stop pouring me drinks I probably can't afford.'

'I think I can extend you some credit.' He proves it by pouring me a drink.

I accept it with a grateful smile. 'Your payment terms would want to be flexible.'

'My bar, my rules.'

'Thanks.'

'Of course we both know someone who'd blow his weekly pension on an hour with you.' His eyes fall on Owen and I cringe.

'I'd be better off hitting the streets. Most of the homeless people I used to know had better hygiene.'

'Yeah but they can't afford you.'

'Depends on how desperate I get.'

I know I've come off a little too pathetic when I'm suddenly being studied like a bug under a microscope. 'Things aren't that bad are they?'

I don't really want to tell him how desperate it'll be next week when the rent is due, so I shrug. 'I'll pick up a new guy. Haven't had to do that for a while. Out of practice.' And I am. I could probably get my old job back at the brothel but going back to work for less pay and under someone else's rules isn't appealing. So where does one even advertise these days? Can't be too difficult to find out. I just don't really want to. I'm getting soft.

'Hey, here comes a possible.'

I look around and see the cop Bailee had confirmed was Finn. *What is he doing here and how did he find me?* runs through my head before I consider sneaking out, but he looks around at that moment and sees Tom and me watching him.

'Hey, maybe he *is* interested,' Tom whispers as Finn heads straight for me.

'I'm just guessing, but I don't think that's what this is about.'

'Lexi,' Finn says pleasantly enough.

I swallow my drink, put the glass down. 'Yeah?'

'We didn't get properly introduced before. I'm Detective Finn Carson.'

'*Sergeant* Detective Finn Carson,' I point out for the hell of it. 'I know.' I look back at my glass, then up to Tom hopefully. Tom rolls his lips over his grin and pours me another, then walks away to serve another customer.

'Great. I was hoping I could talk to you.'

'I'm pretty sure you are.'

'About Jonathan Davies.'

Could this evening get any shittier? 'Can we not do this here, please?'

'Sure. Where then?'

'I'll let you know. Later.'

'Look, I've been chasing after you all night. I'm not leaving until we nail something down.'

I have a suspicion he means it. He looks tired and pissed off. I wonder how long it took to find me. 'If I promise to think about it, will you go away?'

'This guy hassling you?' Tom says, returning.

'Yeah.'

'You might want to move on, mate,' Tom suggests.

'I could say the same thing.' Finn pulls out his ID and shows it to Tom.

Tom's brow lifts. 'What have you been up to?' he asks me, eyes wicked.

'This is what you get when you try to be helpful,' I complain.

'Ah, the Bailee stuff.'

'Quiet,' I threaten, but he's opening the Pepsi he got out for someone else and is pushing it at me.

'It sounds like you might need to sober up.'

I pull a face but have a sip. It's ridiculously sweet. 'Thanks.' To Finn I say, 'What exactly do you want to know?'

'For starters, I want to know how to get into the website you found Davies on.'

I pat my little dress and shrug. 'I don't seem to have it on me. Sorry.' I take another mouthful of Pepsi and shudder. 'Enough of this sober shit.' I push the soft drink away and drag back my JD. 'I'm drinking. We'll have to do this some other time.'

'I can wait,' Finn says as Tom reappears, and he orders a beer.

Tom glances at me as though asking permission. Cute. I shrug, so he serves Finn, who takes his beer somewhere else.

'I wonder how long it will take for him to give up and go home?' I yawn and cover it. 'Sorry. Is food included on that tab? If I'm going to wait out the cops, I'd better have something in my stomach.'

'One nachos coming up.'

'You're an angel.' I'm not entirely sure what to do about the cop. I think back to the conversation Bailee and I ended up having on Saturday. She'd downed a couple more doubles, thinking it would loosen me up to talk. It's not like I've been back in her life all that long but I didn't think she had it in her. She's way more tenacious than I gave her credit for. I can't even begin to imagine how she felt afterwards and I haven't heard, but I ended up telling her the Jonathan Davies story, mostly to see if I could convince her I'm not the saint she's made me out to be in her head. But she handled it better than I thought she would. I'm impressed, but also very, very worried. I probably shouldn't have told her. I'm worried that what she found stupidly funny under the influence of several shots of JD might not be quite so amusing now she's had time to consider it without a hangover and a clear head. Maybe I should have called her. Found out. But I didn't.

I keep drinking, pick at the nachos.

On my third trip to the ladies' room I notice the cop seems to have gone, so I decide I should get home while I can still walk.

I stumble into the house fifteen minutes later. I've had way too much to drink and I know I'll pay for it tomorrow. Thank goodness for the nachos. Maybe I should take some pre-emptive Panadol. I head to the kitchen, but I can't see straight enough to find the pills and the room keeps moving.

I'm still rummaging uselessly through the drawers when an irritating, repetitive banging finally penetrates the fog of my mind. It takes me another minute to figure out the sound is coming from someone knocking on my door. I get there, eventually, only to find the cop standing on the other side.

'How did you find me?' I ask, annoyed.

'I followed you home.'

'I don't need a puppy.' I try to close the door but he puts his foot in the way. I see him wince as the door connects with it and feel a small sense of satisfaction.

'I told you I wasn't going away until we get this sorted.'

'But you left!'

'Far enough to encourage you off your stool.'

'And now it's late.'

'It's not like you've passed out. Yet.'

'I'm working on it.'

'Okay, then. Now I know where you live, how about I come back stupidly early?' he says.

I grit my teeth and step back inside.

He follows, looks around. 'Thanks. I won't take up too much time. Can I make you a coffee or something?'

'No!' Who does he think he is? Because it's easier than staying on my feet, I flop onto my lounge. 'Caffeine's only going to wake me up when I've invested all those drinks into knocking myself out.'

'You were drinking Pepsi at the bar,' he pointed out. 'You can't possibly be worried about caffeine.'

I point loosely in his direction while he searches through my cupboard. 'No one likes a smartarse.'

'I don't need you to like me,' he says, finding a glass and getting me some water from the tap. 'I need you to work with us. Rachael and I.'

'Not gonna happen.' I ignore the water and kick my feet up on the lounge in case he's considering sitting next to me.

'Is that cannabis?' he asks as though astounded.

I follow his line of sight to the plant by the window. It's the only thing other than myself I take care of in any way. I even have a name for it: Mojo. And yeah, it's cannabis. Shit. 'Of course not. That's just my pot plant. Are we done?'

His attention falls back to me and his expression isn't encouraging. 'Will you be in a better mood in the morning?'

'There's nothing wrong with my mood,' I lie. 'I've been drinking JD all night. I'm happy.'

'Oh, yeah? What's sad?'

'Bourbon.'

'Pissed off?'

'Vodka. The good stuff. Maybe. Or I might go back to JD.'

'Great, now I know what to bring to every occasion.'

'There won't be any other occasions. I've given you the link to the Spider's Web website but I'm not giving you the forum, because if you guys start poking around in there, they'll know something's up and all my hard work will be ruined. I'm going to bed.' And because the room really is spinning, I drag my feet off the lounge and head forward-sideways towards the bedroom. 'That wasn't an invitation,' I add, just in case. 'Go away.'

'Okay. But we need you to come into the station tomorrow. What time should I pick you up? Eight?'

'How about never.'

'Okay, nine then.'

'I don't get up before ten!'

'So I'll pick you up at ten.'

I drop my head back and it bangs on the bedroom door. 'This is why I don't like people knowing where I live!'

'Life's full of disappointments. Ten, Lexi.'

I'm still objecting when he lets himself out.

CHAPTER TWENTY-THREE

Monday, March 15

It's not often that I have a bad night's sleep after ingesting that much alcohol, but I've tossed and turned, feeling like death warmed up, for most of the night. As I stumble out to the kitchen for coffee I'm pretty sure that, despite my body's best efforts to remove every trace of everything it's had in it for the past twenty-eight years, I'm still drunk. The shower helps a bit, but the toothbrush and mouthwash that already stood little chance against the furry covering in my mouth make me heave.

I keep telling myself I have to stop drinking. And yet here I am. Again. At least I don't have a Jonathan Davies to contend with like I did the last time I felt this bad. But shit. The cop. Did he say eight, nine or ten? As it's already after nine, I have to go with ten. And there is no way in

hell—none—that that's going to happen today. If ever.
I call Bailee, and her bright answer has me squinting.

'Lexi, hi.'

'Don't "Hi" me in your pretty little innocent tone,' I warn
her. 'Do you have that cop's number?'

There's a pause. Then, 'Rachael's?'

'No, the other one.'

'Finn's? No, I don't, why?'

'Because you need to tell him if he comes near me this
morning, I'll find the bluntest knife I own and stab him
with it until he's dead. And Bailee, I'm not kidding.'

'Ah ... hangover?'

'Even for me, I was stupid,' I admit. I need to go hiber-
nate in the toilet. 'Make sure you tell him because I really
think there's a chance if I see him I'll follow through with
that threat. And that would be a shame, considering I've
avoided incarceration for eighteen years.'

'How does he know where you live? And why are you
pissed off at me?'

'He found me at the bar. Followed me home. Who else
would I have to thank for that? I mean, what kind of sidekick are you, anyway?'

'He what? I didn't tell him anything!' There's a pause,
then 'Mike!' she growls. 'I'm going to kill him.'

'Get in line. Actually, on second thought, you do it.
I need to lay in the dark and feel sorry for myself.'

I've just managed to settle my head and stomach to a dull
agony when the banging on the door starts. I need to buy a
doormat that tells everyone to fuck off. I lift my head and
squint towards the window by the front door. Not the cop
this time. Dawny.

'Not a good time!' I tell her.

'Sorry about that, but we need a bit of assistance!'

I wait until my stomach has completed another long roll, then manage to say, 'What kind?'

'Need to get the freezer on the truck. My dodgy knee won't let me do it. Desmond could use a hand.'

Oh, God. 'Now?'

'Yes, please.'

If it had been anything but the freezer … But I get up. I reluctantly enter the outside world. The fresh air is like being slapped in the face with a cricket bat. There's a small hire truck with a ramp on the back and the freezer has been rolled out to the bottom of it.

'Morning, Lexi.'

'Desmond.'

'Got a spare few minutes today?'

'Not today, Desmond. Hangover. It's bad.'

'Ah. You need an ox testicle and yoghurt smoothie.'

I heave-cough. 'Tell me you're not serious.'

'Supposed to make you chuck at the thought of it. A good hurl's always the best cure for a hangover, no matter what anyone tells ya.'

'You've very nearly succeeded. Let's get this thing up on the truck and … ah, shit.' It's the cop. He's pulled up in my driveway and he's getting out.

'Hi,' he says, buttoning his jacket as he steps out of the car.

I try for a cool smile, which I think probably more closely resembles a grimace. 'Hey. Did you not get the message?'

'Rachael passed on a message from Bailee that you weren't feeling well. I wasn't surprised. And yet here you are, moving appliances.'

I shake my head in disappointment. 'Trust Bailee to give you the polite version. What I said—no, promised—to do if you turned up was stab you repeatedly with a blunt knife until dead.'

'There's a nasty prison sentence attached to that sort of thing. Not a good idea.'

'I don't work with cops!' I say, mostly to make Dawny and Desmond aware of who he is, because Dawny seems to think he's hysterical and is doing her big barking laugh.

'Oh now, Lexi dear, don't be rude,' Dawny says. 'Especially when we're in need of a big strong pair of arms.'

Is she kidding? She has to be kidding! Jonathan Davies is in this freezer. What if the lid moves while it's going up the ramp or, despite the salt, Finn manages to get a whiff of something dead or ... I have this fleeting but horrifying image of the freezer falling over and a semi-decomposed, semi-mummified body falling out at his feet.

'I'd be happy to give you a hand.' Finn comes in around me, puts his hands on the freezer and pushes the thing up without any assistance. Desmond walks in behind the freezer to secure it with ties.

'Many thanks,' he says.

'Heading for the tip?' Finn asks.

'Spare parts,' Dawny tells him. 'We've been cleaning up. And gardening. Lexi has been helping with all the work. Such a good girl. Look at my pansies!'

He turns around and examines them. 'They're lovely.' I can tell something's amused him. I'm guessing it's the comment that I'm a good girl, but maybe he just finds flowers funny.

'Now I feel I should offer you some refreshments, Lexi, dear. Time for a cuppa, eh?' Dawny says. She grabs Finn's arm. 'Goodness! Those are some shoulders you've got there, detective. From catching all the bad guys, eh?'

Finn looks over his shoulder as he's led away. I'm tempted to let Dawny continue to verbally molest him while I make a quick exit, but I really just want to get him away from her as fast as possible. She's obviously lost the plot.

'Dawny, hold up. He doesn't have time for tea. I have to go find some stuff for him.' Predicting the next round of questions, I add, 'No, it's nothing exciting and, yes, I'll tell you all about it later. Can we hurry up and get this over with, detective?' I don't like the suspicious look Desmond is giving me.

'Yep,' he says, disengaging himself at the doorway. 'Nice to meet you Mrs …?'

'Dawny, dear. You come back and have some pie another day.'

'I might just do that. Nice to meet you, Desmond.'

'And you. Best be off.'

Resigned to the fact I have very little choice, I get into Finn's car.

He sends me a sideways look at he does up his seat-belt. 'After threatening to cut me into small pieces with a dull implement you're going to just come quietly?' he asks suspiciously.

'On the condition that if I say stop, you stop. I may need to throw up once or twice on the way.'

He grimaces. 'It's really that bad?'

'Worse.'

'I have a good hangover recipe. Tomato juice, a couple of raw eggs and—'

Repulsed, my stomach convulses. 'Okay, people really need to stop with the hangover cures,' I manage. 'We're not even out of the driveway yet and it's about to get ugly.'

'It works,' he says with a grin. 'There's also Berocca. Berocca works pretty good.'

'So do cheeseburgers.'

'Then we'll hit Macca's on the way. I need you functional.'

Not sure what to say, or even if I want to say anything, I put on my sunglasses and stare out the window. I'm pretty sure a part of me realised this was inevitable, but I don't have to like it.

'So, you like gardening?' he asks as we hit the main road.

'Huh?'

'Dawny said you've been gardening.'

'Oh right. Yeah. She needed the help so ...'

'She seems nice.'

'She's an ex-con.'

He shoots me a sideways glance. 'Someone arrested that sweet old lady? Over what?'

'I don't actually know. Why?'

'Just curious.'

'Cop trait, right?'

'Curiosity? Sure, I guess.'

When I don't answer the car falls into silence for thirty, maybe forty blissful seconds. My eyes just manage to close when he says, 'Are you good at it? Gardening, I mean.'

'There's that curiosity again.'

'Maybe I like gardening, too.'

I press my fingers to my temples hard, as though I can push the headache away. 'Good for you.'

'But I live in a flat. Even my plastic plant died on me.'

I frown because, well, ridiculous. 'How can a plastic plant die?'

'I think the thick layer of dust it accumulated finally toppled it.'

I can't quite hide the grin. My stomach gurgles loudly. If it'll stay down, that cheeseburger might actually help.

'My mother was a great gardener,' Finn continues. 'I like the idea of it. It's like surfing. I can't do that either but I enjoy the idea of it.'

'So learn.'

He flicks me a sideways glance. 'I'm thirty-three. That's probably be a bit late to be starting from scratch.'

'Oh shit. You're right. You're way too old.'

'Thanks.' Then after another minute of silence, 'You don't talk much, do you?'

I forcibly bite back the nasty words that want to erupt from my mouth. 'Luckily, you do enough for both of us.'

He shrugs. 'Passes the time.'

'I don't talk to cops.'

'Cops are people, you know.'

'Seriously? Who knew. You just drove past Macca's.'

'Shit.' He went around the next roundabout, back and into drive thru. 'Cheeseburger, right? Anything else?'

'Coffee. Black. No sugar.'

He orders, adds a coffee for himself.

'Thanks,' I say when he passes me my order. As he pulls back out onto the road I try and decide if the smell is making things better or worse. I take a tentative bite.

'Any better?'

'I'll let you know when it hits my stomach.'

'So, you're going to talk to Rachael, right?'

'Do I have a choice?'

'Of course. And can you drop the attitude? Please? We've all had shitty things happen in our lives.'

'You too? Good to know. Now we can bond over our tragic pasts and be best friends forever.'

'Sarcasm is the lowest form of wit.'

'Oooh, point scored, detective.'

'Rachael isn't the enemy.'

'What do you care?'

'I'm her nephew.'

'I'm so sorry.'

'I'm going to ignore those responses from now on. My mother was your teacher, Kayla Carson.'

I open my mouth then change what I was going to say. 'What do you mean was?'

'She died a couple of years after your case. Rachael took me in.'

'Mrs Carson died? Sorry. She was a nice lady.'

'Yeah, I thought so. I'm telling you this because I've known Rachael my entire life. She looked after me after Mum died and I saw what the Spider case did to her.'

'Oh, of course,' I say, taking another bite of my burger. 'Poor Rachael.'

He hisses out a breath. 'Do you know how many achievements she has, how many awards she's won for service? She could fill walls with them. You know what takes pride of place in her office for everyone to see? Your picture. That creepy drawing you did of the Spider. Not because she's proud of her work on that case but because she sees it as her greatest failure and she will never let herself forget it. She's looked for you ever since. You've been like this ghost that wouldn't let her go. Now you've turned up when all that is about to blow back up in her face and you're tied up in it again. So yeah, I'm hoping you can help out because the sooner we can close this case, the sooner you can both put this behind you once and for all.'

I scald my mouth on my coffee. 'Behind me? I don't get to put it behind me! I don't have walls of awards and achievements because I never got the chance to get them. Rachael might be able to go back to her cushy little life once this is sorted, but this is as good as it gets for me. Keeping a roof over my head by fucking strangers so I don't have to go back to the streets. So please, spare me the "poor Rachael" bullshit.'

'She was right behind you that night. She was on her way. You didn't have to run.'

'Oh, right, it's my fault.'

'That not what I meant.'

'Look, I don't actually care what you do or don't mean. It doesn't matter.'

'I'm getting that vibe,' he says, pulling into the station. 'Here we are.'

CHAPTER TWENTY-FOUR

In her office, Rachael stared at the text from Ed.

Biddle's appeal has been granted. Biddle's lawyers are seeking for his conviction to be quashed with no fresh trial ordered.

She wasn't exactly surprised. It should have taken months to get to this point. But with a monster on the loose claiming to be the real Spider and almost insurmountable evidence her investigation had gotten it wrong, there was little basis left for disputing Biddle's innocence. The public were demanding answers. The media campaign to free Biddle was no doubt embarrassing those in power. She had been waiting for it, but having it confirmed didn't make the news any easier.

She put her phone away to deal with the long list of things she could actually do something about and went to find Debbie.

'Debbie, I have a message here from Van Zettan saying you sent over Davies's remarks and conclusions, not the actual copies of the lab results.'

'I sent everything we had. But I couldn't find anything that looked like copies of actual test results, only Davies's reports on them.'

'Slimy bastard,' Turner muttered from his desk before looking up. 'Davies was in charge of providing the police with the evidence that could have caught the Spider. And he's tampered with and destroyed evidence, made up whatever results—or lack of them—he needed to hinder the case.'

'Everything's certainly pointing to that,' Rachael said.

'And I'm back to wondering if the wife found out,' Turner said. 'There was a party going on a few doors down from Davies's place that Saturday night. I've pulled a load of photos from social media. Police were called, so I have some video as well. There's a silver Audi S5 parked outside Davies's house at midnight.' He showed her a copy of the photo. 'Same make and model as Charmaine Davies's. Only she said she wasn't there.'

'There's a lot of cars on the street,' Rachael said, examining the photo. 'No chance of a plate. Didn't you say her sister verified her whereabouts that night?'

'And I'm sure her sister wouldn't lie,' Turner said wryly.

'Charmaine's tiny,' she said, thinking out loud. 'I can't see her being able to overpower her husband in a fight or lift his body into her car and get rid of it alone. If she was involved, she must have had help.'

'There could be evidence in her car,' Turner added.

Rachael thought about it, then nodded. 'Okay. Show her the picture, see what she has to say, and have forensics go over her car.'

Turner looked pleased. 'I'll get it organised.'

'You really think Charmaine offed her husband?' Debbie asked.

Rachael shrugged. 'I'd say she has plenty of motive. Without any knowledge of what he was up to, he was still making her look crazy, fighting for custody of their daughter and kicking her to the kerb with as little as possible. If she did find out, I guess that's even more motive, though surely she would have come to the police with anything solid. It's certainly worth looking into, and it'll keep Turner out of my hair a bit longer, but I think it's more an exercise in ruling her out than catching a killer. Lexi seemed pretty adamant Charmaine had nothing to do with it.'

'Right. Hey, is that Lexi Winter that's just come in?'

Rachael turned and saw Finn and Lexi by the entrance to the room. 'Yeah. Thanks Debbie.' She studied Lexi's face, the discomfort hidden behind the bored expression, and forced a smile over her own nerves. 'Lexi, please come into my office,' she said. 'Thanks for coming.'

'Yeah, fine. But can you call off this one?' Lexi said with a glance at Finn. 'Since he followed me home, I can't get rid of him.'

'She's full of them,' Finn warned. 'It's funny for about five minutes.'

With some of the tension broken, Rachael's smile became more genuine. 'Please sit down.'

Lexi dropped into a seat across from Rachael and Finn took the one next to Lexi.

'So you want the forum site, right?' Lexi asked. 'The thing is, it's not something anyone can join. It's a private site for members and there aren't that many, maybe twenty or thirty all up. You can't get in unless they know you and you've been invited.'

'So how did you do it?' Finn asked.

'Sorry to interrupt,' Turner said, poking his head around the door and taking an interested look at Lexi.

'No, it's fine,' Rachael said. 'Lexi, this is Detective Turner. He's running the investigation into the disappearance of Jonathan Davies. I think he should hear any information you have pertaining to this.'

Lexi shrugged. 'Doesn't bother me.'

Turner stepped further into the room and leant on the wall, arms folded. As he stared at Lexi there was a notable lack of warmth that leant towards disapproval in his expression that Rachael didn't quite understand.

'So you want to know how I found Davies,' Lexi continued. 'I didn't go looking for him, I went looking for Doc on a site I'd caught another guy on for Bailee. It has a lot of Aussies on it. They share threads about where to pick up the youngest prostitutes in Sydney, that sort of thing. So it was really just a matter of "Hey, I heard this guy called this was posting this sort of shit, anyone know where I can find some more?" Then you throw in a sweetener like a video share and someone in their close-knit little community is going to know something. Turns out Doc had visited the site several times and once I was pointed in the right direction I just had to jump on an old post of his and contact him, get him talking. Then I offered to share a video I thought he'd like and sent it to him. The file contained spyware, meaning I could keep an eye on his online activity. He went to the party site nearly every day.'

'Wait,' Turner said. 'You shared child pornography videos?'

'Yeah. Guys like that don't do stuff out of the kindness of their hearts.'

'That's illegal.'

'And here I was, a law-abiding citizen.'

'This is not a joke,' Turner said. 'You don't have a right to be in possession of that sort of content. It's an offence.'

'I have every right!' Lexi snapped. 'They're mine!'

'You made them?'

'You fuckwit. I starred in them. And anyone who has cash and a reasonable knowledge of the dark web can get their hands on them—whether they have the right to or not. Thank you for reminding me why I hate cops.' Lexi got up. 'I'm out of here.'

'Lexi, wait, please,' Rachael asked.

But Lexi waved over her shoulder and walked out.

Rachael glared at Turner. 'We were just starting to get somewhere! If you can't be civil—'

'Me? She calls me a fuckwit and I'm copping it for civility? She broke the law.'

'And she's the closest we've been to stopping another child from being taken and murdered horribly. Where are your priorities? Finn?' Catching his attention, she looked to the door and nodded. Finn got the message and went after Lexi.

*

Finn couldn't see Lexi, so he decided he'd better check downstairs. But he had better things to do than go chasing around after a hot-headed prostitute, didn't he?

'Out front and left,' the constable behind the desk told him, obviously guessing what he was up to.

'Thanks.' He wondered if Rachael really expected him to chase her down the street, decided she probably did. Stuff Turner and his big mouth.

You fuckwit. I starred in them.

For all that she annoyed him, that had packed a punch. And now she was selling herself to survive, probably because that was what she knew. That sucked. But what about this computer stuff? Where had that come from?

He was about to give up his search when he found her sitting on the low brick wall of the local church overlooking the park and the water beyond. When she spotted him she sat a little straighter, her face closed up. 'Oh good, what now?'

He decided he may as well sit beside her rather than stand over her. 'Rachael's busy giving Turner a mouthful so I get to come out here and talk you into coming back inside.'

'Yeah. Nah. For some reason I'm not feeling all that comfortable with the idea.'

'Not really about you though, is it? Or will not wanting to step out of your comfort zone make it okay when the next girl gets taken?'

'Comfort zone?' she asked, eyes flashing. 'What *comfort* zone exactly are you referring to? How do you think I track down these arseholes? Child abuse videos, dick pics, sick conversations. That's hardly *comfortable*.' Her voice lowered on the last few words and her eyes returned to the view.

He decided she was easier to work with pissed off. It was the only time she said more than three words. 'And do you always wallow in self-pity while you do it?'

'I have never wallowed a day in my life!'

'Right. So why start now?'

He heard her long, indrawn breath. 'I don't like Turner.'

'Join the club. And Rachael barely tolerates him. But we all have to work with him so why shouldn't you? Show him up. It's fun, and honestly not that difficult. Come back in and save a kid's life.'

She eyed him narrowly. 'If I don't want to?'

'Then I'll risk the wrath of Rachael and take you home.'

She seemed to be considering that. 'There's no guarantees I can save a kid's life. I probably can't.'

'You've gotten further than us so far.'

'Ow! Was that as painful to say as it sounded?'

He chewed on a grin. 'We can crack this without you.'

'Guess I'll take that ride home then.'

'But you've already sped up the process and Rachael seems to want you to hang around so ...'

'I don't know how to do things the way you do.'

'I was under the impression you were smart.'

'Was that a compliment? I need a drink.'

'One for every occasion, right?'

She laughed, though it was pretty obvious she didn't want to.

'Come on, you don't want this guy out there any more than we do.'

She eyed him with very little enthusiasm. 'I don't like cops.'

'And that hurts. It really does.' He felt a small victory when the smile crept back onto her face. 'Come on. Please?'

'If you keep Turner out of my way, I guess maybe I could work with you a bit more closely.'

'Great.'

'Tone is everything.'

Now she'd made him laugh, damn it. 'Let's go, Winter.'

When she got to her feet, he figured that was victory number two.

CHAPTER TWENTY-FIVE

Okay, so maybe for a cop, Finn's not *too* bad. I'm far from convinced, but the fact he doesn't like that Turner guy is points in his favour. Jury is still out on Rachael. She's not what I expected at all.

'Give me a minute,' Finn says as we approach the closed door to Rachael's office. 'I'll see if Rachael's ready for us.'

I turn my attention to the next room, wandering a few steps away to peer inside.

The first thing I see is the face of a young girl pinned to the board. *Summer Edgely* is written above. Underneath the portrait is another photo. Summer dead in the water in that stupid mermaid outfit. Poor kid.

I skim the notes and a brightly marked map to land on the next wall. Three more portraits sit there and underneath more photos of girls lying on beds of flowers as though sleeping. I know these images. They're just as heartbreaking.

I ignore the scattering of people at their desks and move in closer so I can see more. This wall is full of the old case. Biddle's first murders. I have to admit I'm interested in filling in some of the blanks I never discovered; I'm also curious to see where the cops are in the current investigation. Because no one seems to be paying any attention to me, I move across the room. Forensic reports, a map showing the location of Summer's house and the dump site, a comparative chart of Summer's murder to the originals and a couple of interview sheets. Then I catch sight of Jonathan Davies's face and, as I move towards the back corner, another I think could be Cody. I briefly wonder how he's going.

'Hey, can I help you?'

A head has appeared over the top of a nearby monitor. The guy gets up and stretches. I decide he's probably closer to Bailee's age than mine, with a crop of red, pointy hair and trendily large glasses. The jeans and tee suggest he's not a cop.

'Hi,' I reply cautiously.

'Are you with the police?'

'Yeah …' I reply, because technically I suppose I am. I mean, I walked in with one. 'With Finn.' Then before he can ask me anything else, I point to Summer's picture. 'Doesn't look much like the girl in the video, does she?'

'What do you mean?'

'I mean she looks like she can't wait to jump off that chair and head off with her friends. Maybe skip school for the rest of the day.'

'Yeah, well, maybe she did. Maybe before her life was cut short she got to enjoy a few of those rites of passage. Even if her father was an arsehole.'

I see a transcript of an interview with Tyson Brewer and I store that piece of information away in case he's part of Davies's group and I get a chance to prove it. 'Anyway, I'm interrupting you so …'

'Not at all. I'm going nuts trying to find something tying Summer's teaser video to the original Spider case.'

'Such as?'

'A watermark or call sign. It's got to be here somewhere.'

Ah, I'm guessing this is the guy Bailee mentioned but I can't remember his name, only that he's supposedly doing the job she thinks I should be doing. 'Why does it matter? You don't need it. You have the Spider's Web and the full version of the video. Don't you?'

'Yes, but I'm looking for differences and similarities between cases so we can decide whether this guy's legit the Spider or a copycat. Rachael's got me combing through and recording every tiny detail.'

Good to know. 'He's a copycat,' I say. 'But he's a good one. The original watermark is there, only a bit more … twenty-first century.'

His face goes pricelessly blank. 'Ah … what … where? I've checked everything!' He's drawn me around to his computer monitor before he's finished stuttering.

Well, I guess this is the sort of thing I'm here for. So why not? I might save the kid a few hours' work. 'Skip to the part just before the arsehole smiles into the camera. Now slow it right down. You want the frame that goes white, like a flash, before his big ugly smile appears. There. Okay. What program are you running?'

'Mine.'

'Which tells me nothing. Can you adjust image colour?'

'Too easy.'

'Okay, so max out your input levels.'

As he does, the shape of a spider appears in the centre of the screen.

'No way!'

'You haven't come across that before? It's a new rough 'n' snuff watermark method. Easy enough to find if you know what to look for, more difficult if you're the cops.'

'What the hell is going on?'

'Uh oh.' Turner's back and he has a couple more cops with him.

'Were you told you could be in here?' he asks me sharply. Every head in the room pokes over or between monitors to watch.

'There you are!' Finn says from the doorway. He comes in with Rachael and everyone at least pretends to get back to work. That's power.

Computer boy stands up beside me. 'She found the watermark.'

'You found it?' Finn asked, moving through the room to take a look.

I shrug. 'No big deal. I was just showing …?'

'Oh, sorry. I'm Jim,' he said.

That's right! And wow, did it suit him. 'Surname Neutron by any chance?'

I see the red creep up his neck. Cute. 'Jimmy Neutron was twelve.'

'And you're not?'

'Why is she wandering around in our strike force room?' Turner asks.

And, oh, if I can't stuff him in a freezer, I'm at least gonna have to have some fun with him. 'Do you need coffee or are you always like this?'

'She shouldn't have access to our case,' he tells Rachael, ignoring me.

'More than happy to leave,' I say.

'What watermark?' Rachael asks.

'The one on the teaser video,' Jim says.

Finn raises his brows at Jim. 'Lexi found it in two seconds and you've been working on it how long?'

'I already knew what I was looking for,' I tell Finn. 'The real Spider didn't use teasers but there you go. The pretend Spider does.'

'That's why she's here,' Rachael tells Turner. 'What else can you tell us, Lexi?'

'What else?' I drag my attention from Turner back to Rachael. 'What do you mean?'

'Look around. Any thoughts?'

I have the attention of the entire room, some interested, some dubious and one hostile. I'm not comfortable with any of it. I move back towards the door without meaning to but manage to kill the movement of my feet when I reach the front board and point to Davies. 'I'm guessing you already know, but this is the guy I looked up for Bailee. He's part of an online group who organise parties for underage kids. They supply food, drinks and drugs, and some other shit a lot of these kids need to survive.'

'And the Spider?' Rachael prompts.

'I'm pretty sure most of the group don't know who he is. There was discussion about it on their site and they seemed pretty clueless. But I think this guy, Davies, knew.'

Finn whistles, like they'd already suspected it.

'Why, Lexi?' Rachael asks.

I can't blurt out that he basically admitted it moments before his death, can I? So I try something else. 'The laptop he was using dated back twenty years and he had all the original Spider files on it.'

'That doesn't prove anything,' Turner said.

'That computer was dedicated entirely to the Spider and the group of paedos the Spider belonged to before. He was one of them. The only stuff that's gone on there since belongs to this group Davies was involved with.'

'So you're sure Davies was involved in Biddle's group from twenty years ago?' Rachael asks.

I can feel the tension in the room and decide I must be missing something. 'Yeah, I'm sure as I can be.'

'And I suppose you're going to tell us who the Spider is next?' Turner asks, sharing a snide grin with his friends.

'Biddle is the Spider,' I tell him, teeth clenched.

'Turner, how about you and your support group find something useful to do,' Rachael says.

Turner's face reddens at the verbal slap. The two officers he came in with exchange smirks, their amusement only inflaming him more. 'Don't mind me. I'm only here as a detective with the experience needed to work this case, but it seems you'd prefer to belittle me and everyone else in this room by handing a sensitive investigation over to a walk-in off the street.'

'Perhaps you'd better take a moment to calm yourself down,' Rachael warned.

'And perhaps you'd better take a moment to decide who's more valuable to have on your team!'

In the ensuing silence, Rachael's measured tone is clear. 'I already have.' Then to me, 'Lexi, you were saying?'

The momentary tightening of Rachael's expression is the only indication she even notices Turner's incensed departure from the room.

'This imposter,' I plough on feeling as though I've just made a very nasty enemy, 'is part of Davies's group. When he hadn't been online for several days, I jumped on the site posing as Davies and no one batted an eye except one guy. He calls himself Victor Rheus.'

'Rheus ... We know from the video this guy is a white male,' Rachael says. 'Is that Dutch? German?'

'Could be either but it could also be a play on words. "Victorious". They all seem to like thinking they have clever usernames. Anyway, he knew I wasn't Davies. With my secure setup there's no way he could have figured that out from my computer information, so it had to be something else. That happened a couple of days *before* it came out that Davies was missing.'

'So this Victor guy knew something had happened to Davies before it became public knowledge,' Rachael said.

'Right. Anyway, because he was so adamant I wasn't Davies, I tried playing a different angle. I said I was a friend of Davies's and he'd said I could check out the group because I was keen to join. I threw in everything I knew about Davies to make it seem legit.' I glance at Finn and grimace. 'Including that Davies kept a laptop that had all his videos on it.'

'Let's get a board set up on this Victor Rheus guy,' Rachael said. 'Lexi, do you know anything else about him?'

'Not yet. I was hoping he'd get back to me about joining, but so far he hasn't. It might not be his decision. I've been collecting bits and pieces of mostly useless information on some of the other members. It's slow work because I have to go through all the forum pages, reading hundreds of conversations.'

'Jim and as many others as you need will assist you with that. Any mention of party times or addresses?'

'None. They're fanatical about it. I'm guessing it's strictly word of mouth or private messaging.'

'Hence why you're trying to get yourself an invite,' Rachael said. 'Excellent. Jim, clear Lexi some space next to you.'

'Yes, inspector.' He looked more than happy to.

'Whoa, I'm not working here!' I tell her.

'Sometimes?' Rachael asked. 'Let's just aim for sometimes. Okay? I'd prefer that any assistance you give us while working this case is done as much as possible with strike force officers present.'

I want to object but everyone's suddenly moving in all directions and they all seem to know exactly what they're doing. Except me. Even Rachael and Finn have disappeared. I can't help but think they've taken off on purpose so I can't argue.

'Excuse me. Is this enough space?' Jim asks.

'Huh? Oh, sure. I guess.'

'We should set up a network. Can you show me this website you were talking about? I'll need to know how to get in so I can help gather the information.'

'No.'

He actually looks hurt. 'Why not?'

'Because I don't trust your system.'

'I swear we're secure. The tech I have is second to none. I promise,' he adds meekly when I don't immediately answer.

It's like talking to a sensitive three-year-old. 'That's sweet. But I'll stick with mine.'

'It's not possible to hack what I have!'

A three-year-old having a tantrum. And I do like a challenge. 'How are you set up?'

'With software you wouldn't have even heard of.'

Another full-on stare sits his bravado on its arse.

'I don't think,' he adds in a small voice.

I'm starting to feel mean. He might have the personality of a kicked puppy but he sounds like he's probably pretty good with a computer. 'You'd better be right.' I flick my fingers at him and he jumps from his seat. And okay, yeah, I have to say I'm impressed as he takes me through his system. I might even learn something.

'How are we going?' Rachael asks, and hands me a black coffee.

'Oh. Thanks.' I pull up the website. 'Okay, the problem is I can log in as Doc, but now everyone knows something's happened to him so they'll know I'm not him. Every time I go on, there's a risk they'll boot me from the site and we'll lose them.'

'Then we need to get in and out fast.'

'Explain to me again how you got onto his computer?' Rachael asked.

'I told you I shared a video with him. I attached spyware to the video file so when he downloaded it, I saw everything he saw whenever he was online.'

'Why not attach a RAT?' Jim asks.

'Considered it but most of the ones I have are more easily picked up by antivirus. This little spyware program seems to sneak under the radar more reliably.'

'What's a RAT?' Rachael asks.

'Remote Access Trojan. Lets you connect to and control someone else's computer.'

'I have one that will sneak past most current antivirus software,' Jim tells me.

'I have one that will sneak through every time,' I counter. 'But it has to be manually installed on the site after running an antivirus corrupting software that mimics the user's real AV.'

'No way. Really? Where'd you get that?'

'I could tell you, but I'd have to kill you.'

He actually looks at Rachael as though to check I'm serious, then shakes his head. 'Anyway, I also have a sweet little program that can copy the contents of an entire website in a very small amount of time.'

Okay, he has my attention. 'How small?'

'Depends on the size of the site. Anything from a few seconds to a few minutes.'

That's got to be a good thing and I'm suddenly more enthusiastic. 'Okay, let's do it.'

I enter the site and Doc appears online. I glance at Jim. 'Whenever you're ready.'

'May I?' He steps around me awkwardly, hammers away at his keyboard. I watch, waiting for maybe a minute.

'Done.'

'Done?' I ask in surprise.

'Yeah, you want me to log out?'

'Yes, do it,' I say, sitting up in my chair. 'Then show me what you got.'

He closes the site and pulls up the copied files. 'You were right about the amount of content,' he says. 'That's an impressive number of conversations and shares for a small group. Though it looks like it's been going on for a lot of years.'

'Well done, boy genius,' I say when he looks at me expectantly. I get the full-effect blush again.

Rachael looks at me with amusement for the briefest moment before she's back to business. 'How many analysts do you need on this?' she asks Jim.

'Depends on how fast you need it sorted,' Jim says. 'I'll run some keyword searches through the data to try and sort content into more manageable loads.'

'I can spare you three for the time being,' she says. 'I'll bring them across.'

'So, where do you want to start?' Jim asks me while Rachael moves across the room.

I take a really good look around because my mind is still having trouble processing what's going on. Everything's happened so fast. I had no intention of doing any of this. Where do I start? Ha.

'I have no idea.'

*

By eight o'clock in the evening, I'm back to what I know. I'm meeting Grady, the least favourite of my clients. I generally see him on Saturday nights and we visit a few clubs before ending up back at my regular. But he's just got back after a couple of weeks on some adrenaline tour in Queensland and because I'm desperate for the cash, I've agreed to see him tonight. There's nowhere much to go on a Monday, but Grady has assured me we're in for a good night and I can only imagine he has something up his sleeve I'm not going to appreciate.

'There you are!' Grady says from behind me at my spot at the bar. 'Hi, sugar.'

I let the smile slide onto my face and turn around. 'Hey there, handsome. Have fun riding rapids?'

'And the rest.' His arm slides around my waist. 'You ready to head upstairs?'

'Sure,' I answer. Maybe I'm wrong. Maybe this won't be so difficult. Straight to business. I lead him upstairs and slip into his arms inside the room. He likes me clingy. I'm against the back of the door in seconds and his hands are all over me.

'I've missed you,' he says against my mouth.

It should be simple enough to ease into my role but tonight something's bothering at the edge of my mind. I shove it aside and get on with my role. Everything else that's going on has left me off balance, that's all. Spending a few hours in a police station, pitting my skills against a brain with degrees in computer science and law and I can't remember what else. I need to get my head back in the right space. I need this money.

There's a tapping on the door and Grady spins me around to the wall. 'I've got a surprise for you, sugar.'

He opens the door and another guy comes in. He's taller than Grady, maybe a bit younger and, from the look on his face, just as horny.

'Thought we'd spice things up a bit,' Grady tells me. 'A bit of two on one, maybe some roleplay. Mick likes it rough.'

I plant my hands on Grady's shoulders when he reaches for me again and hold him at arm's length. 'Hold on. I don't do threesomes and not I'm into rough.'

'Oh, now don't be like that,' Grady croons. 'We'll pay double, don't worry.' His fingers are biting into my arms, tugging me closer while Mick slides around behind me. I try to step away but he won't let go. Panic surges through me. They're coming at me from two sides and not taking no for an answer. I feel Mick's hand wrap around my hair, tug it back. My pulse is racing, my arms hurt where Grady's fingers are digging in. Every sense is focused on escape. I try to calm myself down. To think. I can't overpower them but I need to get away. I need to get this under control.

'Hey! You want to do this, you do it my way!' I try to sound strict but sexy. Heart pounding, I hold my breath as they hesitate. I can do this. I've dealt with similar shit before, just not for a long time. I fight for the cool, the collected, the in-charge me while the guys look at each other.

Mick shrugs. 'What have you got in mind, sweetheart?'

I spin in Grady's loosened grip. Push Mick. 'You, get naked and get on the bed,' I order in a tone that hinders argument. When he doesn't move, I raise an eyebrow. Wait.

'Now we're talking,' he breathes. The smirk returns and he starts to undress. I pull my hair free and let it tumble down, slip one strap from my shoulder and spin again, press myself against Grady. 'I'm gonna start with you,' I purr, hoping he's paying more attention to my voice than the pulse I know is thundering out of control at the base of my throat. My hands slide up his arms to his shoulders while he grasps my hips. I grip his shoulders tight and ram my knee into his groin as hard as I can.

He goes straight down with a primeval sound of raw pain, hands clutched between his legs.

'You son of a bitch. Don't bother calling me again,' I tell him.

'What the fuck!' comes from Mick as I grab my bag and open the door. He gets hold of my dress, drags me roughly back inside. I lose my footing, go down, feel the sharp glancing crack of my cheek against the side table. Then he's coming at me again. I shove at him, kick out and manage to break free, half roll, half stumble into the corridor. He's hopping around, trying to get his jeans on as I flee down the stairs.

Arseholes! I make it to the bar on trembling legs and catch Tom's eye. He's in front of me in seconds.

'What happened?'

'Grady thought he'd bring a friend.'

'Jeez, Lexi, I didn't even see anyone else head up,' Tom says, dragging his hand through his hair like it's somehow his fault. 'Where are they?'

'On their way no doubt, but Tom, just let them go, okay? You don't need the trouble.'

But Tom gives a nod to the other bartender and they leave the bar unattended and head upstairs.

I touch my fingers gingerly to my cheek. Wince. I don't handle injuries gracefully. I know some people are purported to have something called a high pain tolerance. I'm not one of them.

There's a thud from the heavy door to the staircase and it bounces open a few inches, as though something heavy has landed against it with force. A few seconds of general confused movement and sound later, Mick falls through it. He looks like he might have copped at least one punch to the eye as well as his tumble. Grady's still walking funny, but from the eyes pinned to the front doors and the speed in his damaged gait, he seems to be in quite the hurry to leave.

'Crazy bitch!' Mick calls out when he spots me. But his stride doesn't falter as he makes the doors about the same time as Grady.

'Let me get you an icepack,' Tom says, returning to the bar. He wraps it in a clean tea towel and hands it to me.

'Thanks. Tom, really. Thanks.'

'They won't be back, don't worry.'

I try and make the icepack comfortable against my cheek. 'You know—'

'Don't have to say it,' Tom tells me, and puts a glass and what's left of the current bottle of JD in front of me. 'Best anaesthetic ever,' he promises.

'You may just be my soulmate,' I murmur, blocking all thoughts of my earlier hangover from my mind as I pour myself a decent splash.

He winks at me. 'You mean you're only now figuring that out?'

CHAPTER TWENTY-SIX

Tuesday, March 16

Finn bought a coffee and wandered towards work. It was too nice a morning to drive and the walk wasn't a long one. A couple of joggers ran past. He used to run this stretch almost every day when he was stationed here, now the trip into the city chewed up that opportunity, had him spending his workout time inside the walls of a gym.

Sail boats were out already, the conditions perfect. He wasn't really watching where he was going, had his gaze fixed on the water, so he almost walked right past Lexi as she sat on that same low wall by the church as she had previously. The greeting was on his lips when he noticed the swelling under her eye.

'What happened to you?' he asked.

Lexi looked up, clearly unimpressed by his presence. He was getting used to it. 'Nothing. It doesn't matter.'

'Come on, tell me what happened.'

'What's the point? When you do what I do you're asking for it, right?'

'Someone did this to you?' he asked, feeling instant anger towards whoever it was. 'Who?'

'I don't need a knight in shining armour.'

'What about a cop who takes assault seriously?'

'Forget it. I won't be seeing them again. I'm going to have to get some new clients anyway.'

'Why's that?'

'Because I'm obviously not going to be seeing this arsehole or his friend again and I just convinced one of the nice two I had left to take a chance on true love. Now I can't pay my rent.' She looked down at her feet. 'I must be mad.'

'Or just a good person.'

'Yeah, well, good doesn't feed me. And hah. You thought it was funny when Dawny called me that.'

'To be fair I—' He laughed in self-deprecation. 'Okay, you coming in?'

'Yeah, I guess.'

She got to her feet and they walked the short distance to the station.

'So you're not going to tell me who did that?'

'I did it. Falling over.'

'Isn't the standard excuse supposed to be "I walked into a door"?'

She laughed a little, then grimaced as though the movement hurt. 'No, it was definitely a side table. And I don't make excuses for arseholes. Tom took care of it.'

'The bartender.'

'That's him.'

They made their way up in the lift, then Lexi went straight into the strike force room while he went looking for Rachael.

'Morning,' Rachael said distractedly as he appeared in her doorway.

'Morning.'

She glanced up at his tone. 'Something wrong?'

He sighed. 'She's genuinely good at all this computer stuff, right?'

'We're talking about Lexi?' Rachael checked. 'Jim's words were "super, crazy good". He actually asked me why we needed him when we had her.'

Finn couldn't get his head around it. 'And yet she risks her safety working as a prostitute for a living?'

'She what?' Some of the colour seemed to drain from Rachael's face.

'Damn, Rach, sorry, I didn't realise you didn't know.'

Rachael stared into space and dragged in a long, slow breath. Nodded to herself. 'Okay, okay. Well, then.'

'Well, then what?'

'It's a well-researched fact that children who go through what she did are more likely to become involved in prostitution. I'd hoped she might not have been one of them.'

'I want to say no judgement but … The girl's got more options, surely.'

'Intelligence is one thing, self-worth is something else entirely.'

'So, we have a hooker working for us? Fantastic.' Turner stepped into the room past Finn. 'Got time to talk about Charmaine?' he asked Rachael.

'Where are you up to?' Rachael asked coldly.

'She's sticking to the claim she was never at the house that night,' Turner said. 'But I'll know more when forensics have finished going over the car. She seems nervous to me, guilty. I'll give her another chance to talk to me before the results come in. I'm hoping to have something solid on her before the end of the day.'

There was snuffle of wry laughter from behind Finn. Lexi was standing there, her bruised face twisted into disdain.

'Have you got some sort of problem with me?' Turner said.

'Don't take it personally,' Lexi said. 'All fuckwits annoy me.'

Turner's whole posture tightened in disbelief. 'What did you just call me?'

'You're *hoping* a persecuted mother with a young daughter will be responsible? *Hoping* a child might lose the only parent she has left? Wouldn't it be nicer to *hope* it's the nasty bad guy I've already told you about who is responsible?'

Turner shrugged dismissively. 'It's nothing personal. It's a case.'

'It's not a *case*, it's a mother and a child! You have no idea how much difference just one good parent can mean to a kid. To have one person in the world who actually cares about you, who thinks you mean something. So how about trying to be a decent human *and* a cop? Hope for something else. Go find Victor.'

Turner's smirk was smug. 'Oh, but I thought you had him covered? Or is that just men in general?'

'Turner!' Rachael's sharp reprimand echoed off the walls. 'Lexi, give us a minute, would you? I'll come and find you as soon as I can.'

Lexi looked tightly from one to the other then nodded. 'Sure.'

'That was uncalled for!' Rachael said to Turner.

'Was it? How about you tell me why she's still here and why on earth she appears to be setting up like she's moving in?'

'Have you seen what she can do? What she's already got us? She's one step away from infiltrating the group.'

'By breaking the law! And now you're breaking the rules for her. Again. And jeopardising the case. Your relationship with that girl has already ruined my chance at promotion once and I'm not going to stand by while you do it again!'

Rachael couldn't help the blank stare. 'What has this got to do with—'

'If she hadn't called you that night everything would have been different. It was a lucky break, not good police work. Yet here you are an inspector in homicide while I'm still—'

Rachael cut him off in disbelief. 'I understand you have a problem with me, but the idea that you've held a grudge against an abused little girl for eighteen years because she called me for help is unbelievable!'

'What's unbelievable is that you're giving her more credence in this investigation than you're giving me! I had the respect of my peers around here, now they're sniggering into their hands because that prostitute's opinion holds more sway with you than mine does. This case could finally push me up the ladder but once again you're making it about Rachael Langley and Lexi Winter. You put her in my way again and you'll regret it.' Turner walked out, closing the door harder than necessary.

Rachael stared, speechless, at the back of the door while she processed the unexpected tirade. 'Did he just threaten me?' she finally asked Finn. 'And could he possibly be so wrapped up in his own ego he's not seeing the possibilities?'

'Perhaps. You humiliated him yesterday—in front of his own officers. It's already right round the station. A guy like Turner isn't going to take that lightly.'

'Oh, come on, Finn, he backed me into a corner. I know the rules and I know I'm stretching them, but this has nothing to do with stealing Turner's spotlight and everything to do with catching a child killer. We can save the next potential victim with her help. I know we can.'

Finn rubbed the back of his neck and nodded. 'If I didn't think that I wouldn't have brought her back in. Just be careful. Turner's got it in his head this case is going to make his career. Would he use your relationship with Lexi to drag you both down? I'd just about count on it. Especially if he thinks he has the rules on his side.'

'I should boot him off the case.'

'And give him the chance to complain you did it because he objected to you stretching the rules?'

'It would be about objecting to his attitude, but you're right I suppose.' Then after a thoughtful pause, 'What happened to Lexi's face?'

'I got the impression some client got a bit rough. But she's not all that forthcoming with details.'

She grimaced. 'We should go and see what she came in for.'

She followed Finn into the strike force room and found Lexi and Jim poring over something on a computer monitor.

'I'd really like to attach my RAT,' Jim said.

Lexi shook her head. 'It's riskier. My spyware—'

'Doesn't let you control the computer.'

'But at least it won't get picked up.'

'You don't think.'

'It's worked so far.'

'So has mine.'

'Listen, Neutron, if you stuff this up—'

'I won't! Trust me, this will work.'

Rachael cleared her throat. 'What will work?'

Both looked up. 'We found an email address,' Lexi said. 'Rocketman69 shared it with Tumbleseed.'

'Classy,' Finn couldn't help but comment.

'And now you want to attach one of those malware programs to a video in order to gain access to his computer?' Rachael asked.

'Yes,' they replied at once.

'I've never dealt with this exact situation before. Give me time to clear it with legal. We'll no doubt need that signed off on.'

Lexi made a sound of disgust. 'No wonder you guys are so slow. This cop stuff sucks.'

CHAPTER TWENTY-SEVEN

Wednesday, March 17

The knock on the door at five to nine isn't exactly unexpected—Finn had threatened to pick me up. But it's been a long night. I've been scrolling through thread after thread from the forum while I waited for Rocketman69 to take the bait, trying to get a roadmap of each of the members that might lead us somewhere. I have to admit, Neutron's program is sensational. Having all the time in the world to safely look over the conversations is a game changer. When Rocketman69 finally downloaded the video at 2am, I downloaded the contents of his hard drive and called it a night. Now I'm tired and not quite ready to go back to that alternative universe I've been inhabiting for the past two days.

I fling open the door and walk back to my mug in the lounge room. I am absolutely not going anywhere without finishing my coffee.

'Are you ready?' Finn asks by way of greeting. 'I need to get back to work.'

'Well, hello!' I say with a yawn. 'How can I help the world revolve around you today?'

'As I'm driving out of my way to pick you up, I would have said right now it was revolving around you.'

'I told you I'd get myself there.'

'By nine? I wasn't sure you'd show.'

'You might have been right. I have a phone.'

'But you won't give me your number.'

'If I do will you go away until ten?'

'No.'

'Why not?'

'You brighten my day.'

I snort. 'That's terrible.'

'I tried.' He walks over to my pot plant and studies it. Brow lifted, he turns to me.

'That's Mojo. And Mojo's a dealbreaker. You touch him, I'm out.'

'Lexi ... seriously.'

'He's the closest thing I have to a pet! I've kept that thing alive longer than most people manage to look after a dog.'

'This is so totally against the rules.'

'It won't be the only thing.' I scull my lukewarm coffee. 'We going or what? You need to get back to work, remember?'

'Yeah. Let's go,' he says, with one more disapproving look at my plant.

'What time do you start, anyway?' I ask Finn after another drive-thru at Macca's for a proper coffee.

'Honestly? I may as well just sleep there.'

'Aw ... There, there. I worked late too.'

His face tightens. 'Actually, on that. Sorry about Turner yesterday. He overheard Rachael and I talking about your profession. He wasn't supposed to. He shouldn't have brought it up. Like I said, he's a dick.'

'Okay, but I'm really not sure why you're apologising for someone else's behaviour. Besides, it's not a secret. But, that's not the sort of work I meant. I've started a database on each member of the group and all the little bits and pieces they give away about themselves on the forum. I've shared it with Neutron so he and the analysts can all add to it. Also, I downloaded everything from Rocketman69's computer.'

'He opened the video?'

'He did.'

'What have you got?'

'Bear in mind it was the early hours of this morning but I'm pretty sure I have vision of the parties.'

He shot me a look, two looks. 'From inside the parties? Like, with faces?'

I smile widely. 'Like, yeah.'

'I don't even know what to say. Anything else?'

'I guess we'll see.'

Once in the station, Finn herds me towards my temporary work station. Neutron is already working.

He looks up and his cute little face is animated. 'He took the bait.'

'You find the party videos yet?' I ask.

'There's a lot of vision to get through and I honestly don't want to look at any of them. Which ones?'

'What's all the excitement?' Rachael asks, coming in.

'We've got Rocketman69's computer,' Neutron tells her. 'Same scenario as Davies, by the looks of things. Separate laptop and VPN for his paedo stuff so nothing as yet on his identity or location.'

'But we did get some footage from parties,' I add and bring the first video up. 'Take a look.'

The room is dark, with coloured lights flashing and gliding around the walls and floor. Girls who look like they're somewhere in their mid to late teens are mingling with older men. The cameraman is moving through the crowd of dancing, drinking, laughing bodies. He pauses to get past a young blonde who gets a decent touch-up by one of those older men as she raises her glass to her mouth, struggling to drink and dance. As the camera pans right, a brunette is bent over a guy seated by a makeshift bar, her fanning hair not doing much to hide what's going on.

'That's some wild shit,' Neutron murmurs. He drags a hand over his face and turns away, but I'm still watching as yet another girl runs to a bin and vomits violently before stumbling and landing in a heap in the corner. The cameraman bends over to help her up, leads her back through the crowd. Then they're outside. It's dark and he's reaching for his zipper.

'Okay, we get it,' I say, pausing the video before what we all know is about to happen is played out in stomach-turning clarity.

'We need to get stills of as many of those bastards' faces as we can,' Rachael says.

'If he hasn't wiped the data we might be lucky and get a general location,' Neutron says.

'And get as many of the girls' faces as we can, too,' Rachael says. 'We need to identify them.' She takes another look at the image on screen. 'They're so out of it I'm betting most don't even know what they're doing.'

We get to work, spend the next couple of hours capturing, copying, improving the images of faces, then passing the images on to the detectives to try and identify. We study the inside and outside landscapes, look for any clues, any landmarks. It's slow, tedious work and my eyes are aching, but I don't care. We're going to get them.

Rachael turns up periodically to check in. When she places a second coffee in front of me I sit back, take a break.

'How's it going?'

'It's taking a while. Everything's been stripped of any tracing information, but we've got some good images. Your guy Claxton and a couple of others are trying to ID the faces we've shot over there.'

'I feel like we're finally getting somewhere. Thanks, Lexi.'

'It's not just me.'

Turner pops his head in. 'Inspector? Do you mind if I conduct an interview in your office? Downstairs rooms are busy.'

'No problem.'

I freeze as I see who he's got with him. Charmaine's eyes pass almost sightlessly over the room, until she spots me and jolts. Her gaze latches onto mine.

Shit is all I can think. I mirror her surprise, edge it more into the realms of confusion. 'Hi. Do I know you?' I ask.

Now it's Charmaine's turn to look confused before the tiniest flicker in her eyes reassures me she's figured out where I'm coming from. She frowns at me again, shakes her head. 'Sorry, I thought you were someone else.' With a polite but distant smile she returns her attention to Turner.

'That was strange,' Rachael says. 'You sure you don't know her?'

'Nup,' I reply with a shrug. 'Don't think so. Who is she?'

'That's Jonathan Davies's wife.'

'Oh, right. Turner's wasting time again. Surely the poor woman has been through enough.'

'Sorry to interrupt,' Debbie says from behind us. 'Rach, you need to see this.'

I follow Rachael and Finn back to Debbie's computer. There's a news report on pause. A woman who looks to be in her mid-fifties. Her face is red and streaked with tears and her eyes are sad, maybe angry.

'That looks like Maria Frazer,' Rachael says.

'The one who was overseas when her daughter was killed by the Spider?' I ask.

'It is,' Debbie says. 'And you're not going to like it.'

She presses play and Maria Frazer's voice is raspy. 'I buried the teddy bear in his backyard. I know I shouldn't have done it, but we all thought Biddle was the Spider. He was caught with all that other stuff and my baby was dead. I wanted him to pay.' There's a short pause while she breaks down, sniffs and blows her nose. 'It was the wrong thing to do but I thought I was doing it for the right reasons. Now someone else's baby is dead and he's still out there because of me. I can't live with that. How can I live with it?'

The reporter appears on screen. 'You've just heard from Maria Frazer, whose daughter was the second victim of the Spider.'

'Yes, quite a disturbing admission, Michelle,' the presenter in the studio comments. 'That she planted evidence, because it was ultimately that piece of evidence that put him away, wasn't it?'

'We'll certainly be following the story closely over the next few days to see what this news means for Thomas Biddle.'

'Shit,' Rachael hisses and turns in a circle, staring at the roof. 'She couldn't have come to us? What the hell was she thinking, going to the media?'

'When was this aired?' Finn asks Debbie.

'Only about five minutes ago.'

'We need to go and get her. Bring her in.' Rachael scowls. '*Stupid* woman! If everyone wasn't panicking before they will be now.'

'And Biddle just got a whole lot more leverage. Here we go with the whole miscarriage of justice angle,' Finn said.

Rachael's phone rings and she answers, speaks briefly before hanging up. 'Mrs Frazer's handed herself in to Woy Woy Police Station. They're bringing her here now. Shouldn't be more than twenty minutes or so.'

Charmaine walks past again. She spots me and her eyes go round for a split second. The I *need to talk to you* is clear. Shit. I do really need to let her know what's going on, but how?

'There goes our lunch,' Finn said.

'I can order from the café,' Debbie offers.

'Why don't I go pick up some sandwiches?' I offer, because that way I can legitimately follow Charmaine from the building. 'Subway okay?'

I'm not surprised they're looking at me like I've grown another head.

'Well, I'm hungry,' I say. 'And I feel like a teriyaki sub. It's not like I'm going out of my way.'

'Thanks, Lexi.' Rachael manages a smile but behind it I can clearly see the worry over Frazer.

'No probs.' I get their order and head outside, look around. I can't see Charmaine so I start down the road towards the Imperial Centre. It's a bit of a hike, but assuming Charmaine's around here somewhere, I don't want to be too close to the station when I talk to her.

As soon as I hit the end of the street, Charmaine is beside me. 'I'll meet you at Subway,' I murmur as I walk past her and keep going.

When I get to the food court inside the shopping centre she flags me down from her spot at a two-seater table.

'What's going on?' she demands. 'That detective thinks I did it.'

I slide in opposite her. 'He's a tool. But, look, you were always going to be a suspect. You didn't tell him anything, did you?'

'No. But when I saw you in there I thought you might have. Why are you there?'

'I told you I was trying to get information on your husband to bring a down a paedophile ring.'

'You didn't tell me you were working for the police!'

'I'm not! Well, I wasn't at the time. And it doesn't change that what happened that night has to stay between you and me. We have to keep our distance from each other. I'm going to get us all the way out of this, but I need more time.'

Her energy seems to sag a bit. 'Yeah, of course. Sorry. I just needed to know what was going on.'

'Lexi, Charmaine.'

My stomach does a dive. Turner. 'Can I help you?' I load my tone with the amount of disdain he'd expect but my heart rate is a million miles an hour. Did he follow me here? Did he overhear anything?

'I thought you two didn't know each other.'

'We do now. Obviously,' I say, because Charmaine is sitting there looking guilty.

'Something wrong?' he asks Charmaine.

'You pretty much just got through accusing me of murder,' Charmaine says and I see some of her colour return. 'Will that do?'

'And what exactly are you doing here?' Turner asks me.

'I came in to pick up lunch. What are you doing here?'

'You're not picking up anything, you're talking to my suspect. Don't bother telling me you didn't recognise each other earlier, because I know you did.'

'Honestly, I wouldn't bother telling you anything.'

He shook his head slowly in disdain. 'Rachael's got some sort of blinding sentimental attachment to you, but I think you're up to something.' He bends down to talk in my face. 'I look forward to figuring out what it is.'

'You're such a bully!' I say loudly enough to draw the attention of the scattering of shoppers around us. 'Leave us alone!' A couple of tradies eating Macca's look up and stare hard at Turner. A mothers' group is staring too and someone says something about bastards.

Turner looks around, his mouth a hard line. 'I'll see you back at the station.'

'Not if I see you first,' I say under my breath. I guess I was right yesterday about making an enemy. I did a little internal cheer when Rachael snapped at him. Now I'm not sure it was worth it. The idea of someone digging too closely into my life makes me nervous. There's too much at stake.

Charmaine giggles. 'That was awesome.'

'Yeah, but he's not going to let this go. No more contact, okay? I know how to find you if I need to.'

Her expression immediately sobers. 'Okay. And … Lexi, wasn't it? Thanks. My daughter is upset over Jonathan. She's so sad but she'll be okay. If it had gone down the other way, if I'd been arrested … I don't even want to think about it.'

'Then don't. Focus on the future, stick to the story.'

'He says they have a picture of my car.'

'But no plates. They can't prove it's yours. Go home, try not to worry.'

Eyes glinting with tears, she stands, nods, mouths *Thank you* again, and hurries away.

I stand up and look around, paranoid now. I know he's watching, somewhere. I try to keep my expression neutral, order the sandwiches and, on the walk back, plan how to face the attack I know is coming.

At the station I catch Finn and Rachael as they're coming down the stairs. 'Hey, I have your lunch.'

'Great, ta. Better stick it in the fridge. We're going to interview Maria Frazer,' Rachael tells me.

'She's here? Cool. Can I watch?'

'Why?'

'I want to hear what she has to say. That's all. It sounds like this might be important when it comes to the court deciding what to do about Biddle. I need to know she's telling the truth.'

'Why would she lie?' Finn asks.

'I don't know. But why interview her if you're not wondering the same thing?'

'She can watch from the other room,' Rachael says.

'That's not allowed.'

'Come on,' she tells me, 'I'll show you where to be.'

'Rachael ...' Finn says under his breath. It sounds very much like a warning.

I swing slightly on the office chair and sip my coffee as the interview begins in the next room. Through the monitor, Maria Frazer looks even more upset than she did on the television. Her face is beetroot red and her greying hair hangs damp and limp around her makeup smeared face. Her head stays down and partially buried in tissues, even as she talks to Finn and Rachael.

'Guilt got the better of me when I saw that poor girl, Summer. If Biddle hadn't been charged, maybe you might have found the real Spider and she'd still be alive.'

Something's off, but I'm not sure what. I do find it strange that with guilt that bad it took her almost two weeks after Summer's death to come forward. But maybe it was just the knowledge of how much shit she was going to be in that held her back.

Nah, I don't buy it. Her eyes are pleading for them to believe her. It's like confessing isn't enough. There's more at stake here.

Rachael's questioning her over specifics of the alleged evidence planting. Maria is still crying, and between the tears and the nose blowing, she's run out of tissues.

Finn comes out to find more while I'm scrolling through my phone. 'I thought you wanted to watch,' he said.

'I did. She's lying.'

'Why do you say that?'

'She's hiding behind all the theatrics. It looks like remorse but it's not. It's fear. She's scared of something.'

He frowns at me, clearly unsure whether to pander to my amateur detective skills. 'How do you know?'

I shrug. 'You live on the streets, you learn to read people.'

'Right.' He continues his search for tissues, comes back with a box of Kleenex then pauses with his hand on the door before going back in.

'Perhaps you want her to be making this up because you want Biddle to be the Spider. It's understandable.'

'And patronising. Try telling her you know she's lying. That you have evidence she was bullied into doing this and that you can protect her granddaughters if she tells you the truth.'

'Why would I do that? What granddaughters?'

It amazes me these cops can solve crimes yet can't even work Facebook. 'She's so wound up I think she'll crack pretty easy.'

Finn stares at me for one, two, three beats, then goes back into the interview room and sits. But he's looking at the woman differently now. I can tell he's wondering. When the conversation stops, he jumps in.

'Mrs Frazer, you've got granddaughters, haven't you?'

'Two, yes. Why?'

He stares right at me through the camera like he can see me. 'We can make sure you all stay safe.'

'Thank you. But why?'

And damn, I might just be onto something. At least I hope so, because Rachael is looking at Finn like he's grown another head.

'We know you were told to do this. We know it wasn't your idea.'

'Yes, it was!' she says too quickly, surging to her feet. 'I saw the girl and I-I ...' It's like her legs turn to jelly and she falls back into her seat in a fresh flood of tears.

'Who threatened you?' Finn asks gently.

'I don't know! I didn't think anyone knew what I did. No one was supposed to know I buried the teddy in Biddle's yard. It was the one from her photo so I knew it would link him to her murder. But the woman on the phone. She said the real Spider knew I'd planted it and that if I didn't tell everyone what I'd done, he'd come after my granddaughters!' She's wailing now, and it's heartfelt. 'I lost one of my daughters to that bastard, I can't lose them too!'

I feel sorry for her, I do. But the rush of satisfaction of calling it wasn't to be denied. I fist-pumped the air, but only in my mind. Then the reality of being right—no, only partially right—of what that meant, had a chance to sink in. The *real Spider* didn't like what she'd done. And what she'd done was plant the teddy. And that teddy was what had nailed the coffin shut on Biddle's case. What I'd wanted to hear was that she hadn't really planted it at all, had been pressured into saying she had. So now ... what? Was that it? Was Biddle going to get out?

Finn and Rachael leave the interview room.

'Where did you get that?' Rachael asks Finn.

'Lexi,' Finn says. 'She knew.'

'Yeah, hi. Right here,' I say from behind them.

'How did you know?' Rachael asks.

'Just a guess,' I tell her.

'A guess? Really?'

By the look that's pinned on me I have to assume I wouldn't enjoy being interrogated by this woman. I try again. 'I like to read people, that's all. I could tell she was lying.'

Rachael looks intrigued. 'Tell me how.'

I briefly try, but probably not very successfully. 'Anyway, you should get your lunch. It's going to go soggy.'

'Not quite yet,' Rachael says. 'I need to chase something up I organised yesterday.'

She charges up the stairs. Apparently the lift is too slow for whatever mission she's on.

Finn is still standing in front of me, staring.

'Am I in trouble?' I ask.

'You've got a half-decent brain in your head, you know that?'

'That would have sounded so much nicer if you hadn't said it like a revelation.'

He grins at me. 'I'm hungry. Did you get me olives?'

'The full Italian B.M.T. experience,' I promise.

'Sensational. Let's go.'

We head upstairs but I'm summoned into Rachael's office before I can eat my own sub.

'Sit down,' Rachael says. 'I'd like to talk to you about something.'

'Okay.'

'What would you say to being hired as a temporary consultant?'

She may as well have told me I'd be chartering a space-ship to the moon. 'What?'

'It's not uncommon to contract the use of civilian experts for specific tasks. Jim could use some ongoing assistance with this case. The cyber unit is stretched at present and I was lucky to get him, but two heads and all that. You know the case, you've already proven highly useful. I've backdated the start date to yesterday. What do you say?' She pushes some paperwork at me. It's a contract.

I'm desperate enough to consider it. But there's at least one glaring problem. 'The paperwork's going to be tricky. I haven't even got a tax file number.'

'We'll get that sorted. You in?' she says without what I'd consider to be enough hesitation. And I don't really get it.

'Let's be clear. You're offering to pay me to do what I'm already doing for free.'

'We're all getting paid, why shouldn't you? And by officially working for us, I'm not stretching the rules by letting you in on sensitive areas of the investigation.'

'Oh.' I stare down at the paperwork. Do I want this? Do I want to enter into a contract where I'm required to be here? It would take away that safety net of knowing I can walk out at any time. This would be official. The whole situation is surreal and I can't quite take it in. I'm not even used to the idea of working with cops yet. But I do like working with Neutron and his programs, I do want to catch this guy and prove Charmaine didn't kill her husband. And there is the small issue of paying the rent. So …

'Okay,' I tell Rachael, knots on top of knots in my stomach. 'It's just temporary. Why not?'

Rachael's grin is huge. 'Welcome aboard.'

CHAPTER TWENTY-EIGHT

Thursday, March 18

Finn walked past the strike force room, ducked his head back in and stared in surprise. It had only just gone seven and Lexi was already at a computer.

'So you're officially on the payroll?'

'As of two days ago, apparently. And wow, there's a whole lot more to this case than what sits on the boards,' she said without looking up from whatever she was doing. 'Neutron gave me a password that gets me into very cool parts of the system I want to explore and, not so exciting, the pay is a lot less than two-fifty an hour.'

The strangled noise that came from his throat was completely accidental. 'You make two-fifty an hour?'

'Not here I don't. And, damn, I wish I'd had access to some of this stuff from the beginning.'

He decided he'd better go in. 'Why, what have you found?'

'I read over that interview with Isabella and her mum—the kid said they were picked up near Gosford train station at ten. I know from what I read on the forum that the parties start at ten thirty, so they only have half an hour to get from the pick-up point to wherever they're going.'

'Great. So we map out a search area from Gosford station, then,' he said, pulling a chair around beside her. 'It's the only pick-up location we have.'

'Already on it.' He watched her mark out points from a central location on a map on screen. 'Not sure I'm doing this right. I'm using Google maps' estimated drive times along each road so I could be a bit out.'

'Just use the major roads and we'll circle a perimeter.'

'I'm here.' Neutron came in, dropped his tote and set a coffee down next to his keyboard. 'What are we doing?'

'Working out possible party locations.'

They'd been at it only a few minutes when Finn heard Lexi mutter something under her breath and saw her shoot Jim a sideways glare. He'd noticed Jim's repeated glances at Lexi and supposed Lexi had noticed them too.

'You want to take a picture?' she asked after a few more minutes had passed. 'You can stare at it all day and creep me out a lot less.'

Jim reddened. 'Sorry, it's been bugging me, I mean, I'm just wondering how I have never worked with you before.'

'I tend to work alone.'

'Oh, well, what uni did you go to?'

'Didn't.'

'On-the-job training?'

'You could say that.'

'Where at?'

'Somewhere that no longer exists.'

'What kind of work did you do?'

Lexi stopped looking at the monitor to glare at him. 'I'm flattered, really but I'm busy so ...'

'Sorry. Again. I'm persistent. It's one of my best and worst traits.'

'No kidding.' She went back to work. 'There. That's it.'

She formed a circle around the furthest points marked on her image and printed it out. 'Okay so that's everywhere it's possible to reach from Gosford station by car within thirty minutes.' Finn walked across the room and pinned the map to the board. Studied it. 'That's a lot of area to cover,' he said, looking at the map. 'We'll do a broader sweep on traffic cams, find out what way they were headed.'

'I'd be starting with Kariong,' Lexi said.

'Why?'

'This photo from Rocketman's computer.' Lexi pulled one up. 'When we enhance it we get a bit of an idea what's outside the window of the party location. It's difficult to tell for sure, but I think that blob in the corner is part of a white fence post. There's something linear in the sky that might be large powerlines, and these reddish blobs in among the bushes look to me like Gymea lilies. They're prolific around Somersby and the Mountain plateau. There's also plenty of places out that way with large properties with post and rail fences where they could party in private. From Gosford, they'd most likely go through Kariong to get up there.'

'Makes sense,' Finn said. 'Good work.'

'Again,' Neutron said. 'So ... have you ever worked with anyone in Cyber?'

'No.'

'And you can't tell me where you learnt all this stuff?'

'No!'

'It's just once I know, I'll shut up, but I have trouble letting things go until I can figure them out and store them away,' Jim said. 'Unless you're a secret agent or whatever you must be able to tell me something.'

'Oh, just tell him already,' Finn said. 'She's an escort.'

Jim's mouth gaped. 'You're a what?'

Lexi glared at Finn. 'Yeah, well, I skipped careers day at high school. Oh wait, that's right, I didn't go to high school. My choices were vast. What could I possibly have been thinking, sleeping with people to survive?'

'I wasn't judging you—just shutting him up.'

'A full-service escort?' Jim asked.

'Sometimes. Look, if there's anything else you'd like to know, ask him, because apparently he'll tell you.'

'You said it wasn't a secret! I didn't think you were ashamed of it or I wouldn't have said anything,' Finn said.

'I'm not ashamed of it any more than I am my other dodgy albeit brief, born-out-of-desperation career choice that taught me about computers.'

'Care to elaborate?'

'Because you're so good at keeping stuff to yourself? No. I need a break.'

She got up and walked out. He felt an immediate stab of guilt. He hadn't meant to upset her.

'How does a chick like that end up getting to work for the police?' Jim asked.

'Honestly? I think the world's a safer place having her on our side.'

'Escort. Huh. I've never thought about using an escort. Maybe—'

'Don't even think about it.'

'But that's what she does. And, man, she's—'

'A super brain on a computer. That's what she is when she's here. Got it? Take that other image out of your head, treat her with the professional respect you would any other colleague and for God's sake stop with the staring and drooling. It's creeping us *both* out.'

'You brought it up,' he mumbled.

'Yeah. I shouldn't have. Can we get back to work now? I need those traffic cams.'

*

Rachael put down the phone and stared at the wall. What a waste. What a stupid, pointless waste. She sent Finn a quick text and, not wanting to dwell on it, she gathered her things and left her office in time to see Lexi walk out of the strike force room. 'Good morning,' she called.

Lexi looked up and did a double take. 'Are you sure?'

Was it that obvious? 'I just heard from the hospital. Cody didn't make it.'

Lexi's face fell. 'Oh, damn.'

'Yeah.' She took a deep breath in, blew it out. 'Bailee said he wasn't a bad kid. Just lost. And his poor mother. I don't know what this will do to her.'

'It sucks,' Lexi agreed. 'Even more reason to get this bastard.'

'You're right,' she said and shook off the lingering sadness of the news. 'On that, I was just about to come looking for you. I was wondering if you might like to come for a drive with me.'

Lexi shrugged. 'To do what?'

'Janie Miller's parents want to report her as missing. I'm going to go out and speak to them and I thought perhaps, if they agree, you could take a look at her online activity. Check if there's any clue what she's up to, where she might be.'

'Sure. Happy to.'

'Great, we'll grab breakfast on the way.'

Janie's parents sat on a wicker lounge and took Rachael through the last time they'd seen their daughter. They talked about the habit she'd developed since her fourteenth birthday of taking herself off without explanation to friend's houses, movies and anywhere but school when she didn't feel like attending. Both parents worked long hours, Patrick as a chemist and Gabrielle at the local day spa, so they weren't home a lot and Janie had been a latchkey kid since age eleven. Got bored easily. They'd been struggling to keep tabs on her and she had gotten into trouble with some petty theft, a couple of minor arrests. But she always, always came home within a day or two. Except this time she hadn't. It'd been more than a week and they just knew something was wrong. Patrick Miller was stony-faced, quiet, serious. Gabrielle Miller was a barely contained mess. Rachael had the feeling she would have contacted police earlier had Mr Miller not been quietly confident she'd come home.

'Has your daughter ever mentioned any local parties?'

The two exchanged glances. 'We overheard Cody and Janie arguing about some parties. She wanted to go but he didn't want her to. She was upset because he was going without her.'

And maybe that was the real reason behind the complaint to Bailee, Rachael thought, jealousy rather than concern over what was going on. 'Could you suggest any other friends of Janie's we could talk to that might know where we should look for her?'

'Just Cody, really. I mean, she had other friends but it's a bit hard to keep up, you know?' Mrs Miller said.

Rachael could feel Lexi's eyes on her. 'I'm afraid Cody was shot by a man we believe is involved in running these parties.'

'That was Cody on the news?' Mrs Miller's voice lifted two octaves. 'What does that mean for Janie?' Mr Miller placed a hand over her clenched fingers but she tore them away to hold them in her hair. 'What's happened to our daughter?'

'There's no indication anything like that has happened to Janie. She'd run away the week before, correct? She wasn't at the scene nor at Cody's place when we went around to speak to him several days prior to the shooting. You need to stay as calm as you can and do your best to think about some of her other friends, anywhere she mentioned she liked to go, to visit. Did Janie have a phone on her?'

'It's off,' Mrs Miller said. 'Her charger is in her room. It's got to be flat by now.'

'I should get the number anyway. Would you mind if we looked at her computer?'

'I'll go get it from the office,' Mr Miller replied. 'But she only used it for schoolwork.' He left the room.

'Do you mind if we also take a look in Janie's bedroom?'

'Of course not. But I don't think you'll find anything very interesting.'

As they were shown into Janie's room, Mr Miller dropped the laptop on the bed. Rachael smiled her thanks and looked around, decided Janie's room was likely kept tidy by her mother. No teen was this domestic. With its pink walls and pretty decor, it was neat as a pin. A few books sat on a shelf above the neatly made single bed, some faint marks on the walls where posters had come and gone. Nothing that gave much away about who Janie was. She started flicking through the books, in case they were hiding anything other than the promised magical tales, then glanced up at the sound of a window sliding open. Lexi had moved it.

'What are you doing?' Mrs Miller asked.

'Sneaks out this way a lot, huh? Lexi asked, wobbling the screenless window on its track.

'Yes. I'm afraid she does.'

Lexi stuck her head through, looked out before closing it. Rachael stopped what she was doing to watch Lexi with interest as she slid her fingers over the headstock of a guitar.

'She plays?'

'Only started in the last few months.'

Lexi acknowledged she was listening with a nod and a short 'Hmm', but she'd moved to the bed opposite Rachael. 'Cute lamp,' she said, then opened a bedside drawer, shuffled around. Her hand stilled, before lifting out three bottles of Advil. 'She suffer from headaches?'

'Not that I know of.'

Lexi opened one of the bottles and her brow lifted. 'Hey, blue Advil.'

Rachael accepted one of the bottles and tipped the pills into her open palm. Blue pills with butterfly logos. 'These look like ecstasy pills.'

'What?' Mrs Miller exclaimed. Rachael didn't think she was faking her surprise.

'Were you aware your daughter was taking drugs?'

'No, they won't be hers! She doesn't do that!'

They wouldn't only be hers, Rachael guessed. Not in this quantity.

'Probably belong to that deadbeat boyfriend. Cody,' Mr Miller growled.

'Want me to take a look?' Lexi asked, indicating to the laptop. Rachael nodded.

'You can't take it with you. It belongs to the school,' Mr Miller said. 'She's barely ever on it anyway. Always has her phone in her hand.'

Lexi sat on the bed and opened it up. She hesitated, looked at Rachael, then turned the laptop around. 'Would you unlock it for me, please?' she asked Mr Miller.

Mr Miller took the laptop and typed in the password before handing it back to Lexi.

'I feel so terrible, I didn't even ask. Is Cody going to be okay?' Mrs Miller asked.

'I'm afraid Cody died this morning,' Rachael said, noting there seemed to be genuine concern on the woman's face that turned to shock at the news. 'Did you talk to Cody much?'

A phone pinged. Lexi's. Lexi smiled apologetically, but Rachael saw something else in her eyes that stirred with intent. Had she reached for her phone before it pinged? Lexi fiddled with the phone for a moment then got back to the computer. What was she up to?

'Oh, not terribly much. But he was polite enough. A bit of a rough diamond, I always told myself. Poor kid. He would have sorted himself out given the chance. Now ... Oh, it's just awful, isn't it, Patrick?'

'Terrible news,' Mr Miller agreed.

'Here you go,' Lexi said, closing the laptop and handing it back to him. 'There wasn't anything obvious,' she said to Rachael.

Rachael nodded, then dug into her pocket when her phone rang. It was Finn. 'Excuse me.' She walked into the hallway. 'Finn, what's up?'

'We've got the van on a traffic cam at Kariong. That's a ten-minute drive from the pick-up area at that time on a Friday night, which leaves no more than twenty minutes from that point to reach the party location. It puts them roughly in the area Lexi and I looked at this morning. She said there were indications of a post and rail fence, bushland and Gymea lilies as well as a lot of large properties around that area that would be perfect for uninterrupted parties.'

'Update the search area. We're coming in.' She finished up with the Millers, promised to be in touch.

'They have Cody's van at Kariong,' she told Lexi once they were in the car.

'Knew it,' she said.

'Yeah, you did. And nice work in there finding those pills. I'll have them tested but I'm pretty sure I know what they are.'

'Maybe look into Mr Miller too. He wasn't keen on handing over the laptop.'

'No, but he did give you permission to search it. For all the good that couple of minutes could do.'

'Oh, I've got all the time in the world. I only needed a minute to pop the spyware on it.'

'I knew you were up to something!' She laughed a little, even as she shook her head. 'Lexi, we're not allowed to do that sort of thing without a warrant.'

'He said we could search it. He didn't say when. He's dodgy. Don't you want to know what he's up to?'

She agreed, and yes, she did. But that didn't change the rules. She was curious to hear Lexi's thoughts on Mr Miller, though. 'Dodgy how?'

'One, the laptop. Not only was he nervous, he knew the password to get in.'

'He was keeping tabs on her?'

'I guess so. Two, there's something wrong in that relationship. They were playing a united front but Mrs Miller wasn't happy about it. He kept angling towards her, getting closer. She was doing the opposite. Edging away all the time. Why pretend? Three, Mrs Miller was genuinely shocked to see those pills, but he wasn't.'

'Ever thought about becoming a detective?' she asked.

'Ha.'

'Why ha? You've got a good eye, a logical mind and a talent for this sort of thing.'

'I'm an escort. I have a talent for that, too.'

Rachael glanced across, saw the amusement on Lexi's face. Saw the bruise still evident from a run-in with one of her clients. She smiled back with difficulty. But the guilt, the regret, ate it up. 'Do you … think we could talk about before? I mean, not now,' she hurried on when Lexi's smile fell, 'but some time? There are things I'd like to tell you about what happened. Things I'd like the chance to explain.'

'It's over with. It doesn't matter.'

'It does to me. I still don't know what happened that evening.'

'Bailee didn't tell you?'

'She doesn't remember much. Fragments.'

'I thought—' She shook her head. 'Doesn't matter. When we get back I'll take another look at the images we caught outside the party location. See if I can find any more markers.'

And that's the end of that, Rachael thought. At least for now.

*

Finn stared closely at the image Lexi was showing him on screen.

'There's loads of properties within the search area that could fit the one we're looking for, so we should go for a drive,' Lexi suggested. 'Look around.'

She was right. Unfortunately. He'd been hoping that a rural area wouldn't provide too much of a challenge, but with the plethora of hobby farms and the high speed limits attached to the country roads, there was no shortage of places to check out. 'Rachael's organising some patrols,' he said. 'We may need a few more cars.'

'I don't get to come?' Lexi asked. 'You get me to do all your research and then take off without me?'

'That's exactly what we do. You're not a cop.'

'But I'm consulting with you.'

'From behind the safety of a computer screen.'

'Oh, come on! Rachael took me with her to talk to Janie's parents.'

He chuckled because she sounded so comically distraught. 'There's a big difference between talking to a couple of frightened parents and dealing with the men we're looking for.'

'Lexi? Finn?' Rachael was in the doorway, Turner behind her. 'My office.'

Finn sighed and stepped away to allow Lexi to push her chair back and stand. 'What have you done now?' he asked conspiratorially.

'Me? He's got a secret crush on me. I bet it's about you.'

He still had the smile on his face when they reached Rachael's office. Turner's smug expression had it dropping.

'Lexi,' Rachael began, 'I'm sorry to ask you again. Did you know Charmaine Davies prior to yesterday?'

He watched Lexi's expression darken. 'Oh sure,' she said, looking wide-eyed at Turner, 'because I spotted her at the shops yesterday after he'd been at her. I dared speak to her because she was sitting in the food court crying over a coffee. I asked her if she was okay, that's all. Stupid question, but she looked like she needed someone to talk to.' She shoved a thumb in Turner's direction. 'So this one charges over accusing us of being secret BFFs who've carried out some sort of gruesome murder together. He put on a show for the entire damn food court.'

'I had every right to!' Turner said, his own expression darkening.

'Do you ever look in the mirror and see what a twat you are?' Lexi fired back.

'And then there's the matter of your car,' Turner said. 'One matching its description was parked a couple of houses down from Davies's place on the night it's likely he went missing, at the same time a car resembling Charmaine Davies's was there.'

'Yeah? Apparently it's a popular car. At least that's what the cop who found mine told me after it was stolen.'

Turner's arms went out to his sides and he looked at the roof. 'Oh, what a coincidence.'

'Yep, disappeared nearly two weeks ago. Got it back, though, thankfully.'

'I suppose you're going to tell me it was missing the night Davies disappeared? That someone else drove it out to Davies's place?'

'Why would I do that? We don't actually know exactly when Davies went missing, do we?'

Nicely done, Finn thought. Turner was trying to trip her up, trying to trick her into giving them information they didn't have themselves, but she wasn't falling for it.

'Where were you on the evening of Saturday, March 6?' Turner demanded.

'With a client.'

'All night?'

'I'm sure I went home at some point. And my car was definitely there.'

'I'd like to take a look at it.'

'Based on what?' Finn jumped in.

'I just explained that.'

Finn shook his head in disbelief. 'You've got nowhere near enough to warrant that.'

'Don't care, doesn't matter. Stay put,' Lexi said to Turner and walked out. She came back a few seconds later with her car keys and tossed them at him. 'Go for it.'

Turner grabbed the keys, considered her for a moment then strode out.

'Lexi, you didn't need to do that,' Rachael said.

'As long as he doesn't go planting anything in there, it's not a problem.'

'I wouldn't put it past him,' Finn muttered.

'Finn,' Rachael said. 'I gave him the task of looking into Davies's murder. You're going to have to try and cooperate with him … a bit.'

'Oh, come on, Rach, after the way he carried on during your last conversation? I can't stand the guy.'

'Really?' Lexi asked. 'You hide it so well.'

'You don't,' he countered. 'And you were being ultra-careful with those answers. You knew he was trying to trip you up.'

'He's not smart enough,' Lexi scoffed.

'Does that mean there's something you're not telling us?' Rachael asked curiously.

'Plenty. So do you want to question me? Rather you than him.'

'Great, did you have anything to do with killing Jonathan Davies?' Finn asked.

'I didn't plan to kill him, I wasn't involved in any plot to kill him, other than via a name on a screen I don't know who did kill him and I absolutely did not kill him myself. Does that cover it?'

'I'm satisfied,' Finn said. 'Rachael?'

'Mmm. Let's move on. We've got a party to shut down.'

CHAPTER TWENTY-NINE

Friday, March 19

I swing the desk chair around in one long loop. 'I need to take a break,' I tell Neutron. The strike force has been divided into two loose groups all day: those working on the faces from the videos and those of us trying to track down the location, zooming in and out of maps looking for any clues as to where this property might be. When we think we might have something, Claxton calls it in and Finn or one of the other detectives swings by to take a look. Decides whether to rule it out or mark it for further investigation. But there's a lot of properties in our search area and it's slow work. 'Want a coffee?'

Neutron stops squinting at the screen long enough to look up and stretch. 'Why don't I get you one?'

'You got me the last one. Two. Actually, all the coffees ever,' I say. 'I need a walk anyway.'

'It's almost time to call it quits,' Neutron says, checking the time. 'They can't search in the dark.'

'Hours of light left,' I say, wanting this property found. But a glance outside shows signs of late afternoon.

I make the coffees and start on what will be my sixth for the day. It's a poor substitute for JD but it's the best they've got. I sit back down in my chair and choose another street to explore. I see the name of the one I grew up on and choose another. I'd looked the old farm up one drunken night years ago and remember it had been sold. I'm almost curious enough to look again, to see if it still stands or if another, more modern, home has taken its place. Our neighbours way back then had bought their place and used the existing cottage as a granny flat, built a lovely— 'Of course!'

'Of course, what?' Neutron asks.

'I need to go back to that property we were so sure was a good match earlier. The one at Central Mangrove with all the white fencing and the powerlines cutting through.'

'Okay.'

When we'd first seen it, I'd been sure we were onto something. But the house hadn't fit. The size, the colour, the veranda. I find the property again, stare at the aerial image. Big house, nice white post-and-rail fencing, lots of paddocks surrounding the place, a couple of large dams. The property boundary is unclear because I can't tell if the wire-fenced land behind it belongs to the same place or is separate. There's another building there, among the trees. I dismissed it initially as a ranger's station or something because the only access seemed to be from the fire trail that heads in from the end of the road. But where does that track through the paddocks go? It snakes around, gets lost in some trees.

Does it come out further down? Close to that building? The image isn't clear enough to tell.

'Hey,' Finn says from behind me.

'You're back.'

'Yeah. Let's go, I'll run you home.'

'Surely my car is ready.'

'Someone will call you when it's released.'

'How long's he going to need it?'

'Until it's been thoroughly searched and he realises he can't charge you with anything.'

'Oh.' And that's the other thing I've been doing all day: mentally thanking Dawny for being so devious. I'll have to let her know about Turner and the search. She'll love it. I'm feeling pretty ordinary for lying to Finn and Rachael, but what can I do? I looked up the penalty for accessory after the fact to murder. It's not much better than murder itself. Unless I want to be cell buddies with Charmaine for the next quarter-century or so, I'm better off proving Victor killed Davies and hoping the rest blows over.

'So there's this place,' I begin as Finn points the car towards home.

'World's full of them.'

'The one you checked out first because I told you it had to be the right one.'

'The one that looks like a rockstar or world leader probably owns it?'

'I guess so. Anyway, I think it has a second dwelling on it. Much smaller. Old. Probably predates the new one and never got knocked down. I really think it's worth a look.'

'Great. It's nearly dark. I'll check it out in the morning.'

I'm kicking myself that I didn't discover it this morning. I'm sure I'm right and I need to know. 'It really wouldn't take long to zip up the motorway.'

Finn smothers a yawn and shakes his head. 'I've been driving around all day. I've already been out there.'

'Finn.' I load my tone with as much urgency as I can. 'I'm as sure as I can be that this needs to be checked out. I'd go myself but I don't have my car.'

'No.' He shoots me a death stare. 'You wouldn't.'

I change tack. 'You know, Rachael and I are both pretty sure Janie's dad knows more than he's letting on about her disappearance and it could be tied to all this. What if she's there? What if she needs help right now?'

'Are you guilt-tripping me?'

'Is it working?'

I can see him thinking. His expression goes from *no way* to *maybe I should* to something I'm sure involves silent swearing but then he's changing lanes like we're heading for the freeway.

'So we're going?'

'Rachael's going to have my head,' he says. 'We'll do a quick drive-by. But that's it. If it looks like you're on to something, we'll get back out there first thing. If not, we're not hanging around to poke around. Deal?'

'Deal,' I say and shoot him a big smile, then I get out my phone to make sure I can find it again. I don't think he's in the mood to be sent the wrong way.

'So how'd that talk with Miller go anyway? Did you look at the computer?'

I roll my eyes to the roof. 'Rachael says we're supposed to have a warrant to do that because installing spyware on someone's computer is illegal. Honestly. I don't know how you guys get anything done.'

He grins. 'So how did you learn all this computer stuff, anyway?'

'I've had more than one career.'

'The one you wouldn't talk about.'

'Yep.'

'Why'd you stop doing whatever that was?'

I consider my answer, decide it can't hurt to tell the truth. 'My boss was arrested and sent to jail.'

The look on his face is almost comical. 'For how long?'

'Couple of decades.'

'It was *that* bad?'

'I hope you haven't fallen under any illusion that I'm some sort of pillar of virtue?'

'But twenty years? That's serious!'

'Mmm hmm.'

The silence stretches out. I can almost hear him thinking.

'Oh, come on you've got to tell me.'

'Nope. And don't bother using any of those prying-cop techniques on me. I won't budge.'

'Prying-cop techniques? Been interrogated much?'

'I watch TV.'

'So how come you didn't get arrested too?'

A tight-lipped smile is all he's going to get. 'Here's the turn off.'

'Got it.' He takes it, then says, 'It had to be worse than regular computer hacking.'

'Yep.' We turn onto a road that used to be the main high-way. I get the occasional glimpse of farmland through the trees and a few minutes pass before he tries again.

'People-smuggling operations?'

He's not going to let this go, I can tell. 'No.'

'You weren't illegally importing weapons into the country via dark web trading sites were you?'

'No again. Okay, now turn left then right. When you reach the crossroads, go straight through.'

We wind our way past farmhouses and rural trade stores. A small school. At the crossroads he brakes, waits for a lone ute to pass, then drives on.

'I know it's not going to be child exploitation or slavery, right? I mean, you wouldn't do that. Not with ...'

'No, Finn. I wouldn't. Even without.'

'Right. Of course not. Hey, look! Wallaby.'

It's hunched over grazing on the side of the road by a barbed wire fence. 'Yeah. Slow down. They're not real smart at avoiding cars.'

'You know about wallabies?'

'I used to live up this way. Saw more dead on the side of the road than I ever did alive.'

'Where?'

'All over the place. There wasn't, like, one spot where they all decided to do the leap of death.'

He pulls a face. 'I mean, where did you live?'

'A little further up than where we're going. A few weedy acres and an old two-storey. The road's just up ahead.'

'Got it. Okay, so was it one of those "we've locked your computer and you need to give us money to release it" scams?'

My hand pauses on the map screen but I don't bother to look up. 'Twenty years, Finn,' I remind him.

'Hmm. Right. Not serious enough.'

'Are you turning?'

'I'm turning!'

'It should be a couple of k's down to a dead end and the place we're looking for.'

'I know. I was here this morning, remember? Will you tell me if I get it right?'

'No.'

'Have I got it right?'

'No.'

'But you'd say that anyway.'

'They should make you detective of the year. There it is.'

'We're not going to be able to go onto private property to find the other house.'

'I know, it's fine. Keep going to the end of this road and follow the fire trail back along the fence line.' Finn clearly isn't convinced so I go for the low blow. 'Scared of a dirt road?'

The gravel and dust at the end of the road turns onto a semi-overgrown track.

'I'm not sure I can get the car down there.'

'Then we'll walk.'

'Stay put,' he orders and begins crawling the car along the track. Undergrowth scrapes under the car as we jostle around. The track heads downhill and Finn narrowly avoids a pothole large enough to hide a body.

'I guess were going to have to hope we can get back up here in the dark in one piece,' I say, less confident now.

'I think praying would be more appropriate,' Finn mutters without breaking his concentration.

'There it is! I can see a light on.'

Finn stops the car a few metres from the old cottage, which bursts without warning into view as the strip of scrub thins. He backs up enough to remain hidden behind the blade grass and tea-tree before turning off the engine.

The cottage is old but in reasonable shape. A veranda frames it. A small bundle of equipment including a cattle prod and a couple of large plastic drums sit by the front door. A shirt's been tossed on an overturned milk crate. On top of that is a shotgun.

'Finn. Gun.'

'I see it.' He twists his head around to look back up the hill. 'It's a long way from the main house. No sign of cattle or yards down here. Maybe the place is used for storage.'

'Or parties,' I say, wondering what the chances of being spotted in the half-light behind the scrub are.

'I see the powerline tower, can't tell if you'd get a glimpse of the white post-and-rail fence from over there or not. Maybe. You've certainly got Gymeas everywhere. You could be onto something.'

'You don't want to check? We're here, it looks right. One good look in the window and I can probably give you a yes or a no.'

'We can't just barge onto someone's property without evidence of a crime being committed. We get permission from the owner or we get a search warrant. If we ask the owner and they say no, by the time we get the warrant anything that might have been here could be cleaned out and gone. There's no evidence of life at imminent risk, so we turn around. I'll come back tomorrow.'

As he speaks, a screen door squeals open, then bangs as it closes. A man appears from the darkness of the veranda. Bare chest, jeans. He swings down and collects his shirt, runs a hand through his dark hair as though to tidy it and goes around behind the cottage. An engine grunts to life before a Hilux bounces off into a paddock.

'Didn't know he was in there.'

'He's not anymore,' I prompt. 'Got a torch?'

Finn lowers his window and studies the house. A muffled scream has him leaping from the car and I follow his lead. And whoa, where'd his gun come from?

'Call Rachael,' he orders. 'Let her know where we are and what's going on.'

'Okay,' I call Rachael while Finn slides through the loose wire fence, using the trees as cover as much as possible as he silently moves towards the cottage.

'Hey, what's up?' Rachael finally answers.

'It's Lexi. You need to get some people up here. I'm texting the address, but the actual cottage is all the way to the end of the road and down the fire trail about half a k in.'

'What's going on?'

I've lost sight of Finn. As I fill Rachael in, my eyes swing back and forth from the house to the darkening grounds, wondering where he is, what's going on. On my second swing back to the house, my breath halts, nerves skidding as I realise what's happened.

'Shit. The gun's gone!'

'What?'

'You should hurry.' I drop the phone and get out of the car. Look closer. No, it's definitely not there.

My heart is hammering in my chest. What do I do? I can't exactly call Finn and warn him. His phone will ring and whoever it is will know where he is. Except, whoever it is already knows he's there, right? Why else would the gun have vanished?

Another thought: Maybe it's not Finn who's been found. It's me. In the car. I look everywhere. Spinning around, around. Straining my eyes to see into the darkening bushland.

Nothing. Silence.

I weigh up my options. Chances of survival if I jump into the driver's side and get out of here? Probably not bad. Chances of same possible outcome if I go anywhere near that cottage to warn Finn? Way, way lower.

'Shit.' I remind myself Rachael is no doubt on the way. Hopefully speeding. I just need to not die for maybe fifteen minutes.

I duck through the old fence, dart across the small stretch of grass to the cottage. This is stupid. I'm not some sort of action hero. I can barely open a jar of peanut butter. I slink onto the veranda and grab the cattle prod. It's not much, but it's better than nothing. I'm not going through that front door. I already know how badly it creaks. Instead I creep around the side, looking in the windows but seeing very little in the darkness. I move around the side where the Hilux emerged from and I'm in a scene straight out of the video. The markers are all there. There's no question this is the place. But where is Finn? I hear talking inside and duck down, simply because it seems like the thing to do. As I slowly come back up, I look in the window. Finn is standing opposite a teenage girl who's holding the shotgun. It's Janie.

'I'm not going back!' she says. 'You can't make me!'

'I'm not going to make you do anything,' Finn says calmly. 'Just put the gun down, okay?'

Behind him another muffled scream. My eyes dart to a television screening an action movie. Shit. Was that the emergency that brought Finn rushing in?

'No way! You put your gun down!' Janie yells back.

'You're Janie, right?' Finn continues in that same, kind tone. 'Your parents are worried about you.'

'I can't go back! My life will be over! They have videos!'

I creep towards them and on the TV a woman almost falls from a helicopter, screams again. Assuming he doesn't die, Finn's gonna kill me. But hey, we found Janie. He'll talk her down. Probably. I should just stay put.

But then I hear the car coming back. I move as quickly and quietly as I can to the other side of the house. This part of the veranda is littered with rubbish and I kick something by accident. Boxes of tools, more cattle equipment, empty bottles, milk crates, an old table that looks like it once graced a dining room, a possum trap. More junk covered in dusty blankets. I carefully place my feet so I don't knock anything else over.

The car engine cuts out and a door bangs, jolting my attention back to the situation. Footsteps hit the veranda. A low 'Fuck', then a crash as the guy slams the door back against the wall.

'Who the fuck are you!'

I shift my position and feel the drag of something I know is going to make a noise against my side. I freeze, my free hand covering a spanner. A quick glance reveals several other tools beside it. I pick up a hammer. I feel the weight of it in my hand and adjust my grip.

'I'm Detective Finn Carson. I just want to talk.'

I peer through the window and see the man walk in directly behind Janie. 'Give me the gun, Janie. Good girl.'

'Put the weapon down,' Finn says again.

But I don't think this guy is going to. He stays behind Janie, sits the gun up against his shoulder, lines Finn up.

'You shouldn't have come here.'

The world speeds up. Too fast to think about what to do. I know what's about to happen and Finn doesn't have a clear shot. Janie's right in the way. I tiptoe to the door. They're right there. How hard do you need to hit someone with a hammer to knock them out? Could I accidentally kill this guy? Maybe I won't hit him hard enough and he'll turn around and shoot me.

'We can sort this out,' Finn says.

'Nah. Got too much to lose. Sorry.' The man widens his stance, aims.

For fuck's sake, Lexi! I scream at myself silently. I raise the hammer above my head then lunge, arms shaking with adrenaline as I bring the hammer down as hard as I can on his head.

The thud is gross and reverberates up my arm. He goes down. Janie screams and jumps away.

'Thought you were going to stand there all day,' Finn said, rolling the man onto his stomach and dragging his hands behind his back. All he gets in protest is a moan.

'He's bleeding,' I say, stomach queasy.

'You hit him with a hammer, what did you expect?'

'I was hoping he'd put the gun down.'

'So was I.' Then, 'Don't you move!' he orders Janie.

She's crying as she slides down the wall into a crouch.

I hear sirens and roll my eyes. 'Now they decide to get here?' I put the hammer down and realise I'm still clutching the cattle prod in the other hand. I sit it against the wall.

'Hey, Lexi,' Finn says, getting my attention back on him as he rolls the guy back over.

'Yeah?'

He looks me in the eye. 'Thanks.'

I nod, realise I'm still not steady. 'Next time I get a gun.'

'Nope.'

'A big stick?'

'Unlikely.'

'Okay, well, what about the stingy spray?'

'Next time you stay in the car.'

Rachael, Rayburn and Claxton run in, a couple more uniformed officers close behind.

'What the hell happened?'

Finn sighs heavily, looks at me. 'You want to tell her or should I?'

I decide I may as well. 'The unconscious guy was going to shoot Finn. I gave him a bit of a whack with a hammer.'

'A bit of a whack?' Rachael points to the man on the floor. 'That's hospitalisation.'

'This is the place,' Claxton says, looking around. 'This is where the parties are being held. We should check if any more of our POIs are up at the house.'

'That would be a lot easier to find out if our suspect wasn't unconscious,' Rachael points out, still staring at me.

My eyes slide back to where I left the cattle prod. 'Want me to wake him up?'

Finn unsuccessfully attempts to hide a smirk.

'Take some men and go check,' she tells Claxton. Then to Finn, 'What was Lexi even doing in this situation? This is a mess!'

'He really was going to shoot me,' Finn tosses over his shoulder as he tries to bring the guy around. 'And there's Janie.'

'Janie?' Rachael looks around, sees the girl for the first time. I'm not surprised. It's almost completely dark in the room. I find the light switch, flick it on.

'Janie, are you all right?' Rachael asks more calmly.

'Sounds like she was here under her own steam,' Finn says.

'Is that true?' Rachael asks her.

'I don't have a choice!' Janie says, crying again.

'We're going to help you, okay? Detective Rayburn will take you back to the car. Annalise?'

Annalise crouches in front of Janie and speaks to her, gets her on her feet and points her towards the car. Rachael walks across the room to a computer under the large TV. She turns it on and it shows the password screen. 'We'll have to examine this. Has anyone called an ambo?'

'On its way,' Claxton calls from the veranda.

'And get forensics out here. I want the place turned upside down. Do we know who owns the property?'

'He does,' Janie says, pointing to the guy on the ground. 'That's Nigel.'

I'm glad we've got Janie, that we've found where the parties are being held. But this is not where Summer was killed. The Spider took her somewhere else and we're still no closer to knowing where that is.

CHAPTER THIRTY

'What were you doing there?' Rachael asked Janie while Finn watched.

Janie's face was red, her eyes swollen, her posture poor as she sagged into her folded arms on the interview room table. 'I'd wanted to check the parties out for ages, but Cody didn't want me to go. I was mad, so I told Bailee about them. Why should everyone else get to go and not me? But then Cody said the guys that run the parties told him to bring me to one so I'd shut up.'

'So you went?'

Janie nodded and dragged her fingers across her eyes. 'Nigel was really nice to me. I'm not stupid, I know they're all hoping to get laid, but you don't have to do anything you don't want. Except he gave me a couple of drinks, I don't know, maybe three or four and I can't remember anything that happened after that. I felt really sick the next day, kind of groggy and then ...'

'Then?'

'I was at school and got a text. There were photos, a video.' Her face screwed up in teary disgust. 'Without my clothes on. Doing things. I don't remember doing those things! I would never act like that!'

'It's okay, take your time.'

'They told me if I ever said anything to anyone again, they'd put all that stuff up on social media. Send it to my mum, my school. Post it on Instagram. Post it everywhere.'

'So why were you there, Janie?' Rachael pressed.

'Bailee kept asking me to tell her more about the parties and I couldn't! So I told Cody and he made it so I could stay there for a while. I'm not the only one. He's been there on and off. Any of us can stay. There's a couple of rooms full of bunks. You just have to help out, clean up, that sort of thing.'

Rachael sighed. 'Do you really think your parents would be more upset about what happened than having you go missing?'

Janie looked from Rachael to Finn, confused. 'Mum maybe. But Dad knew I was there.'

Rachael glanced at Finn before returning to Janie. 'Your father knew?'

'He got Cody the job there. The reason Cody and Dad didn't want me going was because Dad was part of it. He's a pervert and I hate him!'

Rachael covertly signalled for Finn to leave and he got to his feet. 'Excuse me a moment,' he said and quietly left.

Once they were alone, Rachael asked Janie, 'Has your father ever acted inappropriately with you?'

Janie lowered her head and started to shake it, her face screwed up as she swiped at fresh tears. Rachael said nothing, waiting, and after a moment the shake turned to a nod.

'Does your mum know?' she asked gently.

Janie let out an explosive breath, with a more violent shake of her head. 'I don't want her to know! I can't go back! I won't go back.'

'It's okay, Janie,' she continued calmly. 'We're going to help you. I promise.'

Janie sniffed again. 'Can I talk to Bailee?'

'Of course. I'll get her here for you.'

Rachael walked out, held her calm. The moment the door closed her face turned to fury.

'Son of a bitch! Tell Claxton and Rayburn to go get the bastard,' she said to Finn, who disappeared to do just that. Then she noticed Lexi had come out from watching the interview. 'You were right about Miller.'

She saw sadness rather than victory in Lexi's expression. 'Doesn't make this feel any nicer.'

'Could I get some water?' Janie called out.

'I'll get it,' Lexi said.

'Thanks, Lexi. Would you sit with her until Bailee arrives? I'm going to call her now.'

'Of course.'

'Thanks.' She spotted Finn walk back out with Claxton and Rayburn, who nodded at her before continuing.

'Should Lexi be in there with Janie?' Finn asked.

'It's fine. She's keeping her company, that's all. Let's go upstairs.' She led Finn into her office, where she stood behind her desk and planted her hands on it, channelling her frustration into its surface.

'Finn, what on earth were you doing out there with Lexi tonight?'

He lifted his hands, palms out. 'I was taking her home, and she had this idea she knew where to look. It sounded plausible, so I decided to let her show me, just a drive past. But we got down there and heard a scream and it all went from there. I'll write it up, hold my hand out for the slap.'

'She should never have been on that property.'

'I left her in the car! Told her to call you and stay put. But you try working with her, see how that turns out. She doesn't play by the rules, Rach. But she's …'

'She's …?' Rachael prompted after a moment.

He pulled a face. 'She's good at all this stuff. She figured out where to find the house and she saved me from a bullet.'

She didn't attempt to hide the flash of amusement. 'It nearly killed you to say that, didn't it?'

'You have no idea,' he said with a sigh. 'But we need her on this.'

'And if she'd stay behind a computer that wouldn't be a problem. Those are the rules.'

'This is not about the rules, Rach. This is about you wanting to protect her. You haven't forgiven yourself for what happened and you don't want to see anything else go south.'

She opened her mouth to argue, then shrugged. 'Is that so wrong?'

'My point is, you want Lexi involved, Lexi is going to be involved on her terms. No one else's.'

He was right. Time to concede defeat, she decided. 'I need to call Ed, let him know what's happened. If you're worried about leaving Lexi with Janie, head back down, show Bailee

in when she arrives, then we'll head to the hospital and see
Nigel Dempsey.'

*

He wasn't worried. He just didn't want the headache for
Rachael if anyone else—Turner—had a problem with it. So
he jogged back down the stairs and made them both a coffee. When he got back he paused outside the room, because
Janie was talking and he wasn't sure he should interrupt.

'I don't want to go through all that shit,' Janie told Lexi.
'No courts or anything. He'll just lie. I'd rather disappear.
It'd be better to hit the streets than go through that.'

There was a long silence. He almost stepped into the
room, then Lexi spoke.

'I don't think most people really understand what it's like
to live on the street.'

'Wait—you did?'

'Yeah. Mostly it's boring. It's boring and uncomfortable.
It's cold or it's hot and you're almost always hungry. It's
scary at first. You go around with this permanent sick feeling
of not knowing what's going to happen next, of wondering
who's going to grab you and rape and murder you or just
beat you up for the hell of it. Of what monster is lurking
around the corner. Especially after dark. You can't sleep.
You have to be ready for anything. It eventually sort of
dulls, all that fear, but that's worse, that's when you've hit
the phase where you no longer care. You're so sick of the
endless, boring days and all the people that don't look at
you on purpose. It's like being a ghost.' He heard a humourless laugh. 'I'd talk to strangers sometimes to make sure I
really existed.'

'You're just trying to talk me out of it, right?' Janie asked, but she sounded uncertain.

'Hey, your choice. But that was my experience. And the thing is, you've got a mum that cares about you. She's gonna be devastated to find out, but she's gonna want to be there for you. You should let her.'

'How do you know?'

'I met her. I had a suspicion your dad was an arsehole but I knew your mum wasn't. I can tell, you know? The people that do this job, they can tell, too. So don't assume he'll get away with it. I don't think it's going to be easy, but you and your mum can get through it. She cares. And right now she's terrified for you.'

'Okay,' Janie said after a moment. 'Okay, thanks. I'll talk to Bailee.'

'No one better.'

'You know her?'

'She's my sister. You want some more water?'

'Nah, I'm good. Thanks.'

Finn decided not to interrupt at all. Lexi was handling it. Instead he waited by the front desk for Bailee to arrive, then filled her in on the bits Lexi hadn't while they waited for Mrs Miller. From the looks of the tears, the hugs, the words that passed between them once Mrs Miller arrived, he knew Janie's next challenging steps wouldn't be taken alone.

Rachael appeared just after Bailee, Janie and Gabrielle Miller left. 'We can't talk to Dempsey tonight. Doctor says he wants to monitor him overnight. Assuming all is well, he can come in in the morning. Patrick Miller's here. They're bringing him in now.'

As though on cue, the detectives walked through the door with an irate Patrick Miller.

'This is ridiculous!' he spat, eyes full of fury and aimed at Rachael. 'You won't get away with this bullshit!'

'We'll speak to you in a moment, Mr Miller,' Rachael promised.

'I'm not saying a word!'

Lexi appeared. Finn hadn't realised she was still there. Turner had to be finished with her car by now, didn't he? The bastard was probably stretching it out on purpose. He watched her face darken into disgust as Claxton and Rayburn walked Miller past.

'You sick prick,' she said.

Miller just about jumped out of Claxton's and Rayburn's grip. 'What did you say?'

'I called you a sick prick. That's the kind version. Wanna know what I *really* think?'

'Keep walking,' Claxton said with a tighter grip and a shove.

'What's going to happen to him?' Lexi asked Rachael.

'We'll charge him, keep him here overnight, put him in front of a magistrate tomorrow. Mrs Miller and Janie will be back to file restraining orders against him, assuming he gets bail.'

'He's already lawyered up,' Rayburn said, coming back into the room. 'I can't see us getting anything out of him before morning.'

'Then we'll list the charges we're bringing against him and let him stew. We'll play him and Dempsey off against each other in the morning,' Rachael decided.

'Two down,' Finn said. 'That's something.'

'Yeah. I wonder if any of the other members realise what's happened yet?'

'I can check?' Lexi offered.

'Okay,' Rachael agreed. 'Let's do that.'

'Well, what do you know! Victor's online,' Lexi said said a few minutes later as they sat in front of her monitor. She opened a chat window.

Doc: So, know what happened to Doc?

The cursor blinked for several silent seconds. Then—

Victor Rheus: No. Why?

Doc: He's disappeared and his laptop was pinched. Right after I told you about it.

'What are you doing?' Finn asked.

'Just putting on a bit of pressure,' Lexi murmured.

Victor Rheus: The cops took it.

'Oh, he's going to blame the police? Ha.'

Doc: How the fuck did they find it?

'Language,' Finn muttered.

'I'm fitting in.'

Victor Rheus: I could ask you the same question.

Doc: Fuck you. Doc was a bit of a dick but he was my best source of content and you're the only person I told about that laptop. I don't particularly give a flying fuck what happened but I wanted in to that group. Who do I talk to?

'Last time I asked he cut out on me,' Lexi said and chewed on her lip.

Victor Rheus: We need a photo ID and a phone number, 5K in crypto to join and five hundred a month to fund the parties. But the deal is you shut up about Doc. No questions.

'That's a lot of money,' Lexi said. 'And he's worried I'm going to talk about Doc to the other members.' She looked at Rachael. 'Is there any doubt left in your mind that Victor's our killer?'

'Not a lot,' Rachael said, 'At the very least he knows what happened.'

Lexi nodded. 'Can we get what he's asking for? Can I join?'

'Yeah. Tell him you're in, you just need a few hours to get the money together. That'll give me time to get everything sorted.'

Doc: Deal. Let me know where to transfer the crypto. I'll have it to you in a few hours.

A moment later the details appeared. 'There's the wallet address.'

'Can we trace that address?' Rachael asked.

Lexi shook her head. 'The transactions linked to the wallet address can be viewed on the blockchain, but identifying information isn't required to start an account, so you're not going to get any personal details. You can't freeze the transfer like you can with a bank account either, so once the money's in, it's gone.'

'Blockchain?'

'It's basically a ledger.'

'It would be worth having that information.'

'Easy.'

'I'll get the rest underway. Anything on what went down at Dempsey's?'

Lexi navigated back to the main forum page. 'No, not yet.'

Finn noticed Rachael rubbing her temples. 'Headache?' he asked.

'A small but relentless one.'

'Shame all those Advil you seized had butterflies on them,' Lexi joked.

'The pills,' Rachael said, remembering. 'They were Patrick Miller's!'

'Would explain why he didn't seem surprised to see them,' Lexi said.

'I bet he's supplying the drugs for the parties. But we'll deal with that later. I need to authorise this payment, get you an ID.'

'And on that note, I'm going to head off,' Finn said.

Rachael checked the time. 'Aren't you supposed to have Ava this weekend?'

'School staff development day on Monday means she has an extra day off. She's lined up something with one of her friends for most of it but I'm booked in for Sunday and Monday.'

'You've got a daughter?' Lexi asked. 'How old?'

'Ava's ten. Do you need a lift home?'

Lexi looked at Rachael. 'Are we done?'

'Yeah. I'll have this sorted first thing,' Rachael said. 'Go get some rest.'

'Well done on getting an invite into the site,' Finn said in the car. 'Let's hope we get the rest of these guys before too long.'

Lexi made a dismissive noise. 'We might have slowed down a few arseholes perving on teens. We haven't got the Spider.'

'We're closer now. We will.' He navigated onto the street. The roads were empty. Lights were still on in some houses, others were dark. A full moon illuminated everything in a cool glow. It looked peaceful out there. But what was going on behind some of those doors?

'Did you get in any trouble about taking me out to Dempsey's?'

He shrugged, then smiled. 'I've been getting into trouble with Rachael since I was a kid. I'll survive.'

From the corner of his eye he caught the tilt of her head, the smile. 'What was she like as a mother figure?'

'Pretty cool. Overprotective because of what she deals with every day, but cool.' He glanced across, considered his words. 'There was just one thing I could never be.'

'What's that?'

'You.'

She shifted in her seat, the coolness returning to her voice. 'What are you talking about?'

'You left a hole no one and nothing could fill.'

'Don't be ridiculous, I only met the woman a couple of times.'

'That was enough. You made an impression. You became the poster child for every other case she ever took on. You know what still tortures her? She doesn't know the whole story.'

'She knows exactly what happened.'

'She knows the outcome. I'm not going to tell you to dredge it all up again if you can't. But if you can, I know it would mean a lot. It might help close that chapter once and for all.'

'What happened to me wasn't her fault. I blamed her for not coming in time to stop it. But then I grew up. I know she tried. I didn't mean what I said when I first saw her again. It was the heat of the moment.'

'You should tell her that, too.'

'Shit, Finn. It'll get all emotional and I don't do that.'

He smiled at that. 'I'll come with you.'

'I don't need my hand held!'

'Oh, I'm aware. I overheard what you said to Janie. Sounds tough.'

'It had its moments.'

'If you don't mind me asking ... how did you survive?'

He didn't think she was going to answer, but after a moment she sighed and spoke. 'I didn't have much in the way of ideas at first, but I made a friend, Carly. She was fifteen and she got me a place to sleep, taught me about the streets, how to steal. Going to the sports ground on the weekends was the easiest. The change rooms would be open. You could walk right in, grab someone's stuff and have a shower—score some new clothes, some shoes, occasionally some cash. I did that a lot for the first couple of years. Most of the stuff was too big, but it kept me warm, mostly.'

'What happened to Carly?'

'I don't know. She went out one night to score and never came back.'

'Did you tell anyone?'

'Seriously? Excuse me, officer, a street kid with a meth habit didn't come back to her squat last night.' Then in a mock deep voice, 'Oh, that's terrible, rest assured we'll throw every resource we have into tracking her down!' Lexi sighed. 'No one cares.'

'I want to say you're wrong, but it wouldn't have been high on the list of priorities. How long were you on the street?'

'Technically I wasn't. Exactly. I had a little corner in the back room of an abandoned building that I shared with Carly, three other homeless kids and a smelly old drunk who called himself Durkheim. He used to lecture us on the collective consciousness.'

'You're making that up.'

'I'm not. You can't make up some of the stuff I could tell you. Interesting times.'

'What about—'

'What about we talk about something else? What's the go with Ava? You're divorced from her mum?'

'Nearly two years.'

'What happened?'

He shot her a wry smile. 'What about we talk about something else?'

CHAPTER THIRTY-ONE

Saturday, March 20

Rachael hit send on the email, then decided to go see Lexi in the strike force room and make sure she got it. It was only early, but everyone was already working, the room full of busy energy. Lexi was in the back corner, focused on a monitor.

'Morning,' Rachael said.

Lexi looked up. 'Hi. If you're looking for Finn he's somewhere making sure Turner gives me my car back.'

'If he doesn't, I will. I wanted to let you know everything you need to join the forum group is ready to go. There's a driver's licence and the number for a mobile set up for this purpose. The actual phone is on its way. And you have access to a bitcoin wallet, which I'm guessing is how you transfer the crypto. Should all be in your emails.'

'Thanks,' Lexi said and brought them up. 'I'll take a look ... Yep. Okay, let's do this.'

'Are we members yet? Finn asked, coming in behind Rachael.

'Almost,' Lexi answered without looking up from the monitor. 'Okay, I've transferred the money. I'll just strip the ID image of any info and send that across with the phone number. Hey, where was that phone purchased? He's not going to be able to papertrail that number back to the police is he?'

'My people know what they're doing, Lexi,' Rachael said.

'Right. Sorry. Okay ... done.'

'Hey, look what I found,' Turner said, coming into the room with one of the constables she recognised from earlier as Constable Harvey. He had his laptop open in his hand and at the press of a button an image of Lexi wearing something black and tight and straddling a chair appeared on the room's main screen. Then to Lexi, he said, 'I think you should stick to the leather.'

A couple of murmurs and a low whistle were accompanied by covert glances at Lexi. Rachael felt other stares burning into her, wondering what she was going to do about it. Turner had thrown down another gauntlet. Harvey high-fived him.

'Too far, Turner!' Finn said, voice sharp as a blade. 'Turn it off.'

Rachael had her mouth open to order him to her office. He was in for a serious reprimand. But Lexi's quietly spoken 'Don't' held her up.

She got to her feet. Considering Turner thoughtfully, she half walked, half sauntered towards him. 'That photo is from when I worked at Madame Suzie's. I *knew* I remembered you.' She let that hang for a few seconds while she got closer. 'Still paying people to sleep with you?'

Turner's mouth opened and closed twice before the words came out. 'I never—'

'Got through the door?' She straightened his tie. 'Doesn't surprise me. Even people like me have standards. And yet ...' A puzzled expression appeared on her face, before she shook her head and walked back across the room to her seat.

'You don't really remember him do you?' Rachael asked under her breath.

'Pfft. No. But everyone will forever wonder, won't they?' Lexi murmured back.

'Nevertheless.' Then to Turner, 'Let's go. That's harassment. I'm writing this one up.'

'You can try, but I have every right to investigate a person of interest in a murder and share any information I uncover with the team.'

'She's not a person of interest, and she's working for us!'

'Besides, the media are waiting.'

She could have slapped the smugness right off his face. 'Where?'

Turner gestured behind her with his chin. She turned, saw the journalists hovering outside the doorway.

'You brought them up here?' she hissed. 'What is wrong with you?'

'They have an appointment.'

Rachael simmered. What were the chances the media hadn't heard any of that stuff about Lexi? Zero. That was no doubt the point.

'What are they here for?' Finn asked.

'It's the local radio station. People are getting worried about the safety of their kids. With the Spider back in the news, they were hoping I'd do a short piece with them on what precautions they should be taking to keep their kids safe. It won't take long.'

'Inspector, Nigel Dempsey's just been brought in,' Debbie said. 'His lawyer is with him. We have limited time to talk to him. Doctor's orders.'

'Thanks.' Then to Finn, Rachael said, 'Can you prep for Dempsey? I'll be down in five.'

'Yeah, of course.'

*

'You did a good job of sitting Turner on his arse up there,' Rachael said as she walked with Lexi to the viewing room. From the monitor she could see Finn setting up for Dempsey's interview. 'But next time don't touch him. He can claim assault.'

'For straightening his tie? Wow, he must be great in the field.'

'And speaking of that, it was very brave jumping in to help Finn like that yesterday,' she told Lexi. 'But—'

'You're about to tell me it's against the rules to hit people with hammers? Got it. Next time, Finn dies.'

Rachael couldn't quite help the smile. 'I don't want you getting hurt.'

'Me neither.'

Finn looked ready to proceed so Rachael dropped it for the time being and went in to join them.

'Gentlemen,' she said, taking a seat. Then to Dempsey, 'How's the head?'

'I got hit by a girl.'

'With a hammer.'

'I'll live.'

'We're under the impression you're very fond of girls,' Finn prompted. 'Especially young ones.'

'We're just a little local group of guys who hold some parties,' Dempsey told him. 'Never asked their ages.'

'But you like teens?'

'Yeah. I do.' Dempsey slid around in his seat like he was just getting warmed up. 'Girls are fun, out for a good time without an agenda. They come for the music, the dancing. That's it. Women are game players, scheming, out for whatever they can get.'

'Like your ex-wife?'

'Took me for everything. Bitch.'

'Yeah, you certainly appear to be living in poverty,' Finn said.

'So your answer is to hook up with twelve-year-olds?' Rachael asked

'Teens. That's all we do.'

'Do?'

He smirked. 'Invite to party. They never have to do nothin' they don't want to do.'

'Pump them full of enough drugs and alcohol and they wouldn't really know what they were doing, would they?'

Dempsey gave a self-satisfied laugh. 'Mate, they might be young but they ain't innocent.'

'So how is it, then, that a twelve-year-old by the name of Summer Edgely attended one of these parties and never made it home alive?' Rachael asked.

Dempsey recoiled in his chair and lifted his hands in a back-off gesture. 'I didn't know nothing about that shit until the video was posted on the Spider's Web. Seriously! We've been hosting these parties for years. Girls come and go of their own free will. We do some dancing, some drinking. Maybe some of the girls are a year or two too young to be drinking but that's it. I'll cop to that, but not to any of that other shit.'

'How does one become a member of your group?' Finn asked.

'You've gotta be referred by another member.'

'And Jonathan Davies was a member?'

'Yeah, Davies practically founded the group from the remnants of some other one he was involved in.'

'Any idea who killed him?'

Dempsey frowned. 'I thought he was missing.'

'Missing presumed dead.' Finn opened a folder and showed him the crime scene photos from Davies's house. 'It was messy. Not the sort of way you want to go, if you know what I mean. We think someone in your group was responsible for that. Pretty unsettling, right?'

Dempsey's face screwed up. 'No, mate, none of our group would do that sort of thing.'

Rachael heard the buzz of a message on her phone and checked it. Lexi wanting to know what his username was.

Rachael glanced up. 'Mr Dempsey, what's your username on the forum?'

Dempsey dropped eye contact. 'I'm not saying.'

Another buzz from the phone. Rachael bit back the grin at Finn's wide-eyed stare before asking, 'Who's Victor Rheus?'

'Who?' Dempsey asked.

'Cut the crap,' Finn said.

'Mate, there's—'

'I'm not your mate.'

'There's almost thirty of us, okay? A few newbies. We don't always get around to asking people what their real names are.'

Another buzz. Rachael quickly read the message while Dempsey's lawyer objected. 'What is with the texts, detective. My client is not well, so I'd suggest—'

'I understand that. But there's information coming through your client might be interested to hear. Apparently, Victor Rheus just posted on the forum that Mr Squiggle killed Doc and that the police have got him in custody. That if anyone else gets picked up they should stick to that story.'

Dempsey surged to his feet in objection. 'That's complete crap! I never liked that guy! Walked in and took over like he owned the group! Talked down to everyone. He's full of shit!'

'So you do know who he is,' Finn said.

Dempsey sat down, quietened. 'I don't know his name.'

'Can you point him out on any of the videos?'

'You found the videos?' Dempsey suddenly looked much less sure of himself.

'Yeah. We heard you take them to hold over the girls in case they think about telling anyone what's going on.'

Dempsey shrugged, but his upbeat tone had definitely flattened. 'Get enough footage of them doing silly things and they'll keep their mouths shut. They don't want their tits or muffs on social media.'

'If they're just dancing, how would you get those shots?'

'They get hot.'

'And then there's the supply of alcohol and illicit drugs to children.'

'No one forces them to take anything.'

'You never spiked a drink?'

'Me personally? Never needed to.' He ran his hand through his hair as though to show off his good looks.

'So who is it that keeps the IDs and phone numbers the members have to provide in order to join?' Rachael asked.

'Uh ... um.' Dempsey started to sweat.

'Look, we've got Patrick Miller, too, so whoever talks first gets the deal. Understand?' Finn said impatiently.

'Deal?'

'Yeah. Cooperating with the police could knock a lot of years off what you're looking at. Got anything else you want to tell us?'

'What kinda deal are we talking exactly?'

'That depends on what you're prepared to do for us and how this all turns out. Where's the personal information on these guys? The IDs, the phone numbers? Who's got them?'

Dempsey hesitated, then blurted, 'I can give it all to you. But I want my deal first.'

'Can you give us Victor?'

'I really don't know. Doc brought him in. Said he didn't need to provide it. But I have all the others.'

Rachael got up and walked out. 'How did you know all that?' she asked Lexi a moment later.

'Mr Squiggle always calls everyone mate, so I guessed it was him. The rest I made up.'

'You made it up?'

'Worked, didn't it?' she said and her grin flashed. 'Shame he doesn't know who Victor really is though.'

'We'll get the sketch artist to work with him on Victor's likeness. At least we'll have an idea of what the bastard looks like,' Rachael said. 'This is a long-established group who've been getting away with this for years, and from the girls we saw on the video, I'd say they are all slightly older teens. So the fact that shortly after Davies brought Victor into the group we suddenly had a dead twelve-year-old adds to the likelihood Victor's our guy.'

Lexi nodded. 'He used the party to give Summer the drugs to subdue her. The group is a means to an end.'

Rachael chewed her lip. 'I need to work out what kind of a deal I can offer Dempsey to make sure we get our hands on that information.'

'How about freedom in return for castration?' Lexi suggested.

Finn came out and closed the door behind him.

'We can't waste any time moving on this,' Rachael said. 'I want these members picked up as soon as possible, so no one has a chance to warn anyone else we're coming. I'll have Turner take one of his constables and head back up to Dempsey's property. I need eyes on the place. If anyone shows up, they can grab them. Finn, let everyone know it's going to be a long day, and get us some help. We're going to need it.'

'Got it.'

Here we go again, Rachael thought. Just like the raids on the Spider's group.

Only no paths to choose between this time, no difficult decisions. No little girl depending on her.

'I said to her, "What's this? A spider?"' Kayla said over the phone, 'and she said, "No, he's the Spider."'

Rachael froze, the chaos of the strike force room fading into oblivion. 'What?'

'She's here, with me. She wants to talk to you.'

'Hello?' the little voice said over the phone.

'Hi Lexi. So, you drew me a picture?'

'Mmm hmm. If I promise to talk to the people that come and ask the questions, will you come and get us today?'

'Yes, sweetie, I'll come get you both.'

'And we'll never have to go back?'

'Never.'

'You promise?'

'I promise.'

'Okay. Bye.'

'Something happened yesterday,' Kayla said, back on the phone. 'She's got new bruises. Looks like it might have been a rough night. When are you coming to get her?'

'I just have to clear it with my boss. We've been tipped off about a group of paedophiles we think have been associating with the Spider. The raid on the houses is being organised in the background as we speak.'

'Rach, don't mess this up. I've never seen Lexi place her trust in anyone before.'

When the line went dead, Rachael slipped back into the strike force room, listened while everyone was assigned their duties. As everyone sprang into action, she approached Sanders, blurted out the story. 'So you see, I need to check this out. I need to get these girls. They could be the Spider's next victims.'

Sanders held a finger up to ask her to wait while he answered a question, then shook his head at her. 'Not tonight, detective.'

'But I promised her! She's relying on me, I have to. Please.'

'This Lexi. She's ten?'

'Yes.'

'And she calls a man a spider and says he makes bad movies? Anything more specific?'

'She calls him *the* spider and no, not yet but she's promised to—'

'Have you seen these movies?'

'No, but—'

'You can't remove children from their home based on that. We need more.'

'At least let me talk to her. Get DOCS involved.'

Another interruption, another pause in the conversation. 'And then what?' he asked. 'You've just told me they've already investigated.'

'But she didn't want to talk to me back then,' she pressed. 'She trusts me now. Sir, please.'

'We'll discuss it again tomorrow.'

'But, sir!'

'Raid first, Langley. This is the break we've been waiting for. It needs to happen fast and I need everyone on this. One of these lowlifes will crack. One of them will know enough about the Spider to bring him down. Once we get that, no little girls will have to worry about the Spider ever again.'

She considered taking a car, to hell with the consequences. But she knew the boss had a point. If someone could tell them who the Spider was, they could go get him. And if he really was associated with Lexi's arsehole of a father, they could go and get him, too. They couldn't afford for anyone to slip through the net because she wasn't doing her job. But, damn it, she'd promised.

'Roasted by the boss, eh?' Turner teased.

'Shut up, Turner.'

'He's right, you know. You have to do things by the book. One kid versus a network of scumbags is a no-brainer.'

'You don't get it.'

'I do. You made a stupid promise you can't keep. Rookie mistake.'

She wanted to slap the condescending smirk from his face. 'Who says I'm not going to keep it?' She'd get this done, bang on BJ Winter's front door at midnight if it came to that. She'd promised. She'd be there.

'Let's move!' Sanders ordered.

'You keep that promise, you won't have a career afterwards,' Turner said. 'Get your head where it's supposed to be. I'll drive.'

CHAPTER THIRTY-TWO

Sunday, March 21

I'm not sure how waking early got to be a habit, but in spite of this being a day off for most of the team after last night's raids, I'm up before eight and I'm not even in a bad mood about it. I'm kind of antsy about not being at the station, which is odd enough for me to ponder as I find myself something to do to keep me occupied. I clean my house and consider going to the shops to buy an outfit or two more suited to the job I'm doing. No one has said anything about the jeans and tees yet, but I can probably do better without spending too much at Target or Big W.

My car is finally back and sitting in the drive and I'm in a pretty good mood when I take out a bag of rubbish, until I see what's standing in the Parkhursts' driveway. Turner. He's getting into his car and when he spots me, the polite smile aimed at the Parkhursts turns smug. The Parkhursts wave him off and, seeing me, go inside and close the door.

I need an explanation. I'm betting the Parkhursts won't talk, so I get into my car and follow Turner to the station. What the hell had they told him? He's off to an early start after being part of the arrests last night. At last update Rachael had had twenty-four arseholes in custody. The best part about it was she was able to round them up without giving Miller the chance at a deal. There's little good about Dempsey getting one but as far as I'm concerned, Miller is worse.

So no more parties, but that doesn't solve the real problem, does it? Those arseholes have been useful to Victor, but their capture wasn't going to put him out of action. And the police were still no closer to finding him. Surely Turner should be putting a bit more effort into that? He must really think he has something on me. The idea makes me nervous.

I see the media parked outside the station but I don't think too much of it. They're here every day now that the Spider case is making constant headlines. So I'm caught by surprise when a woman in a dress suit spots me and practically runs in my direction with her cameraman.

'Lexi Winter? How did you escape Biddle? Was he the Spider, Lexi? Or do you think he was falsely charged? What happened that night?'

Another pair of reporters follow her over and start shooting similar questions at me. 'Is prostitution a direct result of your abuse as a child?' one calls out, turning the heads of pedestrians on the street.

My stomach lurches. How do they know who I am or that I'd be here? Now another is on his way over. 'I don't know what you're talking about!' I say and duck around them, but they're following closely, firing questions at me. I get inside the station and I'm fuming. I don't wait for the lift, just take the stairs.

Rachael is in her office, she and Finn talking about something that's going to have to wait. Both look up in surprise as I barrel in without knocking.

'Why did I just get mobbed by a bunch of reporters who know who I am?' I demand.

Rachael's surprise turns to a kind of pissed-off resignation. Her fingers go to her eyes. 'I was afraid of this. Turner invited the media up here to talk to me while he did his little show with your photo, remember?'

'Great. Speaking of Turner, any idea what he was doing at my house this morning?'

The surprise was back. 'None.'

'Happy to fill you in,' Turner said, appearing behind me. 'I was talking to your neighbours.'

'I gathered.'

'They had some fascinating things to say.'

'Lexi, why don't you sit down?' Rachael says, so I reluctantly take the spare chair.

Turner looks around for a seat and Rachael's snapped 'You can stand' marginally levels my mood.

'What were you cleaning out of your car on the Sunday evening of the weekend Davies disappeared?' Turner asks me. 'Your neighbours said you killed their grass.'

'I replaced it.'

'This is bordering on harassment,' Finn said to Rachael.

'I want an alibi for the night Davies disappeared,' Turner says.

'I'm not dragging my clients into this,' I tell him.

'So you're out on the Saturday night it's probable Davies disappeared and won't give me an alibi, then on the Sunday morning you're seen lugging a fuel container home, which you say is for a motorbike you never got, and shortly after that, you had the sudden urge to clean your car with strong enough chemicals to kill your neighbours' lawn.'

'It really wasn't much of a lawn.'

'What was in the car that required such a harsh clean?'

'The carpet. It stank. And I admit I probably overdid it on the chemicals. Sue me.'

'It was Davies's body, wasn't it?' he said, eyes narrowed in on mine. 'And the fuel was to dispose of it.'

Shit. Shit. Shit. I know Finn and Rachael have so far been on my side, but they're listening intently and they're anything but stupid. I'm surprised they can't see the guilt written all over me. I need to deny it, but omitting details of my involvement in the Davies situation is different to lying to their faces. I can't do it. 'You know the Parkhursts must be enjoying the hell out of this, right?'

'And then there's the freezer you and your neighbour disposed of.'

'It was broken,' I say as though he's an idiot, but I'm struggling not to panic. 'And there was nothing convenient about disposing of that thing. It weighed a ton. Ask him,' I say and look in Finn's direction.

'You helped move the freezer?' Turner asks Finn in surprise.

'It was broken,' Finn repeats.

Turner's attention swings back to me. 'You knew about Davies before any of us. You told your sister you were going to find him. That you did find him.'

'Oh, for fuck's sake!' I say, the nerves coming out as frustration in my tone. 'I found him online. I can't exactly drag him through a laptop screen and put him in a broken freezer. Or have you got some theory about that, too?'

'You think this is a joke?'

I need to turn it into one. Where's my fabulous sarcastic sense of humour when I need it? I'm struggling. 'Kind of. Yeah. I mean, you're trying to tell me I somehow found this guy's residential address from a picture online, and I'm going to say that with enough clues I could potentially have done that. But then I killed him. A man I'd never met but apparently hated enough to—what did the pathologist say ... likely bludgeon or stab? Then I burned him *and* froze him? Kinda overkill isn't it? And then I got a sixty-something-year-old woman to dispose of the body for me. And actually that last one's bound to be true because I know I couldn't be bothered doing it myself. I'm lazy as it gets and that whole scenario screams way too much work.'

Turner's hard stare doesn't budge. 'Where did the freezer go, Lexi?'

'I believe it went for parts, but I really wasn't that involved. Couldn't tell you. Why don't you ask Dawny?'

'I did.'

'And you think you'll get a different story from me? Good try.'

'You spoke to the male driver of the van. I need a name.'

Like hell I'm crossing Desmond. 'No, I need a name, like the Boston Strangler. Maybe the murdering, freezing, burning ... No, wait. The burning, freezing ... oh shit, I've lost track. You'll think of something.' I get up, because I need to breathe and I can't in here. I smile. 'Meanwhile, I have a child killer to finish bringing down. Actual work.' I frown at Turner. 'What is it you get paid for?' Then I'm heading for the door.

'I'm not finished with you,' Turner snarls.

'Yes, you are,' Rachael tells him. 'No more, Turner. That's it.'

'You can't stop me investigating her.'

I pause, sigh. 'Okay, but when you come up with a motive, can you make it bizarre enough to be memorable? If I'm going down for something that took that much effort, I want someone to make a movie out of it. Oh, and don't leave out the part where I turned up here after killing him to help you figure all this out.'

'Lexi, stay here, please,' Rachael says. 'Turner, you have interviews to do.'

I don't catch what he mumbles under his breath, but it comes with a decent glare.

'What?' I ask Rachael, still fired up over Turner.

'I wanted to give you an update on last night.'

'Oh, right. Sorry.' I flop back down on my chair. 'You rounded up all the arseholes?'

'All bar four. But we're confident we'll get them. Unfortunately, like Dempsey said, Victor's name wasn't on that list. And there's still the issue of Miller and the drugs to tie up. He's not talking and he's going to get bail this morning.'

'So let me use the spyware I already have on his laptop to monitor his use. Even better, let Neutron install his RAT.'

'I never got that warrant.'

'No one needs to know we've done it.'

'Yes, they do,' Finn says. 'Spying on people is illegal.'

'Let's move on, shall we?' Rachael says. 'If we were to get this RAT onto Miller's computer—'

'Rachael!' Finn exclaims.

'Once the judge has signed off on it,' Rachael counters calmly, 'we might find out where the drugs are coming from.'

'But unless he opens a file you sent him, how do you get this thing onto his computer?' Finn asks. 'He's bound to be more careful now.'

'We'll do it manually,' I tell them. 'The laptop's still here, isn't it?'

'It'll be password protected,' Finn reminds me.

I send him a withering look. 'So?'

'So you won't be able to get in.'

'I don't need that sort of scepticism in my life.' And because I can see his laptop is sitting on Rachael's desk, I say. 'Give me yours.'

'What? No!'

I extend my arm and wiggle my fingers. 'Hand it over.'

Rachael ignores Finn's objection and slides it to me. I open it up, get to work. 'Worst-case scenario, we stick with the spyware. He'll have to contact his source eventually.'

'He might not do that online,' Rachael says. 'It could be face-to-face.'

'So that means stakeouts, right? Could be fun.'

'They're anything but fun,' Finn says.

'They always look exciting in the movies.' Then I can't help but grin. 'You have Domino's Pizza on your shortcuts? How many times a week do you eat that stuff?'

'What?' He spins the screen around to see his computer unlocked. 'That's just wrong! What's the point of a password if you can just—how long was that? A minute?'

'Maybe.' He's staring at me like he doesn't understand me. So much so I have to ask, 'What?'

'Why aren't you doing something constructive with your life?'

I pull a face at him. 'I thought bringing down a child-exploitation ring, a drug dealer and child killer would qualify as constructive.'

'You could be doing this sort of thing every day. Making a massive difference.'

'It's not complicated, there's just a lot to remember. Once you know it, it's easy. Anyone can do it. Besides, I have a job.'

Finn examines his laptop. 'You didn't do anything else to it, did you? How do I know you're not spying on me now?'

I smile. 'You don't.'

'Lexi ...'

'Better be nice to me, Finn!' I threaten wickedly, then answer my phone when it goes off.

'Lexi, dear, it's Dawny. Are you expecting company?'

'What? No. Why?'

'Channel Nine is out the front of your place.'

'Oh my God.' My gaze bounces off Rachael before I close my eyes and hope this is some stupid nightmare.

'Is there a problem, dear? Anything I should know about?'

'Nothing for you to worry about,' I reassure her. 'Nothing to do with you.'

'Just checking. My, you are popular these days. Shall I tell them when you'll be back?'

'No! Don't tell them anything. I'll explain everything to you later.'

'I'll make a pie,' Dawny says. 'Bye, dear.'

I end the call and I'm fuming again. Do I have Turner to thank for this too? Was he actually allowed to get away with this stuff?

'What's wrong?' Rachael asks.

'I have Channel Nine at my front door.' I get up, walk to the window and look down on the street below. 'And every other reporter in the country is still camped outside the station. Don't they have anything else to go report on?'

Rachael gets up to stand beside me. 'Where's your car?'

'On the street. They saw me get out of it. And if one reporter knows where I live they all will before long, right? What am I supposed to do now?'

'I'll have Debbie take your car into the secure parking,' Rachael says. 'Finn, do you still have Ava today?'

'Viv's dropping her at my place in about an hour, yeah. Need me to cancel?'

'No. But can you take Lexi back to your place for a couple of hours while I get this sorted?'

'Yeah, no problem.' Then to me, he says, 'Let's go.'

*

'I like your apartment,' I tell him when he shows me inside. 'The view is nice.'

'Thanks. There's tea and coffee stuff over there, the television, obviously, I have the wifi code if you want to jump online.'

'I don't have my computer. Do you have a VPN?'

'Yeah.'

'Do you mind if I install some software?'

'How about, "Do you mind if I use your computer?"'

I smile brightly. 'Thanks. Just a Tor browser, some extra security. I want to check on the forum. See if there's any chatter from Victor or the remaining members.'

'Okay, I suppose. As long as you can undo what you do.'

'Of course.' I set it all up, log in. 'Damn it!'

'What?'

'It's gone.'

'Not really surprising.'

'Hold on …' I log into the email account I set up for this purpose and audibly sigh when I see the ad for Viagra. I click on it, log in with my old details and up comes the link to the site. 'It's still up, just changed address.'

There's two guys online, neither is Victor and there's only one new thread.

'Oh, look, I really am popular today,' I tell Finn when I find my name in the title. I click on it.

Tumbleseed: You think it's true the cops have got Lexi Winter working for them?

'Well, that's interesting. Was that on the news?'

'No,' Finn says, looking over my shoulder. 'And if we can prove Turner's behind it, he's going to be in serious trouble. I wouldn't mind betting Rachael's working on that right now.'

'She has enough on her hands today though, right? All those arrests, charges, interviews.'

'Most of them were bailed early this morning, the rest are staying put until they can be transferred to remand.'

'Right. Let's see where this goes,' I say and type Nah. She's a prostitute.

Tumbleseed: You know her?

Doc: From what I gather, for $250 anyone can know her.

'What are you doing?' Finn asks.

'We set this up right, we might be able to get Victor to come to us.'

'By dangling you as bait?'

'He's deliberately dragged Rachael and Bailee back into this and Rachael thinks he's got it in for anyone who stuffed up his old empire. Why wouldn't he be interested in finding me? Anyway, I guess we'll know soon enough.'

'You want a coffee? A cold drink?' he asks when nothing happens for a minute or so.

'Got anything alcoholic? It might stop me going after Turner later—'

A chat window pops up.

Victor Rheus: Got your money and ID. You're in. I'll send instructions for changing your screen name shortly. How do you know about Lexi Winter?

'Well, well, what do you know? Victor's online,' I tell him.

Finn hurries back over. 'What's he want?'

'I'm in. And he wants to know how I know about me.'

'Okay, log off. We should check with Rachael before going with any more of your crazy ideas. Look what happened last time.'

'We … brought down a bunch of paedophiles?'

'You know what I mean,' Finn says. 'Just do what you're told for once, please? This is dangerous.'

'Okay, fine.' I huff out a breath as a knock at the door has him moving away.

I watch him cross the room. He's answering the door, not looking, so I make a rash, executive decision.

Doc: I know someone who knows where she is. Interested?

Victor Rheus: Tell me where to find her.

Doc: On it.

I log off and twist in my seat as he opens the door to a gorgeous woman and a cute kid.

'Hi Dad.'

'Hi sweetie.' He takes a bag the woman hands him then steps aside to let Ava through.

'Can you meet me at Tuggerah for drop off?' the woman asks. 'I have to do some shopping. Around two?'

'Yeah, no worries.'

The kid stops midway into the room when she spots me, her face puzzled. 'Hi.'

'Hi.'

'I'm Ava.'

'Lexi.'

Some sort of understanding washes over her features. 'You're Lexi! I heard about you.'

I'm wondering what on earth she could have heard so I look at Finn for a clue and notice I'm getting a hard stare from the woman in the doorway. It's one of those 'and who the hell are you' looks I usually see on the faces of jealous girlfriends.

'I've heard about you too,' I tell Ava, deciding to ignore the woman and let her imagination do its thing.

'Okay, well, bye, Viv,' Finn says and closes the door. Then he winks at Ava. 'You'll get grilled about that later.'

'You're not a cop, are you?' Ava asks me.

'No.'

'What do you do?'

'I'm ... I'm an ...' I'm stuttering because Finn is shaking his head at each answer before I can get one out. 'I help lonely people feel better.'

Ava perches on the back of the lounge near where I've been working. 'How do you do that?'

I have to forcibly choke back a laugh at Finn's distressed expression. 'Say someone hasn't got a partner but they need to pretend they do. Or they want one, just for a day or a work thing or whatever. I fill in.'

'That's nice of you. Do you get paid for that?'

'Yep.'

'That sounds like a nice job. You should hire her, Dad.'

'Oh my God,' he mutters, tossing Ava's bag into her room.

I can't help the laugh because it's just that funny. 'Your dad need a date, honey?'

'Yeah, it's been, like, forever!' she says with an eye roll.

'Ava!' Finn sighs. 'Look, there's gotta be a better way to pass the time. What do you like to do?' he asks me. 'TV? Movies? Boardgames?'

'*Anything* that will stop this conversation?' I tease, mimicking his almost desperate tone.

'Ava, you have a homework assignment you need to finish, right?'

Ava rolls her eyes again but grins at me before heading in the direction of her room.

'You know, there's nothing to be ashamed of,' I tell Finn. 'Plenty of hot guys have dry spells.'

'I'm not ashamed of anything,' he hisses. Then says louder, 'So what do you want to do?'

I look around, spot an impressive library. 'I like books.'

'You like books?'

'Yeah. Even the ones with big words,' I reply to his tone of disbelief.

'Sorry, I didn't figure you for the type.'

'Because I'm a prostitute with a fifth-grade education?'

'Escort,' he automatically replies, shooting a look towards Ava's room. 'And no, more because you never seem to relax.' He goes to the bookshelf. 'I just finished this one. It's good.'

He hands me a murder mystery. 'Thanks.'

'Dad! I need help,' Ava says, coming back out.

'Sit at the table, I'll get you a drink.'

I take the book out onto the veranda to read while Finn sits and helps Ava with a maths question that leaves me feeling like they're speaking another language. She's ten, the same age I was when I stopped going to school. Maybe I would have learnt that stuff if I'd stayed.

I give up on the book after about half an hour of my mind wandering back to Victor and go inside.

'How's the story going?' Finn asks me. He's at the table with Ava, watching her complete some sort of geometrical artwork.

'Oh. I gave up. It's boring.'

'How is that boring? It's full of exciting, dangerous, who-dunnit stuff.'

'It's too predictable.' I put the book back where I saw him take it from. 'It's obvious the wife did it.'

'What?'

'Am I wrong?'

'I'm not going to tell you!' he objects. But I can tell I've picked it.

'You don't have to. The heroine was coming back from the murder scene in the first chapter, right? I mean, it doesn't say that but she took a back road, noticed the fuel was low but when she passed a petrol station she didn't stop. First two clues. Also, the next morning she ran into a neighbour and gave some story about falling from a ladder to explain some bruising she had. Why would that come up unless it had relevance to the story? Then, when the police came round to talk to her she pulled on a cardigan, hiding the bruises right? And when they told her what had happened she—'

'Okay, okay, Sherlock. How about a biography?' He leans across to a side table and holds it out to me.

I look at the front cover and the politician's face is familiar. 'Oh good, more fiction.'

He drops it back onto the table, then gets to his feet as his phone rings. 'Sorry, this is Rachael.' He wanders out to the veranda to take it just as Ava closes her book with a satisfied slap.

'All done?' I ask.

'All except ... I have to pick a topic that interests me and write three hundred words on it. But I have a week to do that. I'm too starving to think about it now.' She goes to the fridge and takes a look then shuts it in disdain. 'There's never any food here.'

'I'm pretty hungry too.' Finn's laptop is on the table right in front of me. I look outside. He's sitting now, still on the phone. I sneakily slide it around. 'Pizza?' I ask.

Ava grins. 'Pepperoni. And those garlic scroll things. Maybe ... Coke?'

I can tell from the look, the tone, that it's probably a no-no, but what the hell? May as well continue to corrupt the kid. 'Can't have pizza without it.'

'You're awesome, Lexi,' she says, grinning.

'I'm not sure your dad's going to agree.' As I open his laptop another thought pops into my mind. 'Want to learn how to bypass a computer password as that topic of interest?'

'Cool!'

'Okay, pay attention. Then you can order the pizza.'

We're finishing off her three hundred words by the time Finn comes back in. 'Sorry,' he says. 'I know that took forever.' He keeps walking right past us towards the kitchen when there's a knock on the door. He opens it and a young woman says hi and hands him a bottle of Coke before pulling pizzas from a thermal bag.

'Hold up. We didn't …'

'Yes we did!' Ava rushes over and takes the pizza. 'Thanks.'

'Yeah, thanks,' Finn echoes before closing the door. His gaze narrows in on my expression of pure innocence. 'You ordered pizza?'

'I did,' Ava said happily.

'And Coke? Ava, your mother doesn't like you drinking Coke.'

'Can't have pizza without it. Lexi said so.'

Finn sends me a chastising look. 'You broke into my laptop again, didn't you?'

'All in the name of homework, Dad,' Ava announces and hands him a pizza. 'Here you go.'

'Homework?' he asks, then looks down at Ava's book when she proudly spins it around. 'You taught my daughter how to break into a computer? She can't use that for homework!'

'Yes I can! Topic of interest!' Ava objects.

'She might forget her password one day,' I tell him. 'It's a handy skill to have.'

'You …' He looks from me to Ava and back, obviously speechless. 'We'll talk about this later,' he says to me, then to Ava, 'Eat up. Rachael's coming over. She wants to take you shopping. She called it girl time. I'm going to take Lexi home then I'm going to meet you later for dinner—if you can fit it in—and a movie.'

'Yay!' Ava says. 'Can't Lexi come?'

'Nah, I have stuff to do,' I say, because I can see what a bad idea Finn clearly thinks that is. 'But thanks.'

*

'I like your kid.' The car ride back to my place has been almost entirely silent. It's starting to wear on me.

'So do I,' Finn says. 'I like her innocent, on the right side of the law, and looking to do something other than escorting for a career—no offence.'

I try not to be offended because everything he's saying is perfectly reasonable. I guess it should just go without saying. 'She's all those things. And none taken.'

'You made one hell of an impression.'

'And that's the last thing you want. I'm guessing you'll be sure to keep her away from the bad influence from now on.'

'That's not what I meant.'

'Yes, it is. It's exactly what you meant.'

'To be fair, you taught her how to hack a computer.'

'I taught her how to recover a lost password!'

'Sounds almost innocent when you say it like that.'

Oh, screw being reasonable. 'Because that's what it was. Ava needed help with her homework and you were too busy to deal with it. Ava was hungry, and you were too busy to deal with it. We resolved a couple of issues in one hit. I'm not her mother, I'm not her teacher, but I did the best I could.'

He pulls up outside my house and rubs a hand along the back of his neck. 'Lexi–'

'Fuck you, Finn,' I answer tiredly and get out of the car.

'Lexi, wait.'

'It doesn't matter!'

There's no media in sight. Bonus. I go inside, grab my JD and flop onto the lounge. Remote in hand, I kick my feet up and flick on the television, determined not to stew on the conversation. Instead, I'm immediately confronted with a news story on Biddle.

A female reporter is outside Long Bay prison. 'The Court of Criminal Appeal will decide in the morning whether or not to overturn Thomas Biddle's conviction. The fifty-five-year-old cancer patient has always maintained his innocence and with recent new evidence and new testimony, Biddle may soon see freedom for the first time in eighteen years.'

'Any word from Inspector Langley on the possibility she got this very famous case wrong?' the presenter in the studio asks.

'Well, no, Simon, the inspector has remained notably silent on the issue, which could turn out to be one of the biggest miscarriages of justice in the New South Wales courts' history. Lawyers say the case against Biddle was weak, depending on unreliable evidence and flimsy corroboration. They claim the trial miscarried because of errors including the Crown's inappropriate attempts to persuade the jury to draw inferences of fact based upon false evidence, and that they're confident their client will shortly walk free.'

'Evidence?' I mutter, taking a deep gulp of JD. 'I guess you needed to be there.'

'Lexi! Bailee! Get down here!'

I hear the shouted command after the bang of the front door as Mummy and Daddy stumble inside. I sit up and rub

my eyes. I figure it must be some time past the middle of the
night if they've just gotten back from the pub. I don't know
when I fell asleep. I was trying to stay awake. I was waiting
for Rachael. But she didn't come.

There's a burst of loud conversation. It sounds like they've
brought back a friend. Mr Biddle?

A shuffling of feet at my bedroom doorway has me sitting
up and squinting. It's Bailee, her long blonde hair messy
from sleep, her hand-me-down Sesame Street pyjamas
crooked over her little shoulders. Dangling from her hand
is her favourite stuffed rabbit that had been singed by the
heater last year.

'Get your arses down here now!' Daddy roars.

'Lexi, do you hear that?' Bailee races over to the bed and
tugs on my sheet, eyes wide with fear. 'I don't wanna go
down there.'

I don't either. There's a crash. Then another. I know what
will happen if we don't show. 'Come on, we'd better.' I swing
my legs out of bed and stand up, lift Bailee and settle her
on my hip. She's getting so big. Her legs are dangling close
to the floor. 'Are you warm enough?'

'Not really.' Her frail arms wrap around my neck as she
cuddles in. 'They're mad again.'

'It's just the drink.' Hopefully it's just the drink. That was
better than when they took the drugs. When they took the
drugs things got really bad.

'Bad drink.'

A heavy footstep on the bottom of the stairs has me hurrying. If Daddy comes up here it'll be worse.

'Coming!' I call out. I jog down the stairs, Bailee bouncing against my hip. I can't help but hold my breath as I get
closer to Daddy at the bottom.

'Get in there!' He gives me a shove towards the kitchen. What have I done? What haven't I remembered to do? I can't think of anything.

Mum's waiting. She looks skinny in the singlet top and torn jeans, but I know how strong she is when she takes the drugs. Her eyes are black and mean and her face is sweaty and kind of a blueish white. Behind her—it's him. Mr Biddle. His mean eyes skip over me and rest on Bailee.

'What's this?' One of Mummy's long pointy fingers jabs at the milk container on the bench.

My tummy feels funny because I know we're about to cop it. I try to put Bailee down, to get in front of her, but she's clinging to me.

'It … it was out of date,' I explain. 'I meant to tip it out and put it in the bin. But Bailee needed her bath and I … I'm sorry, Mummy. I'll fix it.'

Mummy hits me and I stumble back. It stings so much. I hear Bailee start to cry and plead with her in my head to be quiet.

'Shut up, you little bitch!' Mummy is moving from side to side. She's taken the drugs. I hope she falls over but she doesn't. She holds on to the kitchen bench and snatches the milk. 'Mummy and Daddy don't need this shit! You think we can afford for you to waste stuff? Stuff we buy with our money? You're ungrateful little bitches! That's what you are!'

She grabs two plastic cups from the sink and pours in the milk, keeps pouring even when the cups overflow, until the bottle is empty. The lumpy milk is running along the counter and dripping onto the floor. 'You sit, and you drink it!'

Bailee looks up at me then lets me go. She tiptoes around the milky floor and climbs up onto the stool. She picks up the cup in both hands and has a sip. Her face screws up and she shudders. 'Yucky milk, Mummy,' she whines weakly.

'Spoilt brat!' Mummy forces the cup to Bailee's mouth, begins tipping it in. Bailee's choking and crying and Mummy starts laughing.

'Stop it!' It bursts from my mouth before I can control it. 'Please! Daddy, please!' I yell because Daddy's always nicer to Bailee.

The room goes really still and quiet. Mummy puts down the glass and I know I'm in trouble. But Bailee is already off the stool and running for cover. She's okay.

'What did you say?' Daddy asks.

Mr Biddle laughs. 'I think she's asking for it.'

Daddy smirks. 'Get upstairs,' he orders. But Mr Biddle is shaking his head.

'She's too old. Money's not there.' His eyes sneak across to where Bailee is hiding. Already sick, my chest starts to hurt. He's looking at Bailee. Looking at Bailee the way Daddy always looks at me. Before he ... 'I'll give you some serious money for a go at that.'

'Well, go on then,' Mummy taunts to Daddy. 'Good enough for my kid, good enough for ours.'

'No!' I yell again. 'She's too little! Daddy, don't let him! No, please!' But Mr Biddle is already across the room.

'Lexi! Lexi! Lexi!' Bailee screams as he tosses her over his shoulder. He's heading for the stairs.

'Daddy!' I plead again. For a second I think he might listen, then he turns and heads up the stairs after Mr Biddle. Mummy is laughing again.

'You're jealous! Ha! What's wrong, Lexi? Not Daddy's little girl anymore?'

Usually I'm too scared to talk back. But not now. Now I'm desperate and angry and I don't care if I get in trouble as long as they leave Bailee alone. 'Why are you like this?' I yell at Mummy so she can hear me over Bailee's crying. 'You're supposed to care about us!'

Smack. My head spins back with the force of the slap.

Mummy takes a few steps sideways to keep her feet underneath her. Grabs me. 'You think you matter? You don't! You're just a pay cheque!' she says in my face. 'Why the fuck would I care about you? No one cares about you, got it? You're nothing!' She drags me over to the bench and gets Daddy's gun. I'm so scared I can't breathe. 'I could kill you right now and no one would care!' She waves the gun in my face, unlocks it. 'All you did was take my man away from me. Make him prefer you to me! Little slut! You're an ungrateful little slut that doesn't matter!'

She points it under my chin and I feel her hand convulse against my neck. I jerk, expecting the bang, but Mummy's eyes are rolling back in her head and she's falling into me. I scramble back out of the way. The gun clinks on the tiles.

I stare. I can't move. I feel numb, like something inside my head that lets me think and feel things has gone away. Then Bailee cry-screams and I can move, I can think, but not quite the same way.

Rachael promised she'd come. She didn't come. Mummy's right. No one cares. I'm nothing. And nothing I do matters. I pick up the gun and walk up the stairs.

Daddy is setting up the video while Mr Biddle holds Bailee down on the bed and tries to get his jeans down.

They don't even see me. Bailee has her eyes closed tight but tears are still coming out of them. I lift the gun.

'Hey Daddy, guess what?'

'What?' He looks over his shoulder and his eyes go really big.

'Mummy's right. I'm not your little girl anymore.' I pull the trigger. It jolts my arm and hurts my ears. Daddy just keeps staring, even as he falls down. I use both my hands to reset the gun the way I've seen Mummy and Daddy do it. Mr Biddle is trying to get his pants back up. I pull the trigger again. He jumps away, but the bullet hits him anyway. They're both on the floor, both bleeding. And I don't feel anything.

Bailee is screaming. Not just cry-screaming but an ear-splitting sound that outdoes the bullets. She crawls over the bed and holds her arms up, throwing herself at me.

'Lexi! Up, pick me up! Lexi!' She jumps up and down, dragging at my gun hand.

I lower the gun, carefully put it on the bed and pick her up. It'll be fine. It won't be a problem.

I'm nothing. And nothing I do matters.

CHAPTER THIRTY-THREE

Monday, March 22

The room was silent. Not even the traffic outside seemed brave enough to make a sound. Rachael's ear was stuck to the phone. She was aware of everyone watching, waiting with her. Then she heard the words that turned her stomach and left her hollow. She put down her phone and looked around the room at the faces of her colleagues. 'The court has overturned the jury's verdict due to several issues in the Crown case. The appeal court entered verdicts of acquittal, ruling out a second trial. They listed a few reasons but the big one was the testimony on the planted evidence. They're letting him go.'

The room erupted into objections, but Rachael caught the stares and speculative glances from some of her team. Turner was positively beaming. She'd resign. After this she'd have to. No one would ever look at her the same way again. How could she lead a team that had no faith in her?

'Not unexpected,' Ed said, putting an arm around her like it suddenly didn't matter that he was her boss. Maybe it didn't matter. Not anymore. He'd turned up unannounced this morning to be here. She'd said it wasn't necessary. Now she wanted to collapse into his arms and hide from the world. From the news that Biddle was a free man. From the media no doubt about to break the doors down wanting her reaction to it.

'It's not just that they let him go, Ed. It's that I got it wrong. I didn't need the Court of Appeal to tell me that.'

'Rach, it wasn't just you. You couldn't have known someone else planted that evidence on Biddle. But now we know who we're looking for. Let's get moving on this!'

She shook her head. 'I'm out, Ed.'

'What? You can't be out. This is your team, your case.'

'I've lost credibility with everyone in this room. I can't afford for this case to slow down because everyone starts questioning my ideas, my choices. Finn should take over.'

'No one's questioning anything. You're taking this too personally. Evidence was planted that fooled the entire justice system.'

'Maybe,' she conceded. 'I need to clear my head.'

She went down the stairs and out the back, away from the media and into the sun, pulled her sunglasses down and kept her eyes on the pavement as she walked aimlessly, the crushing realisation of her mistake weighing on her. Too many mistakes. Too many that matter. Just like last time.

*

'You ready?' Turner asked as they waited in the car. The house in front of them contained a suspect they were supposed to be arresting in the next five minutes when given the go-ahead. The boss had wanted them to wait until midnight, when they had the best possible chance of finding their suspects at home.

'Yeah.' Rachael's phone rang. An unknown landline. 'Hello?'

'Why didn't you come?'

'What? Who—Lexi?'

'You said you'd come!'

'Lexi, sweetheart. I'm sorry I didn't get there tonight. Why are you calling so late? Is everything all right?'

'Doesn't matter. I fixed it. You don't need to come now.' The call cut off.

'Lexi— Shit.'

'What's wrong?' Turner asked.

'Something's happened. Damn it! We need to go out there.'

'No way,' Turner said. 'We're finally about to go in.'

Turner got out and Rachael followed, Lexi's words spiralling in her mind. Fixed it? Something was wrong. Very, very wrong. She could feel that sick knowing in her gut.

'I'm sorry, Turner. I'll call you backup.'

Before he could do anything about it, she slid into the driver's seat and took off, leaving him standing on the kerb.

'Where are you going?'

Startled, Rachael looked up to see Lexi sitting on the low wall of the church. After a hesitation she joined her, looking out over the water. Lexi would have to find out sooner or later and it may as well come from her.

'What are you doing out here?'

'I like it here. You look like someone just ran over your dog.'

'Biddle's being released. I'm stepping back. I'm done.'

When Lexi remained silent, Rachael turned her head to look at her. Lexi had lifted her eyes to the sky, seemed intent on studying the clouds.

'You want to know the reason I sit out here in front of this church? It's not religious or anything.'

Rachael tilted her head. 'Sure, why?'

'I used to walk to and from the school bus and there was a little church on the main road I had to pass. Almost every afternoon, the lady that lived in the cottage at the back and looked after the place would be there.'

'Margaret,' Rachael said. 'The woman you left Bailee with.'

'Yeah. Margaret. Whenever she saw me she'd smile and wave and say hello. I always ignored her, stayed on the other side of the road. I didn't trust anyone. Not her, not my teachers. But your sister was a nice lady. I'm sorry to hear she died.'

'Thank you.'

'But I didn't really trust her either. Because she didn't know. She didn't get it. And I didn't want to get in trouble by telling her. Then she brought you to talk to me.'

Rachael felt the smile touch her face. 'You didn't trust me either.'

'But I hardly had to tell you anything, because you already seemed to get it.'

'I was bluffing.'

'What?'

'I didn't really have a clue.'

'Nice to know.'

'So, churches?'

Lexi looked down to where her feet were scuffing the grass on the edge of the path. 'Okay, but it's stupid. If you tell anyone I'll deny it and kill you in your sleep.'

'Nice to know,' Rachael mimicked. 'But?'

'This one day Margaret was putting letters on the church board outside. It said, DON'T WORRY, GOD LOVES YOU. And ... look, I was just a kid, okay? The night before at home had been pretty bad. Dad said God was rubbish but I was curious. Because I'd spoken to you I was feeling a bit braver, so when Margaret said hello this time I broke the rules and spoke to her. I asked her who the sign was for and she said it was for everyone. And it was like ... this little glimmer of childish hope because the other kids at school—they said they had people that loved them. I thought what if there really is someone that loves me too? So I asked, "Does He love you even if your mummy and daddy don't?" And she looked so sad and she said, "Even more, baby".'

Rachael could feel the emotion of it choking her, the anger welling for the little girl whose only comfort had been found in a chance church sign. 'I wish I could go back in time; do something, say something. How could I not have saved you?'

'That's the whole point. It got me thinking that if one person cared, maybe you really did too, and I started to trust that a little bit more. The next time I went past, Margaret had baked these chocolate chip muffins and we sat on the little church wall and ate them. I still remember that first bite. I'd never tasted anything that good. She even let me put a couple of extras in my bag to smuggle home for Bailee. From then on she'd always have something waiting for me and we'd sit on the little church wall together and chat.

'After I shot—after that, Bailee was so upset, so hysterical, and I didn't know what to do. I called you to tell you I'd taken care of it, then picked up Bailee and just started walking. All I could think of was to get to Margaret's. I didn't have to tell her what happened. It was the middle of the night and she took us in and gave us some milk and made us sandwiches. I couldn't eat anything but Bailee ate like a starving person. Margaret was so good with her. I could see she'd take care of her. So when I heard all the sirens coming, I snuck out and ran away and left her there.'

'I was too late.'

'Would you just listen? If there'd been a case before mine where something had gone wrong and you'd quit, then I wouldn't have met you. I wouldn't have begun to believe anyone might actually care. I wouldn't have spoken to Margaret, I wouldn't have left Bailee with her and Bailee wouldn't have had a happy childhood. If it hadn't been for you, I would never have understood that I didn't have to put up with being abused. I wouldn't have been able to pick up that gun and stop it. The nightmare would have continued, and Bailee would have suffered the same fate.

'So when I feel a bit shitty, sitting on a church wall reminds me of you and Margaret and chocolate chip muffins and of that first time in my life when I felt like maybe I was worth something.' Lexi finally looked at Rachael. 'You can't quit, Rachael. Because you did that for me. There are other people out there who need you. Who even knows how many or how much?'

The tears Rachael had wanted to hold back spilled over and she swiped at them uselessly. They weren't going to stop in a hurry. 'Sorry,' she said.

'You'll be sorry if you ever repeat what I just said,' Lexi threatened.

'You have no idea how much it means to hear you say it.'

'Sure, and that's more than enough emotional shit for me,' Lexi said, just about bouncing back to her feet. 'It better not be for nothing. You should get back to work.'

'I'm not sure if I can lead this case.'

'Don't think of it as leading, think of it as finishing. Wrap it up.' Lexi's smile returned, challenge and determination stirring in her eyes. 'Let's get the bastard.'

'Lexi, right now I'm not sure how.'

'He wants to find me. I spoke to him online at Finn's place. So why don't we let him?'

CHAPTER THIRTY-FOUR

Tuesday, March 23

I walk into the strike force room with Finn and can't help but stare at Turner's attempt at casual bar clothes. Finn clears his throat and nudges me. 'Cut it out,' he mutters under his breath.

'Sorry, did I make that face out loud?'

'Lexi, you were supposed to be here twenty minutes ago,' Rachael says coming in.

'Well, the best things take time.'

'Not going as a cheap whore tonight?' Turner asks, taking in my jeans and tee.

'All in my bag. Thought I'd change here rather than walking into the station looking like I should be under arrest.'

'I'll be waiting downstairs,' he huffs.

'He's pushing his luck,' Finn says to Rachael.

'Why?' I ask. 'Cheap whore sums me up, right?'

Finn frowns at me. 'Not even close.'

I wasn't expecting an answer. 'Huh?

'You're a survivor, Lexi. You've had to take whatever shitty opportunities life threw at you and make them work.'

'Um.'

'Not finished. You're a damn genius and more than that, you're someone who cares about other people even though no one particularly ever gave a shit about you, which is why you're doing all this, right? What I hope you're not is insecure enough to take on board the pissy remarks of a resentful old twat like Turner. Go get ready. I'll be waiting to take you over.'

I realise I'm imitating one of those open-mouthed cartoon caricatures and close my mouth.

Rachael is chewing the inside of her cheek, eyes glittering. 'And so say all of us. If you don't want to work with Turner tonight, I'll understand.'

'He's only watching, right? This might be our best chance.' I go into the bathroom and start unloading everything I need to transform into the ultimate slut. But I feel strangely weird about it. I've never particularly cared what anyone thought of me but something's changed. I feel like a different person when I'm here. I like what I'm doing. I like that the people I'm working with respect what I do.

Police consultant versus escort. It's like two worlds that don't fit together. Are abrasive to each other. I can comfortably be one person or the other but not both at once. Maybe that's why Turner gets to me so much, why I snapped at Finn when he mentioned my other job to Neutron. I ponder that as I get ready. I don't think I've suddenly become ashamed of being an escort. But maybe I prefer the computer geek persona a bit more.

Whatever. I shrug the thought off. It's completely the wrong time to be worrying about that now.

I finish getting ready then look in the mirror. My little red dress is barely there and what is doesn't cover much, my hair is messed up around my face and my makeup is as heavy as I can get away with. I load myself with the most sinful scent in my collection and slide on my heels, forgetting all about being a computer geek and preparing to wow a sleazebag sociopathic child murderer.

I take a couple of deep breaths, then walk out of the ladies' and into the strike force room and watch several set of eyes go wide. Finn looks like he's having some sort of spasm but I realise he's trying to untangle himself from his jacket. Once he's free of it, it's around my shoulders in seconds.

'I, um …' Neutron begins. 'I have the surveillance things—cameras, I mean the …' He stops talking and walks away.

'Is Neutron okay?' I ask.

'Yeah. No. I don't think so,' Finn says.

'I think your wardrobe is a bit much for him,' Rachael says.

'Okay, but is he turned on or traumatised?'

'I think we're all a little of both.' Finn follows Neutron and I'm not sure whether to follow or stay put. 'Let's go, Lexi,' he calls.

'Hey,' Rachael says, holding me up. 'You sure you want to do this?'

'Absolutely. He took the bait, he'll be there. Let's get this arsehole.'

'We think he'll be there. We told him where and when to find you. There are no guarantees he'll show.' Rachael stuns me by putting her arms around me for a brief hug. 'Be careful. If he does turn up, don't take any risks. Please.'

'You coming or what?' Finn calls again.

'Okay. Gotta go.'

*

'You ready?' Finn asks outside Tom's Joint.

'Yeah.'

'We'll be everywhere, watching and listening, but don't go off by yourself with anyone. Stay in the main area of the pub, okay?'

'Got it.' I wriggle out of his jacket and hand it back. 'Thanks.' I look at the doors to Tom's. I am nervous, I realise, or maybe a bit wired from the thought of coming face-to-face with Victor. Of hopefully catching him. 'Show me that sketch of Dempsey's one more time?'

Finn brings it up on his phone and I commit the features to memory.

'Turner and Rayburn are in position inside. Rach and I and a few officers will be ready out here.'

'He might not even show, right?'

'He probably will.'

'I don't suppose I can have a gun?' I ask, only half joking.

'You've got a wicked sense of humour.'

'You want to send me in there unarmed?'

Finn's brow hits his hairline as he looks me up and down. 'You're enough of a weapon as is.'

I'm not convinced. 'What about the stingy spray?'

He makes a strangled sound in the back of his throat. 'There's nowhere to put it!'

'Handbag?'

His face is suddenly very serious. 'You say the word, I will get you out. I promise.'

I tell myself to stop being a sook. I want to do this. I want this guy caught. 'Okay.'

'Okay. Good luck.'

The bar isn't all that busy, but then it never is early in the week. Once the throng of after-work drinkers move through, it's only really the lonely, the bored gamblers and the alcoholics who tend to hang around. I know most of the faces. They're regulars. The two that aren't are Turner and Rayburn. I spot Tom. He winks, jerks his head in a 'come on over' gesture.

'Hey. Looking hot. Need a date?'

'Drink. I need a drink.'

'Coming up.' He pours me a single shot. It's so ridiculous I cough and stare.

He glances at Turner. 'Can't be too smashed, right?'

'Oh, if there's a bigger reason to get smashed, I've yet to meet him.'

A couple of men walk in. I haven't seen them before. Neither look anything like the sketch we have of Victor.

'Newbies.'

'Leagues club is renovating. The displaced keep popping in here.'

Which probably explains the next three guys and the young couple that come in soon after. By the time I've sipped my way through two singles, five more men of various looks and ages are hanging around. Most are checking me out. But the way I'm dressed that doesn't really mean much more than that they're contemplating their chances of a cheap lay. So much for spotting Victor a mile away.

One of two guys sitting in the far corner of the lounge gets up and walks towards the bar, leaving his friend doing more than his fair share of looking. The Osama bin Laden lookalike sports dark hair, a long beard and moustache. The eyes are hazel though, direct and considering, and they don't bounce off but hold mine.

I want to drag my eyes away but I remind myself I'm in character and instead cross one leg over the other, my dress riding high up my thigh as I raise one eyebrow and send him a small smile before returning my attention to the remnants of my JD.

'Can I buy you a drink?' the guy who left bin Laden asks, sliding onto the stool beside me. He gets Tom's attention, points to my empty glass and holds up two fingers.

I pull Victor's sketch to mind, his description. This guy's got the hair colour, the strong jaw and I'd place him somewhere in his fifties so, yeah, if Dempsey isn't great on getting a likeness too spot-on, he's a definite contender. My pulse elevates.

'I'm never gonna turn down a free drink,' I purr. 'Thank you.' Tom refills my glass, gets another and makes one for my new friend. But I notice he's not quite his charming, friendly self. We probably shouldn't have told him what was going on. He's one step off playing big brother. One quick warning glare from me has him attempting a cool smile and taking the guy's money.

'And who might you be?' I ask as I clink my glass to his.

'Todd.'

'Todd, you're never gonna convince me you don't have some gorgeous wife or girlfriend tucked away somewhere.'

He slides his elbow along the bar, rests his head in his hand. 'Does it matter?'

I lean in, a whisper away from his lips. 'Not to me, baby.' My gaze skips over the security camera as though to remind myself I'm not in this alone. I notice the guy with the facial hair is still watching me, finger sliding around the rim of his glass. He has a definite creep factor, but assuming I have Victor sitting four inches away, this is the king of all creeps right here.

'And who are you?'

'I'm Lexi.'

'And how old are you, Lexi?'

'How old do you want me to be?'

He leans in, a hand on my thigh, and whispers in my ear, 'Will you call me Daddy?'

Revulsion, its putrid taste hits my mouth, its creeping, sickly fingers crawl along my spine. Am I looking at him? Victor? 'I'll call you God for two-fifty, gorgeous,' I whisper back.

'Perhaps you'd better tell me what else you'd do.'

I force my eyes to heat, my smile to suggest all manner of things. 'Perhaps you'd better tell me if you're on any form of medication.'

'Fit as a fiddle.'

'Well, this could be fun.' I slide my hand along his leg, hear his sharp intake of breath. He tosses back his drink and I do the same. 'I have a room upstairs.'

'I have a room at my place. Much nicer. Let's go.'

I'm expecting Turner and Rayburn to jump in about now, but it's Finn who's suddenly beside us. Rayburn joins him.

'Excuse me, sir,' Finn says flashing his badge. 'We'd like you to come with us, please.'

Todd looks around. 'Fuck,' he says and gets off the stool. 'Why?'

'We just have a few quest— Shit,' Finn swears as Todd ducks and bolts. He's fast, but two other officers and Rachael are outside. I see Todd hesitate, look left and right. Before he can make a decision, Finn tackles him to the ground.

'Ouch,' I whisper, grimacing for both of them. Finn has a knee on Todd's shoulder as he handcuffs the still struggling arsehole.

'Was that him?' Tom asks as they lead him away.

'I hope so.' I drag in a breath. I haven't taken a proper one since Todd approached me.

'I'll run into the office, copy the surveillance. Finn said they'd want a hard copy to take it with them if he showed. I think your best ever reason to drink is hanging around for it.'

'Okay but first …?'

He grins and pours me another drink before disappearing.

I knock it back, knowing Turner's probably about to be over here. But the sound of glass breaking has my head jerking around.

'Good one, dickhead,' one of a group of three says to Turner. It looks like Turner's knocked the guy's glass over moving past them.

'Sorry,' Turner says.

'What the fuck is sorry supposed to do? Get me another one. Actually—get us all another one.'

'I'll replace your empty drink,' Turner says. 'I'm not buying rounds.'

The guy gets slowly to his feet. 'It wasn't empty.'

'Funny. I don't see anything but glass down there.'

'You calling me a liar?'

'I'm calling it like I see it.'

Drunk guy pushes a finger into the table. 'We need three scotch on the rocks, and you can make them doubles because you're a stupid fuck.'

'Sit down, dipshit. I said I'll replace your drink.'

'Three.'

'Fuck off.' As Turner walks away, the group look at each other and get up. Then they're cutting Turner off, going out the back door.

Shit. Now what? The guy really needs to learn to shut up. Should I go and see what's happening? Probably.

The cool air hits my face and blows away the remnants of sitting and drinking. I can hear Turner copping it in the alley at the back of the pub. I peek. Yep. That's gonna bruise. Turner gets one back, cops another. I pull out my phone. Unfortunately, I'm going to have to save his arse before this gets too ugly. The phone lights up before I can dial and I put some space between me and what's going on with Turner.

'Yeah?'

'We have Todd. Looks like our guy. We're taking him back to question him. Remind Turner to bring the security footage.'

'Okay. Um, that could be a problem. He's busy being roughed up behind the pub by some pissed-off drunks who look like maybe they play football in their spare time.'

I hear a gasp of disbelief. 'And did you have the intention of helping?'

I contemplate that as a loud 'oof' suggests one of them got another shot in. 'Seriously? I can't stand the guy but I think three is probably enough.'

'Lexi!'

'Yes! I literally had my phone in my hand to call you when it rang.'

'Go back inside and wait there.'

Another smack has me grimacing. That one had to hurt. A lot. While part of me, a very, very bad part of me is keen to let him see out the next couple of minutes, I can't do it. What if he dies or something? One misplaced king hit and …

'Damn it.' I put the phone back into my purse and remind myself I came out the better side of a few unfortunate street fights as a kid—mostly by aiming for the balls then hooking it the hell outta there. I even threw a decent punch once. I take another peek around the corner at the combined three-hundred-kilos of muscle in use on Turner. Nup. Not throwing a punch at that.

But being drunk, now that's something I'm good at.

Idea established, I stumble out around the corner and fall into view. Sway. 'Hi, boys. Anyone looking for a good time?' I deliberately slur my words, then beam them all a smile. 'Oh—good it *is* him! I hate that guy. Can I watch?'

Turner throws me a furious look and narrowly avoids another gut punch.

'Piss off,' one of the big guys growl. 'Mind your own business.'

'Someone's talking to the cops. They said the big ugly dude looking for a hooker is getting his arse kicked and I thought, I bet it's that dick that didn't pay me last time. And yup. That's him.' I stagger over closer. 'Let me give him a little …' I kick out at Turner, stumble again.

'Someone called the cops?' big guy number one asks.

'Yep. Oh—there you go.' I wave my hand in the air as the sirens sound not too far off.

'Fuck.' Big guy lands one more boot to the ribs that even has me flinching and sends Turner to the ground. The three men look at each other then straighten their clothes and head towards the alley.

'That'll teach ya!' I taunt Turner as one hesitates to see what I'm up to. I pretend to try another kick.

The guy sniggers. 'Maybe I'll be looking for a good time tomorrow night, babe.'

I smile, sway again. 'I'll give ya a discount.'

The alley is dark, but I hear the slap of feet fleeing down the alley.

Turner gets up, gingerly presses a finger to his side, then kind of limp-jogs after them. He's stubborn, gotta give him that.

Sharp, burning pain sets fire to my scalp as my head is jerked back by my hair.

'You think you can outsmart me? You think you're smarter than I am?'

I can see the flashing of coloured lights bounce faintly off the fence, then turn brighter as the sirens get louder.

'I know you went online as Doc, and I played you. I tricked the cops into giving me five untraceable grand.' He pulls my hair back even harder. The pain is excruciating. 'I got to you, here, with cops everywhere, just to prove that I could. I know everything you do. Always. Don't *ever* think you can outsmart me.' He uses his grip on my hair to catapult me into the brick wall. 'I'm smarter.'

I get my hands in front of me just soon enough to send shooting pain from my wrists to my elbows, but the move takes much of the force from the bang to my head. It still glances, stuns me enough to have me turning and slumping to the ground, a shaking mess.

I take a few breaths to try and steady myself then stumble to my feet as Finn and Rayburn round the corner.

'Lexi, I told you to go inside! What happened?'

'I'm okay. But Turner's gone after them.' I lean back against the wall, still unsteady, hands on my knees for balance.

'You're bleeding.'

'Doesn't matter. He was here. Victor.'

'We have him. Rachael's taken him into the station.'

I shake my head, see twin drops of blood hit the ground at my feet. 'That's not him.'

'Was he one of the men who beat up Turner?'

'No he was ...' I'm dizzy. I feel nausea rising in my stomach.

'Who was he, Lexi? Did he come from inside?' He turns as two paramedics hurry around the corner to join the chaos. 'Can I get someone over here?'

'Finn, it doesn't matter! It's just a graze,' I tell the hovering ambo, but I feel the sting of something pressed to my forehead. I automatically hold it there.

'Think back. Did you see anything at all?' Finn asks.

'I don't know.'

'Was he taller than you?'

'Uh ...' I think about the shadowy face in my peripheral vision as he loomed over me and talked in my ear. 'Yes. Taller. Deep voice. And ...' Scratching. I remember the rasp against my cheek. Beard? A lot of beard. 'The guy in the corner.'

'Guy in the corner?'

'Tall, lots of facial hair. It was a disguise. It had to be.'

'Let's go in, check.'

I bat the ambo away with a distracted 'Thanks' and move on unsteady legs through the back door, down the corridor, into the pub. The corner booth is empty.

'He was sitting there.'

'All right. We'll take a look at the video.'

'The guy you caught. He was sitting with him.'

'I'll let Rachael know.'

Finn's name is called and I continue to stare at the empty place where the man had sat. He'd been watching me, had creeped me out more than Todd. But he hadn't matched the profile. Todd had. Damn it, he'd been right there, sliding his finger around the rim of his glass. He hadn't even finished the amber stuff inside it. And then it occurs to me.

'Finn!'

'Yeah?' he says over his shoulder.

'That's his glass.'

I can almost see Finn's mind click into gear.

'I need an evidence bag!' he calls out.

CHAPTER THIRTY-FIVE

'The man we initially arrested is Todd Kent, one of the four remaining members of the group we were looking for,' Rachael told the room. 'He was paid by Victor to participate in what he termed "a little game". He wanted to let us know how clever he was.'

'Excuse me, inspector!' Claxton called out. 'Apologies for interrupting, but we just got a match on the fingerprints from the glass.'

'Who?'

'His name is Damon Vaughn.'

'What do we know about him?'

'In 2004 he was sentenced to fifteen years for possession of an indictable quantity of a drug of dependence for the purpose of trafficking and a further five years for the serious assault of a police officer during capture. It's worth noting that the drugs in his possession were the same date rape drugs used to subdue the Spider's victims. He was released early eighteen months ago on good behaviour.'

'That's why he dropped off the radar,' Finn said. 'We had him all along and didn't realise it.'

'And sharing time in the same prison as Biddle could explain why Biddle was in on his plans,' Rachael added. 'Do we have an address?'

'Last known place of residence was a rental in Erina. Should be current.'

'Let's get ready.'

'Can I come?' Lexi asked.

'Not on this one,' Rachael said. 'But you can watch the interview once he's here in custody, okay?'

'Or you could go home and get some rest,' Finn suggested. 'You've gotta have a headache from that bruise.'

'It doesn't matter.'

'She's not going to go home, Finn,' Rachael told him before her phone pulled her attention away. 'Langley.'

'That was quite the stunt earlier,' the man she now knew as Vaughn said.

She sent Finn a look that had him quietening the room, then she put the call on speaker.

'Didn't know you enjoyed a night out at the pub,' she said. 'Have fun?'

'Needed something to do. I had my next girl all lined up and no party to go to.'

'Another one of Bailee's?'

'It was a fun twist, don't you think? Using Bailee Winter's girls. Of course, that was before I knew about your niece.'

Rachael's blood turned to ice. 'You won't be getting near her, either.'

'Oh?' There was a quick laugh. 'What makes you think I haven't already got her?'

The call cut out. Rachael stared at Finn. Then Finn snapped out of his paralysing terror, dragging her with him.

'I want units at the house right now!' she ordered, shouting out Vivienne and Ava's address.

She watched Finn try to call, hang up. 'Viv's not answering,' he said unnecessarily.

'If they're not home where would they be?'

'Netball—Ava had netball training tonight. But it should have been well and truly over by now. They sometimes eat out after, at Mingara. Maybe they did. That might have slowed them down.'

'So they're on their way home. We'll have a team head backwards along that route, see if they can spot them. Keep trying Vivienne.'

'Someone else can keep trying. I need to get out there.'

'The guy was at the pub an hour ago. That wouldn't have given him much time to grab Ava. And how would he know where she was?'

'How does he know any of what he knows? What we're up to, your phone number, your favourite restaurant, the press conference … he's watching us, doing his research. And let's not forget about our leak!'

'Finn, you need to calm down,' Rachael said quietly.

'This guy might already have Ava! He could already be … be …' Finn raked his fingers through his hair in torment before shaking his head. 'What do we do? What do we do next?'

'Excuse me, inspector?' Claxton interrupted. 'We've just intercepted a report of a single vehicle accident on Tumbi

Road. Silver Landcruiser, female driver with a significant head injury and lacerations. Conscious and breathing. Trapped in the car. Firies and ambulance are en route, police arriving on scene now.'

'Is there a child with her?'

'None reported.'

'It might not be them. I need to talk to the police on scene,' Rachael said.

Claxton nodded and got to work on his phone before handing it over. The look on Rachaels face a moment later was enough to tell him it was Vivienne.

*

'He's taken her. Hasn't he?' Finn said as they sped towards the accident site.

'It's Vivienne's car. But we don't know that. It could be a simple accident.'

'Seriously, Rach, what are the chances? And where's Ava?'

Rachael's lips were pursed, her expression grim. 'We'll know more when we get—'

'There it is!' he said, spotting the lights of the emergency cavalcade on scene.

They passed a police car, two ambulances and a fire crew before pulling over.

'This is not good.' He swallowed the nausea and sprang out of the car. It was difficult to see anything past the lights and vehicles and before he could get a good look, the senior operations manager appeared. 'How bad is it?' Finn demanded. 'Did you find Ava?'

'There's significant damage to the car,' the large man in fluro said calmly. 'The windows and windscreen are smashed and the passenger seatbelt has either snapped or been cut. There's a chance she was ejected from the car on impact. You don't want to go over there until we know more.'

'Like hell I don't.' Finn pushed past to see for himself. The car had gone through the railing, down into a ditch, and hit a tree. It was a mess. He skidded down the bank. 'Viv!'

She was still in the driver's seat, a paramedic holding a cloth to her bloodied temple.

Her head was back against the headrest. She wasn't moving.

'Viv!' he said again, coming in closer.

'Finn? Finn?'

'Yeah. It's me. I'm here.'

'Ava! Find Ava!'

'She keeps asking for her,' the paramedic said. 'But we can't find a passenger. We tried asking what happened but she's not making a lot of sense.'

'Why is she still in the vehicle?'

'She's trapped by her legs and the ground underneath is unstable. We don't want to cause a slide. We're trying to figure out how best to safely secure the vehicle and get her out.'

'Ava!' Vivienne's slurred cry was all he needed to get him moving back up the bank. It was dark beyond the reach of the flashing lights, but he could see torches bobbing through the bush on the dangerous slope. He pulled out his own torch and joined them. 'Ava!' He wasn't sure what was worse, the idea she'd been ejected from the car at speed or the idea she'd been taken by Vaughn.

There was a shout as the tree the car had been leaning on fell. The car slid further and came to a stop against another tree a couple of metres down. Finn sat, shaking.

'Finn! That's not safe,' Rachael called out.

'I don't know what to do. I ...'

'We need to go. We need to assume she's been taken. Her seatbelt's been cut. Someone took her out.'

A fresh and welcome burst of adrenaline hit him full force. It made the shaking worse but it got him on his feet.

He paused beside the car for a second. 'I'll find her, Viv.'

'Please, Finn. Please. Our baby. She's our baby.' Viv's head lolled and she fell into unconsciousness.

'I'll bring her home,' he promised then he powered up the hill to meet Rachael.

CHAPTER THIRTY-SIX

Wednesday, March 24

'Where are we on CCTV?' Ed asks from behind me. I yawn. It's close to six in the morning and we've all had about three hours of patchy sleep after spending most of the night chasing down dead ends. The raid on Vaughn's rental had turned up nothing and CCTV footage was getting us nowhere. Ed turned up about five minutes ago to take over the investigation. Apparently Finn and Rachael, as family, weren't supposed to be involved, but so far no one had been able to stop them.

'There's none where we need them,' I tell him.

'Constable Rowan is checking all vehicles and plates in the vicinity of the closest camera but at this time of night, it's busy,' Jim adds, barely lifting his eyes from the screen he was monitoring. 'Lexi and I are screening cars for signs

of impacts on the three cameras within a ten-k radius. It's
dicey at best. We'll need luck to catch Vaughn this way.'

'Keep going. Have we spoken to the driver who reported
the accident?'

'A mother with three kids returning from swimming lessons. She noticed the damaged kerb and the headlights in
the ditch. That's the only reason she stopped and saw the car.
She said it had already happened by the time she arrived.
No one else was around. Vivienne regained consciousness a
couple of hours ago but has so far been hazy on details due
to her concussion.'

'Has the media been alerted?'

'Yes, sir. Ava's face is all over the newsbreaks, her description is on the radio. Every police station has been advised
and patrols are crawling all over the coast. Roadblocks are
in place.'

'He could have already gotten around them,' Finn says,
startling us. He looks like death warmed up. Understandable. It might already be too late for Ava. Even if Vaughn
hadn't killed her he'd had time to do other things I don't
want to spend too much time thinking about.

'Sir,' Rayburn calls out. 'There were bullet casings found
at the scene and further examination of the car reveals the
front was hit at least four times in the vicinity of the bonnet.
Unfortunately, the scene was too disturbed by emergency
vehicles to turn up any evidence of car tracks or footprints
but the belief is our POI probably stood on the corner as the
car came around the bend, firing from the front and forcing
the driver off the road.'

'There goes the chance of spotting a second damaged car,'
I say, rubbing my eyes. What a waste of time.

I listen to Ed as he continues to direct and question and the room around me vibrates with urgency. A thought pops into my head. Biddle did time with Vaughn in the same prison, knew about Summer's video, about the drinks and drugs and parties. But then everyone got caught up with him not being the Spider and he kind of got forgotten. 'Maybe Biddle knows more,' I say to Ed when he finishes speaking.

'We already tried that,' Ed says. 'Biddle's being released this morning and won't talk. His lawyers are blocking us access to him at this point.'

'He said he was going to live out his days in the country,' Rachael said, appearing beside us. 'Quite enjoyed the idea of farm life. That's the only thing he said last time I spoke to him that didn't link back to all this. He's not going to help us. There's nothing at Vaughn's known address either. We're trying to track down relatives to see if anyone knows where he might be.'

I turn over Biddle's words in my mind. Going to the country. Liked the farm life. There was something there. Something on the edge of my mind. Country. Farm. Country …

Farm. It's the farm comment that's bugging me. But why? Where had I seen …

It hits me. I saw it on the laptop. Davies's laptop had contained files on someplace called The Farm. There's no way that could be a coincidence. And then another thought: What if the laptop belonged to Biddle? That would certainly explain its age.

I think back. What do I remember? Paperwork, maybe some bills. I didn't pay attention. Damn it, I always pay attention! But it wasn't what I was looking for. I didn't have much time. And now the laptop is gone and—stupid! I put the drive I copied everything onto back in Jonathan Davies's pocket.

I hadn't wanted any further part of it, hadn't wanted anything on me that could tie me to it. And now I've as good as killed Ava.

A sinking feeling of guilt drags at me. Is there any chance of getting it back? I think about Davies's body, about how the drive would have been soaked in blood, in whatever else got on it as his body started to decompose. Then it would have been frozen, partially thawed and damp. Maybe the salt might have dried it out? Who was I kidding? It was never going to work. But if, just if, it was the least bit redeemable, I bet Neutron would know someone who could take a look at it.

But Dawny had told me the body was well and truly gone forever. I'm guessing probably destroyed along with the contents of his pocket.

But I don't know that. Not for sure.

I press the heel of my hand to my forehead and squeeze my eyes shut against the toing and froing of my mind. Ava's image comes into view, the smiling face with the little gap from the missing tooth. *You're awesome, Lexi.*

I have no choice. I can't live with anything other than the decision I've already made. I can't afford to worry about what's going to come from that. But how am I going to explain it?

'Sorry to bother you with this right now,' Turner says, striding into the room like he's anything but sorry. 'I have evidence Mrs Davies was involved in the murder of her husband. I'm going to pick her up.'

'What evidence?' Rachael asks.

'I've been putting some pressure on the sister. I tripped her up during questioning and she caved. Said she'd been covering for her.'

'She didn't do it!' I blurt out. Because it's all going to come out now, anyway. It has to.

'How do you know?' Turner scoffs.

'Because I was there!'

'What?' Rachael gasps. Everyone is staring at me like I've grown another head.

'Vaughn killed Davies because Davies refused to cover up Summer's murder the way he had all those others years ago.'

Still no one speaks. I keep going. 'I overheard a conversation just before Vaughn killed Davies. Vaughn wanted Davies to help in some way with his special event—which was Summer's death—and Davies said last time was a nightmare and that he wasn't putting his job on the line like that again. We now know he tampered with the evidence. We know Davies had been actively involved in ensuring the Spider wasn't caught last time and he was murdered by Vaughn because he refused to do it again.'

'And you're only telling us this now?' Rachael asked.

'I hadn't put it all together back then! At the time no one was going to believe Charmaine wasn't responsible for her husband's death. No one knew Vaughn or what he was up to and Davies had already made Charmaine out to be a lunatic so he could get custody of Kelli. She would have gone down for his murder for sure, so I took care of it.'

'What do you mean?' Finn asks. '"Took care of it"?'

'I moved Davies's body. I took it away.'

'Oh my God,' Rachael murmurs.

'I was right!' Turner exclaims triumphantly.

'The freezer?' Finn demands. 'The freezer you had me help load on the truck?' His voice is rising dangerously.

'So the neighbour was in on it,' Turner says.

'No,' I say. 'I told them I hit the neighbour's dog and she told me I could stash it in the freezer because they were getting rid of it.' It sounds lame even to me but I have to hope it'll hold.

'I can't deal with this right now,' Finn says, throwing his hands in the air and walking away.

'You don't have to.' Turner's eyes light up. 'Lexi Winter, I'm arresting you—'

'You can't arrest her, Turner,' Rachael says as though suddenly tired.

'I'm sorry to interrupt, inspector,' Claxton says. 'We have a possible sighting of Vaughn and Ava at a random RBT checkpoint at Somersby. Officer said a man matching Vaughn's description had a sleeping child in the back of the car. Saw the alert just minutes after he let them go. Kid looked like Ava.'

'Any description on the vehicle?'

'Red Nissan Patrol.'

'How long?'

'Ten minutes, give or take. Heading south.'

'Make sure roadblocks are in place at both entrances to the motorway, another on that road out to Cessnock. I want every available unit scouring the mountain. Keep us updated!'

I watch Rachael and Finn leave the room at a run before I can tell them anything else. My right hand is grabbed roughly. I feel it encased in cold steel a moment before the other.

'Listen,' I say to Turner as he drives me from the room. 'I think I know a way to possibly find Ava.'

'Okay, where is she?'

'I have to go and get the information.'

'So you don't know.'

'There's a chance I can get it! But you have to let me go.'

'Why would I believe you?'

'I wouldn't lie about this! You can say you found her yourself, that you figured it out. That you dragged the information out of me. I don't care. But just let me go get it.'

'No. You're not having a chance to get yourself or Rachael out of this.'

'What?'

'I warned her to leave you out of it. She didn't listen. I'm sick of playing second fiddle to a lying whore. She's going to get her arse kicked over this and I'm finally going to get some recognition.' He smiles coldly. 'I'll see you when we have Vaughn in custody.'

'You're not just an idiot, you're a dangerous idiot,' I tell him as he puts me in a holding cell. 'You can't risk Ava's life for this!'

The panic hurts my chest. Crushes it. I should have kept my mouth shut. I could have gone looking for the damn thing. But I'm useless here. And then a thought. I bang on the perspex or whatever the hell I'm caged in. 'Hey!'

A uniformed officer comes in. 'Yes?'

'I'd like to call my lawyer, please.'

'One moment.'

One moment becomes at least ten minutes, then Turner and Claxton appear.

'What do you want?' Turner says.

'I want to call my lawyer,' I tell him.

'Shut up, Lexi.'

'She has a right to a lawyer,' Claxton says. 'You want to stuff this up?'

'Fine,' Turner says reluctantly. 'Who's your lawyer?'

'I want to see Neutron.'

'What are you playing at?' Turner asked suspiciously.

'He's my lawyer.'

'Guess I'll go get him,' Claxton says with a thoughtful frown.

Neutron is down in under a minute. 'Lexi. What?'

'I'm appointing you as my legal representative.'

'I don't do criminal law. I'm not practising. I said I studied law not that I ever took it up.'

'Can you take it up now, please? For five minutes?' I send him a look that threatens all kinds of terrible ends if he doesn't do as I ask.

'Ah ... it's not actually that simple.'

My glare holds.

'Sure.'

'This is bullshit,' Turner groans.

'Let's go then,' Claxton says and lets us into an interview room.

'Lexi, all I can do is recommend someone good,' Jim tells me once we're alone. 'I can't actually help you.'

'Yes, you can. Just listen. I need a pen and paper. This is what you have to do.'

*

I spend the next hour sitting in my cell, wondering if anything could possibly go right from here on in. I've heard nothing from Neutron so I can't be sure how that went. I just hope he came out of it all right. I'm still not sure about Desmond.

Turner pokes his head in again. He's been doing that sporadically since returning me here. It's like he can't quite believe he's got me. Like a kid who's caught a prize bug in a trap.

'Comfortable?' he asks.

'Rachael told you you couldn't arrest me. Now you're getting in the way of my ability to provide information that could save Ava's life. What do you think is going to happen when they find out?' I reply.

'Turner,' Debbie says before he can answer me. 'Rachael wants you patrolling an area I've just sent to your phone. There's been another possible sighting. Residential area. You're looking for a red Nissan Patrol.'

'Finally! Okay, I'm on it. Enjoy,' he tells me with a smirk.

'Arsehole.'

'You're out of here,' Debbie says when Turner's gone and unlocks the cell.

'What's going on?'

'Rachael asked me to get you. You need to come with me. Fast.'

I follow her to her car and get in. My hopes are teetering towards the possibility that perhaps my plan might be working after all. 'Did Neutron find an address?'

'I have no idea what he's up to. I'm working on other orders.'

'Oh.' I guess she's used to not being given the whole story. But she seems tense, is driving fast. 'Is everything all right?'

'I don't know. But we can't mess this up.'

Fair enough. Because she's driving pretty recklessly, I shut up and let her concentrate. We're going up the mountain. This must have something to do with The Farm, surely? Neutron *must* have come through. Or are we going back to Dempsey's place?

We turn off the main road, head in the wrong direction for Dempsey's, far enough for the farms and paddocks to become bushland. Then down a side road that quickly becomes a dusty dirt track. At the end of the driveway that winds twice before revealing a clearing is a small red brick house. There's a car in the carport by the side of it but no other signs of life.

'Are you sure this is it?' I ask.

'Yep, get out.'

Something about her tone has me turning to look at her. It's harsh, and her face is set in a cold smile. Then I see the gun pointed at me across her lap.

'I said get out.'

'I don't understand.'

'Vaughn wants to see you.'

'Vaughn does?' The hairs on the back of my neck prickle, my breathing speeds up. This can't be right. 'Why does he want to see me? Why are you doing this? The guy's a monster! Debbie—please!'

'He's not a monster. He's an artist. An entrepreneur.' She waves the gun in my face, reminding me she's probably not as harmless as I've always thought her to be. 'I said get out!'

I climb out, look around, but she has the gun back on me before I can do more than see there's nowhere to go.

'Move.'

I walk as slowly as I can towards the house. Debbie comes around beside me to push open the door and shoves me in.

'Lexi! Welcome. It's so good to finally meet you in person.'

And there he is: the evil-eyed pub guy minus all the crazy facial hair. My heart is hammering in my chest and I don't trust my voice so I say nothing.

'Sit down. Please.'

I sit on the chair he indicates. It's at a wooden dining table in the middle of a room with little other furniture. What is here is practical and old. A desk, a rustic kitchen, a couple of doors off to the side. The handcuffs go back on around the rails in the back of the chair.

'I have to go,' Debbie says. 'I don't want them to figure out I'm not where I'm supposed to be.'

'Keep me posted.' Then to me, Vaughn says, 'May as well get comfortable, Lexi. You won't be going anywhere for a while.'

'Where's Ava?' I manage.

'Oh, the kid.' He walks over to one of the doors on the far wall and pushes it open. He goes inside, comes out carrying a chair containing Ava and drops it a few feet from me. Ava has a gag in her mouth, tears on her cheeks.

Anger rips through me hot and fast, replacing some of the fear. 'Terrifying children make you feel like a man, does it?' I ask. 'It's gonna be okay, Ava.'

Vaughn seems to think that's funny. 'It's really not.'

'Why am I here?'

'Firstly, to witness my work.'

'And second?'

'We'll worry about that later. Time to get changed, Ava.' He goes back into the other room and brings out a dress. 'What do you think?'

All I can think about is how to stop this from happening. The idea he might actually do this is too horrifying for my brain to process. I can't allow it. But what can I do? About the only thing I can do is stall. 'Who are you dressing her up as?' I ask.

'You don't recognise it?' He turns it back to him and frowns as though he can't quite believe it. 'It's Gretel. I get to play Hansel. Only Hansel's not quite the devoted brother everyone thinks he is. At least, not devoted in the brotherly sense.' His smile makes me sick. 'We're going for a walk. We're going to get lost in the woods and find this nice little house. It's not quite made of gingerbread but it is full of lollies and sweets.' He picks up a Woolworths bag and tips it on the table. An assortment of bagged and wrapped lollies spill out. 'But first, because we don't want anyone running away …'

He picks up a small white packet, peels it open. A syringe. Another rustle reveals a needle. He attaches the needle to the syringe, walks over to the fridge and brings out a small bottle.

'What is that?' I demand.

'Just ketamine. Nothing to worry about.'

'Don't,' I can't help but plead.

His eyebrows shoot up as his eyes hit mine. 'It'll help her relax, chill out. Better this way, right?'

'Don't do it!' I say again. If Ava's going to have any chance, she needs to be alert while I come up with a way out of this. But how? What can I possibly do?

'Okay, okay. If you want her to have the full experience. We'll see how we go. Could be more exciting, I suppose.' He puts the needle down next to the sedative and moves back to the dress. 'We'll change first.'

He leans over Ava and she tries to scream through her gag. But she's not looking at him. She's looking at me.

Her eyes are begging, pleading, tears pouring from them. Cutting me to pieces.

'I'm going to untie you, Ava, and you're going to do exactly as I say. Understand?'

Ava nods.

'If you don't, I'm going to hurt Lexi. I'm going to hurt her really bad, Ava. Do you want me to do that?'

Ava's head shakes from side to side. I pull at the cuffs but they're too tight. Then Ava's wrists and ankles are free and he's lifting her T-shirt up to take it off.

'You're going to look so pretty, Ava. So pretty.'

As I struggle against the cuffs, the rails on the chair wobble. I get to my feet and grip the frame behind me. It's awkward, but I'm able to lift the chair out and away from me enough to swing around hard and fast against the corner of the wall. The impact radiates painfully up my arms but along with the thundering bang, I hear a crack and the chair feels less solid.

Vaughn spins around. 'Can't just watch the performance? Have to be involved?' He grabs the tranquilliser and the syringe, draws some up.

Heart racing, I adjust my grip, lift the chair out again, spin. This time it splinters but in the time it takes me to shake myself free, Vaughn gets hold of the cuffs and jerks them up. I feel the needle thump against my forearm as he drags my arms higher up my back.

The pain is agonising. I can't help the cry as I tip myself forward to take some of the strain from them, tucking my head a second before I faceplant the floorboards. The back of my heel connects with some part of Vaughn as I fall over and we both go down. I kick out again and again, flailing my legs madly from my position on the floor as he tries to untangle himself from me. Every kick that connects spurs me on, keeps my legs moving.

I hear a cry. Ava.

'Ava. Run! Hide! Get out of here!'

'But ...'

'Go!'

For a moment I don't think she's going to move but then I see her flash past us. Vaughn gets to his feet as she throws open the front door but then she hesitates again, glances back at me with a tear-streaked, terrified face.

I stick my leg out again, tripping Vaughn. 'Go!' I yell again.

She does.

Vaughn gets his feet under him. I can see at least one of my kicks has connected with his face as blood pours from his nose. He swipes at it and his gait to the front door has a dazed quality that slows him down. He leans on the door. 'Fuck!' For a moment he doesn't seem to know what to do next. I use that time to shove my cuffed hands as low as I can get them, wriggling my aching arms under my butt, my thighs.

I have one leg through when he comes at me, eyes wild and furious. 'You bitch!'

My other leg catches on the chain, then slips through just in time for me to roll away as he dives at me. My hands clutch a splintered chair leg and as I roll back, I swing hard. He falls against the wall and I surge to my feet, hit him again with the chair leg. Clutching it like a bat, I prepare for the next swing. But he's not getting up. He makes it to a sitting position against the wall, head lolling slightly as he tries to lift a hand to his injured face and drops it. I wonder how many of those kicks connected with his head. I pounce on the keys to the cuffs as my head starts to spin. My arms and legs feel heavy, weird. I'll get the cuffs off later. I stumble towards the door. I have to find Ava. Make sure she's safe. I'm almost there when a gunshot splinters the doorframe close to my head.

'Stop right there.'

I'm close enough I could risk running through, but my body refuses to cooperate, disabled by the sedative Vaughn gave me. I'm not going anywhere. I sink to my knees as the darkness overtakes me.

CHAPTER THIRTY-SEVEN

'We'll find her,' Rachael told Finn as they drove as quickly as Rachael dared towards Ava's last known whereabouts. 'They're up here somewhere. They're not getting off the mountain.'

The phone rang and Finn pounced on it much like he had every other time. 'Yes?'

'It's Turner. Lexi is gone. Did you order her release?'

'I never ordered her arrest!' Rachael snapped.

'I don't have time for this shit now, Turner,' Finn said. 'We'll deal with Lexi later.'

'But—'

'How about a little less worry about your personal vendetta and a little more about the fact the Spider has my daughter!' Finn cut the call. 'What a dick.'

'I wonder what did happen to Lexi though,' Rachael said. 'She can't have let herself go if he'd locked her up. Unless

Ed's realised what he's done, but I thought he was going back out to conduct a more thorough search of Vaughn's property.'

'I don't care. She lied to us all the way along. Who knows what else she's capable of? I'm done.' Again the phone rang. 'That better not be Turner again.'

'Finn, dear? Is that you?'

'Who is this?'

'It's Dawny, dear. Lexi's neighbour.'

'Dawny, I'm sorry but we're in the middle of an emergency.'

'Yes. I know. That's why I'm calling. Lexi has sent a young man to my door requesting an item she thinks might help save your daughter. You're very lucky we have it. Desmond is curious about things like this and thought he'd have a peek before destroying it, you see.'

What the hell was she on about? 'I don't get it. Who is there and what do you have?'

'Yes, we'll get to that. Just one thing. You need to let Lexi go.'

'I don't have time for this. A monster has my daughter!'

'That's right. And if anyone other than Lexi had asked for my help I'm not sure I'd be all that keen to get involved. So, I need to know she's not going to jail.'

'Dawny, this is Inspector Rachael Langley. I can promise you Lexi isn't going to jail.'

'Ah. That's all I needed to hear. I'll pass this on then. Ta-ta.'

Finn pressed his fingers to his eyes. 'All this and a nut-case? I can't deal with this, Rach. I can't.'

'You have to. Ava's depending on it.'

Another call. He takes a breath. Answers. 'Yes?'

'Detective, this is Jim. I have a thumb drive Lexi asked me to collect. It has the contents of Davies's second computer on it. Lexi thinks it could help find Ava.'

'You're at Dawny's?' Rachael asked. 'That's what she was talking about?'

'Yes. I'm actually sitting in my car outside her house with my laptop. I'm getting in now.'

'Where is Lexi?' Rachael asked.

'Turner arrested her,' Jim said. 'He wouldn't let her act on her info so she called me down as her lawyer so I could get it for her. Crazy, right?'

'Are you telling me Lexi had information that could save Ava's life and Turner refused to let her get it?' Finn barked.

'That's exactly what I'm telling you.'

'What is it?' Rachael asked.

'You told her Biddle had said something about going to a farm and she remembered seeing something to do with a farm on Davies's computer,' Jim said. 'She said I have to look for deeds.'

'Are they there?' Finn asks after the silence stretches too long.

'I—yes, I've got it. A private road in Bucketty.'

'I'll get more units organised,' Rachael said.

'I've pulled the address on maps. There's a pool,' Jim tells them. 'Solid fence around it. Same shape to the backyard as Summer's video. House is the same colour. It's the same property. I'm sure of it.'

'That's good enough for me,' Finn said. 'Send us the address.'

'Lucky we stayed on the mountain,' Rachael said. 'It's a lot closer from here than the station.'

The drive still felt excruciatingly long. 'Half an hour from civilisation and it feels like the back of beyond,' Finn complained, as Rachael navigated the winding road as quickly as she dared.

'The perfect location.'

He was energised and sick to his stomach, but the most intense fear he'd ever known overrode everything else. Was Ava alive? Had Vaughn done anything to her? Was he too late? He needed to know. And yet he was terrified of finding out.

When they turned onto the dirt road they'd been looking for, Rachael drove onto a relatively clear area on the verge. 'We'll stop here. The house isn't much further in. Backup's still another fifteen minutes out.'

'I'm not waiting.'

'Okay. But, Finn, keep your head.'

They left the car and skirted the roadside on foot, kept close to the bushland until they reached the driveway. Finn took out his gun, kept it low and ready. Rachael followed suit and nodded to go in.

'Where's the damn house?' Finn hissed.

'Around here somewhere. Wait, there.'

They paused as the house came into view. It was surrounded by a clearing. No cover.

A noise in the bushes beside them had them both spinning.

'Dad?' A tiny voice, teary and hopeful. '*Daddy?* Aunty Rach!'

'Ava! Finn holstered his gun and barrelled into the bush where Ava stood, trembling and crying. He scooped her up, held on, breathed her in. 'You're okay? Are you okay?'

She nodded violently as her small arms held as tight as she could and the tears started in earnest. 'He had me, Dad, he had me tied up and he was going to hurt me.'

Rachael smoothed a hand over Ava's hair. 'Where is he? Ava, where is the man who took you?'

'I don't know. I think he left. I heard a car but I don't know.'

'He let you go?' Finn asked, confused.

Ava's head shook from side to side. 'Lexi told me to run away and hide.'

'Lexi?' he asked as his eyes shot to Rachael. She looked back blankly.

'You need to make sure she's okay,' Ava said.

'Okay, one thing at a time,' he said, but his mind was racing and some of that crawling panic was back. Was Lexi still in there with Vaughn?'

'Dad! Mum was hurt in our car. She was bleeding—'

'She's okay, sweetheart. She's in the hospital but she's okay.'

Ava's whole body gave one long shudder. Shock, he realised. She needed to be seen to. 'Let's get you back to the car. More police will be here soon.'

'But Lexi! She should have come out by now!'

'We'll get Lexi, baby. We will. Back to the car. Are you cold?'

'No.'

There was the sound of another car at the edge of the drive and Debbie and Claxton came into view. Rachael flagged them down.

'Okay, I'm going to go find Lexi,' he promised Ava, carrying her across to the second car. 'You're going to just stay here with these police for a minute. Is that okay?'

''Kay.'

'What's happening?' Debbie asked, a note of panic in her voice as she got out of the car.

'We don't know yet,' Rachael said.

'I'll suit up,' Debbie said, 'head around—'

'No. Stay here and keep Ava safe,' Finn said to both Debbie and Claxton. 'Put her in our car and keep her warm.' He looked at Rachael, who had her eyes pinned on the house. 'Ready?'

She nodded, and they crept towards the house. There was no sign of life, no movement, no sound. Finn checked one window, then the next. A chair, destroyed, fragments littering the ground. And then he saw Vaughn, trying to pick himself up off the floor.

He signalled to Rachael he was going in and launched himself through the door. He was on Vaughn in seconds, dragging him to his feet and cuffing him.

'Where's Lexi?' he demanded.

Vaughn gave him the kind of stare that made Finn think the man was probably seeing double. 'I need to sit down,' he slurred.

'You sick prick, you think I care? Where's Lexi?'

Vaughn managed a smile. A slow, wide grin that looked drunk. 'I guess if you don't have her, he does.'

'He?' Rachael repeated. 'Who's he?'

A laugh now. It brought up blood. 'I'm not the Spider.'

Rachael's 'What?' wasn't much more than a whisper.

'It was Biddle. It was always Biddle. You knew it, you had him. And you let him go.' He laughed. 'You idiots.'

When he would have sank down, Finn hefted him roughly up against the wall. 'Tell us where he is.'

'I don't know.'

'No?' Finn slammed him against the wall again. 'Get out of here, Rachael. You don't want to see this.' He had the satisfaction of seeing an edge of fear flash in Vaughn's face.

'I don't know!' Vaughn said again.

'I knew it.' Rachael came in close. 'You could never have been the Spider. Not even a worthy apprentice. Just a rather ordinary wannabe. The Spider would give us a clue. It's the game. He was smart enough to outplay us. But you're not that smart, are you?'

Vaughn remained silent. But the drunken smirk had disappeared.

'Let's get him out of here,' she said in disgust.

'I need an ambulance.'

'You're getting a cop car instead of a bullet. Be grateful,' Finn snarled.

Finn led Vaughn to the back of the police car. He went in without a fight.

'Hey, Rachael,' Vaughn said as she closed the door. 'Maybe you should go back to the beginning.'

'What?'

Vaughn dropped his head against the seat and closed his eyes. That was clearly all they were going to get.

'We'll see you back at the station,' Debbie said.

When the car drove away, Ava got out of theirs. 'Dad.'

Finn wrapped her in another tight hug. 'I'm so glad you're all right. You're so brave.'

'Thanks. But Dad ...'

Another police car came into view. 'More reinforcements,' Rachael said and moved to speak to them.

'Dad!' Ava said again, louder.

'What is it?'

'The lady. Debbie.'

'What about her?'

'She sounds like the one who brought Lexi.'

'What?'

'I didn't see who brought Lexi but it sounded like her. I think it was her.'

A sinking feeling hit him. Lexi had been under arrest at the station. They'd wondered how she could possibly have been out here. 'Rachael!' He jogged over. 'Ava thinks it was Debbie who brought Lexi out here.'

He saw the denial on her face a moment before it dropped and was replaced with a frown. 'Hold on.' Rachael got on the radio and attempted to contact Debbie and Claxton's car. There was no response.

'Get after them,' she ordered the police who had just arrived. 'I'll have Jim track the vehicle and keep you informed.' To Finn, she added, 'I'll coordinate from here until the next unit turns up to guard the scene for forensics. You get Ava to safety. Get her checked out.'

Finn hesitated. 'I'm not sure I should leave you here alone. We don't know who else might turn—'

'More units are on the way,' Rachael insisted. 'Go.'

'Okay … Thanks. Be safe.' Then to Ava, 'Let's go, sweetheart. I'm going to take you to the doctor for a check up.'

'But aren't you going to get Lexi?'

'I'll do that next.'

He got Ava in the car, buckled up. 'You okay?' he asked, noticing her eyes on him.

'I don't want to go to the doctors. I don't need to.'

He didn't know how to ask. If he should. In the end he came out with it. 'Ava, did he do anything to hurt you?'

'He tied my hands up really tight.'

And even for that he wanted to kill him. 'Anything else? He didn't touch you in any other way?'

'No. Except when Lexi was brought in and he wanted me to get changed into the dress. He was going to give me a needle.' The recollection was enough to restart the tears. 'But Lexi told him no and he said he'd get me changed without the needle. He was going to put the dress on but then Lexi smashed the chair apart and they had a fight. That's when she told me to run and hide.'

Had he written Lexi off just minutes earlier in the car? Had he condemned her for lying to him? He owed her everything. Everything.

'Okay, sweetheart. Okay. But you still need to see a doctor, because that's what happens when you get rescued from a bad man. Okay?'

'Grandma could take me. Then you could get Lexi.'

He stroked her hair from her damp, flushed face. 'Are you sure?'

'Maybe while we see the doctor, I could see Mum.'

'You know what? That's a great idea.' And he just had to lean across the seat and hug her again. Because she was alive. She was safe.

He called Viv's mother from the car as they drove away from the cottage. He felt a tug of guilt at not taking Ava himself, but he thought of what he owed Lexi and that was enough.

He'd barely made it down the dirt road when he saw the police car Rachael had ordered after Debbie and Claxton. Claxton was beside it talking to the officers. Finn pulled over. 'What happened?'

*

Rachael saw Finn's number and put Jim on hold. 'Yep?'

'We've got Claxton. They only got to the end of the street and Debbie pointed her gun at him and told him to get out,' Finn said. 'He's just glad she didn't shoot him.'

'I don't know that she's a murderer, and it would have taken more time to shoot him, get out of the car, drag him out and dump him than it would have to make him get out.'

'Lucky for Claxton. Viv's mum's going to meet us back near the motorway and take Ava to the hospital for a check over then take her in to see Viv. But ... he didn't touch her, Rach.'

'That's good. That's great. But if she needs you to be there ...'

'She'll be okay with Eleanor. They're close. I need to catch that bastard. I need to help find Lexi.'

'Okay. I'll see you soon.' She was relieved. She wasn't looking forward to doing this without him.

She went back to her call with Jim. He was tracking the car Debbie was driving, which had stopped a few kilometres down the road. By the time Rachael had organised cars to get to the location, it had been dumped, another taken from the nearby general store. Yet more police turned up at the house and she directed them as necessary. Van Zettan and his team were still thirty minutes out.

And as she worked, her mind kept screaming, *Lexi, Lexi, Lexi.* They had to find Vaughn. They had to make him talk. Between everything else she was juggling, she'd been putting some thought into his words. *Start at the beginning.* But what was the beginning? The first video? The first victim? Or did he mean the beginning for *her*? She only came in after the third victim. Right before Lexi came to her attention.

If her beginning was Lexi, then the most likely place to look was ... the school? She dismissed the idea. The school was still running. So what? Where?

Or ... did Vaughn mean the beginning of what came after: the night at the house when she'd finally caught Biddle and the beginning of Biddle's plan for his freedom and revenge against the child who ended his empire?

The house? It wasn't too far from here.

She called Jim. 'The house on Waratah Road. Lexi's old home. Is anyone living in it?'

'Ah ... give me one sec. Just jumping into the case files ... The Winter home ... Waratah Road ... Got it ... Okay, the property was purchased right after the Spider case by the adjoining property owners. Let me get back to you in a sec.'

She didn't want to stand around waiting for an answer. It *had* to be the place. It was the only thing that made sense. Vaughn could be lying, throwing her off track, but it was worth a look. She got in the closest police car and took off.

When Jim called back she hit the button. 'Yep.'

'The current owners bought the property to extend their cropping business. The house is still there but it's empty, heading towards derelict. They haven't had the money to knock it down and get rid of it.'

'Thanks. Finn's dropping Ava with her grandmother then coming back to assist. Let him know where I'm going. Ask him to meet me there.'

'Will do.'

She moved through the floor plan of the house in her mind as she drove closer. Front door, lounge to the right that led through to a kitchen. To the left a small dining room, a study and a set of stairs. Upstairs. Landing. Two bedrooms to the left, a bedroom and a bathroom on the right. Lexi's bedroom was first on the left. Pink and white teddy bears on the walls, a steel-framed single bed. Shelves of dolls and storybooks served as props. The girls weren't allowed to play with them, got beaten for touching them.

A rug had been spread out in soft tones along the floor. Gone with forensics. Covered in Biddle's blood. BJ Winter's had stained the floorboards in the corner of the room where the camera had stood waiting for its latest horror show.

Yes, she remembered the house. And if they were there, and she hoped to God they were, they'd be in that room. That pretty pink and white room. And again, the phone began ringing.

'What?'

'Inspector, we have eyes on Debbie and Vaughn.'

'Where?'

'Somersby shop, just off Peats Ridge Road. They tried to swap cars again. A member of the public is following. You're the closest to the scene.'

Ten minutes with lights and sirens to Vaughn, about the same in the other direction to Lexi's house.

A confirmed sighting versus a guess. A real shot at capturing Vaughn against a fingers-crossed hope for the best.

'Damn it!' she hissed. And making a decision, the only decision she could make, she made the turn.

CHAPTER THIRTY-EIGHT

I'm floating. I want to reach for the clouds as they drift by, but I can't move my arms. My body. Everything is too heavy, too difficult. My eyelids feel weighted down by some inexplicable force as I struggle to see, to focus on the colours and patterns amid the fogginess. Where am I? What's going on?

As my eyes adjust to wakefulness, the hazy lines and colours start to make sense. Everything is pink and frilly. It all seems familiar and yet completely ... wrong. Like either myself or my surroundings are somehow out of time and place. I know this room, I do, it's ... I'm in my bedroom, except ... I'm not. This is my old bedroom. The one my parents dressed up, not because they cared about me, but because the pretty frills, the pink, the props, made me look younger in the videos. The memory rolls in my stomach and sharpens my mind. My blood begins to pound in my ears and my vision clears. Now I see that the roof is polka-dotted with mould, the pink and white wallpaper is stained and yellowed with water damage, and a fine layer of dust coats the windows and the limp, faded curtains.

I lift my head and look down. I'm wearing pink fairy pyjamas. They're out of place too. I've never seen these before. As the upside-down image of Tinkerbell stares up at me, I try to make sense of it all. But my head is heavy, my mind fighting for clarity against the clawing drowsiness that hovers close to the surface, threatening to drag me back under.

Something moves. No more than a shadow in my peripheral vision. A familiar voice penetrates my consciousness.

'Welcome home, Lexi.'

I drop my head to the left and spot the camera first. Set up on a tripod in the corner of the room. Behind it, the Spider. Enough of the old version left to recognise the new. He's older, thinner, and the lines that had been faint all those years ago have deepened, his eyes sinking down into them. The jolt of recognition is powerful enough to shock my mind back into full memory, kickstarting it right alongside my pulse. I make a much more violent attempt to get up, get out. My arms won't shift from above my head, my legs won't lift or slide. The movement has a painful cramp arcing up my left arm into my shoulder. I shift, roll it around as much as possible to loosen the muscle against the stabbing, clenching agony. I hear whimpering and it takes me a moment to realise it's coming from me.

I remember Vaughn. Ava. The injection. And now this? Now I have to deal with this?

'I knew it was you!' I tell the man smirking at my struggles as he fiddles with his camera. 'Vaughn was never the Spider. Was he?'

'No one could ever be me, Lexi. He's perhaps a poor second. Well done helping Ava escape. So clever. So feisty. But then, you always were.'

My whole being shudders with fear. I can't let those memories overtake me now. I need to think. To concentrate on getting out of this. I wriggle my hands and feet in their ties, hope for some give, but I feel none.

'We're going to make a video, you and I. Do you remember the poem?'

'Completely forgotten.'

'I bet your sister remembers.'

'Actually, she doesn't.'

'Of course she does. Ready?' He presses a button on the camera, comes towards me. '"Will you walk into my parlour?" said the spider to the fly. "'Tis the prettiest little parlour that you ever did spy."'

'You never did get around to telling Bailee what was so special about it.'

'Did you wonder, Lexi? Did you ever want to know why I preferred Bailee?'

'No.'

'Age, just age. In every other way, you were my pick. Feel like a trip down memory lane?'

'No!'

His tongue slides across his lip and I cower back on the mattress before I realise I've even done it.

He smiles, satisfied. 'You're a special girl. This was all for you. Did you know that?'

'I wouldn't presume to know what sort of sick shit goes through your head.'

He sits beside me on the bed. 'I'd dreamed about you for so long. Dreamed about what I would do to the little bitch who shot me. Who ended all my fun. It kept me going—*you* kept me going.' He reaches down and lifts a gun from the floor. Terror ices my veins, shoots through me. All I can think to do is keep him talking.

'And Vaughn?'

'I met Vaughn in prison. It was serendipitous. He wanted fame and fortune and I happened to be in a position to be able to give those things to him. Oh, he's not so much into the little girls as I've always been, which is a shame, but he sees them as an added bonus to the charade and he did a fairly good job on the first video, don't you think?'

'I think he's almost as disgusting as you are.'

'So we made a deal. He gets me out, gets me you, and I give him my fortune. I'm dying. I'm not going to need it. Win-win. But enough of this.' He moves away, restarts the video. He doesn't like what I'm saying, I realise. He wants me scared. He wants the show.

'Let's play,' he says, coming back to stand at the foot of the bed. 'I'll just close my eyes and pretend you're that cute little girl again.'

'You're so full of shit.' I laugh the words out, and something stirs in those evil little eyes.

'And you're a desperate little girl who never grew out of fucking men to survive. Tell me, do you remember what I used to do to you? Do you remember how it felt when Daddy and I—'

I fight for anger, for derision, for anything that would stop those memories from dredging up the old feelings of helplessness and crippling fear that would only help him win. 'Yeah, yeah, blah, blah,' I taunt, but I'm shaking so hard I can barely control my voice. 'Here's the thing. You're not scary. You're just a sick old man and if you wanted me, dreamed about me, why take Ava?'

He lets out a sharp growl, throws his hands in the air and stops the video. 'You're ruining it! You want me to gag you, is that it? Will I shove a sock down your throat until you can barely breathe? Ava was a distraction,' he answers impatiently. 'Vaughn takes Ava and Debbie grabs you while everyone's focused on the kid.'

'You couldn't have known I'd get arrested!'

'It didn't matter. You would have gone with Debbie either way. She just had to ask, to pretend Rachael needed you.'

'She's a police officer. Wants to be a detective. I don't get it.'

'Not everyone wants those things for the same reason. Let's get this done.' He walks back to the camera, restarts it. Then he's coming towards me, stalking me. He lets his cotton robe fall to the floor. Every inch of his aroused, naked body is on show in front of me. A large, deformed area of pink skin marks the place I'd put the bullet all those years ago. Revulsion and terror explode inside me, roar in my head.

He picks up the gun and leans one knee on the bed, brushes the hair from my face with the gun barrel. 'So, Lexi. Whose little girl are ya?'

I thrash violently, my forehead connecting with his in a painful, dizzying crash. It stuns us both and I hear the clatter of the gun hitting the floor. He recovers quickly and picks it up, waves it at me. A nasty smile spreads across his face. 'Whatever will you do now, Lexi? This time I have the gun. This time, you can't shoot me.'

'This time she won't have to.'

My head jerks around to see Rachael standing in the doorway, arms extended, gun pointed at Biddle. Before I can do more than spot her, three explosions blast through the room.

Biddle sways and sinks to his knees. Then Rachael is standing over him, her gun still trained on him as she kicks his from his limp hand.

The shock dims from his face, a weak but smug smile replacing it. 'I still won,' he says. 'I'll be famous forever. I'm the Spider.'

''Fraid not.' Rachael's tone is clipped as she bends to look intently into his eyes. 'I have no interest in officially being right about you. I'll make sure my report states you were nothing more than the pathetic little scapegoat you claimed to be when you set this all this up. Vaughn has publicly admitted to being the Spider and that horrific dishonour will go to him forevermore. In the history books, you're already forgotten.'

The smile drops and his eyes widen on one last adrenaline-fuelled flash of panic, desperation. 'You can't do that! I'm the Spider! It's my fame. Mine ...'

He's already toppling when she shoves him with her foot. He crashes, sprawls motionless on the floor. Then she's beside me, working the knots loose on my wrists.

'Are you all right?'

I nod because I can't speak. The emotions well low in my gut and surge dizzily to my head. Tears bank behind my eyes. My body trembles and shakes. Reaction, I tell myself. Of course there's going to be some reaction. But it's more than that. It's the realisation that I'm not about to die. That Rachael arrived in time.

She saved me.

CHAPTER THIRTY-NINE

Rachael helped Lexi struggle down the stairs and outside, down the scarred, weathered wood of the steps and across the overgrown front yard to the car.

'Wait,' Lexi said when Rachael opened the car door. She turned, looked up. 'I need a minute.'

Rachael waited, studying the house that loomed over them. Two storeys of timber and asbestos struggling to hold its shape against time and the elements. Looking at the house now, she couldn't help but feel it had died that day long ago—or what was left of its soul had. It would be a kindness for its fractured remains to be knocked down, laid to rest once and for all.

'Okay,' Lexi said after a minute. 'I just needed to … I don't know.'

'Say goodbye,' Rachael suggested. 'Close the book.'

'Yeah. That.'

'Hop in the car. Rest. As soon as the other units get here we'll get going.'

Lexi did as instructed, dropped her head back against the headrest and closed her eyes. 'Did you get Vaughn?'

'Initially, yeah but then … I'm sorry, Lexi. We sent him off with Debbie and they escaped.'

Lexi's tired face screwed up. 'Damn!'

'He hasn't won. He just thinks he has.'

'You know, I never picked Debbie. I don't know why I didn't see it.'

'None of us did. But it explains a lot. How he knew everything we were up to, how he had my phone number … all of it. What I'd like to know is why.'

Lexi opened her eyes and turned to look at Rachael. 'When she pulled her gun on me she was a different person. Her face, her tone, everything changed. She was almost unrecognisible in a way. Hard. Cold. She called Vaughn an artist. I was trying to stall Biddle, asked him about her. He just said not everyone wants to be a cop for the same reason.'

'I see,' Rachael said. 'Looks like we're going to be doing some major digging into Debbie's background. Don't worry, I'll get both of them.'

'*We'll* get them. I'm helping,' Lexi said with a smile that looked just a little forced.

'Does that mean you're going to continue to work with us?'

'On Vaughn? Of course.'

'And beyond?'

She saw the surprise in Lexi's face and, she thought— hoped—the interest. 'I don't know. Should I?'

'Yeah. I think you should.' Rachael looked up at the sound of sirens. 'Here comes Finn with reinforcements. I'll have to go through all the rigmarole here, so I'll get Finn to take you to the hospital.'

Lexi made a dismissive noise. 'It's not the first time I've had drugs in my system. I'm okay.'

'This wasn't exactly courtesy of Mojo.'

More surprise. 'Finn told you about my pot plant?'

'Yeah.'

'He's off limits.'

'I know. What was it Vaughn drugged you with?'

'Ketamine. I'll sleep like a baby later.' Then she said, 'Rachael, thanks. You made it.'

'I went with my gut this time.'

'It wasn't your fault. Before.'

She looked away, the guilt still there. 'I told you I'd come.'

Lexi's hand came up to rest on her arm. 'And you did. You couldn't have predicted how fast that was going to unfold.'

'You were just a child.'

'And you were just a detective doing her job.'

Rachael swallowed the emotion the forgiveness brought to the surface then smiled as Finn pulled his car up behind hers, jumped out and closed the distance between them in long, loping strides. 'Are you both okay?'

'We're fine,' Rachael said.

'Biddle?'

'Dead. Upstairs.'

'You?' he asked. She nodded once. He absorbed that, then nodded back. 'So it's done, once and for all. Good.'

'I need you to run Lexi down to the hospital,' she said. 'Get her checked over.'

'Rach, really—' Lexi began.

'You were dosed with horse tranquilliser. You're going!'

'I'm fine. It doesn't matter.'

'You always say that!' Finn said. 'But it does matter, Lexi. You matter. To all of us. You know that, right?'

She didn't answer, but her eyes went suspiciously damp.

Big day, Rachael thought. Big, emotional day.

Finn walked around to Lexi's side and opened the door. 'Now get your drugged butt out of that car and get into mine.'

'You're both so bossy,' Lexi complained half-heartedly.

'We're cops. Do what you're told,' Rachael teased and gave her a nudge to get her moving.

*

By the time Rachael finally made it to the station, Finn was back and waiting with a coffee in her office.

'How's Ava?' she asked.

'Shaken up, teary on and off. Exhausted. She's going to need some counselling, some time. But she's safe. We'll get her through it. Viv's going to be okay. She's got a concussion and a broken leg but considering everything, she's pretty happy. I'm just waiting for Lexi to get the all clear to be released, then I'll run her home, get Ava from her grand-mother's and take her home with me.'

'So Lexi hasn't been released from hospital yet?' Turner demanded from the doorway.

Finn surged to his feet and got in Turner's face. Every-thing about him radiated aggression, his knuckles white where he clenched them. 'If my daughter had died today, you'd be dead. Understand?'

'Finn,' Rachael warned.

'Because I didn't let Lexi go running off in the hope she'd return?' Turner's sneer emerged. 'She would have bolted.'

'She was trying to save Ava's life!'

'She's a criminal! An out-of-control vigilante with her own agenda! I want her back here under arrest as soon as she's released!'

'Finn, please sit down,' Rachael said. She couldn't have Finn do anything that would interfere with her current course of action. Even if she did want to see Finn land one on Turner. Then she said, 'You won't be arresting her, Turner.'

'I'm sorry, Rachael,' Turner said, 'but you can't protect her this time. She and Charmaine Davies blatantly flouted the law. Committed a serious crime!'

'Charmaine Davies was in shock, grieving. Not only for her husband but for the idea she was going to lose her daughter, her life, over what Davies had done. Lexi took over in a misguided intervention that the courts are willing to waive in return for her help with the case.'

Turner's mouth opened once, twice, before he got the words out. 'You got them immunity? You've lost your mind!'

'I believed stopping a child killer was worth more to us than the opportunity to bring a few much lesser charges up against Lexi. If a persecuted mother and a dependent child escape more heartache because of that, so be it.'

He laughed coldly. 'Ed and the old AG, eh?'

Rachael's tone turned stone-cold. 'They're friendly enough, why?'

'I expected more from you.'

'I wish I could say the same. The Attorney-General is a decent man. Greater good means a lot to him within the boundaries of the law. I petitioned for this myself. Ed wouldn't do me any special favours and I wouldn't ask him to.'

'This is not over.' Turner stalked away, fists clenched.

'Not by a long shot,' Rachael murmured to his back. 'Starting with an enquiry into your conduct.'

'Did, ah, Lexi know about that immunity?' Finn asked.

She turned from the empty doorway back to Finn. 'No. She risked everything to get Ava back, even knowing what it might cost her.'

'I won't forget it.' He smiled, his face relaxing out of its earlier anger. 'Were you ever worried about what that immunity might have encompassed?'

Rachael shook her head. 'I never thought she murdered Davies, if that's what you're suggesting. But Bailee had told me Lexi'd had to do some dodgy jobs to survive and that those jobs were what gave her the skills to assist us in this case. What I was worried about was the vendetta Turner had against me and if that would spill over onto Lexi. I didn't want our investigation slowed because Lexi had to look over her shoulder every time she opened her mouth in case he got the handcuffs out. I couldn't employ her with all that hanging over our heads.'

'Good call. The one today must have been difficult to make. You could have had Vaughn but you went after a hunch instead.'

'I followed my gut, not the evidence. Like I should have done the first time. The thing is, I can't help but question that clue Vaughn gave us to go back to the beginning. It was almost too easy.'

'Bordering on stupid really.'

'And he's not stupid. I think he wanted us to find Biddle.'

'Why's that?'

'Biddle wanted to use Vaughn to help him play out the final act of the Spider. His last moment of glory. But Vaughn's as manipulative and narcissistic as Biddle. He didn't want Biddle to succeed in killing Lexi. It would have taken the spotlight off what he's been doing. He didn't want Biddle getting the attention and risk being seen by the world as some sort of means to an end for a dying has-been. He had his own agenda: To get his hands on Biddle's money and be bigger than Biddle ever was. He's been feeding off all this notoriety and making a name for himself. He's shown everyone how clever he is and he loves it.'

'It's been a game to him all along,' Finn said. 'To win. To be Victor Rheus.'

'Except he won't be. Not for long. Lexi wants to help find him.'

'I think she's decided she likes working with the cops after all.'

'And more than that, she's forgiven me. Even told me it wasn't my fault.'

'Great. Then do you think maybe you can finally forgive yourself?'

Rachael held up a finger and walked into the strike force room, came back a moment later with Lexi's drawing of the Spider. She stared at it a moment, then dropped it into one of the empty boxes awaiting the clean up. 'I think it's time we all moved on, don't you?'

'Past time, if you ask me. Vaughn is a new enemy, a new profile. And we still have to track down Debbie. We've got plenty of work to do.'

His phone buzzed and he checked the message then got to his feet. 'That's my cue. You're welcome to stay with Ava and me tonight.'

'Thanks, Finn, but Ed's going to stay.'

'Okay. 'Night.' Then he called, ''Night, Neutron!'

'You know I've bonded with that stupid nickname now?' Jim said from the strike force room. 'It's going to stick. Good night. Oh, wait!' He appeared in the doorway and handed Finn a piece of paper. 'You asked me to look into Lexi's neighbour. Dawn Smith. Interesting read.'

'Thanks.' Finn started skimming the paper on his way downstairs. What he saw stopped him in his tracks. 'You've got to be kidding me.' He sat where he was on the third step from the bottom and read it through. When he was done, he hurried to the car to pick up Lexi.

She was in the waiting room when he got there.

'They kicked you out?' he asked in surprise.

'I kicked me out. There's sick people in there. I don't want to get sick.'

He laughed. 'Come on then, let's get you home.'

She was quiet on the way back. He suspected she might have been dozing. 'You sure you're going to be all right?' he asked her when they reached her front door.

'Yeah, I just need to sleep.'

He had to say it one more time, and he still didn't quite know how. 'Lexi … there are no words.'

'You mean no more words? Good. Because I've heard them all. You're welcome,' she said in about the tone he'd expected. Then more gently, she said, 'I'm glad Ava's okay. Goodnight.'

''Night.'

He waited until she'd shut the door and he'd heard it lock, then headed for Dawny's place, found her waiting for him before he reached the door.

'How is she?' Dawny asked.

'She's going to be fine. Rachael got him. Biddle. He's dead.'

'Well, that's fabulous, but what about your little one?'

'She's fine too. Safe.'

'You'll come in, of course, have a cuppa. I want to hear all about it.'

CHAPTER FORTY

Thursday, March 25

I don't think I had quite enough respect for horse tranquilliser. My yawn is huge as I half slide, half fall out of bed. It's still morning—just. I've had possibly the longest night's sleep in forever and I feel like I'm moving through thick mud. I head straight for the shower in the hopes it might un-fuzz my brain then, still mostly dazed, head towards the kitchen in search of coffee. On the way past, I notice something on the floor by my front door and take the few strides necessary to pick it up. It's an envelope with Dawny's scrawled writing on the front.

Lexi, dear.

'What the?' I glance over to Dawny's place. All is quiet. Curious, I open the envelope and a key slips from a folded note.

Lexi, dear,

Desmond and I are taking a little road trip. Someone's bound to knock on your door sometime soon with terrible news. Don't worry about it. It's bullshit. But keep that to yourself, please. Sorry I've left you to clean the house out for me, but it'd look pretty suspicious if I did it before the accident. Take what you want of what's left. Make sure you check the oven for a small parting gift.

PS Keep in well with those coppers in case we need a favour one day.

PPS I might have spun a white lie or two. Hope you can forgive me. I do like my fun.

Dawny xx

'What?' I stare at the note. I read it again. She's gone? I feel a sudden shock of unexpected emptiness. How can this dreary little corner of nowhere survive without Dawny? That cheerful, crazy, probable sociopath who brightened my day even while annoying the hell out of me. I'm gonna miss her. I already do.

I open the front door and hurry across the driveway on the chance she hasn't left yet, but I can tell she has. The place has a strange abandoned quality to it. Like the energy has been sucked out. I know how it feels.

I use the key and go inside. Bits and pieces are missing, but the furniture and larger items are all still there. I open the oven. Inside is a garbage bag. Curious to see what this small parting gift could be, I take it out. Whatever's inside is heavy and solid. I place it on the table. A shoebox. The lid reads ALWAYS BE PREPARED.

The 'Oh shit!' kind of falls from my mouth as I stare at the contents.

Most of the box is filled with neat stacks of bundled fifty-dollar bills. On top of that is a mobile phone and a handgun. I pick the gun up, turn it around in my hands, then cautiously put it down in case it might somehow go off. I'm not sure how to check if it's loaded, but it wouldn't surprise me. A quick fiddle with the phone reveals it has one number stored in it under *For emergencies.*

As far as presents go it's as ridiculous as it is over-whelming. I laugh a little. Damn it, I am *not* going to cry. As I look up, blinking rapidly to make sure the tears don't fall, a car outside catches my eye. It's Finn and he's got Ava with him. I throw everything back in the box and shove it back in the oven. After one more moment to get myself back together, I go outside, lock Dawny's door behind me.

'Lexi!' Ava calls out and runs over to me.

'Hi, kid.'

'Thanks again for ... well, you know.'

'Yeah. You're welcome.'

Ava smiles again, then gives me a hug. *'Really* thanks.'

'Ah ... You're ... *really* welcome.' I pat her awkwardly on the back. I've already had my quota of emotional shit for the decade.

I think Finn can read the 'help' in my expression because he puts a hand on Ava's shoulder. 'Give us a sec?' he asks Ava.

'Can I play handball against the wall?'

'Sure.'

'How are you today?' he asks.

'Yeah, fine. Why?'

'Something going on at Dawny's?'

'Oh, she's, um ... taken a little road trip.'

I frown, puzzled, when he chuckles. 'Not surprised,' he says. 'She got you through the Davies thing, didn't she?'

'No, of course not. Why would you say that?'

'From what she told me on the phone and' —he reached into his pocket and pulled out his phone— 'because Dawny Smith is the alter ego of Catherine Dawn Delaney.'

'Catherine … Delaney? No. She was friends with Catherine. She knew Catherine, but she's not—' He held up a mug shot on his phone and, damn, it sure as hell looked like a young Dawny. 'Her.'

'Catherine Delaney was a battered wife turned solicitor. She worked for Legal Aid and represented abused women in court. She helped put away quite a few monsters, however one of the ones who walked, Isaac Malone, went after his girlfriend the same afternoon and beat her to death. He then disappeared. A similar incident occurred four years later. Darren Sventon shot his girlfriend and their three-year-old child at point-blank range, killing them both before taking off. Cops couldn't find him, but a couple of days into a massive manhunt two detectives went to see Catherine regarding the case and found her in the backyard, burning something. It was Mr Sventon.'

While my mind struggles to take this in, Dawny's words float back to me. *But burning bodies beyond recognition isn't as easy as you might think.*

'Ha!' It bursts from my lips without thought.

'Something funny?'

I clear my throat and pull back my amusement. 'No, nothing. Continue.'

'Over the course of Catherine's trial, police suggested that her first husband might have met a similar fate. He's been missing for thirty-five years.'

Don't know why she ever got married again after she killed her first husband.

'But they were unable to find any evidence Catherine was responsible for Isaac Malone's or her first husband's disappearances.'

They only found the last one, dear.

I'm grinning from ear to ear. It's wrong, but I can't help it. She's been dropping me clues all along and I didn't see it. 'But her second husband is alive. That's Desmond, right?'

'Yeah. Another colourful character. He has a couple of warrants out for his arrest.'

'I'm surprised Dawny ever got out of prison.'

'Yeah, well, the thing is, though the police could prove Catherine disposed of Svenson's body, they couldn't prove she killed him. When it came time for the trial, just about every woman she'd ever helped stood up in court and gave her alibis for the days leading up to his murder. It was either charge thirty or so women and turn the courts into a circus or offer her a deal, to take the lesser charge of accessory after the fact to murder. Then she got a sympathetic judge and did about half the time she could have on that one, then less again with good behaviour.'

'Shame,' I say, unable to cover my smirk.

'Regardless, she's done her time, and as finding a thumb drive isn't a crime, unless there's anything you'd like to formally share with me in relation to where she found it or her possible involvement in concealing Jonathan Davies's body ...?'

My face goes blank. 'I've got nothing.'

'Hmm. Thought as much. But cops'll be here soon looking for Desmond.'

I'm thinking how lucky it is they've taken off in time when my eyes narrow on another thought. 'You warned her! Because she risked going back to prison for Ava's sake. I saw you go over there last night.'

He shoots back a blank look, accompanied by my words. 'I've got nothing.'

We're both silent with our thoughts for a minute, watching Ava bounce her handball against the front wall of my house.

Finn clears his throat. 'Speaking of the law, what are you going to do about working for us?'

I sigh loudly. 'The very idea is stupid.'

'No, it's not.'

'Really? Because I think I kind of prefer vigilante. I broke the law to help Charmaine and I don't regret it, and I couldn't care less that I helped the body of that disgusting human end up in a freezer at the tip.'

'Is that where he is?'

'Ah, just … guessing.'

'I see,' he says, but I'm pretty sure he doesn't believe me. 'Well, it's hard to regret any of that, really.'

'My point is I don't work well within confines of the law. What kind of civilian employee of the cops would that make me?'

'Probably a pretty shitty one.'

'Exact— thanks,' I say, making him grin.

'You need to learn a better way to go about saving the world.' He leans into his car and grabs some paperwork, hands it to me. It's information on joining to police force.

'You're not serious? You smoked my pot, didn't you? Mojo better still be safe at home.' Because I'm not sure it is,

I shove the paperwork back at him, deciding to go inside and check.

'You like catching the bad guys, yes?'

I stop, turn. 'Well, yeah but ...'

'You want a big stick?'

A small smile escapes. 'I wouldn't mind one.'

'The stingy spray?'

A bigger smile. 'Yeah.'

'And—God help us all—a gun?'

'You know, I don't actually need one because D—'

'Don't tell me!' He takes my hand and puts the paperwork back in it. 'Think about it.' Then he says, 'Come on, Ava. Let's go get ice cream.'

Ava grabs her handball and runs back to us. 'Are you coming?' she asks me.

'Ah, no. I have ... stuff.'

'It'll wait,' Finn says. 'Let's go talk about catching bad guys.'

'But we just finished!'

'Tomorrow's a new day. Vaughn's still out there. And you'll want to find Debbie too, right?'

I groan as I look down at the paperwork in my hand. 'Sounds like I'd be mad to turn down all this cop stuff.'

Ava runs ahead to the car, turns. And it strikes me: She's alive. She's happy. She's safe. I made a difference.

What I did mattered.

Maybe it wouldn't be all bad.

'Can't we just eat ice cream and be happy it's all over?'

'Over?' He throws an arm across my shoulders and propels me towards the car. 'Lexi, my friend, this is only the beginning.'

ACKNOWLEDGEMENTS

I'd like to say an enormous thank you to everyone who worked with me on *Unforgiven*. My special thanks to Jo Mackay for your ongoing support of my writing, to Nicola Robinson for all your help, advice and general brilliance. To Annabel Blay for the million, magical things you do, and to Kylie Mason and Chrysoula Aiello for helping to make the story the best it can be. Thanks also to the design team for my fabulous cover and the sales team who take my books out into the world.

A special, heartfelt thanks to all the survivors of childhood abuse who share their stories and shed light on what some would prefer stays hidden. Your courage is astounding.

As always, a big thank you to my family and friends without whose support I wouldn't be able to write. To Sergeant Tony Jones, I can't thank you enough for always being available to help with my endless police questions. Tea Cooper and Charles Smith, thanks as always for your brilliant critiquing. Thanks also to Richelle Conlan, a cherished friend and librarian who is always ready and willing to promote my books.

And last but not least, my eternal gratitude goes to all the wonderful readers, bloggers and reviewers who have taken the time to read my stories and share them with the world. You are all priceless.